∞ ∞ ∞

LETHAL PRACTICE

For:_____ANYONE_____

Address:____ANYWHERE_____

Date:_____ANYTIME_____

Rx Use liberally when in need of a good read . . .

SIDE EFFECTS: May cause engrossment, excitement, feeling of "being there," and occasional hilarity . . .

CAUTION: May cause stiffness due to long periods of sitting and turning pages.

PLEASE NOTE: This is *not* an imitation. This is the REAL thing.

REPEAT: As often as you can!

MICHEL TÉTREAULT, M.D., Emergency Physician
Former President, Canadian and Quebec Associations of
Emergency Physicians

∞ ∞ ∞

"LETHAL PRACTICE goes beyond the drama of practice in an emergency department with a gripping, suspenseful plot that keeps one riveted to the pages, fearful and expectant of the outcome in Dr. Earl Garnet's deadly medical world."

NORMAN A. SMITH, M.D.
Emergency Physician
Hattiesburg, Mississippi

*Please turn to the last page of the book
for even more rave reviews. . . .*

LETHAL PRACTICE

Peter Clement

FAWCETT GOLD MEDAL • NEW YORK

A Fawcett Gold Medal Book
Published by The Ballantine Publishing Group

Copyright © 1998 by Baskerville Enterprises Ltd.

http://www.randomhouse.com

Library of Congress Catalog Card Number: 97-93255

ISBN 0-449-00281-0

Manufactured in the United States of America

First Edition: April 1998

10 9 8 7 6 5 4 3 2 1

This book is dedicated to my friends and colleagues and to my "New York angels"—Beverly, Carolyn, Danelle, Jeff, and Denise—for their generosity, guidance, and wonderful expertise. Thank you.

Chapter 1

"I'm going to die, aren't I, Doc?"

Christ, they always seemed to know.

"No, sir," I lied. "Your lungs are filling with fluid. We're going to give you medication to clear them out."

Openmouthed and gasping beneath the oxygen mask, the patient was frantic for air. All the muscles in his chest and abdomen heaved with every attempt to breathe, but each breath was shallow and ended with an ominous gurgle. His skin felt clammy and had turned the color of a dead fish's belly. I guessed he was about fifty, though he looked almost twice that age now.

We were in the resuscitation room, a large, tiled chamber, cold, full of echoes, harsh light, and harsher verdicts. Crouched over the patient's left arm, Susanne Roberts, head nurse, was struggling to find a vein and get in an IV.

"Damn," she muttered.

"Get Ventolin and eighty milligrams of Lasix. I'll try to get a line in his right arm." I was already reaching for a tourniquet as Susanne moved fast to follow my order. The patient's skin was slippery cold. I moved my fingers to his neck and found a pulse. It was very faint and rapid, but at the wrist, there was nothing. Shock. "And dopamine!" I yelled after Susanne. She and I had run this race together a lot of times during the fifteen years she'd worked in the ER and, like familiar sex, she'd know exactly what I wanted.

The patient's respirations were getting faster, the gurgling louder. He was literally drowning in his own fluids. An IV, the drugs, and intubation might empty the lungs in time but, then again, might not.

I tourniqueted his right arm but got no bulge at the vein site. I'd have to make a blind try. I anointed the chosen spot with alcohol and went in. Still nothing.

His chest was heaving harder now. He could no longer utter syllables. I advanced the IV. Blood started to come back up the catheter. I was in, but he was looking bluer. The cardiac monitor showed extra beats.

Susanne was back at my side with the drugs.

"I got a line," I said. "Give me the IV."

She passed me the clear tubing that dangled from overhead sacks of fluid. I shoved the tip through the blood running from the end of my needle catheter and opened the line. The skin bulged with overflow from a broken vein.

Shit. When it goes wrong, it really goes wrong.

His eyes began to roll.

"Call ICU stat, please, and inhalation therapy." I spoke in that phony, calm tone we use when we're losing it. I've always wondered if it fools anyone.

Susanne hit the phones, and I abandoned trying for an IV, reaching instead for the intubation tray. The man's lungs were filling up much faster than I'd expected. Bloody foam started bubbling out of his mouth. Too late for medication. My only hope of saving him now was to pass a tube down his airway and blow the fluid back out of his lungs with pressurized oxygen. Susanne finished her terse conversation, then started hooking up the tubes and equipment we'd use.

The overhead PA screeched, "ICU and inhalation therapy, *stat*! Emergency department!"

Now the whole hospital knew we were in trouble.

So did the patient. He dropped his head, seized, and quit breathing.

"Call ninety-nine!" I yelled. The code would bring the cardiac arrest team.

The heart monitor showed the jagged dance of ventricular fibrillation. Susanne was shoving a board under the patient's shoulders as I grabbed for the paddles, then set the machine for two hundred joules. Susanne slapped some lubricant on the man's chest and turned back to the phones.

The current hit him with a loud thwack, arched him, but left the heart dead. I shocked him again. The jolt hit, but still no response. I tried a third time. Nothing.

The inhalationist arrived.

"Move in!" I commanded.

She was already at the man's head, pulling off the clear mask and tubing we'd applied earlier. She plopped a black ventilating mask on his face and attached it to a rubber bag that she squeezed to give him a few puffs of oxygen. Next she reached for a laryngoscope, flicked it open like a switchblade, and went into his mouth. Foam and vomit spilled out. She grabbed a suction catheter and probed through the mess in the back of his throat. Noisily it sucked the debris clear. After reopening his airway with the blade, she smoothly slid a long, curved tube into his trachea.

"Got it," she reported matter-of-factly.

After she hooked up the bag and began forcing air into the guy's lungs, more bloody foam came bubbling up at her with each puff. The oxygen was pushing out what had clogged his breathing. She grinned cockily. "Having a good day, Dr. Garnet?"

"Smartass," I said, smiling.

Susanne was pumping his chest. The ventilation and cardiac massage began to pink him up a bit, but the monitor looked like the stock market ticker on Black Tuesday. We still didn't have an IV line.

I heard the crackling of the PA.

"Ninety-nine, emergency! Ninety-nine, emergency!" the anonymous voice called, requesting help for us again.

As much as I may need it, I hate it when help arrives. Everyone in the hospital with nothing better to do shows up. They all come thundering in, and my job changes from resuscitator to traffic cop.

The first through the door was James Todd. As always, his clothes were disheveled and the expression on his face was intense. A lot of the interns adopted that over-worked and earnest appearance because they hoped it would compensate for what they didn't know. Just looking at one of them made me feel exhausted. Todd was buckling up his belt as he came toward me. He'd probably heard the call in the can.

"Dr. Todd, good to see you. Can you get me a central line?"

Todd had a reputation for magic hands. Under the clavicle is a major vein that passes to the heart. I knew he'd have a needle in it with no trouble. With a quick nod, he started gloving up while I hoped he'd washed after finishing at the toilet.

As I waited, I broke open a few ampules of diluted epinephrine and poured them into the endotracheal tube. The inhalationist resumed bagging. Normally this would have forced the epinephrine all the way down to the small air sacs in the lungs and through their walls into the bloodstream. But in this man fluid was pouring back from the bloodstream into these very sacs; the way was blocked. I had Todd, Susanne, and the inhalationist stand clear while I shocked him again. Just as I feared, it didn't work.

Two medical students rushed in, and I got them busy drawing a blood gas. The noise level was rising. A third came in and I stationed her at the door, telling her not to let anyone else get by, but almost before the words were out of my mouth, the priest, a regular in the ER from nearby Blessed Trinity Church, darted under her arm.

"Is he Catholic, Earl?" the priest asked, trotting with me back to the patient. When I merely shrugged, the priest reached over my shoulder, touched the patient, and started muttering the last rites. Real confidence boost, that one.

"Ready," Todd said. He had his line.

At my order, Susanne broke open another ampule of epinephrine and injected the contents through our IV. I recharged the paddles, placed them, and fired. The patient arched as before, but this time the scribbled line on the cardiac monitor untangled itself and formed the steady, organized pattern of a functioning heart. I put my fingers to his neck; there was a pulse again.

"Could I have a blood pressure reading, please?"

Susanne pumped up the cuff on the patient's left arm and listened with her stethoscope while slowly deflating the bulb. "Ninety over sixty."

Everyone relaxed a bit. Still a long way to go.

I ordered some small Xylocaine boluses, one to use immediately and another in ten minutes to prevent any more defective rhythms. Susanne hung up a drip without my even asking. The BP rose to 110/70.

The room was quiet except for the rush of air with each squeeze of the respirator bag and the welcome steady beep from the monitor. It's always like this at the end of an arrest, whatever the outcome. I broke the spell. "Get this patient up to ICU before he crashes again."

For the last twenty years it's been my job to take patients like this and try to make them better. Trouble is, I'm no St. Jude, and whether they are routine problems, potential miracles, or already lost causes, they all come through the door together. We do triage to sort out those people who have seconds from those who have hours. I'm forever behind, it's always catch-up, and in a chaotic profession of desperate moves with precise skills, the fear of failure never leaves. By the time I get to them, they inevitably have the same unspoken prayer in their eyes. "It's come to this, and you're all I got, Doc. Please be good."

I accompanied him and the nurses for the short elevator ride up to ICU. It was Sunday evening, and only a resident would be there. Sometimes the resident had enough experience to handle a difficult case until a staff supervisor could be called in from home, but I wanted to make sure. Though my patient was making it out of the ER, the real trick now was for him to get out of the hospital alive.

At first, after the stark glare of emergency, the shadowy darkness of intensive care made it hard to see. A hushed place even in the daytime, the ICU at night is a gallery of backlit souls, each hooked into a wall of blinking red and amber lights and bound in a tangle of tubes and wires. The curtains that divide the cubicles hang like shrouds. Now and then a soft beep gets the attention of the nurses. The monitors at their dimly lit station flicker in fluorescent green and show a dozen jagged lines furiously writing the fate of each fragile heart.

While I huddled with the young resident, the nurses quickly signed over to their counterparts and returned downstairs. It took me five minutes, however, to explain the case to the increasingly nervous trainee spending his first night on duty in the ICU. By then I needed a stretch, so I decided to walk back down the three floors to the ER.

As I headed for the staircase, I noticed that the hallways glistened from a fresh mopping, then spotted a deserted mop and pail near the door of the doctors' lounge. I glanced at my watch; it was only seven P.M. Less than three hours on the job, I thought, and already one of the housekeepers was occupying an overstuffed leather chair in the sanctum forbidden her during the regular day hours. Each to her own perks.

Around the corner, I literally ran into our esteemed chief executive officer and two-hundred-pound resident souse, Everett Kingsly. He grunted with surprise and let me know in one breath what he'd been drinking. He normally had a well-groomed mane of white hair, but now it had become tangled and tufted into peaks like whipped meringue. His white beard, full more from neglect than by design, stuck out in wiry bristles that made me itch. Overall, he looked as if he'd been caught in a windstorm.

"Dr. Garnet!" He said my name as if he were identifying an out-of-place signpost.

"Evening, Mr. Kingsly," I replied, quickly steadying him, then stepping aside—considerably aside. He had that aroma of alcohol-soaked sweat that inevitably gives secret vodka drinkers away.

"Yeah," he answered after what seemed like a lot of thought.

"Can I help you?" I asked.

He gave me a hurt look and gazed off into the space behind me. He appeared to take a reading on the next wall extinguisher, then lurched toward it. He was hanging on to this latest handhold, surveying the next leg of his journey, when I left him. I was feeling guilty for not helping him at the moment, but I had to get back to emergency. I did a quickstep to security and told the guards on duty where they could pick Kingsly up.

"Christ, someone should do something about that guy," I heard one of the guards say as I turned to head for the stairs. "It's the second time this month."

"Somebody said he tried to paw Agnes from housekeeping last week."

"Kingsly's an alcoholic. Why don't they—"

The stairwell door swung closed behind me, cutting off their conversation. That guard was right though. While the rest of the world had given up the three-martini lunch, Kingsly had become increasingly devoted to it. Over the last year he'd deteriorated. Some days he was a dead loss after lunch in terms of hospital business—but a menace to reasonably attractive women of any age who dared to go near him. This weekend he must have been drinking at home and come into the hospital . . . for what? To grope some woman on staff?

I felt another twinge of guilt at my increasing impatience with Kingsly. Eight years ago he'd been a vigorous administrator and an enthusiastic supporter of making me the new chief of emergency. "New blood! New ideas, that's what the place needs," I remember him declaring shortly after my appointment. It was pathetic he'd become such a liability to the hospital now, but someone definitely should have done something about his drinking months ago—and, since no one else had done so, I suspected the others he worked with were as shamefully preoccupied with their own problems as I was.

It was almost eleven-thirty. I'd taken care of a cut hand, a few sprained ankles, and four dozen other minor cases that had accumulated in the waiting room during the resuscitation. For the Buffalo area, this was quiet, even on a Sunday night. The few ambulances that did arrive brought mostly elderly patients with the flu. Serious, but not life-threatening. Nevertheless, I was feeling the fatigue of keeping the cases all straight in my mind, and I was glad my shift ended at midnight. At twelve-twenty my replacement still hadn't arrived.

Kradic! The other evening-shift physicians had complained that he'd been turning up later and later. I'd talked to him, but he'd only scoffed. He was almost always so damn belligerent that the only way to make him admit any problem, let alone correct it, was to hit him head-on with undeniable evidence. So when one of the other doctors came down with the flu the day before and asked me to cover for him, I hadn't been reluctant, because of Kradic. If he was late, he damn well couldn't deny it to my face.

"Think you'll get home tonight?" Susanne asked, coat on and heading out. The grin on her face gave me less than even odds. Even my resident had disappeared, probably to get some sleep, but at least there weren't any patients waiting to be seen.

Forty minutes later Dr. Albert Kradic sauntered in. He was tall, a bit overweight, and had a pasty complexion from working nights. He kept his black hair combed flat except for a bit in the front that he let fall forward over some old acne scars. He was in his late twenties, but he looked older, and judging by the expression on his face, I could tell he hadn't expected to see me.

I decided to fire first and fire loud so the nurses could hear. I knew Kradic had money problems, badly needed this job, and was fanatical about his reputation. I didn't think that in front of all the regulars on the night shift he'd have the nerve to deny he was repeatedly late. The smirks of those nurses could make even him cower.

"Dr. Kradic, you have a problem starting at midnight?"

"What do you mean? My alarm didn't go off, is all." He had the nerve. One of the nurses snorted and Kradic shot her a hard glance.

Christ, I thought, they'll be at each other worse than usual now. Whenever spats between staff got out of hand, they invariably sent me notes later, each side complaining about the other person's offensive behavior. I'd have a few on my desk in the morning for sure, especially with Kradic trying to find out who had squealed about his being chronically late.

But tonight I was too tired to prolong the encounter. "Make sure it doesn't happen again," I snapped, and started right into sign-out rounds. I kept the synopsis on each case short and fast enough to cut off any attempt Kradic might make to come up with more alibis.

Five minutes later I was out of my white coat and lugging my briefcase toward the front entrance. My feet hurt, my back ached, and I needed a week of sleep. The security guard was just opening the door when my escape was thwarted by the PA.

"Ninety-nine, administration! Ninety-nine, administration!"

Shit!

The night air flowed cool and fresh through the still-open door. I could keep walking . . . let the others take care of the arrest.

But I'd never sleep.

Resentfully, reflexes taking over, I charged back to the ER and met the nurses coming from the resuscitation room with a crash cart. A startled-looking Kradic tried to wave me off.

"You stay here and manage emerge!" I told him. I turned to the nurses. "Meet you there!"

I ran for the stairs. They would follow with the arrest team in the emergency elevator and arrive thirty seconds behind me. This was our automatic protocol for any cardiac arrest not in an admitting area.

Climbing the steps two at a time, I wondered who'd be in administration this time of night. Then I thought of Kingsly. Perhaps the guards hadn't found him earlier and he had knocked himself off during one of his attempts at sex. As I entered the carpeted hallway unique to the administrative part of the hospital, I wasn't surprised to see the hushed gathering of cleaning people, porters, and security guards at the far end of the corridor outside Kingsly's corner office. Still puffing from racing up the stairs, I slowed to a brisk walk and prepared my mind to run an arrest. However, as soon as I stepped into the large and windowed reception area that was the antechamber leading to Kingsly's inner office, my nose told me there would be no use offering life support, basic or advanced. Mixed with the stink of feces and sour urine was the odor of early rot.

A clutch of pale, wet-eyed cleaning women in greens huddled in the doorway, staring into the office, cloths pressed to their noses. The scene inside matched the smell. On the floor, in the middle of a thick powder blue rug in front of a mahogany desk, lay Kingsly, nearly naked, a mound of white belly below a purple face.

Two other women were alternately gagging, pumping his chest, and trying to blow air through his gaping blue lips. There was vomit running out the side of his mouth, but whether it was his own or one of the rescuers' I couldn't tell. His undershorts, the only thing he was wearing, were halfway down his crotch and sodden with excrement. Some had bulged out between his legs. Jesus, what a mess.

I moved to his side and felt for a carotid pulse in the neck. None, and he was cool, even in the stifling heat of the room, which I absently noticed. His two resuscitators were still pumping, blowing, and choking. They had obviously been taught CPR, but the leap from training to the real thing wasn't usually this bad.

With him long out of his misery, I was about to put the women out of theirs and stop the arrest when I noticed something odd. Every time the woman pumped, a thin jet of bubbly blood squirted out onto his abdomen. I knelt down and stared. The blood came from under a recently formed scab the size of a blueberry that was just to the left of the tip of his sternum and had lifted loose. Under the scab, with each press on the chest, the small silver end of a broken needle rose out of the ooze and then receded back into Kingsly's innards.

More bubbles and thin jets of blood appeared with every chest compression. The bubbles indicated the channel of the wound was deep, burrowing at least into the lung. The jets of blood told me that unless the man had been trying to turn himself into a voodoo doll, someone had driven a cardiac needle into the center of Everett Kingsly's heart.

Chapter 2

Despite the atrocity on the floor, I was almost unable to accept what I'd seen—that Kingsly had been killed—and I dreaded pronouncing it even more. I gently put a hand on the shoulder of the woman next to me to stop her attempts at CPR. Her companion made a few more futile puffs into Kingsly's flabby mouth, then pulled back. They were both visibly shaken.

"You did everything you could," I said as I helped them up.

"Are you sure?" one of them asked.

"Absolutely," I answered, patting her arm.

I ushered the women to the door, where other comforting hands waited, and saw the cardiac arrest team racing with their cart down the corridor. I waved them off.

Then I blanked. What to do now was not familiar. Death yes, but not the management of what I'd discovered here. I was still the only physician in the room and, therefore, in charge of the body. But being the only person who knew that Kingsly had a broken needle in his heart left me thinking back to old detective novels for guidance. I figured blurting out that he'd been stabbed wouldn't help.

More people were peeking into the office from the outside reception area. A security guard pushed to the front, saw Kingsly, and went a little pale. Two nursing supervisors caught him as he swayed and helped him to a chair.

"Don't touch anything" was what I finally said, trying to sound authoritative. One of the night supervisors gave me her who-do-you-think-you-are look and dropped a dust cloth over Kingsly's partly exposed privates. Somehow, it didn't help.

I tried again. "I want this room cleared now, please, and someone find our chief of pathology and tell him to get here fast." After they'd had their peek, and a whiff of the body, everybody was eager to get out anyway.

Two orderlies came and helped the still-woozy guard to a couch in the reception area. The supervisors took turns with the phone on the secretary's desk. I was just leaving Kingsly's office when I thought again about how hot it was. I glanced at the thermostat mounted beside the door frame. It was set at the very top; the room must have been at least a hundred degrees. Unthinkingly, I turned it down.

"Did anybody turn up this heat?" I shouted to the people in the reception area. I got only incredulous stares. Was it always so hot in there? I wondered. I didn't recall from my previous visits, but I had kept those as rare as possible. Or had the heat been jacked up to prevent the loss of body temperature that would reveal time of death? And then I cursed myself. While pompously ordering everyone else to touch nothing, I'd gone and fingered the very dial that might have held a killer's prints.

As I closed the door, I saw Madelaine Hurst, associate director of nursing and the chief night supervisor, arrive and walk over to her assistants. The one on the phone immediately hung up, and I watched as they began talking to her in hushed voices. She was senior, discreet, and, I figured, best able to handle the next step. She was also the sister of Paul Hurst, former surgeon and now the medical vice president for the entire hospital.

I went up to them. "Miss Hurst," I interrupted, "I need

a private phone, and then I need you to get the medical examiner for me. After that call the police—in particular a senior officer from their homicide department."

She looked at me like I was nuts. "The only person I'm calling is my brother—which I've already done. He'll be here any second." She didn't add "so you'd better watch out," but I still felt like a kid in a school yard.

"Please, just do what I asked," I said in a low but forceful tone.

She backed away as though I'd let out a bad smell, but went to the secretary's desk and started dialing. I spent the next fifteen minutes arguing with groggy clerks at the medical examiner's office, being put on hold, and quarreling with Miss Hurst over calling the police until she suddenly shut up. Her brother had arrived. He had obviously dressed hastily, because his raincoat hung open over a wrinkled white shirt and baggy pants. His normally pale complexion had become even more pasty and shone with a sheen of perspiration.

"Oh, Dr. Hurst, thank God you're here." In public Madelaine Hurst always addressed her brother formally. "Poor Mr. Kingsly has died in there. He's lying on the carpet with most of his clothes off, and now Dr. Garnet is making me call pathology, the medical examiner, the homicide squad. . . ." She let the indictment hang there, in the air, while Paul Hurst slipped his arm around her shoulder and joined his sister in frowning at me.

Just then, thankfully, Robert Watts, chief of pathology, entered the reception area with his usual sense of quiet command.

"Where is he?" he asked calmly.

Tall and gray-haired, Watts retained his ease even during the toughest crises. He stood there, glancing first at Hurst, then at me, ready to get down to business.

Hurst, clearly annoyed with me, said, "Sorry, Robert, but Garnet here is out of—"

"Gentlemen," I interrupted. "If you will step in here, you can see the situation yourselves." I opened the door to the office and showed them Kingsly.

It took Watts thirty seconds to agree with me that we had cause to suspect murder and must notify the medical examiner. Hurst's whining wasn't going to change the law. Watts was also pretty sure the medical examiner would order us to call the cops immediately, but he went out to phone the city morgue and speak personally to the chief pathologist. Being a colleague, Watts might rate more attention than I'd gotten earlier from the clerks.

Hurst hung around in a sullen silence to make sure I didn't cause any more harm to the hospital's good name. He'd cover up the murder of his own mother to avoid a scandal, and this was going to be a tabloid special.

"What do you think happened?" I asked gently. The sooner he accepted the truth about Kingsly's death, the better he'd help everyone at the hospital deal with it. Starting to analyze the gruesome situation would give him the start of the objectivity he was going to need . . . or so I hoped.

"Lord knows" was all I got in reply.

Watts returned. "The medical examiner's seeing to it that the chief of detectives is sent over. We can do the autopsy here, but he wants his own man on-site to take special forensic samples. Finding clues to a murder isn't what we usually do."

"Murder?" Hurst winced. "Surely you're jumping to conclusions!" He looked around for corroboration. Watts and I looked at Kingsly. Hurst's shoulders slumped. "Should we just wait here?" he asked.

Watts glared at him. "Wait in the reception area if you want."

"Robert," I said, "when I came in here, the room was hotter than Hades. I think someone must have turned the heat up to try to obscure the time of death."

"How do we know it wasn't suicide?" Hurst asked, pathetic now, still staring at Kingsly's corpse.

Hurst's question startled me, but Watts stepped over and gently took his arm. "Look, Paul, maybe it would be better to wait outside." He spoke in that tone we too often use while dealing with geriatric cases; it inferred feeble-mindedness and was grossly insulting, but Hurst didn't seem to notice. He let Watts and me guide him out of the room and sit him down in a chair by the secretary's desk now commandeered by his sister.

She'd been sternly snapping off a string of orders over the phone, presumably to the floor nurses, when the sight of her brother being so acquiescent must have sparked her hurried good-bye and quick move to comfort him. "Paul, are you all right?"

"It's awful," he said almost to himself, as if she weren't even there. "Just awful."

"Paul!" She stroked his hands, then awkwardly touched his cheek.

Finally he seemed to notice her. "I'm fine, really, I'll be all right," he said weakly. But he continued to slouch in the chair where we had put him while his sister made nervous fluttering movements. By the time she finished, she had also realized her brother was no longer in charge. She looked to Watts and me for orders as angrily as if we had just staged a coup d'état.

Watts continued the takeover. "Miss Hurst," he asserted, fully formal now, "would you please get your brother a cup of tea? Dr. Garnet and I will stay here and wait for the police."

She grudgingly nodded and left, but on the way out she gave me a sullen look to make it clear I didn't rate similar respect. Gray hair again. It conveys automatic seniority in our business and, in this case, not wrongly. Watts's excellence with the living reflected his years spent as a general practitioner before he became a doctor for the dead.

We stationed ourselves at the doorway of Kingsly's office. I continued bothering Watts about the thermostat and a time of death. "I saw him earlier tonight, around seven. He'd been drinking and was stumbling along the hall, so I alerted security. We can check why they didn't pick him up or, if they did, why they didn't take him home. But the room here was an oven when I arrived, so the heat must have been on for quite a while before the cleaners found him."

Watts looked at me intently as I talked, probably thinking he was hearing the raving of an amateur detective.

"Maybe," he finally said. "Room temperature wouldn't change heat loss much though. Besides, there are other signs to estimate the time of death. Leave that for a moment. Where's the blood?"

He looked at me, saw I hadn't a clue what he meant, and went on. "If that bit of metal in his chest turns out to be the cardiac needle we both think it is, then there should be at least a few spurts of blood that shot out during the time it took the pressure to fall. Even if the stab stopped the heart instantaneously, which is unlikely if the needle broke off, then a stream of blood would still have sprayed all over the place for a few seconds. Think back to the times you've put a needle in a patient with cardiac tamponade."

I did think about it. Tamponade is a condition where the sac around the heart becomes filled with fluid. The tension prevents the heart from beating even though the electrical impulses keep firing to organize the pump of a heartbeat.

We would routinely get the pumping action back by sticking a special long needle attached to a syringe into the swollen sac around the heart to pull off the constricting fluid. If we went too far, the tip of the needle would enter the heart muscle and set off an electrical disturbance that if allowed to continue could degenerate into ventricular fibrillation and a full cardiac arrest. But Robert was right; this took time. In Kingsly's case the needle would have passed directly into the center of his heart and set up the fatal dysrhythmia. Unless the needle had been attached to a containing syringe until Kingsly had died and the needle had been broken off afterward, there should have been a lot of blood, streams of it everywhere.

"And," Watts said, "if the needle hadn't broken off in the struggle but was intact, then whoever stabbed him simply could have removed the needle with the syringe attached. A neat withdrawal leaves a minimal mark and would have been the logical way to try to hide that Kingsly was murdered. No one would deliberately snap it off after and risk the broken fragment being found in the body."

"I suppose you're right, but once the needle had broken off, why not just pull it out then?"

He frowned at me as if I were one of his residents and should have known the answer myself. "Because the killer wouldn't know how deep in it was without probing for it," he explained not too patiently, "and that would enlarge the puncture site, making the wound obvious." He paused and looked around. "And where are his clothes?"

I shrugged. Watts had noticed the most obvious inconsistency, which I'd completely missed.

"Probably far from here," he added, "and I bet they're covered with blood, maybe even burned already."

"What do you mean?"

"I mean he was attacked, and broke off the syringe either thrashing to death or struggling when he was stabbed. Blood must have been flying everywhere, all over his clothes, the walls, ceiling, and floor."

Watts suddenly bent over the bloated belly and sniffed. "His chest's been washed clean with rubbing alcohol."

I resisted sniffing for a telltale aroma of isopropyl.

"That's why the heat was up," he went on. "To dry him off." He shook his head. "No, he wasn't murdered here." He glanced around the room. "But I have a good idea how to find out where."

So did I. Kingsly's lonely killing ground would be in whatever part of the hospital the walls and ceiling had gotten an unscheduled cleaning.

"Has anyone called his wife?" Watts suddenly asked. "Or has she called here looking for him?"

I'd forgotten the long-suffering Mrs. Kingsly.

"I'll phone her!" It was Hurst's voice, calling to us from the chair outside, where we had left him. He began to straighten from the slouch he had sunk into when we'd deposited him there, and started to take back the control he'd lost.

"Thanks, Paul," said Watts.

"I'll do it from my office." He left to perform what was probably the worst job in medicine.

Madelaine arrived an instant later with a silver tea set and an array of china cups. No Styrofoam here.

"Where did he go?" she demanded protectively. To her, Watts and I were now guilty of even more than insurrection: we'd shooed away her brother from her custody. Moreover, we appeared to be about to steal his tea. She didn't offer us any.

But Watts undid her with his most lethal weapon— blarney. "Why, Miss Hurst, you always know the perfect thing to do in any situation."

Watts had suggested the tea, but he made it seem as if it had been her idea, and she beamed. He helped himself, sighed in appreciation at his first sip, and added, "I don't know what this hospital would do without you and your brother."

Only Watts had the skill to make this crap work. If I'd tried the same line, she'd have started counting the silverware. Instead, her protestations begged Watts for more of his nonsense. I had to look away and chew my lip to keep a smile off my face.

"Tea, Dr. Garnet?" asked Watts, seeing my difficulty and cocking his head away from Madelaine so only I could catch his smug grin.

As I took the cup, I glanced through the reception area window. Cop cars pulled up. Behind me Watts chatted quietly with Madelaine. Bless him. Sometimes celebrating the absurd was the only way through the pain and dying.

Watts was a remarkable man, I thought. He enjoyed his role as the final diagnostician and keeper of clinical truths. His word on each and every physician's performance was absolute. Some saw him as a teacher and guide. Others hated and feared his verdicts on their competence and character. The pathologist is key in every hospital in the world, and if he or she is a jerk, stay away, because it means incompetents in the place can get by with murder—and probably do. Have a good pathologist in the house and dangerous fools don't last long. Borderline incompetents are more subtle creatures, however. Never blatant enough to lose their licenses, they can weave and bob for years. Sometimes nurses can keep very sick patients out of their grasp by unofficially suggesting other doctors, but it's a good pathologist who really keeps those incompetents in check; they can't hide their fatal mistakes from him. And Watts was the best.

Hurst, Watts, and I looked up at the commotion coming from the entrance to the hallway. Two so-called plainclothes detectives stood at the open door. They were dressed almost identically in raincoats, gray slacks, and black shoes. Probably the outfits came in sets with the unmarked cars these guys cruised around in. No one in Buffalo reaches legal age without the smarts to pick cops out of a crowd.

"Dr. Watts?" asked the stout one with gray hair.

"I'm Watts," Robert said.

"Detective Bufort," he introduced himself. Turning to the younger and much taller man standing at his side, he added, "And this is Detective Riley."

Watts made the introductions on our side, and we all shook hands as politely as if we were meeting for a round of golf. Funny thing about police. The more serious the crime, the more polite the cops. In some neighborhoods, if you were too poor, drunk, or hostile, you could end up down at the station being pounded with a telephone book around the ribs for peeing on the sidewalk. But commit a murder and it's first-class treatment all the way.

Detective Bufort and I were the last to shake hands, then Dr. Watts invited them in to meet Kingsly.

The two officers quietly and competently took charge. They quickly inspected the body and the room, then questioned Watts and me. When I told them I'd seen Kingsly staggering down the hall earlier that evening and reported it, Detective Riley made a note. I guessed he was going to check with security and housekeeping to see if they'd found him or if I was the last person to see him alive—besides the killer, of course. Watts mentioned the raised room temperature and explained that it wouldn't interfere significantly with his ability to estimate the time of death.

"But a nonmedical person wouldn't necessarily know that," Bufort said.

"No," Watts said, "but even a killer who did know might have jacked up the temperature to dry off Kingsly's body after cleaning it up in a hurry with alcohol." He explained about the blood, suggesting that the detectives confirm what he was saying by smelling. Bufort hesitated, then gestured for Riley to do it. The younger man's jaw muscles bulged and he seemed to bristle, but he got down on one knee, gingerly sniffed Kingsly's chest, then nodded.

While Watts and I told what we figured had happened to the clothes and how we thought the police could find the site of the killing, Riley took notes. I watched the muscles in his jaw slowly relax as he wrote.

"Do you have any idea who did this?" Bufort asked when we'd finished. Hurst and Watts shook their heads. I thought of the abandoned mop and bucket I'd seen outside the doctors' lounge but answered, "No."

Bufort frowned at the three of us, then flipped his own notebook closed and warned everyone in the room not to talk. "None of you should discuss the details of what you've seen here tonight, not even with your families. We don't want the killer to have any idea about how much we know."

Hurst cornered Watts and me before we could leave.

"We will carry on business as usual," he said, his voice hard now that he had regained control, "including this morning's planned budget meeting at seven."

I flinched. That was only four hours away.

"And I," he continued, "will announce Kingsly's death, not you two." He glared at Watts and me for a second. "Is that clear?"

Chapter 3

An all-night rain had slicked down the city and left a misty halo around each street lamp. The stoplights at Main and High streets bled their reflections onto the shiny blacktop. It was November, my least favorite month. No snow yet, just sodden leaves and the smells of autumn long gone. I routinely drove to work in the dark and drove home under wet black skies. Sometimes the hissing of the tires nearly put me to sleep, but tonight, thinking of who had killed Kingsly kept me awake, wide awake.

When Bufort had asked if I could come up with of any reason for the murder, I'd immediately thought of Kingsly's reputation for hitting on the female staff. I'd heard more and more gossip about it, escalating in the last six months or so . . . but I'd never received a formal complaint on which I would have had to act. I gathered that he mostly accosted secretaries and lab technicians, and his pawings had been pretty feeble. Someone said he usually passed out before anything got too far, and his victims anonymously called security to pick him up. It was possible, but unlikely, he'd been killed by one of those poor women trying to fight him off—clerks and lab workers didn't have cardiac needles. Yet Detective Bufort and his team were sure to find out about Kingsly's escapades, and would also learn that the housekeepers had always been his particular targets. I simply didn't want to be the one who singled them out.

Fifteen minutes from the hospital I was safely in my driveway and bracing for the full force of Muffy's welcome. I even took off my glasses and pocketed them for safekeeping. As soon as I opened the door, fifty pounds of wiggling black poodle and bad breath were all over my face. "Down, Muff! Down!" I ordered, trying to calm her, but it did little good.

After we greeted each other, we went out for the mandatory walk, the dog perky and jumping at her own puffs of frosted breath, me slouched with cold and envying her endless capacity for play. Finally she finished, and we closed up the house together.

As I entered the bedroom and undressed, Muffy immediately headed for my pillow. I was too tired to kick her off. Hell, she'd been sleeping there all night anyway. Instead, I located Janet's blond hair in the dark and slipped alongside her curled form. I snuggled up enough to steal a corner of her pillow. Only four months pregnant, she described herself as "still disgustingly slim, compared to most of my patients."

"Did you take out the dog?" she murmured.

"Yes."

"Did you lock up?"

"Yes."

I was thinking my day was finally done, but Janet partially rolled toward me and flopped her arm onto my face.

"Kitzle me."

Roughly translated, *kitzle* means I'm to stroke her arm.

"I'm tired, Woof."

"And I'm carrying your child!"

I kitzled.

I awoke at six to the sounds of my wife barfing in the bathroom.

"Can I help?"

"Yeah. Next time, *you* get pregnant!"

Muffy found me a little more useful. We made our out-door tour together, still in the gloom and predawn mist. My head ached from lack of sleep and visions of Kingsly, and that coupled with Bufort's instructions made me figure this wasn't the best time to tell Janet about Kingsly's death.

I once swore that I would never marry a doctor. Two impossible schedules in one relationship would never work, I'd predicted back in medical school, with the dubious certainty I possessed in my early twenties. It took fifteen years before I met and fell in love with Janet to put an end to that myth. Both of us thrived on the demands of medicine, and though we didn't see each other as often as some other couples might, it was enough for us. I'd tried once to show her an article in one of my journals that had suggested *professional couples needed the distance provided by work so as not to feel smothered, yet still stay close.*

She had smiled, walked over to where I was sitting, and straddled my lap. "You balance me," she'd said while taking off my glasses. Then we'd made love, and the subject never came up again.

Back in the kitchen I wiped Muffy's paws, filled her bowls, and listened to Janet put on her Dr. Graceton voice and phone the OR at her hospital—we deliberately worked at different institutions. She was halfway through setting up her operating schedule when I finished with the dog and blew her a kiss on my way out the door. She promptly indicated on which part of her anatomy I could place my affection. This was one of the reasons we worked separately.

The road back to the hospital wasn't quite as deserted as it had been on my trip home a few hours earlier, but the sound of the tires and my opinion of the wet hadn't altered. It was usually about this time of year when I considered a career change.

The meeting Hurst had refused to cancel was our annual slugfest to divide up the budget for hospital equipment. I could understand why he wanted us to carry on as normally as possible, but his rather fierce insistence that only *he* would announce Kingsly's death was a little odd. Hell, everyone would know soon anyway. I didn't even think it would take long for word to get out that it had been murder, no matter what Detective Bufort might want. Our gossip network was one of the fastest east of the Mississippi.

My walk across the parking lot did little to lift my spirits. Over me towered the lights and windows of St. Paul's. Eight hundred beds, and from each of them I could imagine a plea by its occupant that this not be the final stop. I shivered as I felt these entreaties add their weight to the morning chill.

Normally a seven o'clock meeting would sputter to a start at seven-thirty. This morning the brightly lit boardroom was positively cheery with the smells of fresh coffee and hot danish. The usual cast of departmental chiefs was already into second servings and exuding a gaiety more befitting a cruise ship than our yearly squabble over money. Obviously, they hadn't heard about Kingsly.

Hurst and the director of finance, Thomas Laverty, came in, slammed their Dickensian-size ledgers bulging with computer printouts onto the table, and sat down. The air changed. An odor of stale flesh and out-of-date thinking wafted through the room as they assumed their places.

"Gentlemen," Hurst said, "the meeting will come to order."

People coughed, scraped their chairs, and settled into the glazed trances they normally needed to endure these sessions. I noticed that Watts was absent. He was probably downstairs, already starting the postmortem on

Kingsly. I wondered how the rest of the chiefs would react when Hurst announced his death.

"Okay," Hurst said. "The first order of business is the hospital deficit. Mr. Laverty?"

Son of a bitch! He wasn't going to tell them. Incredulous, I stared at Hurst, who caught my eye but looked pointedly at Laverty. Business as usual? That was obscene. Why was he waiting? And from the calm way Laverty started off his remarks, I could only presume Hurst hadn't told him either.

I sat there stunned by Hurst's callousness. I caught snippets about "services provided," "managed care plans," and "rates below what we've traditionally charged" as Laverty droned on about deficits and abandoning fee-for-service remuneration. I couldn't tune in to a review of issues that were standard for most hospitals in the country. Whatever all of us thought of Kingsly, he had been a colleague, and nothing justified pushing on with a meeting like this within hours of his murder. My outrage grew as Laverty started showing pie charts and announcing figures while Hurst carefully fixed his baggy eyes on first one chief, then the next—his usual maneuver whenever he wanted to intimidate and stifle criticism. Most hadn't the balls to challenge the numbers anyway, and "a two-point-five-million deficit" slipped by without pause for questions.

Laverty started a familiar review of how bigger hospitals had bought and closed smaller indebted hospitals to increase patient volume, but I had stopped even trying to pay attention, and his voice rumbled into the distance. Instead, I sank into a fugue of exhaustion and gave way to feeling sick at heart over the murder and Hurst's brutal indifference to it. Finally, some of Laverty's words again penetrated my fatigue.

"Therefore," I heard him say, "we have no choice but to close a hundred beds immediately—and indefinitely."

My first reaction was that I'd heard wrong, that I'd missed something by not keeping track of his little lecture. I knew immediately what the impact would be. Previous closures of other hospitals had overloaded the remaining emergency departments, and beds everywhere in the county were scarce. As it was, we had patients waiting one or two days in the ER before they finally got admitted. Now no one would have rapid access to beds, and we could expect the corridors of emergency to be littered with rows of stretchers.

But I hadn't heard wrong—the uneasy look on Laverty's face told me that. He kept glancing nervously at Hurst, but Hurst's expression remained hard, cold.

Murmurs of alarm started coming from the others around the table.

"What about electives?"

"We'll never get our cancer patients in."

"Christ, our gallbladders'll have gangrene by the time—"

"Are you out of your little minds?" Sean Carrington, seated next to me, boomed. His muscular physique and red, bushy eyebrows made him look more like a Highland chieftain than the chief of surgery.

"Oh, of course I'll accept any reasonable alternative," replied Hurst as he made a pyramid of his fingers in front of his mouth.

Sean went red at Hurst's sarcasm, and I had to catch his arm while he took a few gulps of air to tame his well-known temper. Hurst just stared back at him as if Sean were a besotted fool to care about our patients.

Hector Saswald, chief of anesthesia and our leading opportunist, picked this awkward pause to test where he would be politically safe. "Uh, Mr. Laverty, you estimated a deficit of two point five million. Are you able to say how much we will save by closing a hundred beds?"

"Not exactly."

"Not exactly?"

"Well," Laverty said, "we can't fire anyone because of the unions, so we won't save in salaries, but we *will* use less power and linen, and of course laundry and food costs will fall. We just haven't broken out these costs per bed yet. Haven't had a chance to get to it. However, I can assure you the savings will be significant."

We were speechless.

Saswald quickly made his political choice. "Well, that explains any questions that I had. I commend senior management for its initiative and leadership in solving this problem for us, and I wish to have it recorded in the minutes that I give my full support for any additional budget-trimming measures of these kinds they come up with."

Beaming at Hurst, he sat back in his chair.

Hurst still didn't seem to care.

The rest of us needed a few seconds to realize the jerk was serious. I felt Sean start to tense again beside me, but I leaped to my feet before he throttled someone.

"Mr. Laverty, let me make sure I understand what has so thrilled Saswald here. Basically, you have no idea how much money will be saved by closing a hundred beds, and you don't have any idea how long they will be closed. Is that right?"

Laverty stared at me as if it would have been obvious to a half-wit the first time. "So?" was his only reply.

"So since the savings are to come from the laundry, linen, and food normally used by the patients in these beds, you must be planning to keep them in emergency unfed, unclothed, and sheetless."

"Dr. Garnet, I object!" shouted Laverty, flapping his hands at Hurst for help.

Hurst responded by slamming his hand on the table as if it were a gavel. "You're out of order, Garnet!"

"Like hell I am. There hasn't been an elective admission in medicine for a decade—they're all emergencies

—and we've twice as many of them since those other hospitals were shut down. Closing a hundred of our own beds now and letting even more patients pile up in the ER is nuts."

I looked around for help. There were mutterings of approval and nods in unison from less than half of those around the table. The rest of the chiefs, the scared little political shits in the room, wouldn't even look at me. They watched the extent of Hurst's indifference, then accepted the inevitable and stayed silent. I felt the fight going out of me as their inertia and my own fatigue weighed me down . . . until I saw Hurst start to smirk.

I slammed *my* fist down.

Now Sean put his hand on my arm. Everyone else shrank back. Except Hurst.

"Really, Dr. Garnet—"

"Days and nights in emergency corridors, sir, are not funny, with the noise and stink of overcrowding, on top of the pain and fear that patients come to us with. That's the *reasonable alternative* that you and your cost cutting have gotten us."

"That's not fair!" Hurst snarled.

"When you and the mighty minds that run health care in this county got together two years ago, we ended up with the bright idea of closing hospitals. Except the boys with the calculators—the experts who assured us we could absorb the increased load and not let care suffer— goofed! You've done a lot of talking since, but not much has changed. Hell, some days we're so jammed, we've had to refuse ambulances and hope nobody died trying to make it to the next ER."

I stopped myself then. The litany of screwups was endless, and heaping it on Hurst wasn't entirely fair. In giving vent to my fury and attacking him personally, I'd succeeded only in making an ass of myself. Everyone at the table except Sean started easing away from me, even my few allies from minutes earlier, their eyes shifting or hooding over with embarrassment. Yet as I fought to control my rage, I could have sworn Hurst looked pleased by my outburst. I couldn't reconcile the devastated man from last night with the cold cynic who seemed to be gloating at me now. And still not a word about Kingsly. Why was he waiting?

"Gentlemen!" The soothing tones of Dr. Gil Fernandez, chief of psychiatry, poured onto our troubled waters.

Standing by the doorway, he must have slipped in unnoticed before I'd started my rant. He was tall and impeccably dressed in his trademark dark suit with a scarlet handkerchief elaborately puffed up in his breast pocket. He wore his black hair swept back from a high, balding forehead. A thin, carefully trimmed mustache seemed to give him three lips.

When every eye was on him, he completed his entrance by stepping to a vacant chair beside Hurst. "For the record," he declared pompously, distracting everyone from my hysterics by his own strangeness, "as I have pointed out many times, psychiatry returns funds to the hospital from our pool to cover our own operating expenses, and therefore I feel we can in no way be held responsible for the deficit and must be excluded from any bed cuts. I assure you I've briefed Mr. Kingsly fully on our unique situation."

I almost blurted out *Kingsly's dead, you pompous prick,* but I made myself keep quiet. I wanted to see if Fernandez's use of the dead man's name would force Hurst to finally tell everyone. It didn't. Hurst simply gazed benignly at Fernandez, then said, "Of course, Dr. Fernandez, your situation is unique. Our calculations suggest the new measures in your department will be limited to a few beds at most."

The smug look between the two curdled what was left of the milk in the few sips of coffee I'd gotten down.

"Speaking of Kingsly, where *is* our chief executive officer?" Sean asked. "Has he permanently withdrawn from these meetings?"

This wasn't an innocent inquiry. At every meeting over the last couple of years, one of us had made a point of asking where Kingsly was. We hadn't wanted him present; we'd wanted him fired. So we'd taken turns putting his absences on the record. But Hurst basically ran the hospital the way he wanted in Kingsly's absence and had no interest in getting him fired. He was fully aware of our impotent little game but dutifully excused Kingsly each time to keep his absences off the record. For this crap, we'd become doctors.

But that was over now.

Despite my orders from Hurst, I had to let Sean know. I leaned toward his ear and quietly warned, "Stop it! Not anymore."

He gave me a puzzled look. "Wait a minute," he protested. "The guy should be here! If he can't cut it, get him replaced! We decided—"

"He's dead!" I whispered, trying to get him to shut up. "They found him last night in his office." But it was too late.

Hurst leaped to his feet. "How dare you speak ill of the dead!" he roared. He didn't even wait for a collective gasp before adding, "For years I've put up with your snide remarks and outright insults about the poor man, but this morning, it's too much!"

Sean and I were frozen. The others kept darting their eyes to us and back to Hurst. For a moment I thought he'd snapped. His cheeks were violently red and his body shook. Then he stiffly drew himself straighter, just as I'd seen him do in Kingsly's office earlier that morning. But now, unlike then, his eyes were hard and focused. This was an act, and I realized what he'd been up to all along.

"It is my extremely sad duty," he began, in a low tone

now, with just the right tremble in his voice, "to announce the untimely passing of Mr. Kingsly. He was found dead in his office last night."

No lies there. The expected "Oh, no," "That's awful," "How sad" broke out around the table, but no one asked a single question about cause of death. I guessed everyone simply assumed it was related to his drinking.

"And I am doubly shaken," Hurst continued, his voice again rising, filling with a carefully honed anger, "by the insulting words of Drs. Garnet and Carrington regarding our poor friend and leader."

He gazed slowly around at his audience so none would miss the look of hurt he wore because of Sean and me. "I tried to carry on business as usual in the way I know the man would have wanted us to, but now simple dignity demands that we adjourn this meeting." He wearily sat back in his chair and covered his eyes.

The better to hide his triumph, I thought.

He'd rammed through the cuts, used Kingsly's death to shut off debate, and made Sean and me, his two most troublesome chiefs, seem like malicious malcontents.

Tic, tac, toe.

One glance around the table told me they'd all bought it.

More futility, but I had to try. Again for the record, in case there ever came a time when it might actually matter, I asked, "Are the closures a fait accompli, or are you asking the chiefs to vote?"

The incredulous stares of everyone leaving the table confirmed I was the village idiot.

The only person not looking at me was Fernandez. He was staring off into space with the relieved expression of a man who'd just gotten a negative cancer test.

Chapter 4

A thin, gruel-colored light seeped through the end window and down the still-deserted corridor. It made everything look gray. As I swung into a better lit stairwell leading to emergency, I glanced at the wall clock: 7:45. It normally took until noon before I was this mad.

It was a relief to hit the bright, familiar bustle of our department after the idiocy upstairs. I walked through the sounds and smells of morning signout rounds, a ritual at dawn carried out in every ER in the world where the night people hand over their patients to the day staff. The aroma of coffee mingled with the smell of toast, scrambled eggs, and the overnight odor of unwashed patients. An even worse stench came from the unemptied bedpan on a nearby stretcher.

The nursing station, a large central room, had huge windows with views of the department and the area just outside, where ambulances rolled in and unloaded patients. Wide countertops ran under the windows and were crowded with telephones, monitors, computer screens, keyboards, and racks of requisition forms. A curl of messages dangled down to the floor from our sole fax machine, but nobody had taken the time to rip them off yet, let alone read them. Parked here and there beside the counters were chairs on rollers, but most were unoccupied. The nurses stood while they scribbled notes, used the phones, or read orders and then hustled back out the open doorways that led to the surrounding stretcher and resuscitation areas. A clutter of abandoned half-full paper cups gave testimony to how busy they were.

In one corner, I spotted Dr. Michael Popovitch, listening intently to the quiet murmur of our residents and interns giving report. I silently gave thanks that this calm, bearded man was on duty today; I'd need both his expertise and humor. He raised a finger in greeting, cocked an eyebrow at the piles of charts around him, and returned to the liturgy being delivered by a sleepy-looking medical student.

"Patient twenty-one is a fifty-year-old male who experienced chest pain that woke him at three this morning. . . ."

Susanne turned from one of the countertop phones she'd been using. "What's this crap? Admitting tells me there are no beds and not to expect any. They've got discharges planned, but orders came from Hurst not to assign the expected vacancies on the floors to us. No patient's gone upstairs since late yesterday afternoon, and we already have twenty admitted and another fifteen—" Then, registering the expression on my face, she stopped. "Uh-oh!"

To underline her point, on the security monitor for the ambulance bay I could see two ambulances wheeling through the garage doors. Within moments our latest guests were rolled in, end to end, with all the panache of a pizza delivery. Both patients were bundled, old, and scared.

Susanne turned from me and pressed the intercom. "Triage!" Through the station windows, I saw Lisa Gray emerge from behind a curtain, put down a bedpan, and approach our new arrivals with a smile that visibly calmed them both. Behind me, the dirge from signout droned on, unfazed. ". . . pain was burning, and when he called his doctor, a nursing assistant advised a bit of Maalox but wouldn't approve an ER visit . . ."

I returned to Susanne and led her outside the nursing station to a quiet spot in the corridor near where Lisa had received the new patients from the ambulances.

"It's that bad, eh?" she asked.

"Yeah, it's that bad. The mighty minds upstairs have decided to close a hundred beds to balance their books."

"What?"

I might as well have hit her.

"Are they nuts," she screeched. It wasn't a question.

Two attendants rolled in another ambulance patient. Lisa, still smiling, met them. Incredulous, Susanne sagged against the wall. I changed topics.

"You know about Kingsly?"

"Yeah, not many will weep for that lech. Was it his heart?"

Her cold indifference to the man's death made me flinch. I shrugged since I didn't want to lie and walked quickly back into the nursing station before she could ask any more questions.

Hospital telegraph had gotten out the news Kingsly was dead, but for the moment only a few of us, the murderer included, knew he'd been killed. I for one intended to keep it that way. The ER had enough problems without my letting the secret out and getting in hot water with the police.

Yet it was Susanne's callous remark that burned at the back of my brain. I didn't blame her. Tragically, I knew, it was how most hospital personnel would react. What stung me was the way it echoed the times I'd also bad-mouthed Kingsly, and I felt ashamed. While Susanne stayed in the hallway to help Lisa with triage, I pretended to study the admissions list as my mind flashed to eight years ago—an era when Kingsly's opinion still carried weight—and I again recalled his welcome endorsement . . . that first smile and handshake. I had to force myself to focus on our immediate dilemma.

"When my secretary gets in," I said to the clerk, "have her call all our docs for an emergency meeting at five." The anger in my voice surprised both of us. "Sorry," I quickly added, embarrassed at the lapse. She just smiled and shrugged it off, probably putting it down to stress over the buildup of patients. "Then have her get me all the chiefs," I continued in a calmer tone. "I want to see them at noon."

But none of this impressed any of the nurses within earshot. What we needed were beds, not meetings and phone calls. Through the open door to the triage area I saw Susanne roll her eyes at the ceiling as another patient was brought in on a stretcher. Lisa had stopped smiling.

I thought of one phone call that might help. "And get me the director down at MAS," I added rather loudly. "I'll try and get him to back off sending us ambulances for a few hours."

With an extreme situation, I could usually bypass the brain-dead twits who "managed" day-to-day operations at MAS, the acronym for Metropolitan Ambulance Services, and go directly to Zak Evans, their medical director. So far I'd been five minutes on hold.

Ambulance services in Buffalo, in all of Erie County for that matter, were coordinated by a central dispatch system run out of city hall, but the staff was managed by a large national corporation that specialized in urban and rural prehospital care. Zak Evans was essential to their operation.

He had worked emergency before the organization had hired him to solve some serious problems they'd encountered with the competence of their personnel. When the company first took over, it had either bought out local ambulance fleets or made contracts with private ambulance companies to acquire the vehicles, technicians, and paramedics needed to serve the city. But with so many different groups involved, enforcing standards of care had been difficult, and while most of the workers were reasonably qualified, some were clearly not. At a few of the smaller outfits, driving an ambulance had been little more than a better paid plum for union truckers to haul patients instead of cabbages. They'd received enough hours of rudimentary training so that legally they could call themselves technicians, but they remained far from adequate. Before the takeover, previous attempts to introduce a test of professional competence and accountability had been seen as a threat and had resulted in ambulances being firebombed.

Zak was asked to pull all these disparate groups into a cohesive unit and upgrade the county's prehospital care. It had seemed an impossible task, but he'd successfully integrated the better attendants and paramedics as team leaders throughout the ranks of the service, then empowered them to ensure their members were properly trained. For the most part, it had worked. A few of the rogue outfits were still on the road, but we all knew who they were, and we double-checked everything whenever we got a patient from one of them. As for Zak, we made him the saint of Erie County ERs.

He finally answered his phone.

"Zak, it's Earl. How are you doing?"

"Me? I'm fine, but I hear one of your great leaders bought it."

"I'm impressed, Zak. Too bad you can't get me an ambulance as quickly as you get the inside dope."

"Hey, don't get dirty, Earl. No mystery though. It came over the police band at dispatch."

Yeah, I thought, and now it's probably all over every ER in the city.

"What happened?" he asked, his attempt at disinterest failing. Zak prided himself on knowing secrets. "And why are the police involved?" he added a little too eagerly. I realized he still didn't know Kingsly had been murdered. Maybe I had something to trade.

I hunched down over the phone so people around the station couldn't hear. "Zak, it's terrible. This has to be kept strictly between you and me."

I also hoped my lower-voice routine would raise the exchange value of my secret. "The mighty minds here closed a hundred beds this morning after we found Kingsly dead. I think, well . . ."

I paused to give the impression of a conspiracy. After a couple of seconds he nibbled.

"What? Tell me. You know it stays with me."

Sure, until the next trade, I thought. I had to be careful exactly how I phrased this so I could still follow Bufort's directive, sort of, and yet get what I wanted for the ER. "Zak, look, I need a ban on ambulances for twenty-four hours. I think Kingsly's death was, well, suspicious."

Hell, if Zak would buy a linkage between closing beds and the mysterious death of an administrator, it could even be useful. Might cause an outbreak of competence elsewhere. Set a trend.

"What?"

"Yeah, and it's going to take at least twenty-four hours to sort it out and get the beds open."

"Murder?"

"I didn't say that!" I blurted out. But here came the offer. I was whispering now. "Of course, with your cooperation so closely tied in to the developing situation here, we'd update you immediately on any breaks in the case."

I winced at how much I was sounding like a Scotland Yard movie. Zak, I knew, loved British mysteries.

"He was murdered?"

"I didn't say that, Zak."

"But if I grant the ban, you keep me informed?"

"Of course."

There was a pause. Then, "Okay, you've got it."

"Thanks. I owe you."

My giddiness at having won a little reprieve was short-lived. I suddenly realized only the residents were signing out. "Susanne, where's Kradic?"

She looked up from the chart she'd been writing in at the counter. "I know you don't need this kind of grief today," she answered, "but Kradic left early."

"What?"

"You heard me. Kradic left as soon as Dr. Popovitch got here. Didn't even do signout rounds. Claimed he had an important appointment. He said the residents knew the cases and could transfer them to Dr. Popovitch."

I couldn't believe he'd had the gall to leave early right after I called him on the carpet for arriving late. That he left on a morning overloaded with patients was doubly unforgivable. The residents didn't know yet how to decide who was safe to send home, who wasn't, and either way, what the best treatment plan was. Popovitch would have had to double-check everything.

"You want my suggestion?" Susanne asked, eyeing a walk-in patient who was bent over with pain. "Fire him!"

"I just gave him hell last night about being late!" I called after her a bit defensively.

I *was* mad enough to turf him out, but I tolerated Kradic in the department because he was a brilliant clinician. His resuscitations bordered on miracles, the residents loved his teaching, and he took every shift I could give him, including half of our permanent nights. Yet with his peers, he could be abrasive, sarcastic, and belittling. As chief of the department, keeping the place staffed was part of my job, and I'd give myself an even bigger problem with coverage if I made him leave. Still, arriving late and leaving early was serious, and I would have to deal firmly with him or discipline would go to hell. Another walk-in patient holding a bloody towel to his head was being led to a stretcher. Thirty percent of our admissions crawled, walked, or taxied to our door without ambulances, and we couldn't redirect *them*. Right now I was going to have to fix the mess in front of me, and fast.

I held the telephone receiver about six inches from my ear. Dr. Valerie Jones, who shared the night coverage with Kradic, was raging at me.

"Why are you calling me on my time off? How dare you—"

"Valerie, I need extra help today. The agreement is, you provide us with backup on the weeks you don't do nights."

Eight years ago I'd hired Valerie to work nights. Since then several other physicians had taken the job with her . . . for a year or two. They were usually recent graduates just starting out who liked the free time during the days to study or to set up a practice. For them the job was temporary. But Jones stayed.

"Hey," she snarled, "I cover half the nights and any other shifts you need me for. I sure don't deserve to be criticized for not pulling *my* share of the load."

"I'm not criticizing you, Valerie, only asking for your help." She was as prickly as Kradic, but where he got loud, Jones got sullen and spiteful.

"Ask Kradic!" she said with mock sweetness, as though she had guessed my thoughts.

"You know very well he's on nights this week," I replied wearily. She had been resentful as hell ever since I hired him the previous year. Until then she had been the solo star of the night shift. Now his prowess with resuscitations matched her own, and she had to share the adulation of the residents.

"Can you please come in?" I asked again, trying not to

sound like I was begging. In a pinch I'd humble myself
to soothe her defensiveness, because when inflamed she
bordered on paranoid. Even though my tracking her
down at home probably made her suspicious. "Look," I
started, lowering my voice to make it sound like I was
revealing confidential information to her. "ER's a mess.
The idiots upstairs closed a hundred beds today. The
overcrowding is already unmanageable, and we need
you."

"Sorry, but I have a research meeting at MAS."

Christ, she was really going to make me struggle. "I
thought this was what you wanted, Valerie, more shifts.
You're always complaining you don't have enough work
since Dr. Kradic joined our department."

I listened to her breathing while I hoped that her jeal-
ousy of Kradic would override her need to punish me.

"I can come in starting tomorrow," she said coldly.

"Why, thank you, Valerie, that will be a big help
today." I hung up before she could answer back or hang
up on me.

I sat there fuming. It's hard to fault research, especially
new cardiac arrest work. But she threw it in my face
whenever she could. The irony was that I was the one
who'd encouraged her to become involved with the study
in the first place.

Four years ago, Zak had enrolled MAS and Buffalo
area hospitals in a large American/Canadian trial of new
drug protocols for the treatment of cardiac arrests. They
had needed emergency physicians to ride the ambulances
and supervise the prehospital portion of the study. Jones
had already worked with them on other research projects
requiring fieldwork by doctors out on the road, so I had
suggested she participate in this, their largest effort to
date. Whatever I thought of her personally, she'd accumulated more experience in emergency care studies
than anyone else in the department and was our best

candidate. I'd even offered to adjust her schedule to accommodate the additional workload, since our own teaching program benefited when a staff member was actively involved in research. I'd actually been pleased when she'd accepted, and doubly so when she did well.

But I'd had enough of my departmental prima donnas for one day. I pushed away from my desk and headed out of my office back toward the ER.

"Of course it's atypical," Popovitch yelled into the phone. "Twenty percent of them are. But the ECG and enzymes confirm an inferior MI and he's on streptokinase. You shouldn't have withheld the ER visit in the first place! You guys are supposed to manage care, not withhold it!"

He slammed down the receiver and then turned to the openmouthed residents and quickly assigned each of them to a new case. When he'd finished, I motioned him to join me in the corridor and told him about the bed closures. This got me more than another arched eyebrow. "Jesus Christ! If it isn't HMO gurus, it's our own damned administrators. What are you going to do?"

"Declare war!" I proclaimed dramatically even though I didn't have a single idea about my strategy or tactics.

Popovitch just shook his head, then ran off down the hall to deal with the rising chaos.

I checked with Susanne to see if I could help her with any immediate problems. She had one.

"It's another DOA from the streets. That's about the sixth derelict we've gotten since summer. I gave MAS hell, but they insist they're spreading them around. They claim there are a lot of them lately."

She handed me a sheaf of forms. "If you do the paperwork, I can at least find him a bed. The morgue always has room."

She gave me a sly smile. "Your patient is waiting in

Room C, Doctor," she told me, and then got out of the way before I could hand back the forms she'd given me.

Sounds weird for a doctor, but being alone with a dead body gives me the creeps, and this was my second in less than twelve hours. It's nothing to do with medicine. As long as there is even a spark of electricity left in some remaining cell, there's still life somewhere, and we can try to treat. But a corpse is just too . . . too final. I find myself holding my breath. It's illogical because, unlike Kingsly's corpse, I usually see one long before the decay sets up an odor.

The cadaver in front of me was middle-aged going on eighty. Sleeping on sewer vents, eating garbage, and guzzling cheap booze had mapped his face with broken red and blue lines. They spread over the gray and yellow parchment that had been his skin like an atlas of the winter alleys and dark streets that had got him here. Once he hadn't been like this, but it was hard to imagine when he still might have had enough hope to avoid such a pathetic end.

Masked and gloved, I shivered and got on with it. I had to declare formally the absence of respirations and pulse. There were no gross traces of violence or trauma, and death was probably due to natural causes, if the living conditions that killed him could be called natural. It would take an autopsy to determine the cause of death for certain, but the autopsies mandated by law on Jane and John Does were often cursory . . . to say the least. Even health care for the dead was overbudget.

I quickly checked the DOA for local abscesses or thrombosed veins indicating repeated self-injection but saw none. Eager to get back outside, I was giving the rest of the body a hurried exam when I spotted a tiny speck on the man's chest.

In normal circumstances, I never would have noticed so small a mark, let alone given it a second glance. Dark, innocuous, it might have been a mole, a bit of dirt even, or an insignificant scab. It was the location that set off the alarms. This man had a mark just left of the xiphoid-sternal junction, the lower tip of the breastbone—the usual site for an intracardiac injection.

I stared at it, wanting it to vanish, but there it remained. It was nothing near as big as the scab I'd found on Kingsly—this was merely a dot—but the location was exact.

I felt increasingly uneasy as I leaned down for a closer look. I still couldn't tell what it was. I took a breath, lifted my mask, and blew on the mark in case the speck was a balled-up piece of fabric or some other foreign material that had ended up stuck there by chance. The spot didn't move.

It might yet have proved to be a particle of dirt that would lift off with a wet Q-Tip and reveal intact skin underneath, but I didn't want to disturb anything until I was sure this wasn't something Watts should see first. Scanning the rest of the skin for similar marks, I found a few sebum-filled pockmarks on his face and neck that were blackheads, and benign moles on his extremities. I started to relax, but went back to the original mark. The surrounding skin seemed to be flat, not rolled or raised as was common with blackheads. I looked at the spot from the side and was able to see a slightly rounded elevation in the center. It could be a mole, but then again, maybe not. Feeling foolish, I gingerly pressed down on the man's stiffened cold chest with the palm of my hand to verify that nothing poked or bubbled out from under the mark as had happened with Kingsly.

Nothing did.

Thank God! I thought, embarrassed at having been so easily spooked by something that was probably as simple as a mole. As I exhaled, I realized I'd been holding my breath again.

I was tempted to lay the matter to rest myself and confirm with a Q-Tip if it could either be washed away like sebum or dirt or was fixed like a mole and couldn't be removed, but I still refrained from touching it. If it came off and was a scab, Watts and the police would have my head for interfering with the site before they checked if there was an underlying puncture mark and needle track—first by gross examination with magnification under a bright light, then microscopically after excising the area and mounting slices of the tissue on glass slides. Better leave it for Watts, I decided, feeling silly to bother him about a thing that was sure to be trivial. The idea of this guy being killed the same way as Kingsly was preposterous.

At the door I deposited my mask and gloves, picked up the death certificate, and returned to the nursing station, where I found a quiet corner to fill out the forms. On the second page was an outline of the human figure, front and back, to let me indicate any significant marks on the man's body. I made a dot in the drawing at the left lower tip of the breastbone, drew a small circle around it, and marked it with an arrow from the margin. There I wrote, "Attention Dr. Watts: Pigmented lesion vs. small scab at left xiphoid-sternal junction. Check it out?" I was sure going to be red-faced if it turned out to be dirt.

As I wrote, the familiar sounds of the department getting busy pattered in the background.

"Portable chest in three, please."

"Right."

"Triage at the desk."

"Has CMU called for the MI in bed three yet?"

"No, and the streptokinase is nearly through."

"Still stable?"

"Sort of. His BP's a little low, but I kept the drip going."

Concentrating on the blanks that reduced the end of a life to a few hasty scrawls, I tried to ignore the chatter around me. But I knew it meant we had a heart attack patient in danger of going into shock from the drugs we were giving to dissolve the blood clot in his coronary arteries.

"CMU on line four; they've no more beds."

"What!"

Now I also knew they had no room for that heart attack patient in the cardiac monitoring unit.

"Ambulance in the corridor."

"Triage at the desk, stat!"

"V. tach. in bed five!"

"Shit!"

Ventricular tachycardia is a potentially lethal cardiac rhythm. Another patient was about to arrest.

"Ninety-nine, emergency! Ninety-nine, emergency!"

Christ, I wondered, could this day be real?

I threw aside the uncompleted forms and ran to help Popovitch.

The cardiac arrest in bed five made it, but during the resuscitation the condition of the heart attack case in bed three had grown worse, much worse. He'd been unattended and gone hypotensive on his streptokinase drip while all the nurses in his area were helping us two beds over. By the time they got back to him, saw what was happening, and stopped the drip, he was in shock.

We gave intravenous volume to try to regain his pressure without overloading his already damaged heart, but he remained hypotensive.

Pale, scared, and young, "the cardiac" became a name. Donald Cummings, denied a cardiac bed and proper monitoring in order to save money, now required an even more expensive level of care in the ICU, and would probably end up with nothing more than a monitored dying. The good news, for a cynic, was that the ICU did have a vacancy. The man I'd resuscitated the night before had died.

My rage at reducing Donald Cummings to economics was replaced by dread as I faced his wife. She was white with fear and trembled as she held her husband's hand and gently stroked his head. Her courage was as limp and frail as his heart. I felt dirty when I finally walked away to go to my office.

My secretary was out for coffee, but she'd obviously been busy.

The first note I saw on my desk confirmed that most of the chiefs whom I'd asked to attend the meeting at noon would be there. Then there was the message to call Bufort. The detective apparently had phoned while I was trying to resuscitate Cummings, demanding to see me *immediately*. He could damn well wait his turn. So could the reporters. All three of them who'd called to get a quote from me about Kingsly's death. Probably wanted a lot more than a quote. I tore up those messages.

The morning's correspondence had been screened, prioritized, and stacked to one side. That signaled it would be mostly calls to meetings and minutes of previous meetings mixed with a few cranky letters of complaint— the stuff of a routine paper-shuffle and even less inviting than a meeting with Bufort.

I looked at the wall unit of files. When I had first chosen emergency twenty years ago, it was because of the allure of high-risk medicine, the chance to literally raise the dead and be part of the medical elite on the front line of care. It also meant freedom. The cowboys who worked in the pit seemed excused from the stuffy social conformity that dominated the rest of the profession. We could do a few shifts, then head off to a rock concert in a VW bus and not get shunned by the hospital elders as long as we performed well in the ER.

Now everything had changed. The profession in general was much freer, largely as a result of medical schools recruiting people from a wider range of backgrounds and encouraging women to join our ranks in equal numbers. The all-male bastion crumpled, and medical thinking reflected ideas from the arts as well as the sciences. And I was a respected chief, forty-eight years old, and weighed down by looking at the paperwork from seven years of talk. Had any of it done anything? So much pointless chatter recorded in dusty stacks of minutes, and yet we still slid into more cuts, more compromise. I'd skip these sessions altogether, but it was a constant fight to limit the harm being done, and that morning I'd failed. Donald Cummings had overcome his HMO trying to deny him a visit to the ER, only to pay the price of the bed closures. It was a far cry from how I had thought medical practice would be back in the shining time of beards and long hair.

I leaned out of my inertia toward the phone, intending to get my call to Bufort over with, but I'd barely picked up the receiver when the door opened after a perfunctory knock and the good detective himself strode into my office, two uniformed policemen trailing him. "Dr. Garnet," he said without preamble, "I want your files of departmental meetings and personnel records. Now, please!"

The demand was like a club slammed on my desk. . . . Or maybe right into my midsection.

"What on earth—" I began, half rising out of my chair.

"You heard me," he snapped. "The minutes of your departmental meetings and your personnel files!" He came up and stood directly opposite me, my desk still between us. I got the rest of the way to my feet, and the two uniformed policemen moved to either end of the desk, as though I might make a run for it.

"What are you doing?" I asked, looking from one cop to the other and then back to Bufort. He put both his hands on the desktop, leaned forward, and said, "Well?"

It took me several seconds to gather my thoughts

enough to answer. "The ER minutes are filed upstairs with all the other minutes of meetings held around here. You can get them there." Why the hell hadn't Kingsly's staff just given them to him?

Bufort stared at me.

I was regaining my wits quickly now. "As for my personnel records, those are confidential. They contain among other things the record of any peer review or disciplinary action a physician has been subjected to. I'm bound by hospital bylaws to protect that information from unauthorized scrutiny. You would need a subpoena, and it would have to be for a given individual. You can't just go fishing through a whole department's confidential files."

"You refuse?" he asked, still staring at me without blinking.

"You know I have to," I answered, growing a little impatient at his obvious attempt to intimidate me.

At first he didn't reply. His expression showed nothing—not anger, not disappointment, not even resentment. But the widened blacks of his eyes warned me he was pumped with adrenaline. I felt my stomach knot as I waited for his next move.

"There's one file you could give me permission to see."

"Oh, whose is that?"

"Yours."

I didn't believe I'd heard him correctly. He'd spoken very softly, but with an edge in his voice that startled me. "Pardon?"

"You could let me see *your* file," he repeated, still in a quiet tone, but I noticed that his beefy cheeks were flushed.

A chill went through me. Before I could speak, he spun around and left the office, his two policemen in tow.

I was left standing behind my desk, trying to figure out

what had just happened. Bufort *must* have been told he could have any minutes he wanted without having to ask me. And more than anyone he would know he *couldn't* go through confidential files for the asking.

Then I got it. He hadn't wanted minutes or files. He wanted me, my reactions. He'd been checking me out. He'd wanted to see how I'd react to him going after old minutes and private files, particularly my own. But why? I felt another twinge of alarm. However crude his bursting in on me had been, he must have had a reason. What had he found or heard about me that interested him? Remembering the parting look on his face was giving me the willies.

My fretting was cut short.

"Ninety-nine, emergency! Ninety-nine, emergency!"

I'd started to run out the door when I heard "Cancel ninety-nine, emergency! Cancel ninety-nine, emergency!"

This meant the arrest code was called off for some reason. I slackened my pace but was still pretty brisk in covering the remaining ground back to the ER.

Susanne met me with an outstretched palm to slow me down. Without my asking, she explained. "One of the cleaning men walked in on the DOA you left in C."

"I left?"

"Yeah. Our cleaning guy just took a staff CPR course. Saw the body, called ninety-nine, and started mouth-to-mouth."

"On a corpse?"

"You know civilians. They can't tell how long somebody's been dead. Hell, they're taught not to quit until a medic or someone qualified says so."

"Where's he now?"

"In the can, barfing. The corpse is on the way to the morgue." She shoved a sheaf of papers at me. "Now, for God's sake, do the paperwork so they don't send him back."

It took less than a minute to finish signing off on the

forms, but then I hesitated. Looking at my note about the mark on the derelict's chest after Bufort's astonishing behavior, I wondered if making a fuss about such an unlikely possibility might draw his attention even more in my direction. Would he see my note as a feeble attempt to send the hospital's pathologist on a wild-goose chase? If I could have erased the entry and had Watts check out the mark first, I would have. I even wondered if I should document the inappropriate attempt to resuscitate a long-dead corpse. To a trained doctor or nurse, it would have been inconceivable to start CPR on an obvious DOA. I certainly had never imagined that an inexperienced civilian with recent CPR training could walk in on one of our bodies and start pumping.

But the same thing had happened with Kingsly. We never would have noticed the blood coming out from around the broken needle if the two cleaning women hadn't started CPR on a body that had obviously been dead for hours. If such a scenario was inconceivable to a doctor or nurse in the ER, could the person who murdered Kingsly have made the same assumption—that by the time Kingsly's body was found it would have been so evidently beyond resuscitation that CPR would never even come to mind, let alone be tried? An experienced resuscitator, trying to get away with Kingsly's murder, would never have guessed that a course for the non-medical staff in CPR would give him away.

Chapter 5

Watts scowled at me. "Look, why don't you leave the detecting to the real detectives?" He'd had to delay Kingsly's autopsy until the forensic experts who'd initially gone over the body for evidence could return from the medical examiner's office. With his other work backed up, he was not thrilled by my surprise visit. I'd taken the half hour remaining before my meeting with the other chiefs to slip down the back staircase that connected to the morgue and the morass of tunnels leading to Watts's office in the basement. In the old days at the beginning of the century, a corpse could be dug up at the cemetery, brought to this back door, and then end up on the dissection table, no questions asked and twenty-five dollars forfeited to the grave robber. A generation of friendly family doctors had learned anatomy on such grisly remains.

"Please answer my question," I said. "What would you have put on the certificate as Kingsly's cause of death if one of those women hadn't started pumping him and exposed the needle? Even with his clothes missing would you have started looking for a needle hole in his chest?"

I waited; he was still reluctant to answer.

"Come on, Robert, what would your first thought have been? Kingsly naked, reeking with booze, found dead?"

He took another moment, but then went along with my invitation to play what-if.

"Finally" was all he said at first.

I waited for more.

"Yeah, me and everyone else in the hospital would say he finally did it. Drank and then screwed himself to death, or, at least, died trying to screw. He never actually raped anyone, at least not according to what I heard."

"Would you expect his clothes to be where he fell, or even be surprised if you'd found him nude?"

"If we didn't know he'd been murdered?" He thought a minute, then answered slowly, "No, probably not. I've heard the guards have found him with half his clothes missing a few other times. The women he'd hit on sure as hell never came up with them."

Watts thought a bit more. "I might wonder about most of his clothes being gone, but I can't say I'd make much of it. No, I wouldn't be surprised. I'd have thought he finally started an MI with his sexual exertions someplace earlier, made it back to his office, and collapsed."

"What about the thermostat being turned up? Would that make you suspicious?"

"Not necessarily, if I wasn't suspicious in the first place. I'd likely figure he'd felt cold, being nude, and had jacked up the heat before he arrested."

"So, with all of us thinking that way, could the actual needle and its mark have gone unnoticed if no one had pumped him?"

"You could count on it. Same thinking as this morning. We all saw how Hurst would have grabbed any chance to cover up and prevent a stink at the hospital. He would have explained it the same way, but in this case we probably would have agreed with him."

"The point is, Robert, not to think of the setup from Hurst's mentality but from the mentality of the killer. To count on all these presumptions is to know about the hospital. I mean *really* know. The way you and I do. Only someone intimate with our secrets and foibles would set up this play, dump Kingsly's nude body in his office with a needle fragment buried in his heart, and still consider it a good plan to cover up a murder."

"What are you getting at?"

"To think like that, it's not just someone who knows the hospital. It's someone so experienced in CPR he never even thought anyone in a hospital would attempt to resuscitate an already stiffening corpse."

Watts gave me a skeptical look.

"Come on," I said. "There was every chance of it being called, even by yourself, a freaky but natural death."

"Okay, Sherlock, so the killer knows the hospital and CPR. Is maybe even one of us. That's at least five hundred doctors, well over a thousand nurses, and God knows how many other trained staff members."

I'd already figured how to narrow that group down considerably, but I needed the postmortem on Kingsly to be sure. The problem was, if we found what I expected, I was going to have a hell of a lot more trouble with Bufort.

"Maybe," I mumbled, getting up to leave. "By the way, we got another DOA that gave me something of a surprise. When I was checking him, I found a mark at his left xiphoid-sternal junction."

"What!"

"Relax, it's probably a mole. But given what I found on Kingsly, I'm afraid I overreacted and noted it on the form, asking you to verify it."

I thought he'd make some parting crack about making moles into mountains.

"Earl, you don't need a goddamn pathologist to diagnose a goddamn mole, no matter where the goddamn thing is located!" he exploded, shocking the hell out of me.

"Robert, I'm sorry. Don't bite my head off. I was just being careful, obviously too careful. Let's forget about it."

Watts took a breath. "Sorry, Earl, this killing's got to

me too. I shouldn't have jumped all over you like that. It's just that it's doubled my work, and I'm behind as it is. The last thing we need around here is someone of your experience and background seeing needle marks every time you spot a mole." He smiled, then added, "We all need to relax, and just do what we normally do. Think horses, not zebras, remember?" It was an old saying from medical school. It was meant to keep the overactive imagination of untrained students from galloping off after uncommon diagnoses.

I grinned at him, feeling pretty sheepish. "Thanks, Robert," I said, then let myself into the warren of tunnels and catacombs outside his dissection room.

Dripping noises mingled with silence; cobwebs mixed with a lot of dust; a jumble of pipes and wires ran overhead. Some of these drooped down in tangles and resembled malignant varices, enlarged tortuous vessels dissected open and left hanging. Several layers of fuzzy mold riddled with scurrying eight-legged life, grown fat on droppings from Watts's table, covered the pipes and wires.

This was where his next two patients waited to receive their final medical act, shrouded, silent, and parked on stretchers. Then I realized one of them might have been our DOA. Watts would declare him yet another victim of the street, and my embarrassing note would disappear onto some dusty shelf. At least I didn't have to worry about Bufort's reaction to it now.

The tunnel stretching in either direction was occasionally pocked with a dim pool of light that added more gloom than illumination. I gratefully fled back up the stairs to the comfort of the noise, confusion, and bright lights of my own department.

Entering my office, I managed to jostle my secretary, who was on her way out with an armload of paper.

"Why, it's Carole Lamont," I exclaimed playfully, bowing as I held open the door to let her pass.

"I'm glad to see you too." She laughed. It was a shared joke. We sometimes went the better part of a day without seeing each other, only a string of notes and phone messages connecting us. Then we'd have a chance encounter and quickly update each other in a shorthand possible only after years of working together. "I'll be back in a minute," she called over her shoulder. "I need to talk to you."

Carole Lamont was singly the person who had sustained me most through my time as chief. She kept the department afloat from day to day. More than a dozen doctors, all our residents, and a team of nurses and clerks deferred to her to coordinate staffing and keep the schedule covered. By slowly taking over most of these logistics, she had freed me to concentrate on teaching, medical matters, and standards of care.

Managing an ER is primarily a matter of managing people: knowing who to stroke, who to push, who to nail to the wall. Yet it was Carole who was the keeper of everyone's secrets. She got them in bits and pieces as she made up the schedule. She knew who was in love, whose marriage was ending, who'd just been dumped, who had a sick child. All of it, even joy, could distract a physician and sabotage patient care. So we watched who wanted more time off, who wanted less, and why. From these requests and the reasons for them—revealed to Carole, not to me—we knew who I could ask to do what and when. Brusque at times, efficient always, Carole had a soft shoulder that was obvious nonetheless and encouraged people to confide in her.

"You heard?" I asked when she came back in the door, unencumbered by paper.

"About the bed closures, yes. About Kingsly, a bit. Is it true what they're saying?"

"What's that?"

She lowered her voice. "That he was murdered?"

The gossip network had finally gotten through.

"I'm afraid so."

"How?"

After my recent encounter with Bufort, I felt no compunction about defying the pompous jerk's previous order not to discuss the case—it was pointless now anyway—so I told her what I knew. But I left out Bufort's little visit. I didn't want her worrying about me.

We got down to business. Although most of the chiefs had agreed to attend the meeting, Carole told me that some of them had complained about the short notice. I thought this over for a minute. "Before you leave for lunch, please tell them to meet me in the center classroom. I want them to walk through the mess out front."

She smiled. We both knew it would save me a few hundred words. I also hoped it would soften their reflexes to resist.

I was wrong on both counts. After I'd told the chiefs my plan, three-quarters of them thought I was as nuts as the scene out front they'd just been made to witness.

"Dr. Garnet, you can't close emergency!" declared Arnold Pinter, a new and very insecure chief of medicine. Usually he slouched; now he was sitting bolt upright, looking nervously around the table. There were murmurs and nods of agreement from most of the others, but a few weren't so quick to react. Arnold seemed puzzled by the lack of unanimity. "*Can* he close emergency?" he asked.

"I don't know," Sean Carrington said, "but maybe he should." Sean was chief of surgery and had come straight from the OR, still in greens. He was peering at Arnold over the operating bifocals he used while performing delicate procedures.

"He can't stop emergencies!" Hector Saswald insisted. As always, he was looking for approval. When it didn't come, he moved to protect himself from being politically incorrect. "And I want it in the minutes that I said you can't close," he declared piously, jabbing his forefinger at me.

"There are no minutes, Sas," I said.

This seemed to upset him even more than closing the ER.

"What exactly do you hope to achieve?" asked the chief of geriatrics. He was a rather humorless man, though brilliant at assessing mental competence. The doubtful frown on his face made me feel he was checking my capacity to develop even the vestige of a plan.

"Look," I answered, "we all know how closing beds is crap, dangerous crap. I just had another cardiac go sour because we were playing ICU down here, and I'm not willing to go along anymore. Besides, it's the goddamn idiots upstairs who need shutting down. They don't seem to know their budget for carfare let alone for running the hospital. What I'm after is a complete review of the finances of this loony bin and an end to these clowns shutting down care every time they screw up."

"You can't do that!" It was Arnold Pinter again. This time his voice cracked. The thought of bucking administration seemed to terrify him.

"One of the real problems, Arnold," I said, trying to control my impatience with this annoying little man, "is that you allow your guys to fill up the beds with soft admissions who are on fee-for-service plans, and then your department dawdles with those patients as long as the premiums allow because it's easy money and little work. The nurses let you get away with it because it keeps the hard cases waiting in emergency and out of their hair." It wasn't blatant fraud, and it was never picked up on the chart audits that were meant to prevent outright billing abuses. It was simply what could be gotten away with if the chief of medicine was a wimp.

Of course, Arnold started to deny it, but Sean leaned in from the other end of the table and cut him off. "What's more, Arnold, you've got the nerve to let other medical cases pile up in my surgical beds, and I end up canceling admissions for the OR."

A brief look of fear crossed Arnold's face as he found himself caught between us—and caught dead to rights. He slumped in his chair, a field mouse within the hawk's shadow, and began his patented squirming.

"I've told you, Sean, many times, that I don't have the staff," Arnold said. "Ten of my specialists have resigned in the last year, and with the resident cutbacks we have too big a load. I can't move cases any faster. We're spread too thin, and it's going to get worse."

Good old Arnold, the prince of whine. Maybe he was hoping we wouldn't expect much of him—certainly nothing hard, if he seemed pathetic enough.

He was wrong. Sean came at him with the keenness of a scalpel edge slicing through bloated flesh. "Look at the stats!" he snapped. "You admit a lot more pneumonias and keep them longer when you're paid fee-for-service than when it's by managed care."

Arnold got a bit white at this shot. He didn't say it, but his questioning expression asked, Don't we all have to diddle a few extra bucks when we can? He shrugged, then looked around at the other chiefs and turned his palms up to the heavens. "What do you want, Sean?"

"What I want, my dear Arnold," Sean said, "is for you to stop running a patient's stay here as a private pet farm to make money."

A look of fury flashed across Arnold's face. He flew out of his seat and stood eye to eye with the muscular surgeon. Fortunately the PA interrupted.

"Dr. Carrington, OR, stat! Dr. Carrington, OR, stat!"

Sean gave Arnold a wicked grin and left without another word.

Arnold slowly recovered his composure and settled back into his chair. I looked at the hostile expressions on the faces of the remaining chiefs, sighed, and said, "You don't have to do anything. It would be better if we had your support, but I'm putting it to our docs tonight, and they'll decide. We'll be the ones who close and who take the heat. Hurst can stop us only if he opens the beds and orders an audit." I felt even more weary as I realized how alone we were going to be during the long fight ahead. I'd nothing left for diplomacy.

"It's this simple," I continued, my voice getting harder. "We're doing it. You can consider this meeting formal notification. I'm not here to negotiate with you."

There wasn't much left to say. Arnold looked deflated, and the rest of them seemed either resigned to my decision or relieved that I'd taken responsibility for it myself. No one had even mentioned Kingsly. Obviously, the hospital gossip about his murder hadn't reached these upper echelons yet. As they rose to leave, I was left wondering if one of them could be the murderer. Each knew the hospital, but so did a few hundred others. Yet I had my hunch, and if Watts found what I was afraid he would find at the postmortem, then by tonight Bufort's hunt for the killer could be narrowed to about thirty people.

The funny look on Fernandez's face earlier came to mind. It still puzzled me. I thought about him now only because he had declined to come to the meeting, telling Carole that the bed cuts didn't affect him much, so he didn't need to attend.

"Will your surgeons support us, Sean?"

Carrington and I were having coffee together in the surgeons' lounge. It was two P.M., and I'd arranged to meet him there when he was between cases again. He looked relaxed and at home stretched out on a couch, still in his greens with a surgical mask hanging loosely on his chest. He'd been operating since he left my meeting.

"I think so," he replied. "A few will be worried about the damage to their incomes, but I haven't heard any other bright ideas to save us from Hurst and his cuts, and in the long run, that will cost them a lot more."

Half of the major surgery done in the hospital came from emergency. Obviously, our closure would affect the incomes of his departmental members. Even in this room, a few of the other surgeons who'd been reading newspapers had put them down and were leaning forward to try to hear our conversation.

"In any case," Sean added, "I'll support you, and I'll talk to the others." He stretched, sat up, and leaned closer to my chair. In a near whisper, he asked, "What's this I hear about Kingsly being murdered?"

"How'd you find out?"

"It's all over the hospital—rumors, cops beginning to poke around. How come you didn't tell me?"

"Those same cops told me to keep my mouth shut."

"Well, now that it's no longer a secret, you can open your mouth."

We had another cup of coffee while I told him what I knew. Again, I omitted that Bufort had singled me out for special attention. Not knowing why he'd done so was making me increasingly uneasy, and I wasn't going to fuel any rumors about myself. I had just finished the story when a nurse stuck her head into the room and called over to a gray-haired woman in greens, "Your case is ready, Doctor."

"Sean, is that Phoebe Saunderson, the gynecologist?" I asked as the middle-aged woman left the lounge.

"Yep."

"I thought she'd retired from practice years ago."

He shook his head. "Became the VP medical of a hospital in the east end of Buffalo. After five years she asked to come back to St. Paul's."

"And she can still operate?"

"Sure."

"After being away from it for five years?"

"Absolutely. She had to work like crazy to catch up on all the new drugs and the latest in reproductive endocrinology, but apart from a few new techniques and instruments, cutting is cutting. Once you're a surgeon and know how to operate, it's like riding a bicycle—you never really lose the technique."

The same nurse who had summoned Dr. Saunderson now poked her head through the door and called Sean.

"You know," he said as he got up, "I bet even old Hurst could still wield a pretty mean scalpel."

My meeting at five that evening with my own staff was brief. By five-fifteen we decided, nearly unanimously, to withdraw our services and shut down emergency in twenty-four hours if the closed beds weren't immediately reopened. I suggested we should consider issuing a press release warning of our hazardous overcrowding in the ER. It would condemn the administration for its irresponsible action and request that patients use other emergency facilities until we could make our own department safe. I said I was going to sleep on the wording of the press release and we'd take it up tomorrow. Then I explained that I would warn our sister hospitals, since our closing would increase their loads. In spite of the added burden to the other ERs, I expected we'd get support from their staffs. Finally somebody would be doing something. I'd inform MAS what we were up to. They would have no choice but to continue diverting ambulances to other institutions.

Initially, the younger physicians were reluctant to go along with the plan. Not having the established reputations or financial security of the older doctors, they balked at putting their jobs at risk.

"You guys can walk out of here and probably find a new position by tomorrow night," one of them said pointedly. "We don't have your options."

But then I explained about Arnold Pinter's "pet farms" and excessive lengths of stays upstairs.

"Do the math!" I said. "We admit twenty-five fee-for-service patients a day to medicine, on average. I doubt they all really need to come in, but even if they do, our length-of-stay data show we keep each of them, again on average, two days longer than a managed-care patient with the same diagnosis. That's sixty beds. Two times thirty. By getting internal medicine off its ass, and these soft admissions out two days earlier, Hurst could close fifty beds and we'd never miss them. And that was just one department. Cut length of stay in the rest of the hospital, maybe we'd have our beds, and he'd have his budget."

As I talked, it all seemed so logical, I suddenly wondered why he hadn't done it this way himself. It would have taken a lot longer and been a lot more work, but it wouldn't have caused the chaos we were in now. And if I could figure out a way to balance the books that wasn't disruptive, so could he. Whatever else he was, Hurst wasn't stupid. So what was so urgent about cutting costs that he had to put patients at risk for it? And if something else that important to him *was* at stake, how hard would he resist backing off?

At least the rest of my department seemed persuaded by the logic of what we were about to impose on him. As I looked around the table, I could see they were talking to one another more freely now, nodding approval, and clearly excited by our chances of winning. All except Kradic. He seemed nervous. He obviously didn't agree, yet for the moment he kept silent. I wondered if he'd heard how angry I was at him for having left too early this morning.

Just then Jones entered the room. Research must be finished for the day, I thought sarcastically. She was tall, thirty-something, and wore her red hair in a ponytail. This evening she was dressed in a green track suit that matched her eyes. Cute, until you got to know her. She mumbled something about traffic and took a seat, but the slight flush still in her cheeks made me suspect she'd gone for her daily run rather than be on time for our meeting. Not wanting to rekindle our fight on the phone, I ignored her and again glanced around the table. "Any more comments?" I asked.

There were no takers. We voted. Secret ballot.

I collected the papers. One against. (Kradic?) One abstention. (Jones?) The rest were in favor of closing down.

Before I could adjourn, there were a few questions about Kingsly. While most of those present had heard the rumors that he'd been murdered, no one seemed aware yet that he'd been killed with a cardiac needle. But they'd all been told I'd discovered it was homicide, and they wanted to know more. My explanation that the police had instructed me not to talk about the case was met with catcalls, a few raspberries. So much for respect for the chief of the ER.

We were starting to leave when I saw Popovitch take Kradic's elbow, say a few words into his ear, and then walk away. Kradic caught my eye, quickly looked down, and shuffled out the door. I don't know what Popovitch had said, but from the stunned look on Kradic's face I was pretty sure he'd be staying for sign-out rounds.

I looked across the table at Jones and my resentment from this morning rekindled. I was undecided whether to confront her now or continue to ignore her. I must have had a pretty unpleasant expression on my face, because when she glanced up and saw me watching her, I could have sworn she turned pale.

The speed of rumor and the reaction from Hurst were equally swift. His page for me arrived at five-twenty.

"What have you done?" he shrieked as soon as I picked up the phone on Carole's desk.

I didn't bother putting it to my ear. Carole started to muffle her giggles.

"Exactly what you heard." I was trying to speak into the mouthpiece and keep the earphone as far away as I could. It wasn't far enough.

"I'll have all of you suspended immediately!"

Obviously I was up against a tactical genius. "We've just done that for you." Then I hung up fast . . . before Carole and I laughed ourselves to tears.

I'd dropped in on Watts again to see if I could get a preliminary on Kingsly's postmortem. Instead, I found him still gloved and garbed in protective gown, mask, and cap. He was stooped over Kingsly's freshly opened and eviscerated corpse with a pile of broken and bent cardiac needles strewn about in the body cavity. Even for this place it was a sight. Watts was too involved to notice my arrival.

"Those needles better not be on our budget," I said, announcing my presence. Out of habit I had grabbed a mask on my way in. I didn't intend to handle anything so I didn't stop for gloves.

"It can't be done. Can't use a cardiac needle like a stiletto. And look at this." He was about to show me some other detail of Kingsly's innards when a quiet knock interrupted, and we turned to see detectives Riley and Bufort on the threshold.

"Ah, gentlemen," Watts greeted them like a fine host welcoming dinner guests. "Come in. Please put on a mask from the counter over there and take a seat. I was about to get started with Dr. Garnet here." He had obviously invited them down to demonstrate, with considerable relish, his exceptional skills.

In contrast, my resentment toward Bufort returned full force. I had an overwhelming urge to demand that he explain himself and his behavior earlier in my office, but I held back and merely glared my disapproval at him instead. He seemed as though he couldn't care less. But Riley nodded at me and smiled, then looked somewhat puzzled. I wondered if he was even aware of what had happened before with Bufort.

The two detectives pulled up the only stools in the dissection room and positioned themselves for the best, though distant, view of Kingsly's inner secrets. I noted how at ease they were with the gaping remains. Watts made some opening comment about our two professions being similar and that this was a room where we solved puzzles and answered riddles of death. He absently gestured to a row of labeled tubes and specimen jars neatly lined up on the gleaming countertop behind him. They were filled with various fluids and pieces of human tissue, presumably Kingsly's.

Watts then began to walk while he spoke. "When you came in, I was just starting to explain to Dr. Garnet that while the murder weapon was indeed a cardiac needle in the heart, there are a few big unanswered questions. First, a cardiac needle can't be plunged in."

To make his point, he handed Detective Bufort an unused needle about a foot long, gleaming and sharp but flimsy.

"When we teach residents," Watts continued, "they all start out trying to hold the needle at the far end. They place the point on the skin and push; if we let them continue, it would just bow and break. Perhaps Dr. Garnet would like to demonstrate the proper technique that is necessary to successfully insert a cardiac needle."

Feeling like a magician's assistant and not wanting to spoil Watts's show, I slipped on a green OR gown and donned a pair of rubber gloves, took the needle from the detectives, and stepped to Kingsly's right side. With my left hand I held the tip of the needle a few centimeters from the end and steadied the rest of the shaft with my right. With a slow but hard and steady force, I punctured the skin at the bottom of what remained of Kingsly's breastbone. Aiming for the inside of Kingsly's left shoulder, I slid the entire needle into what would have been Kingsly's heart, if Watts hadn't already taken it out.

"Whoever got that needle into Kingsly's heart," Watts said, "had to use that technique. It means Kingsly had to stretch out on the floor—or stand there and cooperate—or that he was already out cold. Now look at this."

He turned and took a large Tupperware container off a shelf behind him, then flipped open the lid. A small shower of formaldehyde and pieces of God knows what sprayed our way. He extracted a dripping hunk of meat about the size of a small melon, which I recognized as a human heart, presumably Kingsly's. Watts identified the chambers for the benefit of the detectives and pointed out the long, spindly guy wire sticking out of the muscle. "This is the track the needle took entering the heart." He picked up another guy wire and poked it into the needle hole just below where I'd performed my own demonstration. "This marks the route of the needle when it first entered the skin. By alignment, it started perfectly on course for the center of the heart, but the two vectors don't match. The track in the heart is skewered upward."

Riley caught on immediately. "Could he have been stabbed twice?"

"No evidence of it. I'll have more after I get my tissue samples back for microscopic examination. And of course we'll do the usual biochemical screen, but I'll bet his blood alcohol level will make embalming redundant."

Bufort had seemed to study his hands throughout most of this. I'd already gotten a taste of a ruthless streak lurking beneath that rather gray exterior, but what he said and did next alerted me to an even more formidable threat—his shrewd and cunning intellect. "What you are telling us, Doctor," he began without looking up, "is that the victim, though inebriated, felt what must have been expert hands inserting the needle into his chest and then managed to sit up, or, if he was standing in the first place, buckled forward as he fell. Either way, he would first bend, then snap the needle as it was driven home."

It was clearly *his* show now. "In other words, this was not a woman grabbing the nearest handy weapon to fight off a man who was trying to maul her. No, this was a deliberate, almost surgical act of murder." He paused, presumably to let our own thoughts catch up with his. Even before he spoke, I felt what was coming with an unwelcome chill. "It seems likely, gentlemen, that our killer is a physician; moreover, a physician skilled in inserting cardiac needles."

Exactly as I'd been expecting, and dreading, Watts's findings put every member of my department on a very short list of suspects.

Bufort continued. "In a general hospital like yours, Dr. Garnet, how many doctors would be expert at needling hearts?"

I hesitated. The question sounded offhanded, but it felt more like an opening gambit than a sincere request for information. He still hadn't looked at me, and I sensed that at the least he was setting me up for another round of intimidation.

My hesitation must have gone on long enough to make Watts uncomfortable, because he answered for me. "Outside of ER there are only a handful of doctors expert at needling hearts," he said matter-of-factly. "These specially skilled physicians are found in specific areas. The OR, ICU, and cardiology together might include a few dozen individuals with the ability to have murdered Kingsly—though not every one of those doctors would still be performing the procedure routinely enough to have achieved the perfect entry path we observed here."

But most physicians on my staff could. By far the greatest number of doctors with such skill would be in emergency, and it was the most probable place for Bufort to look for the killer. Yet instinctively I felt protective about the ER—it sickened me that our entire department was about to fall under police scrutiny—and I felt a surge of annoyance at Watts for being so coldly forthright with Bufort. Almost immediately I knew it was irrational. What else could Watts have done?

But as troubled as I was about emergency, I was even more unnerved by the growing silence in the room and by Bufort still not looking at me. The stares of Watts and Riley added to the tension. In those uneasy seconds I slowly became aware I'd just given Bufort a firsthand demonstration that I, too, had the skills of the killer.

While continuing to gaze at Kingsly's eviscerated heart, Bufort began speaking again very softly, very politely. "Dr. Garnet, it is early in the investigation, and I haven't had much time to discover what goes on in this hospital, but it occurred to me that the motive for Mr. Kingsly's murder might be connected to some issue, problem, or conflict in the administration here. I thought there might be some reference to such difficulties recorded in the minutes of meetings he attended." He paused, still eyeing the grisly specimen on the table before him, then added, "Unfortunately, according to the records I looked through upstairs, the man didn't seem to go to many meetings."

While Bufort talked, his partner's unblinking stare remained on me. I suspected this was an interrogation technique they used often, a practiced routine intended to put the person they were questioning on edge. It worked. Even Watts was looking a little uneasy, glancing from me to Riley, then to Bufort as the detective continued speaking.

"But the records did show something very curious, Dr. Garnet. The only two people who appeared to care about his absences were you and Dr. Carrington, the chief of surgery." He suddenly raised his head and stared right at me. "In fact," he added, getting off his stool and walking around to my side of the table, "for the last couple of years, the two of you have repeatedly demanded his absenteeism be recorded." He stopped in front of me, his face a few inches from mine. "Why was that?" he asked almost in a whisper.

I instinctively drew back, uncomfortable at his closeness, and again ashamed of my behavior with Kingsly.

"Well?" he snapped impatiently, leaning a bit more into me.

I was quickly realizing I'd better choose my words very carefully. I tried to swallow before answering, but my mouth had gone dry. "Because," I croaked, "we both felt very strongly that the presence of the chief executive officer at our meetings was important for the hospital."

"Oh, really?" he asked sarcastically. "Dr. Hurst told me it was because the two of you were trying to get *rid* of Kingsly as chief executive officer."

At first I was too stunned to answer.

Then I felt a burst of rage against Hurst for insinuating that I had a possible motive for murder. Yet surely Bufort hadn't taken him seriously. It had to be a joke. But Bufort's cold stare was anything but funny. "Come on!" I protested with rising alarm. "We wanted him fired, not dead." Even having to explain myself against such an outrageous suspicion left me feeling resentful and astonished. I still half expected Bufort to crack a smile, poke me in the ribs, and admit he'd only been kidding.

Instead, he said, "Don't try to keep things from me, Dr. Garnet. If you do, you'll get in trouble you can't get out of." Then, apparently feeling his job of unsettling me was well and truly done, which it was, he backed away and went out of the autopsy suite without saying another word. Leaving me hanging like that must have been a well-used tactic too, except that Riley seemed genuinely caught off guard. He looked embarrassed to be alone with Watts and me after his boss's performance. He left fast.

"Holy shit" was Watts's professional opinion.

I probably looked a little unprofessionally shocked myself, because he immediately tried to cheer me up.

"Don't worry. If they do nail you for the old bastard's murder, you'll be a hero, and we'll all bring you cake."

I managed a weak "Thanks, pal."

On my way out through Watts's anteroom, the scurryings and scuttlings in the corners seemed more menacing than usual. After Bufort's behavior tonight I thanked God Watts had prevented me from drawing attention to the DOA.

Chapter 6

The cold mist felt soothing against my face but did little for my jumbled brain. Just on the edge of the hospital parking lot were a half dozen police cruisers; a small fleet of plain-looking vehicles was in the section reserved for doctors. If I'd known which one was Bufort's, I'd have had it towed. I'd been dodging a couple of reporters who'd barged into the ER in the late afternoon, and I was relieved to see there wasn't a gauntlet of their tribe to run on the way to my car. As I unlocked my door, I noticed that all the lights in the finance office were on. Odd, I thought. Laverty and his staff usually left at four.

All the way home, I kept trying to trivialize the risk of Bufort concocting a murder charge against me, but the black thoughts stayed. And I still couldn't fathom why Hurst had suddenly become so ruthless, even by his usual seamy standards. Had he tried to implicate me in Kingsly's murder because of my blow-up with him that morning over the bed closures? It was certainly strange that within hours of Kingsly's killing, after tolerating our financial mess for years, he'd launched massive and sudden cuts that went way beyond simple economic sense. Or was he retaliating against my threat to close emergency? In either case, his behavior seemed driven by something more than a desire for balanced books. Whatever he was up to, he obviously had no qualms about doing me professional or personal damage in the process.

And then came the question I'd been trying to avoid the most but had to face: Could someone in my own department be the killer?

There were fifteen of us in emergency, and I dreaded the inevitable thoughts and suspicions that were bound to surface once Bufort and his team started questioning everyone. Lose trust in a person working in a high-risk area and immediately his effectiveness plummets. Support and backup, freely given, are what keep patients alive. One of my professors had called it *a magnificent dependency that can perform miracles,* and it had a lot to do with what kept me addicted to ER work. If Bufort managed to clog that synchrony with doubt and fear, our team could fall to pieces and become uncoordinated, even deadly.

One thing was certain: All this *was* going to undermine emergency's fight for beds. The moral high ground I'd charged up to go against Hurst would be muddied with the slimy innuendo and suspicion he'd pushed my way. While Bufort stalked each one of us, Hurst would have the perfect excuse to stall and keep his deadly closures in force. "How can we believe emergency?" he'd say. "A killer lurks in their midst." It wasn't a logical dodge, but it would work when no one wanted to listen anyway. Worse still, he might be right.

I figured it would be hard to sleep this night. I opened my window. The familiar sound of my tires on the pavement only reinforced my dark mood.

Janet's car was in the garage, but I knew she must have already gone to bed, because only the kitchen light was left on. After a wagging, slurpy welcome by Muffy, I snapped on her leash and stepped back outside. She tugged me down the porch steps, but then I turned away from our regular route. I was going to need a much longer walk than our usual circuit if I'd any hope of quieting my nerves. Muffy immediately bounded and pulled ahead in anticipation of different spots and new smells.

Two blocks from our home was the middle section of a golf course. I'd never played the game in my life, but I appreciated the green space, and sometimes in the winter, when it was closed, if it was late enough so no one could see me, I did a little trespassing to stroll the links and give Muffy a run. She sensed where we were headed and nearly choked herself straining against her collar.

The boundary was marked by a line of well-spaced evergreen trees and shrubs. Entering the property was a simple matter of stepping between the branches and ignoring the Strictly No Trespassing! signs. I stopped at the edge of the fairway and looked around. Even at night, there was enough city light reflected off the underside of the clouds to make it possible to see. Muffy could hardly contain herself.

Off to my right and down a gentle slope the open grass stretched at least three hundred yards to a distant green backed by a ring of dark trees. I could see the black shapes of surrounding sand traps. The only sound was the noise of the city in the background. We were alone. I reached down and set Muffy free.

She took off like a bullet, charging over the dew-soaked ground with the happy abandon she always showed in a wide-open space. I strolled along behind her while she ran in ever-expanding circles, my shoes quickly becoming soaked in the wet grass.

I tried not to dwell on Bufort and Hurst but found myself worrying about ER coverage and Jones instead. Would she use her research as an excuse not to come in to work again tomorrow, to punish me for . . . for what? Hanging up on her this morning? Ignoring her at this evening's meeting? For having hired Kradic in the first place? I was finding it increasingly hard to cope with her tantrums.

Before coming to St. Paul's, she'd moonlighted working nights in a variety of hospitals. She'd been competent but insecure and lacking in the confidence I would have expected from a physician of her experience. The cardiac research with Zak, however, seemed to give her a self-assurance in the ER that I hadn't seen before. In addition to providing some very respectable work for the study, she appeared to have parlayed all those obscure night shifts and years of experience on the road into the self-assurance I looked for in an ER veteran. Of course, her added exposure to cardiac arrests had quickly made her our most skilled resuscitator.

Unfortunately, her success had also made her rather aggressive. She'd lorded her new level of skill over the rest of the department as though we deserved punishment for having made her feel inferior somehow in the past.

And work. She'd craved it. I couldn't give her enough shifts. It seemed her new prominence in the department was like a drug to her, and she needed to show off her skills as often as possible to maintain the fix. Then I'd hired Kradic, and she'd had to share the spotlight.

My shoes started to squish, and the bottoms of my trousers were wet and dragging in the grass. Muffy continued her joyous gallop by heading down the fairway in great sweeping curves. I was about to call her back when she stopped dead in her tracks and stared intently toward the distant green, still several hundred yards away.

A lone figure was standing there, completely motionless. But around its feet two black shapes swirled in small circles, then scurried back and forth, moving incessantly, like shadows on the ground. The stillness of the figure was eerie. It seemed to be looking back up at us.

Without warning or a sound, the two shadows began hurtling up the fairway toward us. I had to blink to be sure they were real—their speed made them almost translucent in the dim light. But they were real, speeding at us like a pair of dark torpedoes. Muffy growled, then barked. I heard a returning snarl.

Dogs!

Muffy was twenty yards ahead of me, perfectly still but ears up, and poised to charge.

"No, Muffy!" I screamed, but it was too late. She raced away toward the oncoming animals.

I started to run after her, yelling her name and hollering, "Stop! Come back! No!" but in seconds she was way ahead of me, becoming little more than a shadow herself. With mounting panic I watched the three shapes hurtle toward each other, separated by less than a hundred yards and closing.

I kept running after her, frantically waving my arms at the figure on the green. "Stop them! For God's sake, stop them!" I implored at the top of my lungs. "Call off your dogs!"

Whoever it was continued to watch, and didn't respond. Now I could see the dogs: Dobermans. They could tear Muffy to pieces.

Fifty yards.

Shit! I had to break Muffy's rush.

My throat burned from yelling and I was breathing hard as much with fear as from exertion. They were almost at each other.

Twenty-five yards.

I stopped running, took a deep breath, and let out a roar as loud and fierce and full of rage as my poor vocal cords could muster.

Muffy whirled around to see what beast was coming at her from behind. The two dogs, still ten yards away from her, also stopped, but as their heads went down and I heard their low growls continue, I suspected they'd been more surprised than frightened.

"Get back here, you dumb dog," I screamed at Muffy, trying to shock her into obedience. It worked. Her tail, head, and ears drooped, and she slunk toward me, looking nervously at the growling animals behind her.

They didn't run off, but they didn't approach either.

They started circling us, keeping their heads toward us, showing their teeth, snarling.

When Muffy got close enough, I grabbed her collar and pulled her to my side. Being careful not to hit her, I began twirling her leash over my head like a whip, the metal clasp on the free end.

"Get away! Get back!" I screamed at the circling Dobermans. I accelerated the circling of the leash over our heads until I could hear the metal tip whistling through the air. Muffy stopped cowering and began lunging and barking at the dogs. It was all I could do to hold her with one hand and circle the leash with the other.

Suddenly one of the dogs skirted around behind us. Muffy tried to turn and face the attack, but her collar twisted in my hand, choking her and knocking me off balance. I managed to direct the twirling leash down and behind and felt it connect. The incoming animal screamed in rage and pain and continued to yelp as it pulled back and joined its partner. I was getting ready for them to come at us again, but above the growling and barking, I heard the sound of a whistle—like a policeman's or a referee's—come from way up the green.

The Dobermans immediately broke off their attack, spun around, and raced away toward their master as fast as they had come.

I held Muffy tightly. She was trembling as she barked, straining to give chase.

"No, Muff, good girl, they're gone. It's okay," I reassured her, though I was by no means certain we were out of danger. Trying to calm my own shaking, I watched the two distant shapes run up to the figure and begin their previous pattern of prancing around its feet.

I wanted to scream, "You fucking idiot!" but I was terrified the dogs would be sent after us again. I quickly connected Muffy's leash and started back up the slope from where we'd come. She resisted, whined, and stood on her hind legs to get a final look before we left. When I next glanced back, the green was deserted.

All the way home I kept checking over my shoulder and listening for the padded sound of galloping dogs on pavement. Muffy, on the other hand, trotted along beside me, happily sniffing out the bushes as usual, our ordeal apparently forgotten. I was not so sanguine.

Once we were safe in our kitchen, Muffy raced on upstairs to get the best spot in bed. I began to feel anger more than fear, and wanted to report the incident to the police. That idiot had nearly let his dogs kill us.

I was about to dial 911 when I had second thoughts. What was I going to complain about? I'd been illegally on a private golf course with my dog unleashed and had been chased off. The creep on the green might even have been a night watchman. I knew I wasn't the only person in the neighborhood to use the fairways as a dog run, despite the property being posted. There even had been flyers distributed door-to-door requesting we keep our animals away. Maybe the owners of the club had finally gotten fed up with warning us and had resorted to letting their security staff scare us a little. It was dangerous and stupid, and the idiot who'd been there tonight ought to be charged with reckless behavior, but I put down the phone.

I certainly wouldn't be taking Muffy there anymore, I thought, still angry, but beginning to feel a little foolish as well.

I awoke to heaven. My head was being stroked, and I could smell coffee on my bedside table. I opened my eyes and sleepily smiled up at Janet, who had one hand on my forehead and one hand holding her own cup of coffee. The light was dim outside the window and invited dozing off again, just for a few moments.

I slid into a rush of last-minute dreams denied by too much missed sleep. A large ambulance was driving toward me, bringing Kingsly back, rotted, all in parts. His fluids seeped out the side panels and blew into liquid plumes. Yet I could hear his screams. Piercing screams that over-whelmed the noise of the siren. Screams that kept coming from the yellow bulk looming up over me, a shadowy figure at the wheel.

I woke to my own scream. Janet was long gone, and the telephone was shrieking in my ear. I fumbled the receiver and managed a dry "Hello."

"Nice hours, Doc. Wish *I* could sleep in." It was Susanne, fresh and saucy as ever.

"Oh, God, what time is it?" I'd obviously slept more than a few minutes.

"Eight-thirty, and we're fighting World War Three here while our fearless leader sleeps."

"Bad?"

"Real bad."

"I'll be there in thirty minutes."

I'd barely hung up and was halfway to the shower when the phone rang again.

"Hello!" I answered impatiently, expecting it was the ER.

I heard only static, the kind of noise produced by a car phone.

"Hello," I repeated, more politely this time.

The noise seemed to change. At first I thought it was more interference on the line. But it became a whisper, barely audible.

"Hello! Who is this?" I demanded. "Speak up. I can't hear you."

The raspy voice became louder. "I know, Doc. I know it's you. You've had your warning. Back off!" Then I was listening to a dial tone.

The noise level in the ER matched my frazzled state of mind. Stretchers were end to end in every corridor.

Susanne rushed by and muttered, "We're not doing well," keeping her reputation for understatement intact.

All around me nurses and doctors yelled orders and patients cried for help. Ventilation bags, oxygen masks, and IV sets were tossed to residents waiting alongside still-untreated cases. At first I thought there had been a disaster, a train crash or a downed plane. I tried to huddle with the clerk; she was besieged with calls for ECGs, X rays, the lab, and beds, always for beds. While still listening to someone on the phone, she mouthed my answer.

"We're getting ambulances again."

Zak! Shit! I'm not sure if I said it or thought it.

I was down the hall and in my office in seconds, but there I found more unpleasant surprises, two to be exact.

The first was a foot-high stack of computer printouts, which meant added hours of work going over them.

The second surprise was embarrassed to be caught going through the first.

Jones jumped back from my desk. "A lot of paperwork," she sputtered nervously.

Annoyed, I let silence work her over. It took ten seconds until she caved in.

"I brought you the latest numbers on my magnesium sulfate resuscitation study." She added a thin folder to the pile she'd been sneaking a peek at.

"Find anything interesting?" I knew I sounded cold and sarcastic.

She looked startled.

I wanted her to see she was over the line. I brushed by her to get behind my desk and let her stand there looking uncomfortable while I called Zak and wheedled another ambulance ban.

He demanded payment. "Any news on the murder front?"

"I can't talk now." I whispered, hoping I could still imply goodies to come. Apparently it worked. After we'd exchanged a few sentences, Zak said he'd direct his ambulances to other ERs until noon. I hung up before he could change his mind.

"I meant your study, Valerie," I said, turning swiftly back to her, hoping to get her even more off balance.

Her thin shoulders lowered a notch. I felt pressed to get back outside, but I knew how important the work was to her. Maybe if I gave it a moment's attention now, I'd get her on my side, at least for the rest of the morning. I was dangerously distracted as it was and needed to avoid another fight with her.

"We finished the first phase last month," she said, "and the initial . . ."

I tried to focus on what she was saying and ignore the feeling in my stomach of a fist that kept tightening. I was aware they'd gotten ambiguous results so far. Magnesium sulfate, cheaper than other cardiac agents, had shown initial promise, but hadn't panned out as the wonder drug some earlier California studies had suggested it was. As she spoke, her disappointment showed. Still, to give her credit, negative finds in medicine were important, and the material was timely and fascinating. Even talking about it, her voice reverberated with a quiet authority that I hadn't heard much in our recent exchanges, and her prickly defensiveness was momentarily gone.

"Fabulous for torsade de pointes," she concluded. "Compared to the old magnesium sulfate protocol, our new version improved survival rates by twenty percent. Not much advantage for V. tach. or V. fib. though." She shrugged, then added, "It's too bad."

I agreed. Torsade de pointes was a lethal but rare form of abnormal heart rhythm. I'd only read about it and in twenty years had never seen a case. The usual killers were ventricular tachycardia and ventricular fibrillation.

"But for unstable angina or MIs it might be promising," she continued, sounding enthusiastic. "The study's going to be extended into a second phase, and we're going to see if magnesium sulfate protects these patients against going into V. tach. or V. fib."

Trying to keep myself from glancing at my watch, I responded, "Hope so." I meant it, especially for patients with unstable angina, a condition preceding a heart attack where the blood supply to the heart is increasingly shut off by clogged arteries, but the heart muscle isn't yet permanently damaged. To reverse the process and prevent the impending heart attack, or MI, we use oxygen, nitroglycerine, bed rest, blood thinners, and sometimes surgery, but the patients often die anyway from the deadly rhythms Jones had mentioned. If magnesium sulfate could protect these patients against V. tach. and V. fib., it might improve survival rates and prevent MIs. In some cases its use would avoid the need to use thrombolytic agents costing three hundred to three thousand dollars a dose. Magnesium sulfate cost thirty cents a dose. It was a lot safer too.

But right now I had to deal with the ER. "Keep me informed," I added, stepping to my closet, where I exchanged my jacket for a lab coat.

"I see you finally got the case breakdowns per shift you've been waiting for." She casually gestured to the printouts, adding, "*Everybody's* dying to see them," as if that excused her own prying.

Again I resented her snooping. I was too anxious to have much patience anyway. "Since I haven't had a chance to look at them myself, I've no idea what they are," I answered rather coolly. "I haven't been through my mail yet. Now, if you'll excuse me, I've more calls to make, and they obviously need you in the ER. Tell Susanne we won't be getting ambulances for the next three hours."

With that I ended what had been probably the nicest moment I'd had with the woman in recent months. Neither of us mentioned our conversation on the phone the previous day. She tried to smile. And failed. I noticed that once again she was wearing something green underneath her lab coat, this time with earrings to match. But her attempts to be stylish had always seemed a bit obvious and did nothing for me. At the door she rather pathetically asked, "Please give me any feedback you might have on my study."

"Of course."

I sighed after she left. Difficult was Valerie Jones's middle name. At least she was here to work with Popovitch.

Over the next ten minutes I made the usual calls to admitting, got Sean to cancel elective surgery, and managed to convince a few of our off-duty doctors to come in and help out for an hour or so. When the enraged surgeons whose cases I'd bumped started phoning back to scream at me, I switched the line onto my answering machine. As they recorded their fury, I leaned back in my chair and tried to think what the hell I was going to do about the whispered warning. Back off from what? Even if I wanted to take it seriously, how could I when I didn't know what the hell I was supposed to be involved in?

It had to be about Kingsly's murder. And though it could have been anyone—the voice was impossible to recognize—the first person I thought of was Hurst. He'd already given Bufort the idea that I had a motive for the killing, but I'd thought his insinuation had been a tactic, a despicable move designed to tie me up in Bufort's investigation. Did he really believe I was the killer? *I know it's you!* He had sounded livid last night after learning I was ready to close the ER to fight his bed cuts. *You've had your warning. Back off!* The thought of Hurst being so desperate chilled me. And what was making him so desperate? *You've had your warning.* Was he threatening to give Bufort even more ammunition against me, maybe even try to frame me for the killing? I felt a surge of

panic as I had another idea direct from the depths of paranoia and not enough sleep—the dogs. The attack on the
golf course. *You've had your warning.*

I started to hyperventilate. No! That was off the wall. I
fought to control my breathing. I had to be rational about
this.

Should I report the call to Bufort? Or would it only
make me more suspect in his eyes? I'd have to think this
through when I was calmer. Meanwhile, I had no choice
but to focus on the ER.

As I pushed out from my chair, I considered the stack
of printouts on my desk that Jones had been sneaking a
look at. Normally they would have offered a perfect
bureaucratic escape from the mounting craziness outside.

She'd seen enough to spot the reams of numbers and
diagnostic codes that were our first ever breakdown of
which doctors saw what problems on what shifts and
with what outcome. And she'd been right about another
thing. All of us were nervous and yet irresistibly drawn
to this measurement of our skills, victories, and disasters.
It was like a book of judgment, beyond excuses and
denial. Some called it quality assurance. Some called it
Big Brother.

It was actually paper shuffling I'd been looking forward to, but my moment with our truths would have to
wait. I locked the printouts in my desk drawer to prevent
any of the other doctors from taking a premature peek.

Then I headed for the mess out front. On my way back
to the nursing station, I glanced into the resuscitation room
and saw Popovitch at the right arm of a very pale woman
who was sweaty and having a lot of trouble breathing. He
had just threaded a long Swan Gantz catheter under her
right clavicle, through the subclavian vein, and on into her
heart. It was a more complex version of the technique
James Todd had used on my patient Sunday evening.

As I watched Popovitch's practiced hands secure the

line, the association between skills like his and the skills used by the killer spread over me like a stain of blood. While he was reassuring the gray-faced lady that the tip of the catheter would measure the response of her heart to the medication he'd given her to clear her lungs, I was wondering how many others besides myself would end up on Bufort's list.

Popovitch looked up and saw me watching him. Thank God he had no idea what I'd been thinking. "By the way," he began, "I took care of that matter of Kradic leaving early." He gave his patient a final check and joined me in the doorway.

"Michael, am I going to get an angry note?"

He winked. "I certainly hope so," he answered, whistling the *Godfather* theme right after he brushed past me and started down the hall.

The next hour took all my thoughts away from suspicion and murder.

The ambulance ban I'd reinstated was helping. The staff could face the pandemonium knowing it wasn't going to get worse. The surgical beds I'd commandeered and the reinforcements I'd called in cheered Susanne even more.

"Thank God," she said. "Oh, and you too, of course."

"Good to see you smile, Susanne, even if you are such a smart—"

"Never mind!" She shoved a file in my hand. It was for a forty-year-old man bleeding from both ends. He'd heard daily aspirin would prevent heart attacks but had given himself a GI hemorrhage by overenthusiastically dosing himself. When I found his stretcher, he was pale and smelled fecal. Black diarrhea poured from his rectum while brown vomit the color of coffee grounds stained his pillows and nightshirt.

"Oh, God, I'm going, I can feel it. Don't let me go! I'm going!" His head thrashed around.

"It's okay. We got you." Two IVs raced fluid into his depleted veins. I felt for a pulse at his wrist. Not much, but it was there. "You've already got a pressure," I told him as I jacked up the bottom end of his bed to rush the blood in his legs toward his heart. "This will boost it even more." His oxygen mask had slipped to his forehead; I slid it back over his nose and mouth. Two sacks of type O blood arrived and were being hung up on IV poles. For the moment his pressure was holding, and some IV cimetidine would probably keep him from bleeding. Hopefully. We didn't have a monitored bed for him if he went shocky again.

While writing my own orders at a free place on the counter, I could hear Popovitch behind me arguing with a junior neurosurgical resident. "Look, a thirty-five-year-old woman has the most severe headache of her life right after making love and is now slowly losing consciousness. This isn't a postcoital snooze. She needs a CT of the brain in minutes and most likely neurosurgery in the hour or she'll die."

CT is a specialized X ray used to diagnose hemorrhages of the brain. It had to be done quickly and with a staff radiologist or neurologist present to assure it was interpreted correctly.

The resident stalled. "My staff man doesn't like it when I interrupt his rounds upstairs."

Popovitch lost it. "Your lady has a subarachnoid bleed. If you don't get your staff man stat and she deteriorates, he will kill you. If he doesn't, then I will. If after that there is enough of you left to have a career, we'll both finish that for you as well." The CT was under way within three minutes.

"Good teaching, Michael," I said over my shoulder.

"If he reports me, flunk him."

I heard the nurses out in the hallway greet Sylvia Green, one of the doctors I'd called in to help. Recently back from her second pregnancy leave, she was another veteran known for her technical skills. She could get an IV line on anyone no matter how flat or inaccessible the veins. Her help was welcome anytime, doubly so today.

After passing through the confusion and entering the nursing station, she gave a single comment. "Jesus Christ!"

"Sylvia, a nice Jewish girl like you," chided Susanne, handing her a chart.

"Yeah, I know. After ten years in a Catholic hospital, I swear like a shiksa." Sylvia grabbed the file, smiled hello at me, and went to find her patient.

Twenty minutes later the resident who'd reluctantly obeyed the ultimatum to get a CT was back in the department, proudly showing everyone the films of the subarachnoid hemorrhage *he'd* "picked up in the ER." Popovitch gently handed him the phone and suggested he get on with the transfer to neurosurgery. We got to hear him proudly arrange for life-saving "burr holes" and explain to some wide-eyed students how these would relieve the pressure of accumulated blood on the brain. Popovitch gave me another wink.

Within an hour the place was calm. Well, relatively calm.

Jones had even managed to discharge a couple of patients with abdominal pain. Instead of lying in the corridor with nonacute abdomens and borderline blood results while waiting for a trial of oral liquids, they would do their "observation" at home and be reexamined tomorrow morning in a follow-up clinic. Ironically, they were safer out of the ER. Should something go wrong, a vigilant family member would pick up a change for the worse and get the patient back to us faster through the front door than one of our busy nurses might notice them go sour in a rear corridor. With this degree of overcrowding we were in danger of finding patients dead in beds.

Susanne had a mental filter like mine— get to the

important stuff; ignore the crap—and she showed it now. "Oh, I forgot," she said. "Hurst's secretary called and left a message. You're to meet him in the boardroom at ten-thirty."

I stiffened. I was going to have to be very careful in my dealings with Hurst. From now on there would be no business as usual, and I'd have to decide whether I should report my suspicions about him to Bufort. I glanced at my watch: 10:40.

"Susanne!" So much for time to plan. Now I'd have to improvise my way.

"Hey, we needed you more. You can't save lives from the boardroom."

"I'm in enough trouble—"

"So what difference does it make? And before you run off," she added, stopping me as I was halfway out the door, "we got another DOA last night, a bag lady. MAS figured we'd still have room in the morgue."

My mind was already preoccupied trying to piece together a way to confront Hurst in front of Bufort, but I tried to pay attention. "Another one?" I asked. Two DOAs in as many days *was* unusual. "Any idea what killed her?"

"Probably exposure, alcohol, whatever—like the rest."

"Is the paperwork done?"

"Yeah. We sent her right down to Watts. Funny, he seemed hot to do a full post on this one. Go figure."

"Really?" I winced again at the dressing-down I'd gotten from Watts for my stupidity over yesterday's DOA, then remembered something.

"Dr. Watts thinks if the numbers of vagrant DOAs really are up all over the city," she explained, "the medical examiner's going to push for thorough autopsies to find out what's killing more street people than usual."

Deaths could be caused by new batches of lethal crack or bad hooch. It was important to find the latest poison of choice and issue a strong warning. If Watts was willing to add another extensive autopsy to his workload when he was already so busy, it was because it was a hell of a lot more legitimate than chasing after moles. Even for autopsies handled in a pretty cursory fashion, many of the DOAs were sent straight to the city morgue.

"Did he say anything about the one from yesterday?" I asked.

"Not specifically, but it was getting two within twenty-four hours that seemed to get him so stirred up."

Despite the ban, two more ambulances rolled in. Susanne turned to real work, and I headed off to my meeting with Hurst, trying to plan my next move with him and Bufort as I went.

I was surprised to see it was the detective himself who had the floor. He paused politely as I took my seat. From the poleaxed look on a few of the chiefs' faces, I presumed he'd just announced that Kingsly had been murdered. The others in the room looked appropriately somber, but their lack of surprise probably meant they'd heard the gossip. Hurst, however, was taking a showy look at his watch and all but tapping the dial to make sure none of those assembled missed the outrageously late hour of my arrival.

"I'm late because emergency's a mess!" I snarled, unable to control my anger at him. I noticed some of the chiefs exchanging concerned looks, probably afraid that we were going to continue our fight from yesterday morning.

Bufort seemed kinder. "I was just running through what we discussed in the morgue, Dr. Garnet." He sounded respectful, as though we were colleagues and I was his chosen confidant. But it was bull. I knew Bufort was mocking me with his politeness. The little smirk playing at the corners of his smile made sure I remembered what he could put me through if it suited him.

I felt livid with both of them, but took a seat without saying anything more.

Bufort continued speaking, describing the problems of investigating a homicide in a hospital. Just conducting brief interviews with everyone who'd been on duty Sunday night had taken over twenty-four hours. The site of the actual murder was still unknown. Combing Kingsly's office for prints or other traces of the killer had been fruitless. It was particularly confounding that the body had been washed. When he got to the autopsy results and how the killer clearly knew how to needle hearts, everyone shifted away from me.

He advised us his department would issue a brief press release later in the day, but if reporters approached any of us individually, we were to refer them to the police or to the hospital spokesperson. We definitely were not to discuss any details of the case with the media.

Despite the urgency in his voice as he chronicled all the difficulties they were facing, that annoying little smile kept reappearing. Whatever game he was playing, he looked exceptionally pleased with himself. As if he had an ace up his sleeve.

On the other hand, Riley was sitting at the back of the room, staring up at the ceiling tiles. Even from where I was sitting I could see his jaw muscles repeatedly quiver and tense. I'd begun to suspect this younger detective had little patience with his boss's preening. If Bufort was the kind of man who demanded stroking from his underlings, he certainly hadn't gotten any show of adoration from Riley—at least not in my presence.

In any case, even without his junior's encouragement, Bufort built to his climax. "And so, gentlemen, we must expand our investigation, and as you can see, we need your help."

He didn't look very needy to me.

"Detective Riley will arrange a meeting with each of you to discuss any new information you may have, any further thoughts since our preliminary interview, any rumors you've heard about the killing of your CEO. We particularly want to hear about possible motives for Kingsly's murder."

I repressed the urge to shiver. So, Bufort was going to open up the hampers and turn over the carts and spill our dirty laundry all over the place. I felt sick; so did the other chiefs, judging from the expressions on their faces. But Bufort clearly was pleased with himself. I squinted at him. Damned if his hands didn't seem to be fidgeting as if he were trying hard to keep them from rubbing together in glee. The stocky detective with the big ego could have been funny—if I hadn't already experienced the menace that accompanied his determination to jump to conclusions. Was he the kind of cop who, right or wrong, was more concerned with getting a conviction than finding out the truth? If so, then my own innocence, or anyone else's, might not matter much to him. As I watched him stride out the door, I couldn't help worrying about how thorough or scrupulous his investigation would be once he settled on the first available suspect and saw a chance to keep his solution rate intact—especially if Hurst was trying to feed me to him.

I decided telling Bufort an anonymous caller had whispered *I know it's you* wasn't a good idea right now. He might agree. Nor was I any more encouraged by the troubled expression on Riley's face when he looked over at me before he rose slowly from his chair and walked out the door, shaking his head.

The other chiefs continued to look tense, and a few talked quietly together as they got up from the table. Hurst left the room without a glance at me. There wasn't the slightest hint of the kind of malice I'd felt listening to that whisper on the phone. Still, even if Hurst couldn't get me charged with murder, he probably was angling to get me to resign. In fact, he was probably tempted to accept resignations to get rid of all of us. With trouble-makers like me gone, he could approach the young guys and offer them their jobs back. Then he could reopen emergency with a staff of novices who didn't oppose him. But even *he* must know emergency couldn't survive the loss of all our experienced physicians. At the very least, he'd have to do a lot of explaining, especially when our sister hospitals made him look like an idiot by snatching up our best doctors before the next shift.

On the way back to the ER, I stopped at the vending machines near the front of the hospital and pushed enough buttons to win myself a hot chocolate. I didn't have a clue who had killed Kingsly, let alone why. Nor could I figure out what Hurst was really up to, but for the moment I had to stop dwelling on it and try to face my more immediate worries in the ER.

The machine whirred and sputtered out my order. Trying not to spill the hot brown liquid, I had turned toward emergency when I saw what was left of the Cummings family approaching me in the corridor. Their vigil was finished. A brother supported his brother's wife. She was clutching one of those obscene plastic bags that hold a patient's belongings when it's over. At their side walked two small girls.

I froze, wanting to escape, but on they came until they were right in front of me.

Mrs. Cummings tried to speak, failed, and my own mouth went dry. Then she swallowed harder and reached for my hand.

I flinched and almost jerked it away. I knew what was coming.

"Thank you," she managed to whisper. "I know you did all you could."

The little girls watched me from behind their mother's skirt. Despite myself, I imagined first one, then the other of the girls held high in her daddy's warm, comforting hands. Now Donald Cummings's hands drooped cold and purple from the stainless gleam of an autopsy table—and we'd put him there. The charts of his case would probably show we were watching his blood pressure while waiting for a bed, because shock was a risk, but an acceptable one, with streptokinase. Yet on this day we hadn't caught the drop, and two little girls had lost their dad, all within the standards of conventional care—if you didn't count Hurst's bed closures as the real reason it happened.

Mrs. Cummings still held my hand. I gently withdrew it, mumbling words of consolation. Then, I have to admit, I fled.

I didn't have the stomach to face the ER at the moment, so I went to my office by a back corridor. Carole had begun storing our interminable memos, minutes, reports, and written recommendations—good intentions on paper—in her computer to save space, but the changeover had produced more printouts than I'd ever seen before we'd started putting shelves of words on disks. Her desk was scattered with these leavings, but she was out, probably generating even more copies of copies. I was glad for the moment alone.

I leaned back in my chair and thought about the reams of numbers and coded outcomes of the ER study that now lay locked in my desk. There I would probably find a small number of catastrophes like Cummings, and a few cures. But mostly there would be draws, stabilizing patients by the book and buying them the time they needed for healing.

I entered Cummings's name in our mortality review list. The recorded verdict would be "unexpected" and, depending on the size of the guy's original infarct on postmortem, probably "unavoidable death." The delay in getting a bed in the cardiac monitoring unit would be noted; the importance of monitoring blood pressure while using streptokinase would be reiterated. Then memory would fade until the cuts exacted another life. In a way, those cuts were as much murder as plunging a needle into Kingsly's heart. The computer printouts held all our ghosts . . . except one.

Paper wars, paper cuts. The injunction arrived at 11:10 forbidding any organized withdrawal of service.

Hurst! The son of a bitch had thrown lawyers into our mess. And I'd been stupid enough to be caught by surprise. The injunction would take hours to unravel. Worse, we would need even more lawyers.

The server, a little man in a big-shouldered raincoat, smirked at me. "You weren't expecting that, were you?"

I was stunned; he actually liked his work. As I held the unfolded legal sheets in front of me like a scroll, I realized all at once where he was headed.

I ran out of the office and into the ER yelling, "Hey, you!" Nurses and patients recoiled as if I were the latest psycho dumped on the ward. But I was too late. The little guy with the Joan Crawford shoulders was disappearing out the far door. Popovitch and Jones, papers in hand, looked as if they were about to have heart attacks.

There ought to be a law against serving a doctor legal papers in the middle of an emergency shift, especially one from hell. Our instincts and training keep us making the right moves. Undermine those instincts, introduce self-doubt and second-guessing, and the result can be lethal. Nothing but nothing gets a doctor hesitating and second-guessing faster than the shock of being slapped with legal papers.

"Look," I said to Popovitch and Jones, "relax. It's poli-

tics. It's about not withdrawing services for want of beds.
Go on being doctors and let me handle this shit."

Their expressions made me feel like the idiot I was for
leading them into this, getting them named.

"I know, I know! Another fine mess I got you into."
Before they could say anything, I lifted the injunctions
out of their hands.

"Popovitch, go on a diet or share your food with Jones.
You two are beginning to look like Laurel and Hardy."
Their groans accompanied me halfway back to my office.

Now I was in over my head.

Working emergency always meant seizing control.
With blood, pain, or a bubbling, choking airway, I had a
move for it, knew what to do, could react fast. My
greatest dread was freezing up.

I actually had a recurrent dream. I would be ineffec-
tively struggling to intubate through a bloody tangle of
vessels, nerves, and smashed windpipe when I'd receive
the ultimate condemnation from a Greek chorus of residents. "You don't know your stuff!"

As far as sorting out legal entanglements, I very definitely did not know my stuff. The stand against closing
beds was right, but all I'd accomplished was to galvanize
Hurst into taking legal action. The injunction could have
as big an impact on morale and concentration in the ER
as I'd feared the murder investigation would. Damn
Hurst!

He'd upped the cost of our defiance to a risk of fines,
contempt charges, even prosecution. None of the doctors
would go against that. Even if they threatened to resign
through legal channels, it would take ninety days' notice,
and I shuddered at the thought of how much damage and
death might be caused by ninety days of these conditions.
What number of "preventable morbidities or mortalities"
would it take to force Hurst to back down?

My instinct—one I hadn't felt in years—was to call for help. It was a reality of residency: Go as far as you can, and then get backup. It was harder later, after becoming staff, to admit to needing help. I'd seen experienced doctors actually kill a patient by not asking for support. As a result, I'd learned to fear such arrogance, and was pretty much ready to admit when I wasn't cutting it.

And right now I was not cutting it.

If it wasn't too late already, I had to alert the other doctors who hadn't yet received summonses. I fantasized an army of Joan Crawford raincoats shouldering through the city to find them.

Outside my window a distant siren warned of the rapidly approaching noon deadline when the ambulance ban would expire. I looked at the clock on my desk. 11:15. I wished Carole would get back.

The phone rang. I let the answering machine get it and listened to the message.

"Carole, this is Dr. Hurst's office. Please tell Dr. Garnet that Detective Riley wants to see him as soon as possible."

So much for "arranging convenient times."

I literally turned a few circles and wondered what to do first. The phone rang again, but it was my private line. Only one person knew that number.

I picked up. "Hi."

"Sure of me, are you?" Janet's voice was an island of calm.

"No, just really glad to hear from you."

"Bad day?"

"Eleven-seventeen and I'm down to plan Y."

"Let's see, that's the one where I work and support you in the style you've become accustomed to."

"Hey, I'll raise your kid."

"You'll make the kid a bum, just like his father, or at

least like his father was until I saved him and made him respectable."

"Yeah! You made me so damn respectable, I got this job and all the trouble I'm in."

"I'm the girl in trouble here."

"I love you."

"That's the kind of talk that got me in trouble."

"I thought you seduced me."

"Yeah, well, your virtue will remain unsullied tonight. I'm sleeping over in the case room. I've two ladies in early labor. They'll keep me here till dawn, so I'll relieve one of the guys on call. He'll owe me when I've got a new man in my life and want to spend the night with him."

"Janet!"

"Oh, didn't I tell you? Had an ultrasound this morning. Saw a little thingamajig hanging down. It looked just like his father's—you know, the one that got me in trouble. Bye now."

Carole couldn't for the life of her understand the goofy grin on my face when she came into the office while I still held the receiver.

My mood didn't change even as I went out the door to meet with Riley and Bufort and endure their attempt to hang a murder charge on me. It kept up when Sylvia Green, scared and waving her injunction, listened skeptically to my reassurances. Hell, it even endured the two ambulances that roared in twenty minutes before the ban expired, and it wasn't altered at all by the resulting bedlam.

I was going to have a son.

Chapter 7

"Dr. Garnet, let's review the statement we took from you on the night of the murder. You said you saw the victim alive but inebriated on your way back from the ICU. What time was that?" Riley asked, showing no trace of the uneasiness I'd witnessed earlier. We were in a small, empty classroom. Riley was seated in front of me. Bufort was leaning against the back wall.

"As I said, about seven o'clock."

"Are you in the habit of being here that late?"

"I was on duty. The shift ends at midnight."

"Then why were you still here at one in the morning?"

"Sign-out takes a little while, especially if we're busy."

"Were you?"

"Not especially. But my replacement was late that night."

"Who was that?"

"Dr. Kradic."

And so it went. Riley scribbling away as if he hadn't questioned me already; Bufort hovering in the corner, like a spider watching a protégé weave a beginner's web.

"And what did you say Kingsly was doing?"

"He was walking down the hall on Second Main. That's the center block on the floor above the administrative suites."

"So he had come from his office?"

"Probably."

"Was he in the habit of being here so late, especially on a Sunday?"

They must know by now. "Unfortunately, yes. He had a drinking problem. Lately he'd gotten worse, and was sometimes known to stay late and, well, maybe have a few belts in his office. I figured that Sunday he'd been drinking at home or out at a party somewhere before he came in."

"Did anyone ever have trouble with him when he was intoxicated?"

Despite Bufort's previous warning against keeping secrets, I decided to minimize. I still didn't want his men hounding the women it was rumored Kingsly had tried to paw. "He was pretty harmless. I've heard he made a few feeble moves on any skirt he fell over, but nothing serious. Besides, the postmortem results showed this was not the random stab of some woman defending herself against one of his advances."

"What did you do to help him?" Bufort suddenly asked.

The nearness of his voice made me jump. He'd moved up to stand directly behind my head.

"I told the guards at the door. They usually got him home okay."

"I know that! They didn't find him. I meant what did you doctors do to help him? He was an alcoholic. Who was treating him?"

I was stung. I'd prepared for questions about a murder I hadn't committed, not for a grilling about my indifference to Kingsly's problem. "I don't know," I answered lamely.

"How could it be that this obvious alcoholic was allowed to continue in his job without help?" Bufort's tone was hard, accusing.

"I told you, I don't know. To be honest, I feel damn guilty about it now, but I guess I was just too wrapped up in my own problems with the ER." I was hearing my words at a distance; the truth of my admission unsettled me.

"Hell, Doctor, if we had a cop in his shape, he'd be pulled from his job for treatment. Any half-decent corporation would have yanked this guy. Yet he's been allowed to screw up here, a total incompetent from what I gather, in the middle of a sea of healers—and not one of you bothered to help him?"

His disgust fed my own. I suddenly felt compelled to explain how we ended up so callous—not as an excuse but because I needed to explain it to myself.

"Look, I know it was unforgivable." I was finding it hard to keep my voice from shaking. "But maybe others here felt as I did—his drinking was his business. He had a family. I suppose that if I gave it any thought, I'd have guessed his wife or someone was taking care of him. He'd made such a mess of the hospital's budget, however, I saw him more as an adversary that needed firing."

"You never thought of going into his office yourself and urging him to get help? You never thought of organizing your colleagues for an intervention?"

I felt my face go hot. "No" was all I could say, but the question bored into the heart of my guilt.

"He was one of your own, Doctor. Why didn't you help him?" He let the question hang.

I sat, silent, taken by surprise at the extent of the remorse and regret I felt. Then I began to feel angry. Bufort was peeling away my defenses, layer by layer, like a malevolent therapist.

"Would you answer me, Doctor?"

"I told you, I'm not proud of what I did—or, rather, what I didn't do." It felt like I was being skinned alive by this cop.

By now he was in front of me. He leaned toward my left ear and said very quietly, "You mean you didn't have time for a drunk in your busy, important schedule."

"Hey, you're getting out of line!" I said sharply.

He reared back in a sarcastic show of surprise. "Oh,

really? Since you couldn't get rid of him, you *all* seemed to prefer him ineffectual and inebriated on the sidelines."

I finally lost my temper. "This is really too much!" I instinctively looked over at Riley for help. I watched the muscles in the corner of his jaw tighten.

Riley cleared his throat. "Look, maybe we should get back to the night of the murder."

There was a pause, cold as ice, before Bufort said, "I'm in charge of this interrogation, Riley." He began pacing behind me so I'd have to keep turning my head to see him.

Across from me, the side of Riley's jaw bulged again. He got up and walked over to a desk at the front of the room. There he half sat, half leaned on its large top, fiddling with a piece of chalk from the sill of a nearby blackboard.

Bufort now came around to where I could see him better. "Here's my point, Doctor," he started to say. "It seems everyone in your hospital conformed to a norm of indifference—sort of the hospital's way of institutionalizing an acceptance of Kingsly's alcoholism." He sounded like he was reading from a textbook. "It certainly seems to have freed all of you from any thought of taking the trouble to help him."

By the expectant look on his face, I figured he wanted a reply, so I confessed, or surrendered, or maybe did a little of both. "Yes, I see what you mean."

But admitting my complicity didn't end the ordeal. I tensed as he leaned toward me. "So who gains? Who does it serve to have the administrative head of this place continually out of it? Who could profit by that?"

The obvious name came to mind. It was the perfect time to tell Bufort about the phone call and my suspicions about Hurst. I could throw in my story about being chased by the Dobermans and let the detective make whatever he wanted of it. But even after what I'd just been through, and as tempted as I was to subject Hurst to his own ordeal by innuendo and whispered allegations, I balked. I balked at resorting to the same underhanded level of treatment he had used against me when he first pointed Bufort my way. It wasn't altruism. Being anything like Hurst just revolted me too much. And whatever I thought he was up to, I had no proof. Until I did, if I was going to stop Bufort from subjecting me and the rest of my staff to similar cheap shots and accusations, I couldn't very well indulge in them myself. "I don't know!" I finally answered, my dread about Hurst and what he was capable of in full force.

The rest of the interview was mundane. Bufort asked me if I knew why anyone would murder Kingsly. I said no. Then he wanted to know if outsiders could get into private areas of the hospital at night. Sure, I told him. Sometimes street people hid out in the basement to keep warm or waited in washrooms till after visiting hours. Security wasn't our highest priority in the ER. On the contrary our unit was—had to be—open, free-flowing, and constantly chaotic. Again I thought he was getting a little offtrack, given that the killer was probably a doctor, but I supposed he had to account for all possibilities.

He finished by requesting a list of the doctors I'd seen in the hospital that night, particularly between seven and midnight or so. I presumed this was the estimated time of death that Watts had given him. I said I had seen only the residents scheduled to be there. He didn't have any questions about them as I'd feared he might, and for that, at least, I was grateful.

He didn't once ask me if I'd killed Kingsly, or even allude to the possibility. It seemed he'd convicted me so far only of being a total shit as a doctor . . . and as a human being. I felt deprived of a chance to hear his suspicions and answer allegations about me as a killer. Perhaps he'd even figured I'd feel that way, and not asking was part of his game to keep me off balance.

Riley wasn't any help either in determining how seriously he considered me a suspect. After his reprimand from Bufort, he'd sunk into an unreadable silence on his perch at the front of the room and had given his jaw muscles a good workout.

One point Bufort congratulated me on. During their search of the hospital, they hadn't found the room yet where the walls and ceiling had been given an unscheduled cleaning, but a sweeper had reported that when he came on duty Sunday at midnight, he had found a mop wet and recently used in his basement locker. They were checking it for traces of blood and other bodily fluids that had leaked out and squirted out of Kingsly as he died.

Outside our department window, the afternoon light had dimmed to thin smoke. I was still stinging from the dressing-down I'd received from Bufort hours earlier, but where my own failure to help Kingsly's alcoholism was inexcusable, it *was* passive. However, if Bufort's line of reasoning was right, Hurst may have deliberately counted on Kingsly's drinking going untreated to maintain his control over the hospital. The prospect of our medical vice president being that ruthless no longer surprised me.

I found Sean Carrington talking to some residents near our X ray–viewing box. He'd just plopped an odd film of spindly bones on a lighted screen and was eliciting some very puzzled expressions from his audience. I paused to watch, but when he saw me, he grinned and said, "Go away, Earl, this is private. Shoo, shoo!"

I knew what he was up to.

Recently I'd heard he'd taken to buying racehorses as a tax writeoff and that his latest nag pulled up lame after her first meet. Sean had wanted to shoot her there and then, but the track authorities said he couldn't do that. He'd have to pay a vet for arthroscopic surgery—$1800 plus boarding fees. Sean had looked up the fee for the same procedure on humans: $1200. Now he was trying to snag an orthopedic surgeon who was unfortunate enough to be passing by.

"Marty," he called, "come here and look at this knee for me."

Marty squinted at the films for a few seconds and then gave his opinion. "This is not a human knee."

"So, can you operate on her?"

"Is this one of your horses?"

"Yeah, so what? Will you operate on her?"

"I'm cheaper than the vet, right?" He started turning away.

"No, no, it's your skill. I love this animal so much, I wouldn't trust her life with anyone but you."

Marty chuckled. "Who's going to give the anesthesia, you?"

A demonic light came into Sean's eyes. "Anesthetic death! Sure! Who'd know?" He turned to one of the incredulous residents. "You want to earn fifty bucks? Look, give me an hour. You just stand there. We don't say you're a vet, but we don't say you're not. It'll be over before you'd be expected to actually do anything. Now, we get a scope from day surgery, just to look good, and I'll get some pentobarbitol syringes . . ."

The rest was lost to me as he slipped his arm around the shaken resident and led him to a corner where, obviously, he intended to sell him on his plan.

Funny, I always found his zany performances a breath of relief compared to the pompous demeanor that masked many of our less competent yet more proper practitioners of the healing arts. But today his flash left me empty. He hadn't been physician enough to help Kingsly either . . . and his callousness about the horse disturbed me.

The sound of Carole's long fingernails clicking on her keyboard blended with the steady patter of rain on my own office window. Here too, very little light got through the opaque square of glass. Grime or design, I couldn't tell. The dirt on the outside pane curdled into a greasy sludge.

When Carole and I were using our desks at the same time, our two tiny adjoining offices were cramped, but that happened so infrequently, we rarely found it a problem. We usually left the door between us open so we could easily speak to each other without getting up.

Carole had given me my messages when I came in. A number of the doctors had dropped by, wanting a look at the ER study. She'd even walked in on Kradic and Green hovering over my desk, much the way I'd surprised Jones earlier that morning. Obviously, Jones had been telling everyone about it, and until I sorted out those statistics, the whole department was going to be nervous waiting for the results. It was a good thing I'd locked up the printouts.

But for now I had to deal with the injunctions. I managed to get through to a lawyer at our malpractice agency in Albany. It was an insurance company that specialized in defending doctors against lawsuits. After a few minutes of assuring ourselves we each had equal meteorological misery, the lawyer listened to my recital of our plight and a half-baked plan I'd put together. He said he'd get back to me the next day with a legal opinion.

After we hung up, I let the rain hitting the window lull me into idle thinking. A lawyer's emergency response time could be days; a doctor's was often measured in seconds.

Carole stopped her typing, came through our door, and handed me a stack of mail—mostly ads for equipment we couldn't afford, and one letter from a national recruitment group offering me a career change and a job in Newark. But she'd already opened and screened them, so when she remained turned toward me, looking at her hands as she rubbed her palms together, I knew she wanted to talk. It was what she always did with her hands if something was going to be awkward.

"Okay, Carole, let's have it."

She smiled. "You know me too well." She took a deep breath. "I realize you don't need anything more on your plate right now, but I've heard some gossip I think you'd better be aware of." She paused, looked back down at her hands, and kept rubbing them against each other. "Dr. Jones has been sleeping with one of the residents," she said, obviously embarrassed.

"Oh, God!" I groaned. I definitely did *not* need this now, or at any other time, and especially not from Jones.

Residents were strictly forbidden fruit to our staff. Male doctors had learned that a decade ago, but in the last eight years at least three women doctors in the department had had to be told that sex with the students was, to say the least, inappropriate. And even then they'd been surprised it was any of my business. "It's the whole department's business," I'd explained. "If you split up, and there's any resentment on either side, it can totally poison our working atmosphere. As for evaluations, they're completely compromised, good and bad. Hell, disgruntled residents are already taking us to court if they don't like what we say. Don't hand them a sexual harassment case to charge us with as well." Those women had been reasonable after explanations of that sort. I expected no such luck with Jones.

"Who's she sleeping with?" I asked, feeling even more tired than when I'd finished with Bufort.

"Dr. Todd," Carole answered. Looking relieved to be free of her burden, she returned to her desk and her typing. She never told me her sources, and I never asked.

Shit! Obviously his *magic hands* did more than insert central lines. At least James Todd was a strong resident. His evaluations from the other doctors would be positive, so we shouldn't have any problem with having to defend our credibility there. But I'd have to speak with Jones—and I dreaded doing it.

I took out my frustration on the junk mail by smashing each piece into a tight ball and hurling it into our recycling box. When I got to the recruitment flier, I called out to Carole, "If they ever send one of these recruitment things for a doctor in Hawaii, make sure I'm the only one who sees it."

"So, did you name names?" Sean asked. He'd popped into my office after his own session with Bufort.

"Of course. One glimpse of the bamboo splinters and I immediately gave him your name. Told him you were planning to murder a horse."

"Oh, really. I heard you were still his number one *needler*."

I groaned.

"Seriously," Sean said, "is he going to start coming after your staff?"

"It looks like it." I sighed. "How about you? How many of your surgeons regularly needle hearts?"

"Just four. The cardiothoracic surgeons. They don't actually needle them much, but they do a lot more complicated things to living hearts on a daily basis. Needling them would be a snap."

"What about the rest of you?"

"We were all trained to do it back in residency, but without having done it over the years in real practice, few of us could get the kind of accuracy Bufort seems to be looking for. At least not the younger surgeons."

"What do you mean?"

"Our conversation the other day made me think of it. Up until the seventies, if a patient arrested on the OR table, the surgeon would give an intracardiac injection. It wouldn't happen often, but over the years any surgeon from that era would get pretty good at needling hearts."

I knew where this was going. "Sean, you didn't!"

"You're damn right I did. The good Dr. Hurst is now a suspect on Bufort's list."

"Holy Christ!"

"What? You think I shouldn't have told Bufort that Hurst had the skill to kill Kingsly?"

"Not just to get even, Sean."

"What makes you so sure he isn't the murderer?" he asked, getting a little testy. "Hell, you know how he's a fanatic for covering up any scandal in the hospital. Maybe Kingsly was about to cause a whopper. And what about this crazy agenda for budget cuts that Hurst is suddenly ramming down our throats, literally within hours of Kingsly's death? The speed and size of it make no sense. I tell you, Earl, Bufort should take a damn close look at Hurst!"

Sean punctuated this accusation by stomping out of my office.

I was left totally amazed by his astonishing suggestion.

As much as I detested and distrusted Hurst, and as much as I found his behavior ruthless, bizarre, and, lately, even frightening, I didn't think of him as the killer. I never doubted that his first reaction to seeing Kingsly's body was sincere. But was it? Now I was racing to a different possibility. Had I actually witnessed a murderer reacting with horror as his cover-up failed? And if that was true, then his attempts to frame me for the killing were certain to continue—and have no limits.

I'd begun to sweat. Another possibility reappeared out of my rising fear. The dogs. *You've had your warning!* Had the whispering caller been the figure on the green after all? Hurst? Or someone he'd hired? No! It made no sense. Even if Hurst had killed Kingsly, he wouldn't try to frame me for the murder and then risk killing me with Dobermans at the same time. I had to reign in my paranoia and think clearly. Besides, something else didn't jibe. Something even more contradictory. If Hurst was the killer and the anonymous caller, why did he say *I know it's you*? Or why would he warn me to *back off*?

Suddenly none of it made sense. I tried controlling my increasing panic about what I was up against, but Sean's argument wouldn't go away, and visions of Bufort with Hurst at his ear, pointing at me, pushed in on my mind as oppressively as when the detective had leaned against me last night, warning that I might get in trouble I couldn't get out of.

Damn them both! I had to stop letting them scare me. I needed to get back on familiar ground, where I could shake off all this weird speculation. Only one place would do.

I retreated to the ward, where I saw patients for an hour. The routine was calming, therapeutic even, for me and, at first, for the patients.

I quickly got a young asthmatic breathing comfortably after giving him a mask of bronchodilators. He wanted to go home, but I explained one treatment wasn't enough. He'd need steroids intravenously to dampen down the inflammation that was closing off his lung. Otherwise, he'd be in trouble again and back.

By chance, all the patients I saw after the asthmatic didn't require admission. At least momentarily I was spared the frustration of sentencing anyone to corridor care.

Then a little old lady was brought in because the day before she'd vomited up black liquid, but hadn't told her daughter about it until this afternoon. The daughter had rushed her to ER and was pacing nervously all through the examinations and tests. The mother had had an upper GI bleed but was remarkably stable. Under other circumstances—namely, the hospital being run like a hospital—I'd have medicated the elderly woman and admitted her to a monitored bed in an intermediate unit for safekeeping until she could be scoped the next morning. So once again, just as Jones had done that morning, I tried medicating and discharging a patient who should have been kept for observation and more tests.

I tried to explain to her daughter. "If she starts to bleed again, she'll get a faster response by you calling 911. That'll get our attention by ambulance through the front door."

"You're out of your mind!" her daughter cried.

She was right, of course. "Look," I said, knowing I had to be completely candid, "here she'll be parked unmonitored at the end of a corridor."

"You call this a hospital?"

I looked around at the rows of stretchers, where the elderly woman could slip unnoticed into shock. I remembered another daughter's eyes.

"Not really, not tonight," I answered.

"I want to speak to your director."

"I am the director."

Horrified, she gaped at my name tag. "Oh my God, you are!" She looked around at our controlled panic and asked, "What about another hospital?"

"Unfortunately, that's unlikely. But come, we'll check." I knew it was futile, but I always showed families "the try." According to our management manuals we then "share the frustration" and "demonstrate we are not on opposing sides." The way the daughter chewed her gum and gave me disgusted looks suggested otherwise.

I took her to the computer reserved for a citywide bed registry. State of the art; instant documentation of no beds anywhere; all ERs saturated.

I knew that half the hospitals lied. Some pushed the "code in process" button to reroute ambulances during coffee break. But most of the time it was the same as here: medical patients in beds too long, "pet farms" all over the city. When the changeover to managed care is finally completed, our soft fraud artist Arnold Pinter and his buddies will be out of luck, and the beds will empty out. The trouble is, that's the way they'll stay, and everyone will get to experience the world of withheld care, just like Donald Cummings had.

I punched in a request for a monitored bed. Three came up. Two were obstetrical, one was in a cardiac unit—all three inappropriate.

Still convinced it was better to level, I explained my logic again, said it'd be what I'd offer my own mother given the circumstances, and meant it.

She took my name, called her lawyer on our phone, and then walked out, leaving her mother with us and threatening loudly that I'd be hearing from her soon.

It had worked better this morning.

I had the nurses place the lady as close to their station as possible, and then looked around the department for something else to do. It was packed with admitted patients and teeming with relatives. Cries of pain and calls for meds or bedpans added to the confusion, but there were no new incoming patients for the moment.

I went back to my office. Carole had left for the day. I was alone with my options and with the gloom applying itself to the window like a coat of paint.

I thought I'd better call Zak to make sure he'd go easy on sending us ambulances again that night. I caught him just as he was leaving.

"Sure," he agreed. "But unofficially. Even *I* can't ban ambulances for more than twenty-four hours."

"Thanks, Zak."

"So who killed him?"

Right to the point. Payment.

"Nobody knows yet, except the police think it's a doctor who can needle hearts."

"What!"

"You heard me."

"But that's your entire department!"

"Including me."

"Get serious!"

"Oh, I am serious, unfortunately." And I filled his ears with detail.

"Gee, Earl, I'm sorry," he said when I'd finished. He actually sounded like he meant it.

While I was talking to him, I'd been absently fingering Jones's paper. The whole project was under Zak's supervision. "By the way," I asked, "how's the cardiac study going?"

"Pretty good!" Despite it being the end of the day, he sounded enthusiastic. "Nothing earth-shattering," he began, "but a lot of confirmation of existing treatment protocols, with a few minor improvements."

"Jones just handed me her magnesium sulfate study."

"Nice piece of work, that. Too bad torsade de pointes is so esoteric."

I was about to thank him and say good night when I asked on impulse, "Zak, have you ever had any trouble with her?"

He was clearly taken aback. But when she worked the ambulances on the research study, he was her boss. "With Jones?" he repeated.

I began to feel a little foolish, but pressed on. "Yeah, with Jones."

He was silent for a moment. Then he asked, "What do you mean by trouble?"

So there *was* something. "Look, Zak, this is completely confidential. It would help me if you could answer."

"You mean trouble with her work?" he asked, still cautious.

"With anything."

He was silent again.

While waiting for his answer, right out of nowhere, I suddenly thought that Zak had had sex with her too. That startled me, and I was wondering where the hell it had come from when he finally spoke.

"Never any trouble with her work," Zak said slowly. "She's become our best resuscitator over the last few years. I'd be lost without her."

"What about her personal relationships with the staff?" I asked, still trying to shake off my intuition that he'd been involved with her.

He snorted. "What relationships? The other doctors resent her like hell. She's abrasive and rude, and very defensive whenever I try to deal with their complaints about her."

Just like here. Sort of Kradic in a dress. So it wasn't only me.

"Funny though," he added, "the technicians love her. She's always teaching them, and they can't get enough time with her on the road. She's good with patients too. It's the other doctors she can't get along with. And it doesn't help matters any that her survival rates are way ahead of theirs. Why are you asking about her?"

"I'm having similar problems. I wondered if it was a personality clash between us."

"Well, stop blaming yourself. She's a brilliant clinician and an insufferable prima donna. They exist all over our profession. Patients are lucky to have them, we mere mortals have to endure them. Good night, Chief. I'm going home."

"And I'm blessed with two of them," I muttered as Zak hung up.

I did glance quickly at the summary of Jones's study. As she had said, there were good results for a rare condition, but no clear-cut extra help against our common enemies. The method and statistical precaution against chance giving false conclusions seemed sound. Still, as I filed it, something that I couldn't pinpoint niggled at the back of my mind. If we ever got back to normal, I'd sit down to dissect the paper in detail.

Janet was on duty in the case room at her hospital for

the night. There was nothing more to do here. Tomorrow at noon I had private office hours for patients from my former general practice. I'd kept them on to counterbalance taking over emergency eight years ago. It was shelter from the storm.

But I needed a respite now. If I didn't occupy myself with something engaging, I'd end up dwelling on Kingsly's murder and likely make myself panicky again. I unlocked my desk drawer and eyed the statistics I'd hidden there earlier. They were the perfect excuse to indulge in a guilty pleasure and a way to keep myself calm.

I made a quick call to Janet's answering service and left a message about where I was heading. Pocketing the computer disks I'd need, I scooped the reports under one arm and carried them with me while I gave the ER a final check.

"We're okay for the moment," Popovitch said good-naturedly. He eyed the printouts. "And good luck with the statistics, but you're going to get a hernia lugging all that paper around."

"Take care," added Jones with a slight smile.

I didn't smile back. I still resented her snooping this morning, and evidently talking about it later, but it was her liaison with James Todd that troubled me most. I wasn't going to confront her on the ethics of it tonight, but as I looked at this fierce, athletic woman, I suddenly visualized her writhing naked with Zak, then Todd. It had been little more than a subliminal flash, but thinking anything erotic about her at all surprised the hell out of me, and I turned away, embarrassed, dismissing it as part of my preoccupation about her and Todd. I wished everyone else a good evening and left by the back door.

The parking lot was filled with more mist than cars. At the freight entrance, an ambulance stood in a pool of sodium light, and through its rear doors two attendants were loading a stretcher with a body bag on it. Probably they were making a pickup for a funeral home of a patient who had died recently. I wondered if it was Cummings. Above, the hospital lights disappeared upward into gray. Only the administration wing was dark—except for the finance office. Like the night before, it was still lit. I could even make out a figure moving behind the glass. As I watched, I became aware of someone else nearby. Turning, I saw Gil Fernandez standing beside his car and looking up at the same windows. Huddled in a raincoat, he lacked his usual bravado. It was probably the streetlight, but I'd seen precodes with more color.

I jerked my thumb back at the window in question. "Maybe the good Detective Bufort will fix our budget while he's at it."

I'd expected Fernandez's belief in himself as a brilliant manager to make the crack work. Instead, startled, his face drained further, to the color of lard. He jumped in behind the wheel of his car, slammed the door, and sped away without a word.

I stood there as his taillights disappeared from the lot. Until then, I'd been mildly curious about Fernandez's look of relief when he first heard of Kingsly's death. It had been odd, but I certainly hadn't wanted to read too much into it.

What counted more was the look of fear I'd just seen on his face.

Gil Fernandez was terrified.

My guilty pleasure was a log home. I'd found the place years ago. Originally it was a simple cabin more than fifty years old, lovingly constructed on the edge of an isolated mountain lake surrounded by eighty acres of forest. Janet liked to tell people that I had taken her there before I ever took her on the ritual visit to Mom and Dad. We'd modernized it with carpeting, electric heaters, a pool-size bathtub, and, for real luxury, an indoor toilet. Later we added a large addition and ended up with a log and glass home well over a hundred feet long, full of spacious rooms with high ceilings and magnificent windows. Janet had assumed total control over the kitchen and melded a full collection of electrical appliances with the woodstoves. The lady and the lumberjack was what Janet called us when we were there. More important, it was a sanctuary, a place to find intimacy and laughter, a healing place.

It was also where I kept a computer and fax machine, and was the hideout I retreated to if I needed to do more than an hour of uninterrupted work.

I'd gone home to pick up Muffy and then headed south out of Buffalo toward the mountains, all the while trying hard not to think of the mess and horror I was driving away from. I passed through the clutter of junkyards and failed industries that ringed the city. They formed an urban garbage heap tossed farther and farther out. Even when I reached the countryside there was no clear break. From the highway I could see a jumble of trailer homes and cheap new bungalows built up on top of the broken-down farms of the previous generation. In turn, the grandchildren playing on this land in the dusk would only know how to farm welfare. I caught a glimpse of an old man staring out a window at the barren fields. Probably he'd once made them rich with food. I was willing to bet that in the background a TV flickered, showing pictures of starving kids somewhere in the world.

Starving kids. Suffering kids. Corridors full of suffering people. I couldn't shut out the images or associated thoughts. Hurst. Back in my office I'd figured if he was trying to frame me because he'd murdered Kingsly himself, then the whispering caller had to be someone else. But who? And why? I'd been so sure it was Hurst telling me to *back off* my attempt to close the ER. Could someone else be that angry about it? One of Sean's surgeons upset about the loss of income? Or even one of my own doctors? Could any of them be that crazy about money? Perhaps crazy enough to set a pair of Dobermans on me? Dammit! I was starting to let what I didn't know panic me again. If I was ever going to get out of this mess, I had to stop jumping to conclusions and think clearly.

I reined in my wild thoughts and focused on something familiar. In medicine, when faced with a set of symptoms and signs, we lay out a differential, a list of all the possible diseases that could cause the initial facts of the presenting sickness. Then we do tests to get more data, and in the end we look at which diagnoses fit most of the facts and which don't. I tried to apply that process to my current problems.

Singling out Hurst had only led to confusion. It was time to do a differential, consider all the other possibilities, including the chance that Hurst was neither the killer nor the person on the phone. All I knew for certain was that he'd made sure the police included me on their list of suspects and he was ramming through an illogical set of bed cuts. The rest I'd assumed. Even about the warning. Now that I was thinking diagnostically, I realized *back off* hadn't necessarily meant back off closing the ER. I'd have to keep an open mind there too.

Up ahead I saw some hot-dog stands come into view. Faded and rust-chipped, they cluttered the edge of the highway like litter. They had Drink Coke signs from the fifties that would have been trendy in some downtown establishments, but here they simply marked when the progress had stopped. I couldn't buy a drink. These concessions had closed for the winter. They looked just as dingy in summer, and I never stopped then either.

I let my mind drift onto other possibilities. Images of Fernandez's desperate expression returned to blur in with the passing roadside and persisted on the edge of my thoughts. I made a try at including him in my differential. He had looked relieved when Hurst announced Kingsly's death and not called it murder. Then that relief seemed to vanish when Bufort had revealed it *was* murder. Again behavior perfectly consistent with a killer whose cover-up initially seemed to work and then failed. Exactly what I'd thought earlier about Hurst's behavior.

But now I wanted to think critically and avoid easy conclusions. I was going to have to get used to thinking about murder in this familiar, clinical way.

I continued my new application of an old skill, more for the practice than any real hope it would get me anywhere. There could be other explanations for Fernandez's symptoms. His apparent mood changes could have been coincidental and stemmed from some other unrelated nightmare. His wife might have announced she had a lover, or one of his kids been diagnosed with cancer, or even a malpractice suit been threatened against him. And some things about Fernandez didn't fit the diagnosis of him being the killer. Even though his initial calm had vanished, he still hadn't seemed more obviously upset than the other chiefs when Bufort finally did say Kingsly had been murdered. And why was he panicking now, after Bufort had clearly indicated suspicion was primarily on the ER and those few doctors in other parts of the hospital who could needle hearts? Fernandez might have gotten some rudimentary training about how to administer an intracardiac injection during medical school, but as Sean said, that would hardly be enough to give him the means of murdering Kingsly now.

Occasionally mist drifted across the liquid mud fields on either side of the road. Sometimes it glared in my headlights and hid the dirty pavement snaking out in front of me.

There was hardly any traffic. In my rearview mirror I could see only a single pair of headlights keeping a steady distance. I was glad the driver was being cautious; I didn't want any tailgater humping my car in a fog patch.

By this point in the familiar drive, I'd usually left thoughts of the hospital far behind. But I kept obsessively turning over why I had an uneasy feeling I was missing something about the murder, a connection I was sure was there but had eluded me so far. About Fernandez? I didn't seriously think he could be the killer. But had I forced a case against Hurst to avoid adding the real nightmare possibility to my differential diagnosis—that the killer might be a member of my own department? Again the thought of unchecked suspicions about my staff that I couldn't control sent a chill down my back.

Finally the road left the sodden flatlands for some real rock and pine turf. Climbing one interminably long hill, I was suddenly above the fog. A full moon rippled the mist lapping around the bases of floating hills. It was the first sky I'd seen in more than a week. I opened the window and inhaled deep breaths of clear, frosty air. I laughed and woke up Muffy, who immediately scented the wild. She sat panting expectantly, ready to run out her hunting fantasies in the night woods. I ruffled her ears and got licked in return. Thoughts of murder started to subside.

Soon I slowed for our turnoff. It was foggy again, and remembering the pair of lights behind me, I quickly left the highway for the narrow dirt road leading up to our lake. As I started the climb into the deepening mist, I saw in my rearview mirror the passing taillights of a large square-ended van continuing north through the night.

The road was rutted hard in the mountain frost, but I preferred it to the mush we had left behind. Pointing up the incline, my lights tunneled through swirls of bare tree branches awaiting winter. The beams exaggerated the bouncing motion of the car and gave our progress the feel of a boat plowing seas.

A few minutes later I pulled into the graveled parking

area and was met with the glare of the automatic flood-
light snapped on by movement sensors picking up our
arrival. Muffy was unrestrainable. As soon as I got my
car door open, she bounded out and happily ran into the
woods. I struggled with the computer printouts and made
it to the front door before the timed light went out and
left me juggling keys in the dark. Door open, I plopped
the paper stack on a rickety antique entrance table more
suited to delicate riding gloves than the pounds of data
encumbering a modern man. But the table was a favorite
of Janet's, so there it stayed. Then I switched on the lawn
lights and stepped back outside.

The grounds were a lacy melange of vapor and backlit
trees. The only sound was from the distant creek, the rush
of its swift currents defying the coming winter to turn it
into ice. Muffy trotted up and put her head under my
hand for an ear kitzle.

Our breath joined the general haze. As I turned to put
her in the house, the first flakes of a light snow began to
fall. In minutes I'd chucked my intentions to work and
was asleep under a skylight framing diamonds and mist.

I have no idea what time Muffy went on alert and
roared out of the bedroom down to the front door. But the
ferocity of her bark told me we had a night visitor. Rac-
coon most likely. The barking raged on. I mumbled,
"Good girl," and went back to sleep even before she finished her tirade to scare them off. Good riddance. Rac-
coons made a mess of the place.

I wouldn't call it first light. This time of year it was a
lighter shade of gloom. But it was enough to signal my
sleep-sogged brain it was time for coffee and a start on
the computer with my stack of stats. The coffee was
easy—a form of yuppie instant that involved pouring
boiled water on fresh grounds, waiting a few minutes,
then pressing down on a plunger. It was the only piece of

kitchen equipment Janet let me use. She considers me so technically challenged, I'm banned from cooking.

My first sip coincided with a glimpse through the large windows that surrounded the oversize kitchen. The lake was black, but covering everything else was a powdering of snow. In a magic instant the brown month had been banished and made over. It was one of the annual landmarks of life, the first snow. It never failed to lift me from adult routine back to childhood, inspiring me to play and infusing me with a sense of sweet freshness in which all was possible again.

I was still wearing a smile as I lit some kindling in the kitchen woodstove. It performed like a furnace and was the fastest way to cozy up this end of the house. My computer room was directly above on the second floor, and I wanted it warm up there. When the crackle and scent of wood smoke assured me the fire was well started, I went to the front entrance mudroom to get the printouts. Muffy, monitoring me out of a half-raised eye, saw this move as interesting to her. She arched in a leisurely poodle stretch, then pranced to the door to be let out.

Absently, I reached for the knob, then stopped. Outside on the wooden stoop and stone pathway the white dusting was already beginning to fade. Still visible was a set of footprints. They came up to the door, turned, and retreated back down the path.

Chapter 8

I held my breath. Muffy, sensing my alarm, went still, listened, but didn't growl. I let myself slowly exhale and tried to rationalize. My prints from coming in? No, the snow had started just after we arrived. Hunters were a constant nuisance, but they stayed away from the cabin, out of sight.

The chill of the simple truth sank in. Someone had tried to break in on me. Only Muffy had made the difference.

Her lack of concern now was reassuring. Whoever had been here was gone. But the footsteps were a slash across my earlier mood. Isolation was stark and beautiful, but the wilds were also a place of menace and natural violence. Yet in nature there was reason, usually. Bears lived in the next valley over, but, unspoiled, they stayed away. I'd always felt more people were killed in gun accidents than bear attacks, and so I never considered arming myself. Against human menace, the long drive in was both protection and a trap. Shutters on the windows and a chain gate over the road discouraged casual vandals. To a real creep intent on trucking the furniture away, however, we were vulnerable. But they were cornered if seen. Our defense had come down to a couple of BEWARE OF DOG signs and letting Muffy roar her head off at unwanted guests. Sort of security by the Wizard of Oz. It was damned effective too. I even left the chain down most of the time. It fooled hunters into thinking we were there, and Muffy had actually chased them off enough times that they were too scared to find out for sure. Those prints, however, already fading with the melting snow on the darker stones, were mocking me. A hunter wouldn't come to the door. A kid looking for a place to throw a party, or an intruder with a more sinister purpose?

I know, Doc. I know it's you. You've had your warning. Back off! I felt a chill again, remembering the dogs. But there were no paw prints anywhere.

Why would I be a target? I didn't know who had killed Kingsly, or why, and I hadn't a clue how the murder had anything to do with me. That hadn't meant much to the cops so far, thanks to Hurst, but it sure should have been clear to the killer, and keeping me alive would be what made sense, as long as whoever it was knew I was a suspect.

I was probably overreacting again. It was pretty far-fetched to think the footprints had anything to do with the murder at all. Maybe they were made by a common thief here to steal a VCR.

Nevertheless, I put Muffy on her leash to keep her near me until I made sure no one was still hanging around. We stepped outside. It was frosty, but the footprints disappeared where the graveled parking area ended, and the darker cinder road had already melted the snow. Muffy showed little interest. The hard surface refused to even hint where the intruder had headed. I shivered, this time because I was still in a robe and slippers. I let Muffy off her chain. Me, I needed the warmth of indoor plumbing.

I refused to let my paranoia chase me back into the city after coming all the way out here to work.

Besides, the respite offered by working on the QA data for the next three hours was the only remedy I had at the moment for my paranoia.

Carole had saved me days by entering the data for our major diagnostic categories on a floppy disk. It was pretty routine stuff, and if I needed anything more esoteric, I could still refer to the original printouts.

Studies of lawsuits had identified that two-thirds of screwups came from six types of problems: chest pain, abdominal pain, missed fractures, nerve injuries, intracranial bleeds, and meningitis. Knowing where to look before going in always makes the odds better to find our flaws and to learn.

These major categories were behaving as they should. The classic—chest pain—presented about a hundred and twenty times a week. In this group, only four, statistically and on average, would be real heart attacks, but the trick was to know which four, and which weeks were not average. Sixty would be cleared right off, and be sent home with acetaminophen for sore muscles or antacids for indigestion. But in the remaining sixty, there would be four heart attacks and four unstable anginas about to become heart attacks, statistically speaking. To find one MI, it takes a workup on fifteen suspicious chest pains, according to studies on centers that get it right ninety-five percent of the time.

Out of more than two hundred proven MIs, we had mistakenly sent home only five in the last year. One died at home. The other four, each feeling increasingly worse after discharge from the ER, had made it back to our door. One arrested in the hallway and failed to respond. The other three had survived.

Each case was a different physician. The chart review had revealed an error in judgment, not negligence, in all five cases. Statistically, this was all acceptable. Individually, I felt pretty disgusted knowing we probably would miss another five this year.

Abdominal pain shaped up miserably, as expected. Our initial diagnoses were wrong, or right, fifty percent of the time. This was a national average no one seemed able to better. It just was a reality that initial presentations of abdominal pain were hard to pinpoint and required repeated reassessments and follow-up to finally nail the problem. Knowing this, we could act with appropriate care. Two physician numbers popped out of the norm here. I had no idea who; a code kept identities unknown in the raw data prepared by medical records and submitted to the state health department. An individual physician's performance would then be known only to that doctor and myself, after I analyzed the statistics.

While one doctor had been correct in diagnosing appendicitis one hundred percent of the time, another was only sixty percent accurate. The first physician was actually the more dangerous of the two. Every patient this doctor had diagnosed as a possible acute appendicitis actually had an acutely inflamed appendix when they were opened. That pattern meant only the most obvious cases had been diagnosed and the subtler presentations had been sent home. In a good center where appendicitis was not usually missed, a competent surgeon would usually have to open five bellies to find four acute appendixes, and would take out a perfectly normal appendix twenty percent of the time. The doctor whose initial diagnosis was always right had not been referring enough patients to surgery. Sure enough, further down in the study, this same physician had a disproportionately high number of unscheduled return visits with a ruptured appendix attributed to his or her code number.

The second doctor was calling everything acute appendicitis. As a result, he, or she, wasted time, tests, and money, and had subjected too many patients to the dangers of unnecessary surgery. Of course, an overeager surgeon was partly to blame here too.

I also noted another problem. Too often the diagnosis for abdominal pain was constipation. Repeatedly, I'd stressed to staff and residents that constipation was a symptom and not a diagnosis. It could be caused by anything from colon cancer to not enough fiber in the diet and, if it was unusual for the patient, indicated the need for further investigation in a follow-up exam. Obviously, the message bore repeating.

And so it went—injuries and deaths caused by our mistakes and errors dulled to the dry stuff of tables and numbers. Even then, whatever harm we did was statistically rare enough that we were no worse than physicians in other ERs. In other words, as long as we screwed up within national norms, we could claim enough competence to still go out there and perform.

And occasionally, just as rarely, we achieved those elusive miracles. Still, I was as depressed as I was fascinated. Looking at a year of our cumulative mistakes had a sobering effect on me. Until I broke the code, I didn't even know my own performance. Maybe I was the one sending home the acute appendixes.

It was ten o'clock when I shut down and got ready to leave for the city. I'd gotten barely a third of the way through the main groupings of possible errors.

Outside, I welcomed the frost to clear my head. At least I'd kept myself from feeling afraid for a while. I'd grabbed an apple for a late breakfast and balanced a final cup of coffee on the way out to my car. The footprints had vanished to a glistening varnish on the stone walkway. It was still cold enough that the lawn and surrounding forest floor had stayed white.

I got Muffy into the car, and we headed down the mountain and back toward Buffalo. The prettiness was lost, however, as I started to dwell on those footprints again, and inevitably Kingsly's murder. Even in a hospital where death was common, the grisly killing sickened me. Maybe it was a delayed reaction, postponed like so many other emotions in a doctor's life by all the practical coping we're forced to do. More likely, I'd been trying to deny another question I feared, but Bufort's dressing-down had finally shamed me into facing it. I could still visualize Kingsly's pathetic body, as dissolute in death as was his life. Would his fate have been different if I'd tried to help him? My mood became even more morbid as I swung through shrouds of mist so thick, the wipers had to part the droplets left by them on the windshield. Other memories of death crowded in uninvited like silent accusers in the fog. I remembered two little girls and their dead father. I shook my head and tried to drive away the unwelcome visions.

The practice of medicine could rip your heart out. Most people can mercifully ignore the parade of terrors happening to others and trust that the odds will keep such horrors away from them. But our job is closer to the front, and we see every day the ways life can go horribly wrong and sink into pain and death. Some days I can't keep the images of it all out of my head. And sometimes it makes me think the worst.

I thought again of the footprints. Despite my previous dismissal of their relationship with Kingsly, I now felt a lot less glib here in the fog than I had in the clear beauty of the mountains. Because there was yet another possibility. If the killer feared exposure from me, then I might very well be a target. Had the menace really faded with the melted snow? Or had those prints marked the approaching steps of my own turn with a murderer?

It was less misty by the time I'd reentered the outskirts of Buffalo. There was no vestige of snow here, just gray sludge. The prenoon traffic rescued me from dwelling any further on the darker thoughts I'd had on the way in. I flicked the radio to a traffic report; bad everywhere. I listened to a weatherman assure me this was the worst November in ten years for consecutive days without sunshine. He proceeded to interview three experts who argued with one another over the cause. They couldn't agree on global warming, pollution, or rogue volcanoes, but all of them predicted tomorrow would be more heavily overcast than today and warned that record smog levels would make breathing difficult for people with lung conditions. Janis Joplin then rendered a little bit of therapy with "Me and Bobby McGee."

When I finally got to hear the news, Kingsly's murder was the lead story. It was brief, contained little more than the essential facts, and said nothing about a cardiac needle. There was a brief statement by Hurst assuring the public that the tragedy in no way compromised St. Paul's capacity to give proper care to its patients.

I drove directly to my private office beside the hospital. The patients that I'd kept in my general practice put up with the crazy demands on my time that went with becoming chief of the ER. At least they had me where it mattered for emergencies, if I wasn't in some damn meeting. More than this, I'd known them so long, many had become friends.

Muffy wasn't thrilled at being left in the car. I'd call geriatrics and see if they wanted some pet therapy that morning.

It was 11:55 when I entered the quiet of my still-empty waiting room. Barbara O'Hara, semiretired, a grand-mother, and previously secretary to a half dozen former chiefs, was my receptionist here. It was her judgment and interest in the patients that let me be away so much. She looked up from her crossword.

"Coffee? Or messages first?"

"Coffee, please, and good morning to you too."

"Good, because your first appointment isn't until twelve-fifteen, and I want to hear about Kingsly."

I hadn't seen her since the murder and had forgotten that among the many regimes she'd marshaled, she'd had a short stint as Kingsly's secretary. When he put a move on her, she quit.

I settled into a chair with the cup warming my hands and gave her only what I had seen on the night he was found and later at the autopsy table. I left out my own speculations about Hurst and Gil Fernandez, but when I described how Bufort was starting to focus on the ER physicians, she stopped me with a question.

"What about you? Do you think someone in your own department did it?"

Right to the center of what I'd been avoiding. But my instinctive answer came without hesitation. "No. I don't, and talking to you now, I just realized why."

"You mean besides your not wanting to believe it?"

She was one cagey grandmother. "Yeah." I smiled a little sheepishly. "I mean, Bufort is focused on who had the means, the skills to accomplish the killing, but not on who had the motive. I neither know of nor can imagine any connection between Kingsly and one of my staff that could be a motive for killing him. Until someone finds that link, if it exists, then the fact that we can all needle hearts doesn't amount to much."

She thought for a moment and then commented. "I bet it was one of the women he molested, because it's what I would have done, with anything handy, if he had actually tried to force me into sex that night he came at me."

It was after that encounter that she had come and offered to work for me. She was way overqualified, and I needed someone only part-time, but she'd had it with the seediness of hospital politics and a lifetime of keeping its secrets. Working for me freed her for her husband, garden, and grandchildren. Yet now her voice had a steel in it I'd never heard before, but it left no doubt. If Kingsly had stirred such fury in this gentlewoman's soul, the list of possible killers could have gotten a lot longer.

Except that secretaries and cleaning women didn't know how to use cardiac needles.

"You know, Mrs. O'Hara, it's exactly what I thought at first. But the autopsy didn't show he'd been stabbed blindly by someone trying to keep him from attacking. It was done by someone with the knowledge and skill to needle a heart."

She looked a little surprised, then thoughtful, and was about to say something when my first patient arrived.

General practice is the minutia of medicine. Blood pressure checks, controlling angina, healing ulcers, managing pain, consoling, comforting, and above all listening. It's the opposite of attempts to save a life in a matter of minutes. In general practice, patients' stories are told at the pace of life unfolding. The visits and checkups over the years slowly reveal more than sickness and health.

I marveled at the courage, humor, and toughness of some of my patients who had survived great losses and yet managed to have fun between the disasters. Calamities hit everyone, but these special few showed me that escaping from a life of melancholy to a world of laughter and friends was sometimes a matter of choice. Even the uneventful lives with no big upheavals were fascinating. Visit by visit, a glimpse at a time, I came to know who lived with vigor and joy and who just moodily endured.

The slow pace of the afternoon was restorative. Who was healer and who was healed blurred. As three o'clock approached, however, the distant howl of ambulance sirens began penetrating the inner calm of my office. Each was a reminder that emergency was still getting hit and I was due back soon. The last patient barely got my attention.

At 3:01 my phone rang. I'd taught our doctors and nurses enough that emergency could solve its own problems and leave me uninterrupted when I was at my private office two times a week. Today the deal ended at three. "You on your way?" Susanne asked. No effort wasted; no need to identify herself.

"Nah! I got tickets to Cuba instead."

"Must be the same flight I'm on. See you."

Ten seconds in the place and I wanted to resign. Stretchers ran double down both sides of the hall. I could barely pass. The stench of body dirt had trebled since the day before, and the noise was worse. There was nothing I could even pretend to do, and it scared me. Waiting relatives were looking at me with the expectancy that here was someone, finally, who was in charge and could allay their fears.

"Holy shit!" was all I could say. It wasn't Churchillian.

In seconds they had reached the consensus that I was as useless as I felt, so they went back to arguing with the nurses and doctors. That freed me to start getting mad. I lit out down the corridor of reaching hands and sheeted misery and blasted open my outer office door so hard, Carole jumped and tangled herself in a Dictaphone wire.

"Get me that lawyer in Albany I talked to yesterday," I ordered while marching into my office. "If he's not in, tell them I need him now, even if he hasn't finished lunch." Then I dialed Hurst on my other line.

"Office of Dr. Paul Hur—

"This is Garnet in emergency," I blurted out without letting his secretary finish. "Tell him to get down here now!"

"I'm sorry, Dr. Garnet, but he's in a meeting with senior management, and I couldn't possibly interrupt—"

"Get him to emergency in two minutes or he can senior-manage my calling the media and warning the public away from this meltdown!" I slammed down the phone before the gasp. Carole was at the door indicating she had the lawyer on the line. She discreetly reminded me of his name before I punched the button to speak with him.

"Bill! Earl Garnet here. About that problem I asked

you about yesterday. It's really hit the fan and I've got to move. Any luck?"

His answer started with "Well, here's what I found." The next few minutes were taken up by my saying "yeah" a lot and scribbling a few notes.

At the end I asked for a formal letter containing the substance of our conversation and thanked him. I meant it. He'd just given me the weapon I needed.

Back in the corridor I saw Hurst surrounded by the same desperate clutch of patients, husbands, wives, lovers, children, and friends of patients who justifiably had found me of no use before. While he worked his kind, concerned routine, I caught his eye and gave a mock salute, and left him there. I could sense his hatred pelting my back all the way out the door, where I quickly felt a lot less cocky. I hadn't seen Hurst since Sean had voiced his suspicions and expanded my own wild speculations about him as well, but instinctively I feared him now. I'd no new inkling whether he had murdered Kingsly, or was taking our usual political skirmishes to a new extreme for some other hidden reason. Nor had I any better idea what he was capable of doing to me, or what he was up to. But until I knew why he had tried to make me a suspect, even challenging him on the bed cuts could be dangerous.

I didn't have any destination at the moment, just the intent to let Hurst simmer in the mess he'd helped create while I planned my next move and the best way to use what our insurance agency lawyer had given me. Suddenly I realized my name was coming over the PA. I got to a wall phone and learned that Watts wanted to see me in his lab. I waited while they transferred me through to his private line.

"Earl?" he said on picking up.

"Yeah, Robert, what's up?"

"Are you busy?"

"Am I ever. I've got a meltdown in the ER, and I just

suckered Hurst into an unscheduled meeting with all our angry users. Let him explain budgets and bed closures."

"I think you'd better come down here and see something."

"Hey, Robert, I always learn from your sessions, but this just isn't a good time."

"You've got to see this now!" he said abruptly, and hung up.

It was unusual for Robert to press. Immediately worried, I walked quickly to the elevator, found it an inordinately long wait, and took the stairs instead. As I descended to the basement, then trudged through the tunnel passages that led to the autopsy room, I wondered with increasing dread what my usually friendly mentor wanted to show me that was so urgent.

Watts and I had grown to respect each other's clinical skills, having met regularly about cases over the past twenty years. During the last eight, we'd managed to kid each other through the absurdities of hospital politics as well. In the interludes, with a comment here, a joke there, we had become friends of sorts, not close, but still friends. I knew he loved sailing and planned to escape to it when he retired. His last child had left home years ago and recently had started a surgical residency. One time, waiting for some useless meeting to begin, he'd leaned over and announced, "My wife and I were alone in the house for the first time in thirty years last night. It was weird." Then, a little more than two years ago, his wife died. Colon cancer. Widespread metastases. She was dead within three months of the diagnosis.

I had found it hard to comfort him. His broad shoulders so bent with pain brought a lump to my throat. What could I say? Finally, I had chosen the ancient Irish phrase I'd heard from farmers at my father's funeral: "I'm sorry for your troubles."

His gray eyes had filled with tears, and he'd turned

away. A week later he was back at work. We never spoke of it again.

These patches of insight made a collage more than a portrait. I didn't really know him. But we faced pain and death together, and we exposed our triumphs and failures to each other. Now and then, when it was most needed, we told each other, "You did good." Watts was a guy I laughed with, a guy I liked a lot.

He met me at the door of his autopsy suite in full protective garb and made me stop by the lockers in the changing area to replace my white coat with a green OR gown. I also put on a mask, pulled on a hair cap, and slid a pair of paper slippers over my shoes. He advised me we wouldn't be cutting tissue, so I needn't put protective goggles over my glasses, but that I should double-glove for handling organs. Since the resurgence of antibiotic-resistant tuberculosis in America's inner cities, most of these precautions were protection against airborne organisms as well as parenteral agents such as the viruses causing AIDS or hepatitis. We would also practice reverse isolation on the way out, carefully depositing our protective garb in a bin at the door, to avoid carrying lethal strains of anything into the rest of the hospital.

Stepping into the brightly lit autopsy suite, I noted he had two corpses there, and both were cut open. The insides of the bodies looked the same, the postmortem having reduced them to basic colors. Their trunks were slit from the top of the breastbone to the pubis and the halves spread to expose two red pods streaked with yellow fat and white sinew. The lungs were blue with pollution, and in each abdominal cavity a purple liver and an ochre spleen lay atop a glistening tangle of intestines. On one, the breasts had been parted and laid to each side. On the other, a limp and bedraggled penis hung down between withered legs.

The heart had been removed from the male, but was left in place in the female.

Watts hadn't yet opened the craniums, but in the male, the scalp had been given an incision around the back of the head and peeled over his face. A small circular bone saw lay on a nearby instrument table ready for use. On the left-hand counter by the male were two rows of labeled tubes and small specimen jars containing various body fluids ready for toxicologic testing. Other bottles stood empty and would be used for tissue samples taken later. An open Tupperware container in the bottom of one of the deep sinks held the removed heart. More containers were stacked on wall shelves and would eventually hold other vital organs. On the right-hand counter by the female lay a complete set of tubes and jars, still empty. Over each dissecting table, large venting hoods hummed, doing their best, but the fumes of formaldehyde and other toxic reagents stung my eyes. And, in spite of my mask, there was, of course, the smell of dead flesh.

But I was puzzled. It looked like he was partway through a complete autopsy on the male, then stopped, and had done only a partial "limited look" at the heart, lungs, and abdominal cavity of the female. I waited for him to explain.

Watts pointed to the female. "This is the Jane Doe you got yesterday," he began in his familiar, professorial way. "And this," he added, turning to the male, "is the John Doe from Monday."

He caught my surprise.

"I know," he continued, sounding abject, "I didn't take your concern about the mark on his chest seriously. But when we got the Jane Doe yesterday, I called the medical examiner and he confirmed there really have been too many of these DOAs all over the city lately. He's going to start having all the hospitals look closely at them. Since I had John here on ice as well, the ME said to give him a thorough autopsy." He was putting a heavy apron on as he talked.

"There was nothing unusual on Jane there." He nodded toward her corpse. Then he leaned over John and reached into his chest cavity to what was left of the cut-open sternum, or breastbone.

I was getting a funny feeling.

Watts was folding back in place the two halves of the chest wall he had cut open to start the post. There, like a dancing marionette wire, quivered a thin stylet identical to the one he'd used earlier to trace Kingsly's mortal wound.

"Unfortunately, Earl, you were right. That small mark you noticed was a scab over a puncture mark. Except the needle had been inserted and withdrawn cleanly, unlike in Kingsly's case, so it was even less perceptible. I doubt anyone else but you would have noticed it, even after Kingsly's murder. I feel like a fool for having ridiculed you, because right now we have to assume it's possible the chief executive officer of this hospital and this down-and-out homeless John Doe were both murdered with a needle to the heart, and I delayed the police finding out by forty-eight hours."

It was insane. Crazy. Despite having initially found the mark myself, I was sure he had to be wrong. I started grasping at logical explanations. "Someone must have tried resuscitating him prehospital and it wasn't recorded."

"That was my first thought too, but I already double-checked with MAS. It was a DOA picked up in an alley. Long dead. There was no attempt at resuscitation made." Watts seemed weary and paused, then added, "I know it's hard to accept. I've run it over and over looking for some other explanation myself. But the entry wound on the heart in that container over there is in perfect position. John Doe was stabbed same as Kingsly, by an expert. Of course, I'll need my tissue samples to confirm whether the needle went in before or after death, but without the history of a resuscitation attempt, murder, however inexplicable, has to be our working diagnosis. I'm just kicking myself for not following up on your first impulse."

The shock left me nervous. Since I was a kid, a serious

situation had always made me giggle; I didn't giggle, but my next crack was its verbal equivalent.

"Maybe John and Kingsly were drinking buddies?"

Detective Bufort was not a happy man. We'd pulled him out of the hospital's finance department, where he was hovering over a group of men uniformly dressed in white shirts, gray slacks, and black shoes. Only the ties varied. They had taken their raincoats off, giving a slightly new meaning to the term "plainclothes," and resembling more the members of a firm of certified public accountants than cops.

With all the focus on the hospital books, I realized Bufort must have figured Kingsly's death had something to do with money. I wondered if that was why Gil Fernandez had looked so frightened. But a dead vagrant didn't exactly fit the financial crimes profile.

"Impossible!" Bufort had spat out as we described our find on the way to the morgue. Having to put on full protection against airborne infections made him even more irritable. Actually seeing the guide wire tracing the needle stab to the heart seemed to make him angry.

"Preposterous!" He glared at Watts. "You must be wrong. This goes against everything we've found so far in our investigation. You've obviously made a mistake." He was nearly stuttering, he was so upset.

"My big mistake," said Watts, sounding miserable, "was ignoring Dr. Garnet when he suggested I take a look at this mark two days ago. I practically laughed him out of the room." He shook his head. "I can't believe I was so stupid."

Bufort swung around to face me. "You reported this two days ago! And you didn't tell me?"

"Detective Bufort!" interrupted Watts. "I said the delay was all my fault. If it hadn't been for Dr. Garnet being so alert—"

"Dr. Watts, I'm not interested in your very noble and entirely predictable defense of a colleague," snapped Bufort without taking his eyes off me. "I'm very interested in the fact that Dr. Garnet has once again attempted to withhold information from me." His face was flushed, and the blacks of his eyes widened until his irises became thin brown rims.

"Now, wait a minute," I protested. "I reported a very unlikely possibility to the hospital's pathologist—a mole or dirt on that DOA. Why should either of us have told the police such a wild idea until it was confirmed? You wouldn't have believed us then, and you don't seem ready to accept the finding even now." My accusation sounded a bit hollow, since I, too, was having trouble accepting that the derelict could have been murdered with a cardiac needle.

Bufort turned back to Watts. "I don't accept your verdict, Doctor, because according to our investigation so far, it makes no sense. And with all due respect, while we appreciate the help you gave us with Kingsly, you're not a forensic pathologist. You may be perfectly adequate discovering why people die from natural causes, but to go so far as proclaiming this derelict was murdered in the same way that Kingsly was, well, clearly, you can't know what you're talking about."

Now Watts's eyes dilated, and his cold stare fixed on Bufort. Many a poor fool, resident and staff alike, had invited his or her own humiliation by challenging one of Watts's clinical pronouncements. He struck the pose of a readied cobra I'd seen in previous bouts, but this threatened to get physical. "Would you care to repeat that accusation?" The level of menace in his voice alarmed even me, and I instinctively placed my hand on his arm. He was shaking with rage. With deliberate slowness Watts reached up and switched on his overhead dictating microphone.

Bufort swallowed. He was a tough cop, pompous, close-minded and maybe incompetent, but I suspected he was also a canny bureaucrat. A tape recorder probably frightened him more than a gun. An official record, even on his best behavior, could be scrutinized, picked apart, and twisted against him by the press, or even by someone in his own department settling an old score.

He looked from Watts to me, then very carefully said, "Let's review your findings, Dr. Watts. And if you'll permit me to use your phone, I'll call an officer to come down here and help me take a statement from you and Dr. Garnet. Then I'll get a forensic pathologist on this."

His tone was polite, but his expression was murderous. The son of a bitch kept us in that room for more than an hour making a "detailed report."

It was late afternoon by the time I got out. Between the formaldehyde fumes, the corpses starting to stink, and the cramped subterranean quarters, I had a headache. As soon as I entered the relative freedom of the main floor corridor, I heard my name being called on the overhead speakers.

"Where have you been!" demanded the operator once I got to a phone. The women in locating always sounded like annoyed mothers, but none more so than this woman at this moment.

"In the autopsy room." There were no speakers there. The operators didn't even want to think about what it was we did in that inner sanctum.

There was a pause as my misbehaving was measured. "Well, next time tell us where you're going."

"Yes, mommy. Now can I have my messages please? I promise I'll be a good boy."

"Smartass! Okay, first: Susanne wants you in emergency, then Dr. Hurst has been calling for you, but the most urgent seemed to be geriatrics."

Damn, Muffy had been there since the morning, when I'd had them retrieve her from the car.

"Anything else?"

"Yes, phone your wife."

Great idea. Recalling I had a life outside this labyrinth made me feel better.

A quick call to Susanne confirmed we were still in a mess. "Forty admitted patients," she reported, "and some are on their second day in the corridor."

No surprise there.

"And Hurst is a little mad at you for stranding him in the real world of patients. Mad as in wanting to resurrect his long-faded surgical skills on your carcass without anesthetic."

Normally I would have laughed, but not now. My next thought just slipped out. "They probably aren't all that faded."

"Pardon?"

"Sorry, Susanne. Talking to myself." I certainly wasn't ready to add my suspicions about him to hospital gossip. "And thanks for the warning. I've no inclination to call him anyway. What else?"

"A few reporters have been looking for you. They seem to have picked up that you found the body."

I *very* definitely didn't want to deal with the press. "Oh, God!" I started. "We've been told to send *all* reporters to Hurst and Bufort. And tell the rest of our staff to do the same." That was one order I was more than glad to obey.

"I already have, on both counts. I figured they'd want it that way."

"You do good in chaos."

She gave a little laugh, but then there was a pause, which was unusual for Susanne.

I gave her time. More silence.

"Okay, Susanne, spit it out."

"No. It's nothing. Look, I gotta go, another ambulance." And she clicked off.

Great. If Susanne can't tell me something, I worry. I added it to a growing pile of questions.

Janet's line was repeatedly busy. That left Muffy. I

retrieved her from a regal pose on a love seat in the geriatric wing amid a clutch of elderly admirers. She pranced along, proudly drawing stares as we headed through the corridors for the front door and home.

It was a rare treat to be home at six o'clock, but the back lane was already a channel of mist. Our house was even darker. Neighboring porch lights were fuzzy glares in the gloom. There was no point going in just to sit alone. Muffy happily accepted a chance to walk.

The lane was normally a pleasant place lined with backyard hedges and gardens put to bed for the winter. It had once been a private road leading to the golf course where I'd encountered the dogs Monday night. Now it was shared by all the home owners on our block.

The image of those Dobermans needed no urging to come to mind. I kept pushing away what might have happened if the attack hadn't been called off. The intruder at our cabin didn't help my frame of mind any. I tried to remind myself to stop jumping to conclusions, but out here alone it was hard not to be afraid of the dark.

The fog was so heavy, I could feel its cool droplets on my face, yet it was strangely soothing, and as Muff happily marked her favorite spots, I began churning over the events of the last few hours.

None of it made sense. There was no explaining how both Kingsly and a derelict could have been killed by a cardiac needle. At least I agreed with Bufort about that. Watts's bombshell certainly seemed to have derailed whatever solution Bufort was on the trail of. Or worse, maybe not. I still had the distinct impression no troublesome facts were going to get in the way of his "solution." Heaven help the innocent, including me.

My own thinking was certainly thrown off. As much as I'd come to fear and suspect Hurst, I couldn't even begin to imagine why he'd have any relation to the DOA, let alone a motive to murder him. It was just as inexplicable to try to connect anyone else in the hospital to killing a vagrant. There had to be some other explanation. I kept clinging to the possibility there'd been a resuscitation attempt somewhere during which a cardiac needle had been used, but if not with MAS, where?

Watts wouldn't issue a final report until he'd completed his study of the other organs, subjected all the tissue samples he'd taken to an examination under the microscope, and reviewed the results of the biochemistry and toxicology testing that would be done on the man's blood, urine, and stomach contents. Until then, all we knew for sure was that a needle had been put into his heart. As Watts had said, knowing definitively whether it had killed him or was inserted and removed after something else killed him would have to wait for his findings. But without there having been a resuscitation, was there any possible cause of what he'd found other than murder?

Muffy examined a weed at the edge of the concrete, and I tried to focus on more pleasant thoughts. My head was beginning to ache again.

It wasn't hard to start thinking of Janet coming home in a few minutes. We were going to have an all too rare evening together, and the prospect lay ahead of me like a life raft.

Muffy anointed a suitable bush and made a deposit in a vacant strip of weeds nestled between a telephone pole and the gate to a neighbor's manicured lawn. Since scooping laws were left to towns and municipalities and nobody could decide to whom this patch belonged, we poop troops were uncertain. So Muff and I were free, for now at least, from any degrading bagging routine.

On the way back, she limited her pause-and-sniff checks to an occasional passing snort and was suddenly tugging me home, pulling me hard.

A jerk on the leash set me jogging after her. Even in leather shoes the exertion was welcome, but I was hopelessly outclassed. Trying to keep up with her for thirty seconds left me winded and my heart pounding. I was clearly out of practice.

Then I suddenly thought of how a derelict might have a cardiac needle track in his heart and it be perfectly legitimate. The possible answer was as simple as relief. Of course! I thought. It had to be. But I couldn't check it out now. I'd have to wait until Kradic and the night resident were on call at midnight. More realistically, I'd catch them before they went off in the morning. Now they'd probably be sleeping.

Muff turned the corner of our driveway and scooted up to our well-lighted back door. Janet's car was in the garage, and the kitchen lights promised warmth and welcome. Muffy pranced around me in an impatient circle as I got the door open, then ran in ahead of me to get the first hug. Already, the warm, spicy aroma of Janet's quick goulash filled the place. I stood in line till Muff was finished, then got a kiss.

"Miss me?" Janet asked playfully.

"You and what's-his-name here," I said, reaching down to pat the beginning swell of Janet's stomach. I was periodically pushed away by the head of a jealous poodle. We started to giggle.

Janet looked at the upturned eyes begging for attention. "Muff, you are in for a surprise."

We made a little fuss over her, then Janet shoved us both out of the kitchen and returned to preparing our meal. Muff and I retreated to the living room, where I put on a tape of Joe Cocker and settled down to the strains of "Try a Little Tenderness." As that raspy voice evoked the decade when I had sworn I would never end up domesticated, Muff sprawled out beside me, taking up most of the couch *and* planting her head in my lap for a few kitzles. In the kitchen, Janet had joined Cocker in a duet and was belting out *when love grows weary*. I put my head back, smiled, and loved every corny moment of it.

This was the first real time we'd had together since Kingsly's murder, and I knew I'd have to tell Janet about the trouble I was in. But I resented letting that worry and dread intrude on our lives. I'd at least wait until we finished eating.

The ordinary evening was nothing less than resuscitation of the soul. Simple stew, a beer for me, club soda for Janet, and, by some miracle, no calls for either of us.

After dinner we sat in easy silence in the living room and had coffee. Janet's feet were in my lap, and I was kitzling them.

"What have you been up to?" she asked sleepily.

"You obviously didn't hear the news today. The CEO of the hospital was found murdered in his office early Monday morning."

"What! Kingsly?" Her eyes were open wide now. Janet had met him a few times at hospital social events.

"Afraid so. That's why I came in so late from my shift."

"Who killed him?"

"Nobody knows. There's police all over the place."

"God! That's ghastly. How was he killed?"

"This isn't in the news, and it's confidential as hell. He was stabbed with a cardiac needle."

"Good Lord! That's weird. Who'd use a cardiac needle to kill someone?"

"That's what the police want to know."

"Who do you think it was?"

"I haven't a clue."

She lay back with her eyes closed again, and I was relieved she didn't ask any more questions for a while. Should I volunteer the rest of it? What was the point? It was all suspicion and unsubstantiated fears so far—the shadow stuff of nightmares. Whispered warnings. Cops playing mind games. Dirty hospital politics. Why upset her with vague conspiracy theories, or frighten her with stories of Doberman attacks and intruders in the night, when I had no real evidence any of it could harm us. I'd only be sharing paranoia.

"Is any of it going to be affecting you?" she finally asked.

"Not much," I lied. "Hurst shut down a hundred beds Monday, and emergency's a mess."

This didn't even get her eyes open. She'd come from a family of doctors, two brothers and her father. Whenever we all got together, there was a family rule. "No medicine!"

And she had insisted the same for us. It assured we didn't squander what little time we had together on worries better left at work. But, of course, exceptions slipped in now and then.

"Is that why you went to the cabin?" she asked slyly. She knew I'd use any pretext I could to sneak in an extra trip. "The old I-got-to-use-my-computer ploy," she added with a grin and a toe jab in the ribs.

"Hey, watch it. You'll injure my kitzling arm."

"Kitzle me!" she ordered with more toe tickles.

I started laughing and protested, "Stop it!"

That got her toes racing up and down my rib cage and me guffawing and begging her to stop.

Then her feet fell back in my lap, and I started kitzling again, laughed-out and content. The nightmare shadows had been driven off for now.

Janet was a wonder in my life. We had met nine years ago in London. I was attending a conference on emergency medicine and staying at Brown's, a lovely hotel near Berkeley Square. It had a particularly good tearoom, and one crowded afternoon the maître d'hôtel came over to my table and asked if I would mind sharing it with a fellow physician from New York. I accepted politely, expecting to be paired with some old man, but was delighted to instead find Janet escorted to my table. She was dressed in a sleek beige suit that matched her light blonde hair and fair skin, but what captured my attention were her deep blue eyes and the light that flashed from them. We extended crumpets and petit fours into dinner, and I spent the next few hours learning she was in England on a fellowship year studying high-risk obstetrics at King's Cross Hospital. We passed the next week together going to art galleries and the theater.

After two weeks we became lovers. A year later she took a position at the University of Buffalo, and we were married.

Her toes were stirring in my lap, and I increased my kitzling.

She had wanted to wait until her practice was established before having children. I was seven years older, and already in practice for twelve, but agreed to the delay. It seemed she needed time to feel secure enough with me to have a child. And little wonder. All our colleagues were divorced. But now it looked like we were about to have it all.

"You know," I said dreamily, "an awful lot of happiness for the two of us"—and then I eyed her tummy and corrected myself—"make that the three of us, depended on that maître d' in London putting us together."

More than just her toes were starting to stir in my lap.

"Things that important can't just be left to chance," she answered softly.

"What?"

"I slipped him five pounds and asked him to put me at your table."

"You what?"

"I was feeling like I am now. Take me upstairs to bed."

Her eyes opened and were intensely blue, and not a hint of sleep lurked in them.

"It's okay for him still?" and I cupped my hand lightly over the mound above her groin.

She put her hand on mine and pressed. "Don't worry," she whispered, "I'm a specialist. I'll teach you the ways."

* * *

Next morning I felt rested even when I awoke at five-thirty. Then I heard the garage door closing and felt the emptiness of the house. Janet seemed to defy the pregnancy, daring it to slow her down. I worried when she didn't accept body messages to rest. She scoffed that anything less than her usual workload would drive her mad.

So that morning after showering and dressing, I sat alone with coffee and Muff and planned out my day.

It was still dark, but first I called emergency to catch Kradic's night resident before sign-out.

"Emergency."

"Hi, it's me. Is the resident there? I'd like to speak with him or her, please." I'd had a bit of hesitation calling Kradic directly with my question. Given his usual defensiveness, he'd probably think I was checking up on him, even if, as I hoped, his answer provided a completely innocent explanation as to why the DOA had a cardiac needle track. And my reluctance had a darker cause. I hated to admit it, but I was starting to take precautions with my staff. My logical insistence that no one had an obvious motive to kill Kingsly and my best determination to resist unfounded suspicions were being eroded. An unpleasant wariness was creeping into my feelings about individual physicians, especially with the ones who were difficult. Until Kingsly's killer was caught, that uneasiness would be there.

"He's busy. But just a minute, please, I'll ring Dr. Kradic's room—"

"Hold it! Don't wake him—" But it was too late, and I was left listening to his phone buzz, feeling stupid for not avoiding him as I'd planned. I was relieved when there was no answer.

The clerk came back on the line. "He doesn't seem to be there, Doctor. Should I page him?"

He was probably having an early breakfast. At least

he'd better have been. "No, let me speak to the resident. Is he still busy?"

More clicks, unanswered rings, then finally someone picked up. "Emergency, Miss Claymore speaking."

"Miss Claymore, it's Dr. Garnet. I'm trying to locate the resident."

"The resident's with a patient. But Dr. Kradic should be in his room asleep. Shall I buzz him?"

"No, I've already done that. Could you please see if the resident could come to the phone?"

"One moment, please."

This circling on hold like stranded aircraft over a dysfunctional airport would get worse once the day really started.

Finally someone picked up. "Dr. Todd here."

I didn't groan out loud, but he might have heard me exhale with a bit more vehemence than usual. Sleeping with a staff person wasn't anything I could officially censure a resident for, but it sure raised doubts about his judgment and, in this case, his taste.

I tried to sound casual. "Hi, Dr. Todd. Look, I'm sorry to bother you, but did you or Dr. Kradic do any practice procedures on the DOA early Monday morning? In particular, did either of you pass a cardiac needle?"

"Not me, but I wasn't there. Laura Tran covered the rest of my shift that night. It was my fiancée's birthday, and we had a midnight supper planned."

So much for fidelity, I thought, first thinking of his poor fiancée, then wondering if Jones knew, or cared. Maybe it even aroused her. "Any idea where Dr. Tran is?" I asked, refocusing on why I'd called.

"Tahiti."

"What?"

"Tahiti. She left Tuesday morning. That's why she did the switch; I'm covering her now to add an extra day onto her vacation."

We paid these residents too much.

"When will she be back?"

"Two weeks from today."

Way too much.

I hesitated, then accepted that Kradic would have to be asked outright, whatever he might make of it.

"Dr. Todd, listen, in case I miss Dr. Kradic, could you ask him to call me when he goes off duty this morning?"

He seemed puzzled but answered, "Sure, but Dr. Jones is here early for sign-out rounds. Do you want to ask her?"

God, no! "No, it's all right, just ask—" Again it was too late. He'd put her on the line.

"Yes, Dr. Garnet," she began icily.

"Ah, Valerie, I was just looking for Dr. Kradic. Dr. Todd has the message—"

"I can give it to him," she said, almost like a command to let her do it. "He'll be down from breakfast for sign-out in a minute."

Christ, she was testy. Probably it was her resentment of Kradic and having to do sign-out with him, but I never really knew what fired her nasty moods.

"Thanks, Valerie. Sorry to have disturbed you, but Dr. Todd has it covered." I hung up without waiting for a reply. I wasn't going to risk *her* setting off Kradic with a question about needling hearts. Damn! He'd be surly enough with it coming from me, even if I was asking through a resident. And once again there was that unwelcome cautiousness about who I confided in and what I said. Then, as if for finishers, a frisky afterthought tumbled into my mind. Was Jones in early so she and Todd could have a little morning screw before starting rounds? Shit! I was going to have to make time for our talk as soon as possible.

I felt exhausted and had accomplished nothing. Tahiti! What a great idea. Made me jealous. Especially since I had to deal with the injunction issues.

Our high-priced legal protection from Albany had

handed me a pretty big card, but I had to play it carefully. One chance to knock Hurst off his injunction crap would be all I'd get. Today was going to need a finesse that had nothing to do with medicine but everything to do with protecting our patients from bureaucratic chiseling.

After three cups of coffee, two croissants, a riffle through old newspapers, and a twenty-minute soak in the bathtub, I had my plan. I left a message on Carole's answering machine to assemble our entire staff that afternoon at five o'clock.

It was after six-thirty and time for Muff and me to make our tour again. The weather had changed exactly as the experts had predicted. It was unusually dark for this time under a black, overcast sky, and a thick fog made it difficult both to see and breathe. The temperature must have dropped below freezing as well, because everything was coated with an icy film. My leather soles skidded over broken concrete while Muffy had no trouble getting traction with her built-in four-wheel drive. I mimicked an aging Nureyev trying to keep my balance as she tugged me along on her leash.

I heard the car before I saw anything. If I hadn't already been lurching into the gutter from an unexpected skid behind Muff, it would have hit me.

Black, no lights, and exploding out of the darkness behind us—only the roar of its engine gave me the cue to leap into my forward fall and roll as the tires brushed my face. My left hip took the landing full force on cement and the pain made me yell involuntarily in agony and feel a surge of nausea. By the time I reopened my eyes, the car was past and I could see it disappearing down the lane.

I watched in sick horror as it reached the street, spun around, and, with another roar of acceleration, started back at me.

Chapter 9

The pain in my hip came in waves, like the hot vomit at the back of my throat. It took a few of these crescendos before I even started to move. I could see the grille on the front of the car hurtling toward me, swerving on the ice as it came. There was no time to get up. It careened over to the side of the alley where I lay. I managed to roll farther in under an overhanging cedar hedge and grab the small trunks at its base. I flattened myself against them and felt the wheels whip by my back and legs. The bushy outgrowth above had kept the car from running over me.

It sped on toward the far end of the lane and disappeared into the fog and darkness. I let go of my handholds under the hedge, rolled back out to the edge of the cement, and began scrambling to my feet. I slipped on the ice and went back down. More pain lanced through my hip. I sat there, staring toward the sound of the motor, which was receding into the murk. Then I heard the tires squeal in the distance.

Turning away, or coming back?

The motor roared again.

I realized my hands were empty. I heard the rising yelps begin like the crescendo of a chill. They turned to screams of blind animal panic.

"Muff!" I gasped, forgetting my own pain.

I could hear the car coming back up behind me.

Muff's high-pitched shrieks were pulsing now. Bedroom windows lit up.

I was pleading, "No, please, no" as I struggled to reach her.

The car sounded as if it were on top of me. I glanced quickly over my shoulder but saw nothing coming out of the darkness—yet.

I pushed myself to my feet to look. Muff is black, impossible to see in the dark. How many times had I fallen over her on a nocturnal trip to the toilet? I thought, limping and stumbling toward her cries. I was still unable to see her in the dim light of the lane. The noise of the approaching car was right at my back.

The yelping weakened, but now seemed to come from a black hollow under a cedar hedge.

I hobbled over, reached down, blindly scooped into the shadow with my arms, and came up with her.

Over my shoulder I saw the car, headlights off, looming out of the mist and heading for me.

I stumbled forward again. "Muff, Muff," I repeated, staggering under her weight, looking for a safe place to leap from the narrow alley.

The car accelerated on my heels.

I planted my left foot and lunged right against a mesh of bare branches from a tall lilac hedge. It was like going through the breakaway protective fence behind the end zone in high school football—only this barrier didn't break away. Muff and I crashed to the ground under a shower of roots and sticks.

The car flew by and this time kept on going.

I was thinking only of Muff. She'd fallen out of my arms as I hit the ground. It was even darker here under the hedge, but I crawled toward her sounds, trying to calm her, saying her name. She was reduced to whimpering now.

I touched her; she was trembling, shaking. She struggled toward me but fell back. I found her head. She whimpered again, then gave my hand a feeble lick.

I felt down her front paws. Nothing. I kept talking softly, rubbing her head, and continued to explore. My hand slipped inside the rip in her open belly and into her intestines before I realized what had happened.

They writhed like snakes in spasm from my touch. Her yelps wailed to full crescendo again.

I recoiled and pulled my hand back. I couldn't see what I'd just felt, but I tried to cradle her spilling organs from falling out onto the dirt.

Porch lights were going on.

Muff's cries were weakening again. Someone started screaming, "Help me! Help me!"

Before I passed out, I realized it was me.

I first heard the siren as if in a dream, distant, having nothing to do with me. It was an annoyance. I wanted to go back to sleep and I fought coming to. Then they were shrieking in my ear, and I was awake. My mouth was full of vomit. I was surrounded by a circle of neighbors, most of them huddled in their bathrobes. Two ambulance technicians were trying to move Muffy off me. The shrieks were hers, from fear as much as pain. Through bits of sour particles I tried to yell "No," but nothing came out. I tried again, but managed only to squeak, "Stop!"

They ignored me and continued to pull her away. She started to writhe. Panicked, she snapped at one of the drivers.

"Shit!" he yelled, and dropped her. She shrieked again and tried to struggle up.

I finally managed to shout, "Leave her!"

The two startled techs backed away. I was up on all fours now and crawling to her, comforting her by saying her name, lying that it was okay. I put my hand back on her torn and eviscerated abdomen.

The techs were looking at me as if I were mad. The

older one seemed frozen, undecided what to do. The bigger one said, "Hey, you shouldn't move."

Now the older one seemed to decide his partner was right, and both yelled in horrified unison, "Don't move!"

But I'd already broken every basic rule on page one of their trauma manual. And apart from my hip still throbbing, everything seemed to work all right.

Yet they were on me like a tag team, trying to pry me away from Muffy, immobilize my neck, take my vitals, and tell me in that familiar professional cant, "Lie back, be calm, just let go of the dog, sir!"

"Look, I'm all right. Help me save the dog. I tell you, I'm all right."

"We can't do that, sir," the older man said. "You've been hit by a car, and we have to get you to a hospital. They'll check you out there." His grip on me was getting tighter. Muffy, sensing the struggle, started to writhe again.

"Guys, look at me! I'm chief of emergency at St. Paul's. I know what you're trying to do, and I appreciate it, but I'm okay." They paused; I was going to have to convince them to cut some major corners and violate some biggies. In fact, they should be canned if they listened to me, and I knew it.

"Look, no neck pain, I can move it all around; I fainted, wasn't knocked on the head; my hip hurts but I can move it too; I'm not bleeding, and I know what day of the week it is. I need help with the dog! Will you?"

The bigger of the two had been getting ready to strap me down. Immobilization must have been his specialty. The older attendant peered at me. Of the two, he had seemed the more intent on getting me into the ambulance and to a hospital. I realized I must be smeared with dirt and vomit. But his partner, the one with the straps, appeared to hesitate. He looked hard at my face. I took a chance. "Didn't I teach you prehospital care last year at the university?"

I teach them all every year at the university, sooner or later, as part of Zak's refresher program. I hoped this guy hadn't cut classes.

He took an even harder look. "Holy shit, it *is* you. What the hell happened here?"

These guys respected rank above all else, and I was pulling it. I felt a little guilty. They should have told me to suck rocks and gone by the book.

"I'll tell you later. Meantime, can we get my dog to the Buffalo Animal Hospital? They're equipped for surgery there, and we can still save her." Muffy had sensed the change, to talk from yelling, and was quieter, but she still whimpered and shook under my hands.

The older one looked pretty skeptical, but my former student was a little more receptive. "Gee, Doc, I don't know. I mean, we'd like to help you, but a dog, I don't know—" His reservations were understandable.

"Look, I'll settle it with Zak. I'll take full responsibility; I'll tell him I forced you." The guy still looked doubtful.

"In writing," I added.

It helped. But they were still hesitating. "And of course I'll sign a release of liability for myself," I added.

That did it. Being responsible for blowing my case was apparently their biggest worry. I quickly signed triple forms proclaiming I was an ass and hadn't the sense to do what they thought was good for me.

Muffy was breathing hard; each expelled breath ended in a weak whine. The wound, as best I could see in their headlights and the gray, belated start of dawn, looked surprisingly clean and straight. She must have been sliced from catching a fender edge on the first pass as we both leaped clear.

A few of the neighbors, shivering in their bathrobes,

asked if I was all right. Someone offered to go back and lock the house.

From the ambulance kit I took a large sterile pad and put it over Muffy's abdomen. I held it in place as the other two men lifted her gently, and, now unprotesting, onto the stretcher. I didn't really know if all that stuff I'd said about being all right was true. As I stood and walked beside Muffy to the ambulance, I felt my knees start to buckle. I hoped that neither of the attendants noticed, but I caught the bigger guy checking his shirt pocket to make sure my signed release was handy.

As I climbed through the rear doors, I noticed the sign on the vehicle's side panel. This was one of the rogue private companies we kept an eye on. But for a ride to the vet, I figured it didn't matter, and got Muffy settled down in the back while the attendants climbed into the front.

"Siren, Doc?"

"Why the hell not?"

He hit the switch.

Never had the clientele of Buffalo's leading animal hospital had an arrival like it. We'd phoned ahead in the ambulance, so Dr. Sophie had her team ready at the door. She was an old friend from shared premed classes during university days. Our arrival with full lights and siren raised her eyebrows, but she and her colleagues swept Muffy away and into the OR. I wished my unit were that fast.

I thanked the drivers and assured them I wouldn't forget to call Zak and put in a good word.

After their departure I felt helpless with nothing to do. I was smeared with Muffy's blood and juices from her innards. Awkwardly I took a seat in Sophie's waiting room. Her other "patients" sniffed the gore on my shirt and backed away. The owners looked miffed that I'd gotten priority treatment. Muffy's emergency surgery had pulled most of Sophie's staff from conducting routine visits.

"Car accident," I offered, hoping forgiveness would follow. I got a bunch of "Likely story!" stares instead.

I slunk down in my waiting room chair. It was a lot more comfortable than the ones in the ER.

Finally, I had a chance to think about what had just happened.

Someone had tried to kill me. Deliberately. Savagely. The intent of it scared me as much as having been so close to death.

I was alive only because of a fluke, a random slip throwing me half out of the way on their first pass. There was no logical reason I hadn't been hurt. I couldn't comfort myself much that I'd done anything to save myself— I hadn't had a shred of control over what had happened. Except for sheer blind stupid luck, I'd probably be dead.

My worst fears had been true. Somehow I'd become a target and I didn't have a clue why.

I could no longer explain away the footprints at the cabin or dismiss the figure on the golf green as an overzealous watchman.

And the whispered warning to *back off*? Not knowing what it meant seemed likely to cost me my life.

My panic was reaching new heights, and I realized I was trembling like the proverbial leaf in the wind. So far I hadn't been able to link the warning to Kingsly's murder. I desperately tried to think of other explanations.

A doctor always lives with the possibility of coming face-to-face with a wacko, and it's even more probable for doctors who deal with the walk-ins in emergency. But in twenty years I'd never had anyone try to hurt me. Anger, rage, blame in the face of unspeakable loss, yes— even threats, but never harm.

I had heard one story of a psychiatrist I'd been in medical school with who'd been targeted by a woman suffering erotomania. When he repeatedly rebuffed her obsessive advances, she had used her family connections with the mob to have his car bombed. He miraculously survived, but left town and changed his name.

Now someone was after me, and I didn't know what I'd done. Someone I'd unknowingly crossed in emergency was possible, but unlikely. While I did have more run-ins than most with discontented patients or relatives in my role as chief of the department, as an acting clinician I'd never been sued for negligence. I didn't take much comfort in that. It meant only that my errors in judgment had occurred within the conventions of reasonable care. This distinction didn't rule out personal retaliation over somebody dying, but it lessened the danger of it. When cases did go bad, it was usually the disease that did the damage. I don't know why—the grief and regret remained, including mine—but I had never felt at risk for whatever mistakes I'd committed. A bit of luck, and a lot of being careful, had so far, it seemed, resulted in, if not forgiveness, a lack of someone taking revenge. At least among the sane.

Psychiatric cases were another matter. Here even a slight, real or imagined, could have catastrophic consequences. I'd had my share of those, but again, in some context, with some reason—a diagnosed psychosis to explain it all. There was nothing recent, at least not that I could remember . . . but there could have been a patient with some impending disaster I'd missed and then sent home. I might never know who I'd butchered—the emergency physician's nightmare. And what about the undiagnosed psychos and sickos whom I'd unknowingly cared for. What seething maniac had I treated for tonsillitis and unwittingly enraged?

No. After twenty years on the line, it was a mighty big coincidence to have randomly invoked such wrath now, little more than three days after Kingsly's murder. The most probable reason for the attack on me had to be related to his killing. But why, I asked myself again, would Kingsly's murderer be after me?

Slumped in the chair in the waiting room, I'd stopped shaking, but now I was stiffening up. I realized as I shifted in my chair that getting up was going to be significantly more painful than sitting down had been. I groaned as I stood. The other animals whined, much as their owners waiting with them probably wanted to do.

I limped over to the receptionist and asked her to call in to the OR and get an update. She looked annoyed, but she knew Sophie and I were friends, so she grudgingly complied, punching the appropriate speaker button and asking how long it would be. "Another thirty minutes!" blared out of the receiver, and that was all I got before she pointedly resumed her typing. She didn't offer to get any progress report. I hadn't the stomach to hear the worst from the likes of her anyway, and didn't ask.

I limped back to my chair. The animals shuffled around a bit more and then settled again but watched me nervously. The owners made huffing noises and looked at their watches. I went back to my thoughts.

If not Kingsly's killer, then who?

The only other unusual event was my threat to close emergency. I still couldn't believe any sane person would murder me over that because of lost income. Then I recalled Kradic's obvious but silent rage at our departmental meeting. Did all his unreasonable behavior hide a deeper, deadlier flaw? Had I set him off by publicly calling him on the carpet Sunday night? I didn't know for sure, and this frightened me. Were there others in the department I wasn't sure of? Could I have worked alongside a secret maniac all these years? And what about Hurst? What if he had murdered Kingsly and was coming after me because I was the one who had actually discovered it was murder? What if he thought I was getting too close to something that could expose him? My previous dread at what he might be capable of came flooding back.

I shivered some more, then stopped myself from thinking in this direction. I wanted to concentrate on logic and couldn't give in to groundless speculation and fears. But fear was inevitable now. Until I knew who had tried to kill me, and why, it would pervade everything I did.

If there was a why. Maybe the killer didn't need a reason; maybe he was one of those zombies who killed for the sake of killing. The professional term was a *homicidal psychopath*.

The animals around me must have sensed my distress again, for they whined and shied away some more. The owners looked fed up with my effect on their pets.

Had I been followed? I wondered, as I thought back to that night and remembered the trailing headlights. Had Muffy spoiled the first attempt—or hadn't she? This morning the killer hadn't seemed the type to be put off by a barking dog. If the same person had been at my door two nights ago and wanted me dead, a dog wouldn't have stopped the attack. They could just as easily have killed Muffy and then me.

Perhaps the other night hadn't been a murder run after all. But then why had I been followed? And what had I done in the meantime to up the ante?

Janet! I'd forgotten to call her, and I didn't want her to find out about Muffy from a neighbor.

I asked the receptionist for the phone. I got an icy "Certainly, Doctor." I was sure that the emphasis on "Doctor" was a warning to the civilians in the room that they wouldn't be making any free calls.

Getting through to Janet's hospital was the same pain in the ass as it had been when I called my own department, except Janet's hospital was computerized. A cheery voice kept telling me to punch a number if I wanted one department, another number for the floor, and a third for the exact nursing station. When I finally got to a human voice, it was the janitor in the case room cleaning up between deliveries.

"Doctor not here. Went home in big hurry."

"Shit!"

"Pardon?"

"Sorry. Thank you."

I dialed home. Janet picked up on one ring. She was sobbing. I had never heard her cry.

"Janet, what's happened?" I immediately thought of the baby.

"Please, come home."

"What's happened?"

"Just come home now—please!"

And she hung up.

She never even asked about Muffy. Whatever had happened, it was bad.

I told the receptionist to call me at the house as soon as Sophie had Muff out of surgery.

I got lucky with a cab, but during the ride my sense of dread increased.

Two cop cars flashing blue and red outside our front door confirmed it. I shoved a fistful of bills at the driver, jumped out of the cab, and ran inside.

The first assault was the stink. Feces. Smeared over the hallway and up the staircase. Janet, pale and hunched, sat on the couch beside a uniformed cop. He was shyly holding a salad bowl. More smells; she'd been vomiting.

"Janet!" I moved to her side. A detective seated across from her quickly got up, as if to protect her.

"It's okay, I'm her husband."

Janet took my hand, weakly squeezed, then grabbed the salad bowl and retched again.

I put my arm around her and could feel her trembling. Through chattering teeth she whispered, "Sorry."

Her shaking subsided to shivers. She handed the bowl to me. The uniformed cop looked relieved.

"Mrs. Sharp called me at work," Janet said. Mrs. Sharp was the neighborhood busybody.

"Said you were all right but Muffy was bad. I signed out and came home to this." Her helpless expression as she looked around rendered the destruction even more vicious. This part of the house had been attacked. I didn't know yet if anything had been taken, but the room I was sitting in had been slashed, torn apart, and then smeared with excrement. The wallpaper along the staircase leading upstairs was shredded and the chandelier in the entranceway was ripped out of the ceiling and left dangling from its wires. Broken lightbulbs and pieces of glass crunched underfoot. The stereo I had listened to the night before lay bent and cracked open in the fireplace. It must have been thrown against the bricks.

"It's worse on the second floor." Janet spoke quietly into clenched hands. "The bastards really destroyed the baby's room." She started trembling again. I had my arm around her shoulders. I pulled her to lean against me, but she resisted and stayed rigid.

"I want to know what the hell is going on!" she said, taking back the salad bowl.

The uniformed cop got up and went into the kitchen. The plumbing was intact; I heard him washing his hands.

The detective leaned toward us. "So do we," he said, and then ignored me as he picked up the questioning I had interrupted.

"So, when you arrived, you found the back door locked, and from the outside there was no evidence of forced entry?"

Shit. In the lane. I remembered a voice behind me, indistinct, a presumed neighbor. *"I'll go make sure the house is locked.*" I had never even looked to see who it was; I'd been focused on Muff.

"Oh, God," I muttered.

The detective sighed. Janet gave me her "you again" glance and tried to finish her statement. I think talking kept the heaves away.

But I interrupted anyway. "I know how they got in," I confessed.

The detective got a little more interested.

Janet said, "This better be good," and handed the bowl back to me, still keeping a close eye on it, and swallowing a lot.

"No, I mean it," I went on. "It must've been the person who offered to lock the house."

She looked up, startled. "What?"

"Who did you tell to lock up the house?" The detective was suddenly half off his chair.

"I don't know."

Janet had pulled away again and was holding her hand over her mouth. I think I heard her mutter something about "turkey," but I was explaining to an increasingly incredulous cop that after almost being run down and trying to save our dog, I wasn't exactly keeping tabs on voices in the crowd.

"You didn't report a deliberate hit-and-run to the police?"

"I didn't have time to report it."

Janet was holding her head.

The detective opened a pad. He looked like he was going to write me up for stupidity. "Who's 'they'?"

"The people who tried to kill me."

"Kill you!" This was in stereo. Janet and the detective seemed to move closer to each other to ward off my obvious lunacy.

"You said he'd had an accident." He was talking to Janet now; I wasn't even in the room for him. I cringed at how many times I'd relegated a patient to nonexistence in the same way. On the other hand, Janet took ignoring me as a designated right by marriage.

"That's what the neighbors told me," she answered him. "An accident. Nobody said anything about anybody trying to kill him."

Finally the detective turned back to me. "I think you'd better go back to the beginning, sir." Janet had grabbed the bowl, like I couldn't be trusted with it anymore, and was studying it indecisively.

More cops were coming in the door. Some were carrying suitcases that I presumed contained kits to test for fingerprints and other traces that might lead to finding out who did this. A uniformed woman carried a camera. Another man had a small vacuum. An open case on the floor in front of me contained neat stacks of both paper and plastic bags, a box of disposable gloves, and a jumble of ties and tags.

Janet's indecision was over. She started vomiting again.

Now the detective seemed undecided. He wanted a statement, but Janet's retching kept getting his attention.

I took another look around at the remnants of wallpaper hanging in tatters. Our photos and prints of paintings had been hurled onto the floor, then trampled, leaving shards of glass everywhere. This was more than a violation of our property. It was a display of insanity.

I swung back to the detective. "Officer, of course I'll make a statement, but I need to have Detective Bufort of homicide here. He's probably at St. Paul's."

It took a bit to convince the cops, but one of them finally made the call.

"We got a doctor here who says someone tried to kill him and that you'd want to hear about it. His name's Garnet."

There was a moment's silence. He read out my address.

Then a puzzled look came over his face. Without a word he hung up. He said incredulously, to no one in particular, "Bufort's coming right over."

All the cops now looked at me with new respect. I guess in their circles, anyone who could grab Bufort's attention rated.

Janet was another story. "What the hell have you gotten us into? You haven't said a word about having cozy new friends in homicide. You told me the investigation into Kingsly's murder hadn't involved you much."

I sensed a little sarcasm in how she said "homicide." I'm that kind of sensitive guy.

I started to reassure her. "I've hardly seen you in three days. Besides, you never want me to talk medicine—"

"Medicine!" she shrieked. *"Someone trying to kill you is not medicine!"*

The entire force poking around the house had gone still. Our detective mumbled something about waiting for Bufort out front in case he couldn't read the street number.

Janet looked hurt more than angry, near tears again. I grabbed her, tried to hold her, but she pulled away and said, "We had time together last night. You could have told me."

"Look, I'm sorry. I'm sick this has happened, and God knows I'd die to protect you from harm, but I didn't really know for certain the trouble I was in till now."

She gave me a skeptical glare. I reached for her again. She let me hold her, but kept the bowl in her hands. Regaining her calm, she asked, "What else is going on at St. Paul's?"

"The police think the killer may be a doctor in emergency," I answered, feeling a bit sheepish.

She stiffened and then gave a long, incredulous sigh. "Why in the world wouldn't you tell me *that*?" she demanded. Then, sounding weary, almost sad, she repeated, "We had the whole evening."

The answer was stupid. Embarrassing. Yet I coughed it up.

"I didn't want to ruin the mood." What a miserable excuse. I felt her staring over my shoulder. I went on. "It was so special to be alone and close last night, I didn't want to spoil it. And I didn't have any proof really that this nasty business would ever have anything to do with us."

She pulled back, looked me in the eye to make sure I was as morose as I sounded, and gave a nervous giggle through her tears. At last she put down the bowl and leaned forward to hug me hard. She pressed her hand to the back of my neck and with her lips to my ear whispered, "You're an idiot. A romantic jerk. But I love you."

"I'm so sorry!" I said again, adding, "I haven't a clue what I'm supposed to have done to get us in this mess."

"Are you okay?" she asked softly.

"I'm fine."

"And Muff?"

"In surgery. The car eviscerated her, but it was only the abdominal wall that got cut. Not much bleeding, and I couldn't see any big intestinal perforations, at least not on gross examination. Otherwise she seemed intact. They'll call."

Janet knew as well as I did they'd have to check the entire length of her bowel for any tiny tears or punctures in the intestinal wall and that any leak, however small, could be deadly. "Let's look around and see what's gone," she said.

Ever practical; move on. Don't dwell on what's out of our hands. It's a doctor's hold on keeping the nightmares away. It was Janet's way of waiting out already inevitable endings.

The rest of the house was a replay of what I'd seen in

the front, but the tour still hit me in the guts. Overhead lights had been smashed, some small fixtures ripped out; the upholstery was slashed, small tables and chairs tipped over. Anything made of glass had been dashed on the floor. Again there were great sweeping cuts across the surface of most of the walls.

But upstairs the baby's room was the worst.

Janet had started to prepare it a few weeks ago, working at it little by little whenever she had time. She knew better than anyone what could go wrong even at four months, but the work pleased her, and starting early, she had said, would give her time to do most of it herself. So far she had painted a changing table and crib I'd assembled from a kit, and then had made a set of covers with matching curtains and wall hangings. It was these they had ripped up, defecated on, and then used to smear the walls in the rest of the house. The crib and changing table were broken.

I was seething. A tenderly prepared nest of love and perfect safety had been savaged.

I wanted these animals. That they could come even this near our unborn son unleashed in me a whole new aspect of fatherhood: I could and would kill anyone who threatened him.

Somehow it was even more disturbing that nothing seemed to have been stolen. It would take a while before Janet could do a detailed check of her jewelry or we could sort the clutter enough to verify we hadn't lost small valuables, but so far the destruction appeared senseless. Then I reached my office on the third floor and got a surprise. File drawers were open and papers were scattered all over, but there was no wanton slashing or destruction. The place looked as though it had been searched carefully, thoroughly. Not finding what he wanted, had the intruder gone berserk in the rooms below?

As we returned downstairs, Janet was coldly silent, her own version of withdrawn fury. She paused by the wall outside the baby's room, fingering the slash marks.

One of the cops noticed and joined her. "Funny, eh? We saw they were peculiar. Too clean a cut for a knife. More like a razor blade. But to be wielded with that force, and in those big, sweeping arcs, it would have to be one of those old straight razors. You know, with a handle."

Janet took a step back and viewed the handiwork as if it were hanging in the Museum of Modern Art.

She quietly offered her own critique. "Or a scalpel."

Chapter 10

Bufort arrived resentful as hell. He obviously considered this latest interruption a continuation of my personal campaign to sabotage his investigation.

Seated, silent, legs crossed, he listened to my tale and occasionally made notes in his pad. Once again I felt as if I were being given all the status of a suspect obstructing his speedy version of justice by perpetrating a hoax.

As I laid out the details of the lone figure on the golf green with the Dobermans, the whispered warning by an anonymous caller, and the footprints at our cabin door, Janet was becoming livid all over again.

Admittedly, hearing myself describe the extent of everything else I hadn't told her was making me feel pretty sheepish—a *"How could you be such an ass?"* type of sheepish—if not outright deceitful.

Janet's silence screamed I'd damned well gone way too far into this business, and I'd done it behind her back.

"It would appear, Dr. Garnet," Bufort said coldly, "that you've attracted the interest and now the rage of a very dangerous person."

Janet was a little less subtle. "You idiot! You've been dabbling like some damn amateur detective and brought God knows what down on us."

I winced. Bufort smiled at my discomfort. Then he even tried coming to my rescue.

"Now, Mrs. Garnet—" he began.

Janet bristled. "My name, Detective, is Dr. Graceton," she said icily.

Bufort flinched.

My turn to smile.

Bufort sighed. "I was going to say, I doubt your husband even knows what he did to make such a nuisance of himself that he'd get killed for it."

Some rescue. His tone echoed Janet's verdict perfectly. A bumbling fool. Man doesn't know what he's doing. "In fact"—he looked at me—"I suggest you write a complete account of all your movements, everything you've said and done in the last four days." He leaned back, enjoyed my attempted protest, then quickly cut me off. "Everything, Doctor. Every step, every encounter, and—this is particularly important—log every word you have uttered and to whom."

"You've got to be kidding! Come on. That would take hours, even days."

I turned to Janet, who was no help at all. She was busy suppressing a giggle.

"Ah, c'mon. You can't be serious. I've got a department in meltdown, and a practice, and I don't see enough of either as it is."

No use. Janet was even nodding in agreement. I knew what they both liked best—that I'd be safely out of the way.

I felt I was being sent to my room to write lines—like I should scuff my foot, say "Gee whiz, you guys aren't fair," then surrender to the inevitable and stomp off. Except I didn't have a room. We didn't even have a house at the moment.

Bufort saw me waver and moved in with the clincher. "Listen, you're in danger. Someone wants you dead, and your home and loved ones are obviously of no consequence to this killer. Look around you, for God's sake! The mind behind this is frenzied, out of control. Your only job now is to help us. Until we catch whoever it is, you and your family have no life, no haven for business as usual. Accept that. Accept that and we've got a chance of keeping you safe."

Bastard. He leaned back, smug but right. Then Janet and I got fingerprinted.

They had finally gone. Except Bufort. He hung back in the remnants of our kitchen while Janet and I were in the living room figuring out what to do. He had said he wanted to know our plans before he left.

I reached over and took her hand. She squeezed back gently. The anger was gone, and now she just looked as scared as I felt.

"What do you want to do?" I asked quietly.

"I want to get this mess fixed, fast."

I smiled at her. She had resumed her role as a doctor, fixing the physical, but both of us knew it would take a long time to heal from the other damage done.

"I'll call Doug Perkins," I said, and was relieved to see Janet smile at last. Doug was our contractor, an artist with wood, and he could mobilize a small army in less than twenty-four hours. His men were good, fast, and weren't afraid to pick up a hammer or wrench to ward off goons of any kind. Doug himself was young, congenitally bald, and tough as a bull. Besides this, the man had taste.

"You want me to tell him to meet you at any particular time?" I asked.

"He knows what I like." Janet shook her head. "No need for me to see him. Just tell Doug to get this place back the way it was. Give him carte blanche. The hell with our insurance company."

"And you?"

"I'll live at the hospital and at my parents' house." She called to Bufort. "Am I right, Detective?"

He took her question as a cue and entered the room. "Probably."

She continued. "Don't get me wrong, either of you. I'm doing this to protect my baby. If I weren't pregnant, we'd stay together and fight. Is that clear?"

This time Bufort and I both nodded. She was absolutely clear.

"Now that I'm taken care of, Detective," she paused, "I want to know how you intend to protect my husband!"

Her glare was like a spotlight in his eyes. He looked accused.

"Uh, well, I hadn't figured—"

She abruptly waved him silent. "Whatever my spouse has gotten himself into, it is your responsibility to protect him. Is that clear, Detective? You *will* take all measures to protect my husband!"

Bufort squirmed like an intern, sighed, and said the inevitable words. "Yes, ma'am."

Janet's curt nod of dismissal indicated he'd given the right answer. She touched Bufort's arm. "Let's take a last, quick look around. I'll tell you if anything's missing that I didn't notice before."

When they'd disappeared into the hallway, I called Doug and got him with a cacophony of hammers in the background. He explained he was on someone's roof high in the mountains south of us.

"A cellular phone doesn't fit your image," I teased.

"With clients like you who want it yesterday, what choice have I got?"

It was reassuring just having him around. He listened to my description of the damage. After asking some detailed questions, he lowered his voice. "Earl, are you okay? I mean, it doesn't sound like a routine break-in."

I hesitated before answering. It wasn't that I had any qualms about telling him. In fact, I intended to warn him. But it was just that it all sounded so damned strange.

"Doug," I finally said, "the person who did this probably used a scalpel and probably already killed at least one person at the hospital. Tell your guys to be careful."

He answered with a whistle. Then he showed the class that had always made me like him. "Earl, if you've no objections, I'll move a few of my guys in with you until this is over, as a precaution. You know, mutual interests."

"You don't have to."

"I want to."

"Thanks, Doug."

"Hey, wait until you see my bill. I gotta protect customers like you to get the kids through college."

I told him he could pick up the keys from Mrs. Sharp. He said no problem, he was going to give us real locks this time, and hung up.

Janet and Bufort had finished the tour, and Janet was still sure that nothing appeared to have been taken. Bufort urged us not to stay too long, assured us he'd get added police surveillance right away, then left.

Janet started to compile a list of lamps, furniture, and electrical appliances that we'd need. Neither of us had time to shop, and since Doug had done two expansions on our home up north and some previous work on the city house, he'd come to expect to take on tasks for us that his other clients would do themselves. I think he secretly took pride in our complete trust.

I told Janet of Doug's offer of protection, which made her look relieved. Bufort's cops might be okay, but with Doug's men around we knew we'd have the safest house in Buffalo.

The phone rang. I thought it would be the vet and braced myself. Instead, it was Carole. "Are you all right?"

"Yeah. How'd you know?"

"Ambulance telegraph."

I should have guessed. At least they'd think it was an accident.

"Are we going to see you today?" she asked.

I glanced at my watch. Only eleven. Less than four and a half hours since I'd stepped out the door, blissfully ignorant of what was in motion.

"Yeah, soon. Anything big on my desk?"

She didn't answer. I suddenly felt a twinge of fear again. "Carole, what's happened?" I snapped. "Tell me!"

She took a breath, then answered, "Your office here was broken into sometime last night. They smashed the window and came in from the parking lot, and made a hell of a mess, tossing around our files and drawers. Only one thing seems to be missing, though—our backup computer disks."

I couldn't talk. My throat had gone dry again. I had to try a couple of times before I could swallow. Janet, watching my reaction, started to look alarmed. She must have thought it was bad news about Muffy. "It's my office," I mouthed at her. Then I found my voice. "Carole, what was on those disks?"

"That's the good news. Nothing I can't replace. Only the backup of some minutes and ER lectures that are already on our hard drive. And they didn't get at that."

After repeated thefts, hospital security had mounted all computer terminals on sliding trays in heavy wall units that could be closed and locked at the end of the day. Anyone trying to break in would need a crowbar and a lot of time, and have to suffer the consequences of making quite a racket.

"Did security see anything?" I asked.

"No. After breaking the glass I guess the thief was in and out pretty quickly, probably afraid the noise would attract attention."

"Did anyone in the ER hear anything?"

"It's too closed off. I wouldn't expect them to. But it was Dr. Kradic who discovered the break-in."

"What!"

"Yeah, he was out in the parking lot this morning around six-thirty to get some fresh air and saw your broken window. That's when he reported it to security."

I was unable to speak again.

"Dr. Garnet?" said Carole, obviously puzzled by my silence. But my mind was racing to the earlier doubts I'd had about Kradic back in Sophie's waiting room.

That explained why I couldn't reach him earlier this morning. A lot of ER doctors, myself included, went out in the parking lot at that time, especially if we'd been up all night. By then it was too late to go to bed, and the cool air made it easier to stay awake while waiting for the new shift to arrive. But Kradic could also have been out there doing the break-in and then reported it to take suspicion off himself. And not getting what he was after in the office, did he come after me in the alley?

"Dr. Garnet? Are you there?" asked Carole again.

I hesitated, not sure how much to tell her. She had to know at least enough to be careful. "Carole, my office at home—in fact all of my home—was ransacked this morning as well. They probably didn't find what they wanted here either, because nothing seems to be missing, but I want you to keep our office there locked even if you step out for a minute. They may try again."

"My God!" she gasped. "Who's doing it?"

"I've no idea, but you also should warn security to be extra careful on their rounds. Nobody is to get in unless we say so, not even housekeeping. And I want you to make sure Detective Bufort knows about the break-in there. He left here a few minutes ago and should be back at the hospital pretty soon doing those interviews. If he isn't, track him down."

"Of course," she said quickly, probably puzzled why

someone from homicide had been at my house for a break-in, but she didn't question it.

"Anything else important?" I asked, trying to control my fears while forcing my attention onto routine business.

"No, the usual," Carole answered. "Did you forget you asked me to get the staff together again for tonight at five?"

Forget? Hell, it sounded like someone else's agenda. "Let's just say it hasn't been in the front of my mind this morning, Carole. I'll be there. Anything else?"

"Nothing much. Voyzchek wants our copy of last summer's psych coverage. Can I give it to her?"

Funny. Voyzchek was in charge of emergency for psychiatry, but Gil Fernandez drew up their schedule. I knew they didn't get along, though it would have been easier just to ask him.

"Sure," I agreed, wondering why she'd want a five-month-old roster. "Anything else?"

"Yes, Hurst's called a staff meeting with Bufort for tomorrow morning."

After what I'd been through, it'd be anticlimactic. "That's it?"

"Want to know the place is a mess?"

"Not really. Tell Susanne I'll be there in an hour."

I hung up thinking of Muff. She had to be out of surgery by now, or dead. While I was on the phone with Carole, Janet had gone upstairs. I guessed she was packing some things for the stay at her parents' place in Lackawanna, a small town nearby. When she finally came back down, I measured her optimism by the size of the bag. It was a bit too big for my liking.

"You looked upset by your phone call," she commented without asking outright what was wrong now.

Oh, God, I thought, I don't want to tell her, not after all

this. "Just office crap," I lied, and immediately felt like an adulterer for keeping stuff from her again.

We were in what was left of our kitchen. She stood by the counter picking at an edge of raised linoleum and readying herself for the news as I dialed Sophie's number.

"Hi. It's Dr. Garnet calling about my dog Muff?"

"Oh, yes, Dr. Garnet, Dr. Sophie was trying to reach you. I'll get her." Silence, absurd Muzak on hold. It was bad. Otherwise, the receptionist surely would have said Muffy was all right. Then I remembered the surly treatment from her earlier. Maybe the woman was cruelly perverse. No, I thought, they reserved the bad news for Sophie to give herself. Just like it was in my job.

"I'm on hold," I told Janet. She turned to stare out the back window. She was unknowingly looking at where it had happened.

The phone clicked off hold. "She's alive but gone septic." Sophie got right to the point. She knew the agony of not knowing. "Low blood pressure, lousy urine output, and fever. Same picture as with two-legged sickies, and the same lousy outcome."

Eighty percent mortality in humans. Muff was in bad trouble. "What antibiotics are you using?"

"Usual triple therapy. Amp and Genta, with metronidazole for the chance of anaerobes. The only good news is when we explored her gut, there were no gross perforations we could see."

Again, left unsaid was the possibility of a microscopic hole. The lethality of bacteria from feces was the fear of even modern medicine. Their names raised the specter of horrific Greek gods. *Proteus, Clostridium, Pseudomonas.* Vengeful creatures. If allowed outside the confines of tough intestinal walls, they would marshal their armies and sweep through the bloodstream to infest heart, lungs, kidneys, and brain.

The antibiotics Sophie had chosen were correct but, by human standards, outmoded. They would guarantee the eighty percent mortality.

"Do you want me to get some Triaxone?" This was a new fourth-generation cephalosporin that killed everything with little side effects except to the wallet. The residents called it "gorillacillin."

"It would be a good idea—but it'll be on your card. My patients don't rate that stuff." What Sophie meant was Triaxone had been tested and found to be safe for humans but was unproven for dogs. A bizarre reaction was always possible, and she was merely letting me know the risk was mine.

"I'll send it over."

I hung up, then realized I hadn't thanked her.

Janet knew from my end of the conversation what Muff was up against. She came up, put her arms around me, and kissed me fiercely on the lips. A flash of longing, completely sudden and out of place, surged up and then had to be put down in each of us. Being near death always made me want to make love. We held each other, letting the mutual hunger ebb. Janet put her mouth close to my ear. "Save that for me, and you take care!" she whispered.

I called the pharmacist next door to my private office.

"Carlo, I need a favor. My dog got hit by a car. She's alive but septic, and I want to get Triaxone for her."

"For your dog?"

"Yeah. She's in bad shape."

"Gee, I'm sorry. Listen, the best way is I list it to your office, then what you do with it is your business. Where do I send it?"

I gave him Sophie's address and the daily dose calculated on Muffy's weight, then phoned Mrs. Sharp to warn her that Doug's crew would show up soon, and asked her please to give them the spare key I always left with her. She'd be miffed not to be kept up-to-date anyway. I figured her life was sniffing out neighborhood news and secrets, so why ruin her day?

Soon she'd be out prowling the back lane, trying to engineer a chance meeting with anyone who might have a tidbit of gossip for her. Two steps behind would follow her thin, stooped husband, the curve of his back and nose giving him an odd pecking look, like a heron foraging in grass. In the prewinter light the old couple might be cave dwellers, except millennia of marital training had finally got the man where he belonged.

After I replaced the phone receiver, I hesitated about the next call I had to make. Even thinking about it made my throat go dry again.

I needed to confront Kradic. If he was the monster behind this, I wanted to flush him out now. But I had nothing specific to do it with. I knew he was mad at me, but he was mad at a lot of people. I didn't even have an inkling of what might motivate the man. And I certainly had no evidence that he was the maniac behind the hit-and-run attack this morning. I had to have something if I was going to voice any suspicions to Bufort.

I decided I'd call Kradic about the break-in and ask him if he had seen anything. Or I'd ask him to speak with me before our meeting tonight about practicing with cardiac needles on DOAs. Either way, I'd look for some giveaway, some shred of the hatred behind the attacks on me. If it was him, I figured I might at least sense it.

I called the hospital, got his number, and had them connect me to his home. Busy. I tried again but got the same annoying sound.

I wasn't going to be put off, so I called the city operator.

"This is Dr. Earl Garnet, chief of emergency at St. Paul's. I've been trying to reach Dr. Albert Kradic, but his line's busy. Could you please interrupt the conversation and advise him I have to talk to him?"

"Of course," she replied. I gave her Kradic's number and waited. My hands were getting sweaty as I psyched myself to sound official while being shrewd as hell.

"I'm sorry, sir, but that phone seems to be off the hook."

Shit! He was probably sleeping. I'd have to psych myself all over again tonight.

I cleaned up, found some fresh clothes, and got ready to go. When I went to lock up before leaving by the back way, I found a cop car parked in front of the house. Already? I marveled at the effect Janet had on people like Bufort. I went out and walked over to the driver's side, where a very bored cop was reading a magazine. He barely looked up as I introduced myself. My protection. I advised him about Doug arriving later.

"How will I know him?" he asked without much interest.

"Big, very big." Thank God.

The only sign that my usual predawn excursion to the hospital was now occurring at high noon was a lighter shade of gray and a hundred times more traffic. Buffalo drivers are an ornery lot after three weeks of rotten weather. Ten minutes of the snarl-up in the streets and I was giving the finger and lipping off with the rest of them. By the time I pulled into the sodden parking lot, I felt warmer than I'd been in weeks. The weary attendant signaled me to the special spot he kept for a few of us when we were late and otherwise out of luck. It was the emergency fire lane outside the staff entry to the outpatient department, where we held all our clinics. Since I was also chairman of the Safety and Emergency Measures Committee, it was a slick move. Who was I going to report myself to?

I parked, got out of the car, and opened the trunk to retrieve the computer printouts and disks I'd been working on at the cabin. Then I paused. I hadn't put them there for any specific reason. I was in the habit of lugging a small office around with me, and rather than cart it inside each time I parked, I just locked my briefcase and any other stacks of paperwork in the trunk as a matter of routine.

Could the quality assurance data be why I was suddenly a target? Was that what the night visitor had been after at the cabin? And this morning in my office and at my home? The thought seemed absurd. Yeah, most of the physicians were nervous about their visibility in the study, but that was tempered, I thought, by their curiosity to have their competence measured. The sniff of competition had been irresistible when we'd voted on whether we would enter the QA program. It was the implicit challenge of a rivalry among old friends and colleagues whose job every day meant putting their skills on the line. The vote had been nearly unanimous; only one of the secret ballots had been left blank.

But for any of the reservations expressed then to bubble into the insane fury of the last few hours was beyond understanding. I had to find out more about Kradic, but also, almost in spite of myself, I felt my instincts start to probe what some other members of my department might be capable of as well. Dark possibilities, unthinkable a few days ago, now appeared frighteningly plausible. Had Jones been snooping through the study out of the same nervous curiosity that afflicted most of the department, or was she after something specific? Did the data hide a secret so terrible, someone who had seen me leaving with the printouts felt they had to kill me before I stumbled onto it?

Or did these records somehow connect with Kingsly's killing, or possibly the wino's, and threaten a killer not even in my department? I still didn't know of any relationship between Kingsly and members of my staff that could possibly be a motive for one of them killing him. But this was far less reassuring now, if the attack on me today, as well as the destruction of my house and the office break-in, had been set off by something hidden in the ER statistics. That suggested a motive limited only to the physicians identified by code in that report.

I was still standing at the back of my car with one hand on the open trunk, and I couldn't help giving a quick look around. The lot was filled with cars and mist. An old man struggled out of a nearby taxi, then walked with a cane slowly toward the hospital. I could see other figures moving farther off in the fog, but no one was near me. I looked back down at the pile of printouts and computer disks. I had to keep them safe. If they *were* the cause of the attempts at theft and the hit-and-run try, then it made sense that the perpetrator wanted to keep me from unlocking their meaning. I frowned. The records themselves had been sent out from the state health department and were accessible to a lot of authorized people. But what was in those numbers and symbols that only I was likely to pull out, cross-reference, and look at in such a way that I fingered a criminal? If these statistics could tell me something, maybe they could give me what I needed to find my way out of danger instead of getting me killed.

No one had found them in the car so far. For the time being, that seemed the safest place to keep them, so I slammed the trunk closed and checked the lock.

I was just setting my antitheft alarm when I saw Gil Fernandez. Coatless, he was crossing the hundred yards between the psych building and the main hospital. Now that the daylight was at least equal to the street lamps, he looked even whiter. His forehead had the sheen usually seen in fevers or the sweats of withdrawal. Gone was his jaunty scarlet handkerchief. In addition his suit and his shirt were equally wrinkled—and he wasn't even wearing a tie. Instead of the flamboyant cavalier he had so often mimicked, he slouched by, like a condemned man headed for the gallows.

"Gil, are you all right?" There was no answer. "Gil!"

His head jerked up. The blank gaze I got was far from recognition. I stepped over to him. If possible, he looked a lot worse up close. The man probably hadn't been home, certainly hadn't changed or showered since yesterday. Being caught overnight wasn't unusual for a physician, but by noon the next day most doctors could at least find time for a shower. Even Fernandez's usually crisp beard needed a trim.

"Gil, are you all right?"

He looked at me, tried to smile a greeting, but instead his eyes brimmed over with tears. He couldn't stop himself; his chin kept trembling, and the tears continued to flow.

"Sorry," he muttered, turned, and raced to his car before I could grab him.

"Gil!" I yelled after him, and started to walk quickly over to where he fumbled with his keys.

He saw me coming, whirled, and shouted, "Back off!"

I was so startled, I froze in midstep.

"You can't help me!" he said in a more normal tone.

Before I could protest, he got the car door open, jumped inside, raced the motor on starting, and like a replay from the other night, jerkily sped from the parking lot.

He had seemed afraid then; now I was afraid *for* him, despite the familiar words. *Back off!* Coincidence? Maybe. I'd nearly lost my life passing off some recent events as coincidence. But it was a pretty common expression, and I certainly had no idea why I'd be a threat to him. And what the hell had driven him to this state? I didn't know what to do. Doctors who were sick, whether mentally or physically, had two problems—whatever afflicted them and being assholes who refused help.

Fernandez, at the very least, needed a friend. But I had no idea whom to call. Again, with that peculiar formality of colleagues, we had worked together for years in carefully defended isolation. I presumed he was married, but didn't know for sure. I certainly didn't know who his friends were, or even if he had any. He probably had none in the hospital. Chiefs rarely did.

As I turned back toward the hospital, I had a funny thought. I'd spent the last twenty-four hours becoming afraid of people. But I wasn't afraid of Fernandez.

In emergency the clerks and nurses all greeted me with smiles and told me they were delighted I was okay.

Popovitch and Sylvia Green walked over and started feeling my bones.

"Should we shoot him?"

"Nah, who would we blame this mess on then?"

"Pity, I kinda wanted his car."

"Back to work, schleps," I said, and made my way to my office, feeling slightly restored.

It didn't last. Carole had locked the door as I'd requested. I opened it and found everything as usual except that she wasn't inside. The only evidence of a break-in was a plywood sheet nailed over the window. What bothered me, however, were the notes on my desk. The first was from Bufort. Since he'd dropped me as his number one suspect, he hadn't wasted any time. Now he was going after the rest of my department.

"In-depth interviewing of all emergency room doctors will start tomorrow; we need only a small room near the ER for this purpose; my clerk will coordinate on scheduling with your secretary."

No "if convenient," or "at a suitable time," just "will start tomorrow." Terrific! From court orders to being interrogated as possible murder suspects. What the hell else could be done to disrupt us?

I found my answer in the second note. It was from Jones's reputed bed partner, James Todd. It was hand-written, hastily scrawled across the back of a history and physical sheet.

Dear Dr. Garnet,

    I had a problem with Dr. Kradic this morning when I asked him to call you. His outburst was really embarrassing because it was in front of so many other residents and staff. Please call me immediately when you arrive. I won't be able to sleep now anyway. I don't know if I can work anymore with Dr. Kradic.

                               Jim Todd

I'd forgotten. The beginning of this day was like a distant time unconnected to the present. Obviously Todd had given Kradic the message to call me and been handed his head for his trouble. I wondered if the unfortunate resident had innocently added that I'd asked about cardiac needles and practicing on the DOA. He may have been a fool for getting involved with Jones, but he didn't deserve this. And the last thing I needed right now was a coverage problem with a resident, even one sleeping with his supervisor.

I quickly punched in the number Todd had left, cursing Kradic as I hit each digit.

He answered on the first ring. "Dr. Todd here."

"It's Dr. Garnet. I'm sorry I didn't get back to you earlier, but I just now got into my office. What happened with Dr. Kradic this morning?"

"It was pretty unpleasant, Dr. Garnet, and it took me by surprise."

"What happened?" I asked again gently. Even over the phone I could hear the strain as he was speaking half an octave higher than usual. A resident making a complaint about his staff man was serious business.

"Well, it probably wouldn't have been so bad if *Dr. Jones* hadn't made such a big deal about it." His voice had just gone up the rest of the octave.

"Dr. Jones?" I said, trying to keep my own voice steady.

"Yeah," he answered, sounding a little less nervous and a whole lot more angry. "Right at the start of sign-out rounds she turned to me and said, 'Dr. Garnet wanted me to remind you to give his message to Dr. Kradic here.' Well, we all know those two can't stand each other, however good they are individually, but it was the way she said it that got Dr. Kradic's bristles up, even before I told him to call you." He was practically spitting out his words now. Whatever inexcusable behavior had been leveled at him by Kradic, Todd seemed more bitter and hurt talking about how Jones had set him up.

Damn that woman. She had the highest "fight quotient" on staff, but around Kradic she was at her very worst, always taking shots to put him on the defensive. It was part of her ongoing war to discredit him, but this time she'd used a resident to do it. Not even knowing what I'd called Kradic about, she probably hadn't been able to resist another try at getting him riled just for the hell of it. Not that Kradic was any better. They were like two feuding cats. Even if I separated them, they went looking for each other to fight some more. But for her to drag Todd into it, especially if she was sleeping with him, was too damn much.

"I'm sorry, Dr. Todd, but I assure you I'll speak to both Kradic and Jones about their behavior."

"I'm afraid that's not all, Dr. Garnet."

What now?

"Go on," I said, getting ready to control my own temper.

"Well, when I told Dr. Kradic to call you, he immediately asked why. When I mentioned the cardiac needles and the DOA, he went ballistic. Shouted that you were trying to pin Kingsly's death on him and stalked out."

"How did he know about the needle in Kingsly's heart?" I interrupted. Until yesterday, Bufort had successfully suppressed that detail. It hadn't been part of the general gossip since, as far as I knew, only the chiefs and a few others had known. I'd told Carole and Mrs. O'Hara, but I didn't think those two had blabbed.

Todd seemed surprised at my question. "It was in the papers this morning. You didn't see it?"

Shit! The reporters swarming over the hospital yesterday had obviously gotten someone to tell all. I'd expected the press would find out all the sordid bits one way or another, but I'd somehow hoped Bufort and Hurst might succeed in keeping the lid on things for a while longer. Then I remembered I'd also told Zak. And who knew who the other chiefs had told?

I answered wearily. "My wife and I don't have time for the morning papers."

"In any case," he went on, obviously relieved to be spilling out all the garbage that had happened to him earlier, "Dr. Popovitch was really upset and ran after Dr. Kradic but couldn't catch him. Dr. Popovitch did speak rather sharply to Dr. Jones, right in front of all us residents, and told her to keep her problems with Kradic out of the emergency department. Strangely enough, I think the whole thing made Dr. Jones sick to her stomach. I know she likes to bug Dr. Kradic, but I guess even *she* felt it had gotten out of hand this time. She started looking really pale and disappeared for a while. I think she was in the can, barfing. When she came back, she asked Dr. Popovitch to excuse her so she could lie down in the doctors' room. It was almost an hour before she could come back."

As he talked about Jones, his voice grew softer, and deeper. I wondered if he was trying to find an excuse for her treatment of him, slough it off as a thoughtless mistake that went too far and that he might forgive, for the sake of still getting sex. It suddenly occurred to me that ordering Jones to keep her hands off him might do him the favor he couldn't do for himself.

Quickly smothering my impulse to protect this not-so-innocent lamb, I said, "I'll take care of this crap and they won't bother you again. Sorry, Todd."

He stayed quiet a few seconds, then sounding resigned, he said, "Well, okay."

"Get some sleep," I told him, "and we'll see you tonight. By then I'll have taken care of Jones and Kradic."

After hanging up, I again considered dumping both of them. Before this morning I had always weighed their affinity for trouble against their competence and willingness to do the nights and weekends no one else wanted. Reluctantly I'd admitted life in the ER would be more miserable without their skills and flexibility about shifts. As a result, when I wasn't dreading their fights, I was marveling at their saves in the ER and thanking them for filling the hard- to impossible-to-fill holes in the roster. I had a grudging appreciation of them for the many times they'd kept me from having to work these last-minute shifts personally, most often at night, on holidays, or both. And I was certainly aware no one else wanted their regular load of nights. So, in exchange, I had always forced myself to endure the additional aggravation of smoothing over their perpetual flare-ups. But were they still worth it?

I crumpled James Todd's note and shot it angrily at my basket.

Any other week, sorting all this out would have been my worst problem. This week I was left sitting in my office wondering if Kradic had a secret so dreadful that after his fight with Jones he'd gone out and tried to run me over.

"She's going to arrest," our new junior resident yelled. He was panicky. When I'd come out of my office about an hour before, I'd started seeing patients in the ER to avoid thinking any more about who was after me. Because of the wet, cold blanket of air hovering over Buffalo, we were overwhelmed with respiratory emergencies, and I was using the occasion to teach.

The woman on the stretcher was desperately casting her eyes about for help. Her bronchial tubes had shut down, and her breath was cut off. Her chest heaved. She was unable even to speak. She clawed at her clothes and gave panicky whimpers. Her nicotine-stained fingertips with downwardly curving nails—a sign we called clubbing—told the reason: end-stage emphysema. A lifetime of smoking had come down to a few desperate seconds.

"What do you want to do?" I commanded more than asked, to get the resident thinking again.

"Ventolin?"

"Good answer—except it's too late for Ventolin now." She's so shut down she needs an airway."

"Won't she buck the tube if we try before she arrests?"

"Good question, but I want to prevent the arrest and relieve her distress. We're going to crash her before she crashes on us. Get your intubation equipment ready."

He looked relieved to have a familiar job. I knew he'd just come to us from an anesthesia rotation.

Susanne, anticipating where we were heading, had filled the pancuronium, succinylcholine, and ketamine syringes. Our lady was reduced to useless, flailing movements like a stranded fish. She already had an IV.

As I worked, I talked out what I was doing for the sake of the resident. "First a defasciculation dose of short-acting curare to prevent muscle twitching when we paralyze her outright."

I shot in the pancuronium.

"Never paralyze someone and not sedate them. Though unable to breathe or move anything, she's still conscious—the living dead, so to speak, and terrified. For this scenario we use ketamine."

In it went.

We started to bag her before intubation. I continued to talk. "That sedates, gives analgesia, and dilates her bronchial tubes." I let it take effect.

"Now we paralyze," I said, and injected the succinylcholine.

A few twitches, modified by the preceding curare, and she was flaccid, unable to move a muscle, including her diaphragm. We were committed; either we succeeded in getting an airway or she was dead.

"All yours, Doctor," I said as I stood back to let him intubate. Given his recent training, it was unlikely he'd have any trouble. But in the OR, the resident was used to a calm, well-planned routine for intubation. Here we had to snatch the same technical precision from a lot messier setup.

He moved in and positioned her head. I gave three quick puffs with the bag and mask and then removed it. He scissored open her mouth with his right hand; with his left he slid in a laryngoscope. The curved blade with a light in its tip pushed aside the tongue and illuminated the vocal cords. Through them he'd slide a tube into her trachea. The nurses went quiet. The resident steadied the light in position.

"Do you see the cords well?" I asked him to confirm this crucial step.

"Yep." He picked up the endotracheal tube with his

right hand and slid its tip carefully over the tongue held aside by the blade of his scope. He paused with the tip of the tube aligned at the small opening in the windpipe, then slipped it through. "Got it!" he announced, and the nurses began to chatter again.

He hooked up the bag to the tube, squeezed in a few test puffs of air while listening at the bases of the lung for confirmation. "We've got air entry!" He sounded surprised at his own success.

"Of course, Doctor, good job." I knew he'd build on this case. Respiratory emergencies would no longer frighten him.

We added some Ventolin down the tube, started steroids through the IV to dampen down the underlying inflammation of the lung, then arranged the transfer to ICU. I let the resident continue bagging her and supervise the trip upstairs. He'd enjoy presenting his win. The lady looked pink.

Before this week I never would have thought I'd be using shifts in the ER as a way to relax.

The whole department was present, a first, but then, they'd never been summoned because of an injunction before. Even Sylvia Green, who was on duty, came up to the meeting room, but she stayed near the phone, ready to be called to the ER in an instant. And I'd had Carole make two special calls: to Kradic, who had finally put his phone back on the hook, and to Jones. She'd given them my order to be here, and they were—sullen, withdrawn, and sitting at opposite ends of the table, but they were present. Jones avoided my eyes; Kradic seemed oblivious of me. Finally he realized I was staring at him and looked annoyed, but then, he always looked annoyed to me.

There were a few wisecracks sent my way about the accident. The usual type of stuff—"Anything for a day off." "What'd the other car look like?"

Obviously no one except the murderous driver knew that the hit-and-run had been deliberate. All the banter ended when I mentioned the injunction.

"We'll get to that in a minute. First I need to talk about Kingsly's murder. For those not up-to-date on the situation, when we found him early Monday morning, he had been stabbed with a cardiac needle. No one knows why, let alone by whom." I paused a second, then said, "Because of the way Kingsly died, anyone with the skill or means to perform intracardiac insertions is under scrutiny. Each one of you will be questioned, starting tomorrow."

Now there was more dismay than offense.

"They gotta be kidding."

"That's nuts."

"Christ!"

I waved the noise down. "I know. I share your feelings. But until they get some clue as to what's going on, be careful. Anything unusual, take note, and get back to me."

The initial shared outbursts were being replaced by averted eyes.

"Look, I don't mean I want you to spy on your colleagues or anything. I mean, we all have to remember that after this ends we're still going to be working together and, I hope, continuing to trust one another."

My attempt at perspective sounded feeble even to me. I tried the practical example. "Here's what I mean. This past Monday there was a DOA derelict found in the street and brought here without any resuscitation attempt tried on him. The post found marks from an intracardiac needle. Anyone here know of any practice procedures on the body?"

I had asked this looking directly at Kradic. He swallowed and then quickly glanced down at his lap. The rest of them answered my question by saying no or shaking their heads. All except Jones. She just stared at the center of the table.

"Dr. Jones?" I asked to get her attention.

"No, I don't," she said resentfully without even looking at me.

I turned back to Kradic. "And you, Albert?"

His head snapped up, and he seemed surprised, but that could have been because I called him by his first name, which was rare. "Of course I don't." He scowled, then added even more resentfully, "Why are you asking us about this anyway?"

"Because, as I said, the DOA had a needle track into the heart we can't account for. And, since we can't explain it, I have to think the derelict was also murdered, the same way as Kingsly."

Kradic looked startled. Others at the table expressed their shock.

"Another one?"

"Good Lord!"

"Like Kingsly?"

"What the hell is going on?"

But I just kept staring at Kradic. He looked even angrier now, and leaned forward as he spoke over the noise of the others. "Are you saying the cops will blame that on us too?" he demanded, his voice rising.

Everybody in the room went quiet.

"As I warned you, the police will start questioning you tomorrow about Kingsly's death. I don't know what they're doing about the derelict."

He was red in the face now. "Jesus Christ! What kind of setup is this?" He began pounding the table with his right forefinger as he spoke. "I don't know about the rest of you, but I'm getting a lawyer!" He rose partly out of his seat and used that same finger to point across the table at me. "And you," he yelled, "are letting the staff of this department be hung out to dry!"

Then he shoved back his chair and stomped out.

His accusation hung in the silent room. Some looked at me, obviously nervous; others looked anywhere but at me.

My mouth was too dry when I first tried to speak. I had to take a sip of water and try again. "I don't need to tell you this is a very serious matter. Perhaps each of you should consider legal counsel before talking with the police."

The silence remained, but now nobody was looking at me except Popovitch. He gave me a sad little smile and then came to my defense.

"I'm sorry," he started to say, and got everyone's attention, "but Dr. Garnet can't change what has happened in the last few days. The police are looking for a killer, and until they succeed, this department, along with a few other areas in the hospital, will be under scrutiny. It may not be fair, and it's certainly not desirable, but it can't be helped." He looked around at his colleagues, then spoke rather sternly. "It is absolutely unacceptable to blame the messenger, and I insist, on behalf of all of us, that we dissociate ourselves from Dr. Kradic's inexcusable behavior."

Most quickly came to my defense, but a few still looked pretty worried. Jones was scowling at Popovitch now, probably still smarting from his rather public rebuke of her this morning in front of the residents. I turned back to Popovitch.

"Thank you, Michael, now let's deal with this court-order nonsense." I told them my plan, but I doubted many of them had much confidence in my ability to pull it off.

And I still had no idea who had tried to kill me.

Coming home that evening was more like entering a boys' camp than being at the site of a recent attempted murder. Right away I knew Doug's men were out in force when I saw the number of pickup trucks wedged into my driveway. The warm scent of pizza greeted me as I stepped into the kitchen. "Hi, Doc!" and a chorus of other welcomes came from those filling the room. Someone opened the fridge, which was now full of beer, and handed me a can. Seemed like Doug had made my mental well-being the primary responsibility of his crew.

I recognized some of the guys from the renovation work on the cabin, and the others cheerily introduced themselves. Doug's best. Many had families they were abandoning for the evening to baby-sit me, and I was warmed and flattered.

"Thanks, guys."

"Hey, no problem. Our pleasure. Glad you're okay."

Doug led us into the living room where, clearly, he'd made replacing the large-screen television a priority and had hooked up our still-functioning VCR. He punched Play. *Casablanca*, in all its original black and white, was starting to unfold its tale of love and glory. It was my favorite movie of all time. "How'd you know?"

They answered with pleased, knowing grins. Doug must have called Janet.

"C'mon, Doc, sit down. We've got it cued up so he's about to do the 'Of all the gin joints in all the towns in all the world, she had to walk into mine' bit."

And I did sit down. I watched that famous craggy face and took courage from it. I felt blessed.

It was after midnight when Janet called me from the case room. "How'd you like it?" she asked.

"Would have been better with you."

"Flatterer."

"You okay?"

"Yeah, you?"

"I'll be better when we get our life back."

"How's Muff?"

"I dropped by the vet's on the way from work. Sedated, fever, but pressure and urine output are up. I left one of our pillows. She didn't know I was there, but if she ever does wake up, she'll recognize our smell."

"I'll go see her in the morning. 'Night, love."

" 'Night, Janet. I love you."

Chapter 11

Hurst started his meeting promptly at seven A.M., and almost everyone was present. Not surprising. I was relieved to see that Gil Fernandez had turned up. He was bathed, his beard trimmed, but still he seemed subdued. Even his pocket handkerchief was less puffed up than usual.

Sitting beside him was a uniformed policewoman with a stenographer's pad in front of her. On the opposite side of the long table, but farther down, a second uniformed police officer, a pad also in front of him, sat between Bufort and Riley. A dozen legal-size file folders were stacked near Bufort, and two open briefcases were on the floor near his chair.

I happened to sit by Watts. He leaned over and quipped, "If those are Kingsly's financial records, it'll be ruled justifiable homicide."

Hurst stood, cleared his throat, and we were off.

"Though this special meeting of the chiefs of staff was requested by Detective Bufort, I want to remind you we are under police orders not to discuss the details of Mr. Kingsly's murder. A sordid tragedy such as this is disruptive enough without the appalling sort of headlines we saw in yesterday's paper." As he slowly turning his head, his glare spared not one of his medical colleagues at the table. I suspected he was more concerned about bad publicity than any negative impact a leak might have on

Bufort's police work. "For those of you interested," he added, "a memorial service for Mr. Kingsly will be held next Monday at one o'clock in the hospital chapel." Some of the chiefs made a gesture to note the announcement. I was saddened to think of how few of them would actually bother to go. Hurst sat down with a curt nod at Bufort.

Bufort sat motionless for a few seconds, as if waiting to make sure he had our undivided attention. The two uniformed police picked up their pens and got ready to write. Even Riley had taken out a notebook. "There's a rule of thumb in homicide," he began, "that the most important evidence is found within the first few hours after a crime. Then the trail grows cold quickly." He seemed tense, and I was surprised to see dark shadows under his eyes. Without me as a suspect, I wondered, did he feel the case was slipping out of his grasp?

"The first days of this investigation seemed to go well," he continued. "We discovered a probable motive for Kingsly's killing, and were looking at a few suspects." He looked at me briefly, then continued. "But recent events, some of which were brought to our attention only two days ago"—he frowned in the general direction of Watts—"have made it necessary to widen our investigation. While it's unusual for us to conduct a session like this, we've been forced to do it to try to make up for lost time. We hope that after hearing about some of the evidence gathered so far, one or more of you may realize you have information or insights that will help us find Mr. Kingsly's murderer."

Damn, if he was this desperate, he was really back at square one. Then I noticed something strange. While Bufort talked, neither Riley nor the two uniformed police were looking at him. Each had his eyes fixed on a different section of the group at the table.

Bufort stood as he resumed speaking. "One of the avenues we have explored to find out why Kingsly was killed and by whom is his hospital records. The other avenues, his personal life, his associations beyond hospital life, haven't yielded anything so far. Besides, as you probably know, the manner in which he was killed suggests it was done by someone in this hospital, someone with a special skill."

Hurst was starting to squirm. I wondered if Bufort had questioned him on his ability to needle a heart. The policewoman opposite Hurst watched him for a couple of seconds, then wrote something on her pad.

"In these records," Bufort continued, "we find what I take it all of you are aware of: The hospital's finances are in a mess. Every department, it seems, has a debt. It isn't easy for the auditors we've called in to determine who controls what expenditure. People just forward requests for equipment, tests, and supplies, and other people fill those requests from preauthorized labs and medical supply houses. No one at any level seems to know why existing supply and service contractors were chosen. The authority to question alternatives, let alone actually implement any attempt at more cost-effective measures, doesn't seem to be exercised in any consistent or logical way."

He paused. Around him a ring of puzzled faces echoed my own confusion. It sounded more like a management seminar than a murder investigation. Riley and his two colleagues watched their sections of the table but wrote nothing down. And Hurst was really squirming now.

"The budget of this place is one hundred and twenty million annually. That's a great deal of money by anyone's standards. And Kingsly and the director of finance, Thomas Laverty, alone controlled its allocation."

Everyone at the table looked around. Laverty wasn't present. The police officers watched our faces, and I slowly caught on. Bufort and his people were checking for reactions again.

"The opportunity for diddling the till here is immense," he continued, starting a professorial strut behind the chairs occupied by the policeman and Riley. "Increasingly Mr. Kingsly was ... well, incapacitated. The clerks up in finance kept sending checks to pay the bills as they came in. Overdrawn, why not? A lot of hospitals are these days. The bank relishes racking up interest charges, and loans to the health care system are a cash cow to the moneylenders, so they don't complain. End of the year, there's a deficit. The board screams, then approves borrowing the money to pay the interest and further service the debt. The bank now has interest on interest but assumes that even if the hospital is in danger of defaulting, another institution is likely to buy it out and make good on the loan. So for the time being, who even thinks of paying back the principal? After a few years the entire mess becomes such a routine, it gets no more than token scrutiny. The familiarity gives a false sense that it's all proper, and the diddling continues."

He had us all now. Hurst looked as if his second heart attack had plugged his pump. His first one, ten years ago, was the reason he'd given up surgery. His hands rolled into fists; his mouth made sucking movements. I leaned forward and took his arm. He wrenched it free. I saw the policewoman write something else on her pad.

"We don't have many details yet," continued Bufort, "and we haven't finished looking at all your departmental salary pools, but we have a pretty good example of wrongdoing. The first oddity was a receipt for etchings and prints from a place called Renaissance Art Gallery. More than two hundred thousand dollars' worth, labeled as institutional art, that no one knows about. We have no idea where they ended up. There wasn't a trace of the stuff in Kingsly's home."

He paused, surveyed his incredulous audience, and seemed to particularly savor his next revelation. "There is a single account in all the hospital's bank records and cost centers that routinely holds money. We noticed it because, in contrast, all the other cost centers are continually in deficit. This center, with no designated function, is numbered 0067."

The absurdity exposed. An account rendered peculiar in our madhouse by the simple deviance of actually having some money in it.

He no longer needed a dramatic pause to get our attention. In fact, he seemed taken aback as, one by one, we reacted to the enormity of what he'd told us. We'd endured shortages year after year. Suggesting we had an embezzler in our midst was a flashpoint. Every person at the table seemed to be getting angry. By now some were standing, leaning in on him. Others remained seated, staring at him, their expressions changing from disbelief into disgust and their hands curling into fists. Riley and his two cops occasionally made a note. Names? Reactions? A lack of reaction?

It was Sean who found his voice first. "Do you mean that creep was siphoning off hospital funds?" he asked, barely controlling the rage in his voice.

Bufort clearly hadn't expected this level of fury and still seemed astonished by what he'd unleashed. "We don't know much yet," he said cautiously, "but I'm asking anyone who does to come forward. We're especially interested at the moment to hear from anyone with any information on cost center 0067."

I got my own brain functioning again. "How much do you figure went through this center?" I asked.

"More than a million a year," Bufort said carefully, as if each word were nitro.

I swung on Hurst. "That's the cost of closing fifty beds. Were you aware of this?"

He had a lock on the table's edge that turned his knuckles as white as his face. "Of course not!"

I didn't believe him.

"Is this why you were so hell-bent on attacking the deficit and ordering such excessive bed cuts? Were you planning to use the extra savings to cover some embezzled shortfall of Kingsly's?"

At my accusation his lips trembled so violently that I was sure he'd have attacked me if we'd been alone.

"Well, get this, Hurst," I said before he calmed down enough to speak. "Patients in emergency aren't going to play victim to cover Kingsly's dead ass, incompetent, crooked, or both. Your court order's dead in the water as of now."

I hadn't planned to use that fact this morning. I pulled a rolled fax of legal-size text from my lab coat pocket. It was confirmation that our malpractice insurance group in Albany would assign a legal team to quash Hurst's court order. But I unscrolled to an even more pertinent section. Against the sounds of Hurst's sputters and the counter-protests of Carrington and Watts telling him to "stuff it," I started reading aloud. " 'Specifically forbidden is any action on the part of the county, hospital, or any individual representing the hospital who attempts to coerce a physician to work in conditions unsafe for patients or contributing to patients being subjected to substandard care. Our company deems the long waiting times for emergency patients to get beds as unduly dangerous to their well-being and, as such, a breach in the standards of acceptable hospital practices. Adherence to such standards is the basic tenet under which we grant malpractice policies, and any failure to adhere to them automatically renders our contracts null and void. The probability of costly lawsuits is too great, and we refuse to underwrite in such a high-risk situation.' "

Everyone was looking at me now with very confused expressions on their faces. Even the cops.

Sean asked, "What's that mean?"

"It means if a hospital doesn't have the integrity to shut down emergency services that can't supply timely care, then the insurance company can withdraw malpractice coverage. Without coverage, it's against our own hospital bylaws for a physician to work."

"Wow!"

"Finally!"

"Great!"

Lost in this chorus, Hurst went an even paler shade of his usual white. "It'll never stand!" he snarled at me.

"Then try this," I said, and handed him another document.

All the side conversations stopped. Every pair of eyes gazed at Hurst as he skimmed my latest offering. Probably, I thought, he was going to say we should meet privately later and discuss the matter, try to bury the ruling without the other department heads finding out. I blew that option off the table.

Not letting my eyes off Hurst, I raised my voice. "Gentlemen, what I've shown Dr. Hurst is a letter of intent from our protective agency to defend free of charge any physician subjected to legal action for his or her part in shutting down an unsafe ER. They figure it's cheaper to prevent the inevitable litigation than to pay for it later. And whatever our own financial woes might be, Dr. Hurst and his bean counters aren't likely to go into a court of law to argue their right to force doctors into unsafe practices just to balance their books."

Now I looked at my colleagues. Four days ago they had been cool, outright hostile to any action on our part against the bed closures. A few had probably welcomed the injunction.

Arnold Pinter hesitatingly tried to rekindle their opposition. "Uh, Earl, surely this is completely inappropriate at this meeting, don't you think? I suggest you forget this ridiculous idea of shutting down emergency. Why, the—"

"Shut up, Arnold!" Sean Carrington shouted. "And I'll be raising this same principle of standards with the department of surgery."

The other chiefs came to Carrington's and my support.

"Right."

"Agreed."

"Bravo!"

A few even gave me a slap of congratulations on the back. Their smiles lightened the mood, but only for some.

Fernandez was staring into space. He gave no sign of following what was going on around him. Instead, as white as Hurst, he got to his feet and made for the door. I was startled to see his hand shake as he reached for the handle. I don't think anyone else in the room noticed him leave. Except the policewoman. I saw her watching his departure and making a note on her pad.

I turned back to the table.

Saswald was desperately oiling his sensors to gauge the political swing unfolding too fast for his usual self-serving calculations.

I enjoyed putting him on the spot. "Where are you now, Sas?"

He started weaving the air with his hands. "Well, I . . . of course, I must raise any such serious matters for careful study within my anesthesia department, and I'll make a motion—"

"Forget it, Sas." Gotcha! I knew I was being petty, but it felt good.

In my mind I fancied a perversion of one of those righteous bumper stickers: I DON'T BRAKE FOR POLITICIANS, EVEN IF THEY PRETEND TO BE PHYSICIANS. LET 'EM BE SMEARS ON THE ROAD. Then I remembered that I'd nearly been dispatched to that status myself and sobered up. I turned from the still-blustering Saswald and faced Hurst.

"Forty-eight hours, Hurst, or we shut down. Open the goddamn beds!"

He glared at me but said nothing. I glared right back at him. I was pretty certain now that he'd gone as far as crippling the hospital to cover up a scandal over Kingsly. Was he also capable of killing for it? I still didn't know, but clearly we were now on a different footing about the beds.

Arnold sank morosely into his chair.

Riley broke my second of triumph with a quiet cough, then deferred to Bufort and thus duly returned us to the business at hand. We all sat back down and stopped muttering to one another. Riley and the two uniformed police resumed watch on their respective sections of the table. I don't think anyone else noticed we were being observed so systematically.

"We are questioning the director of finance."

That explained Laverty's absence.

"We are *not* sure yet of the extent of his involvement. Nor do we know how these events led to your former executive director's murder. But we're very sure there is a connection."

I saw the policewoman look at Hurst and make yet another note. I wondered if because of my outburst he'd be questioned now about covering up the embezzlement.

Bufort made his next disclosure very quietly. "Two days ago, as I mentioned, we had to completely change our thinking and the scope of our investigation. That's when we learned from Dr. Watts that there may have been a second murder with a cardiac needle."

While everyone else at the table gasped in surprise, Watts grimaced at this belated acknowledgment of the inconvenient find and leaned back with his arms folded.

Bufort gave him a wary look, then said, "A derelict DOA in your emergency had evidence of an unexplained intracardiac needle stab. We are looking into other explanations, but given how Mr. Kingsly died, we have to keep the possibility of a connection open, though what the connection could be, we've no idea."

More silence—until he added what I wished he'd left out. "Yesterday morning both Dr. Garnet's house and his office here in the hospital were broken into, and he was the target of a hit-and-run attempt."

It was my turn to stare at the center of the table. I heard horrified exclamations of shock from all around me. "Oh my God!" "How awful!" "Good Lord!" Beside me, I sensed Watts tense up.

"The attack," Bufort explained, "was vicious, and barely failed. Again we haven't the slightest idea how the attempt might be tied in with Kingsly's killing. Not even Dr. Garnet has a clue as to what has made him so vulnerable."

Arnold and Saswald nodded readily—probably in agreement to the judgment that I was "clueless."

"For the moment," continued Bufort, "we must assume these extraordinary events are linked somehow. Please contact me if you think of anything that might help us. In the meantime, I would like all of you to be careful."

As the meeting broke up, I got some more patronizing looks from Arnold and Saswald. They made me feel I could have avoided my own misfortune had I just paid attention. They were obviously not going to make the same mistakes I'd made—whatever the hell those mistakes were. What pompous asses.

Sean stood up and gave my shoulder a hearty squeeze as he went by me on his way to the door. A few of the others mumbled words of sympathy while they pushed away from the table, but I got the distinct impression the danger I was in made them feel uncomfortable. I felt a flash of impatience and almost blurted out that it wasn't catching, but I had to admit they had a point. I probably wasn't the healthiest guy to be around right now.

Out of the corner of my eye I saw Watts frowning at me. When he caught me looking, he quickly turned away. Of all of them, his was the opinion I most cared about, but if something was troubling him, he didn't let me in on it.

Chapter 12

It was the type of day when the afternoon light starts fading at one o'clock. Fog and low clouds slid over the city like rolls of steel wool. Even photo sensors on the street lamps had declared most of the sun's effort invalid and left a ragtag pattern of some off, some on, and some flickering feebly in limbo—vital signs of a dying neighborhood on a monitor, part of a city weakening and shutting down.

The daylight filtering through the mist was little more than a dim glow, the kind that emanates from a TV set left on after sign-off. The houses, modest boxes set back from the street, were blurred. The few cars that were out hissed their approach before I could see them emerge and then vanished quietly in the white haze. Each time I heard the sounds I stiffened and hugged the inner sidewalk, then relaxed and tried to shake the previous morning's attack.

But that wasn't why I was out walking, at least not entirely. A bit of it was frustration at trying to dodge a faceless menace. But the real reason was a deeper niggling that had kept interfering with my attempts to work. I'd tried several routines throughout the morning to distract myself. In the end I felt like an actor, restlessly putting on one costume after another and none of them being right for the part.

I'd checked emerge. It was a mess. Did they need

help? No, they needed beds. I called Janet. She was busy in the OR. At least she was safe, if operating on AIDS patients was safe. Her partner had just had his hand sliced by a resident's slip with a scalpel while in the open abdomen of an HIV-positive woman. The risk depended on the amount of the patient's blood that had contaminated his wound, but even if it was minimal, and even if his tests in three months and six months were negative, there would be lingering doubts for years each time he made love to his wife.

My feet made crunching sounds on the remains of a broken beer bottle. I sidestepped the jagged end piece and thought of our wallpaper. I scuffed the smaller glass bits off my wet soles and trudged on, but I couldn't shake off my black thoughts.

I'd called the vet. No change. This was the gray time, hope soiled with dread. On many occasions I'd cast that same sentence over human life.

I'd tried working on the quality assurance study in my office. When Carole had placed all the material on the disks now in the trunk of my car, she had done the work on the hard disk of the computer she locked away each night. With her help—I was hopeless wading through her computer files myself—I had been able to work on the numbers in the office, but the data was frustrating in its monotony. Any answer it held slid beyond my grasp. There were highs and lows, wins and losses, but mostly draws, and all within the norm. I could find nothing to kill for. At least, nothing I could see. But the image of a baby's room slashed and coated with feces suggested madness, not logic.

I'd managed to make the record of my actions and conversations over the last few days for Bufort. The net result was, as he had so eloquently put it, I hadn't a clue who I'd threatened or why anyone thought it necessary for me to die.

I felt a little satisfaction though. By taping the report instead of laboriously writing it out, I'd foiled Janet and Bufort's plan to keep me busy for days. When I'd finished, I had asked Carole to type it up and send it to Bufort.

Then I'd ended up pacing the office, driving her insane. She suggested I go bother Mrs. O'Hara, but no patients were booked that day. Still, I'd shuffled over through the parking lot and found Mrs. O filing lab reports. After having me check a few abnormals and arrange follow-up tests or repeat examinations, she wasn't putting up with me either.

So here I was, walking in the fog, trying to get past the debris of what I knew and tease out what was bothering me. Cushioned by the mist and braced by cold, I kept thinking I had missed something. I reran the morning meeting, and the fuzziness slid into a single focused image: Fernandez. But this time it wasn't his fear and agitation that struck me. I'd just discovered what I'd overlooked. In fact, it was something that was missing from the events at the meeting that was incongruous. I'd missed it because it was a negative find—not there when it should have been. As I told my residents over and over, unless you go after negative signs, you'll miss them every time. I had to talk to Fernandez. It didn't make sense, but what wasn't there that should have been was all I had.

I wheeled around and headed back toward the hospital through the fog. It was growing darker now, and the hospital's lights loomed up over me like an onrushing ship.

I left my raincoat in the doctors' coatroom, dripping alongside other bedraggled wet wear. The place smelled like the inside of a running shoe. Plaster fell out in chunks, pushed by fuzzy green and blue mold that bulged from inside the walls. Maybe Hurst's cost cuts could lead to a new source of income—growing our own penicillin.

Hurrying down the hallway toward psychiatry, I had little idea of how to confront Fernandez other than surprise him into leveling with me. But as I got closer to his office, I remembered him screaming at me in the parking lot the day before and began to rethink the likelihood of startling the truth out of him.

My second thoughts brought me to a stop in front of the coffee shop. After the gloom outside, it looked like a sanctuary of warm light and delicious aromas. Hot soup and a bagel with lox suddenly seemed far more important than ambushing a frazzled shrink.

I slipped into line and caught the attention of the woman behind the counter. She mouthed over the other waiting heads, "The usual?"

I nodded thanks, stayed in line to prepay the order, and tried to think of a better way to question Fernandez.

At the cash register, my musings were interrupted by Bessie. Eighty-one now, and a regular volunteer for the auxiliary, she had been head nurse in emergency when I first came on staff. Trained and seasoned in World War II, she was at ease in a crisis and ever ready for a drink or a poker game after the work. "That'll be six-fifty, Doc. When are you and that other doc of yours going to finally learn how to make kids?"

Janet was her doctor. She'd taken an ovarian cancer out of Bessie two years ago, and Bessie had been back on her stool three weeks later.

"Hey, lady," I said, "shows you haven't kept your appointment with Janet. We finally figured it out. Must've missed the lecture. Looked it up in one of her books. Our first will be here in April."

Her smile and surprise were genuine. "I'm so glad for you." She gave my hand a squeeze after handing back my change. "And my best to Janet. Tell her I'll be in."

"You'd better, Bessie. Skip one appointment and see what you miss?"

Another smile and she was on to the next in line.

I headed for a free table and passed a foursome of retired surgeons. They gathered each afternoon to relive old battles and rehash cases long since dust. Twenty years ago they were my teachers and in their prime. When I took over as chief eight years ago, one of them, Jack Graham, was still working emergency, hopelessly unable to keep up with the increasing pace and standards. He'd become outright dangerous. My first task was to tell him it was time to leave. It was like telling him he had cancer, but for him it was even worse: He was sentenced to go on living without his work.

I greeted them all by their formal names, since I remained an intern in their eyes. Three of them nodded, but all I got back from Jack Graham was an accusing silence.

I passed the very stool at the coffee counter where, as an intern those same twenty years ago, I'd received a hurried cup of coffee and a five-minute orientation from the chief resident. He had raced back to the OR and I walked into emergency for my first shift under Bessie's ample wing. Now I was at the halfway point of my own journey toward the day when one of my current residents would probably tell me the ride was over, that it was time to go home. Would I blame the younger doctor, or only the bitter irony?

"Jack still hold you responsible for his old age?" It was Watts, sitting alone at a table, apparently amused at what he'd seen.

"Hey, for time itself." I noticed his half-empty cup of coffee and an open sailing magazine by his elbow and invited myself to sit. "How's your dream machine coming?"

"Going to be ready when the spring ice goes out, and I'll be out of here with it."

I paused with a spoonful of soup halfway to my mouth.

"That's bad news." I meant it. I didn't relish surviving the rampant rise of hospital bureaucrats without his deflating wit and clinical savoir-faire to keep *some* vestige of sanity. I also knew his term had two more years. "Why?"

"I've had it. My Christmas card this year will include my resignation. They'll have till spring to find my successor."

There was a heaviness about him that didn't surprise me. He'd vigorously carried the load of being the hospital's conscience for thirty years. As keeper of the final diagnosis, he had wielded his knife with a passion to improve care and learn from the verdicts: correct or incorrect, right or wrong, unavoidable or avoidable death. There was no appeal, and no one escaped his theater of judgment. Watts had been our gatekeeper.

All of this had changed forever when his wife died. He still did the job, but his passion and his quiet joy in excellence were mostly gone.

"Some investments I made came through," Watts added. "I'm expecting some more final dividends soon. I don't need the next two years. Enough's enough."

There was a bleakness now to his plan in contrast to the same dream he had expressed to me at a happier time three years ago. He stared at the photo on the open page, a sailboat ad, with a robust gray-haired man and woman at the wheel of a yacht on open seas.

My bagel tasted dry. "What was bothering you at the end of today's meeting, Robert?"

His double-take startled me. "What do you mean?" he asked.

"Your look. At the end of Bufort's soliloquy."

He shrugged as if he didn't know what I was talking about.

"C'mon, Robert, I've seen that look before. Your nose

was definitely out of joint—and that's something, considering what your nose puts up with. So what was it?"

He sat completely still, like a card player weighing his hand, trying to decide whether to play or fold. Finally, he said, "It shook me that an attempt had been made against you."

I waited for more.

"Hey, that's it! I swear! It's one thing to do what I do to strangers. It's another when a pal threatens to become one of my patients!"

He sounded sincere, but I didn't believe him. I also knew pushing him wouldn't help. Over the years I'd seen how stubborn he could be once he decided something.

"What about the derelict?" I asked instead.

He seemed relieved to change the subject. "Funny, that. The tox screen was nonsignificant apart from his maintenance level of alcohol, but it was alcohol, not some cocktail better suited for cars."

He meant no antifreeze or methanol.

"I don't have the trace-element levels yet. We send them out to another lab. The rest was negative, pretty much."

"Pretty much?"

"Yeah. He had hay fever, but some rookie, probably in a street clinic, thought it was a cold."

"You might diagnose chronic allergies from tissue samples on a post," I answered, "but find out the thoughts of people he met too?" I knew it was my expected role to play incredulous. I was going to be taught something.

"Traces of terfenadine and a touch of erythromycin." He leaned back with a smug smile.

I saw what he meant. Terfenadine was a hay fever medication, but alcoholics living on the streets usually spend what little cash they scrounge on booze. The John Doe must have gotten a clinic sample. Erythromycin was a form of penicillin especially for people with a penicillin allergy. It took a prescription, and only a rookie would have given antibiotics for hay fever or been browbeaten by a patient into prescribing them for the symptoms of a viral infection that hay fever might mimic. Worse, a precautionary had been issued against giving the two together. Fatal arrhythmias had occurred with little more than therapeutic doses.

"Do you think it's a drug-induced dysrhythmia?"

"No. But you're right to think of it. These things rarely leave footprints. His anatomy and conduction pathways were normal, and the rest of the drug screen was negative. However, you're forgetting another little feature in this guy's heart that was a lot more obvious cause of death."

He made a stabbing motion with his finger over the left side of his chest. "The slides of tissue samples along the needle track show extensive intracellular bleeding and none of the degenerative changes I'd expect to see if the needle went in postmortem."

In his own inimitable fashion Watts had made a clinical description of the stark way the DOA had died. The needle had gone into the beating, healthy heart of a very live man and then killed him, fast. The mechanical effect of the tip or something injected had stopped his heart cold. Either way, it was murder. The needle definitely hadn't gone in after he was dead. He had been killed just like Kingsly.

"Did you tell Bufort?"

"After our last encounter? Fuck him. I'm submitting my written report as required."

He surprised me; revealing nasty news to people bent on keeping their illusions was Watts's specialty. Besides, this morning Bufort had seemed pretty resigned about what Watts was going to find.

"Do you mind if I do?" I asked. Bufort needed to know as soon as possible.

He hesitated, then replied quietly, "Be my guest. By the way," he added, "I've called a few of our sister hospitals to see if anyone found cardiac needle tracks on any other DOAs, and I suggested that they keep their eyes open."

"My God! And did they?"

"They haven't had the chance. It seems the run has dried up for now." He gathered his magazine, stood up, and said, "Well, back to work." I watched him carry his tray to the rack by the door. He found a slot for it there, then smiled and gave me a parting wave. Always a teacher, he should have been restored from enlightening me. Instead, he looked worried.

Fernandez wasn't in his office. His secretary, dressed like Elvira, thought he'd gone home but wasn't sure and obviously didn't care.

My tactical plan exhausted, I decided to head home myself for an early dinner and movies with Doug's boys. I rescued my coat, which wasn't any drier, except now it smelled bad and hung on me like a wrinkled foreskin.

I peeked into emergency on my way out. I immediately wished I hadn't.

Sylvia Green's eyes were brimming with tears. The nurses went quiet at my entrance. Everyone focused on the floor. It was embarrassing. I waited. No one spoke. Sylvia started to look more mad than tearful, and for that I was grateful. But it was clear that I had to be the one to break the silence.

"Okay, everyone, what the hell is going on?"

The nurses looked at one another, but still no one said anything.

I turned to Sylvia. "Syl, are you all right?"

She looked at me and decided on angry. "No, I'm not all right!" she answered, her eyes flashing. Wrenching a chart off the wall, she strode down the hallway to her next patient.

The silence only got worse after she left.

"Look, I need to know what happened."

Lisa Gray, sheepish, offered, "It's the killings."

"What do you mean?"

She glanced at her friends for support. They continued to keep the floor under observation. Nevertheless, she went on. "Those two detectives, they got us all in a room and started asking a lot of questions."

Everybody got more intent on studying the floor, and I got angry. "What the hell's going on here?"

Silence.

"Lisa!" It was a plea.

"Okay. But promise you won't be mad."

"Lisa!" More like an order this time.

"Okay, okay! Like I said, they asked a bunch of routine questions. You know, how we work, how the shifts are arranged." She shrugged. "They asked about the doctors. At first it was innocent, how you guys work your shifts, who works when . . . that kind of stuff. Then they wanted to know who was really good with procedures, lines, that kind of thing."

" 'That kind of thing' include intracardiac injections?"

"Yes, but we didn't know they'd use any—"

"And you gave Sylvia's name."

"Well, you know how good she is," Lisa said defensively. "We're proud of her."

"Any other names you were proud of?"

"A few."

"Oh, Jesus, who?"

She hesitated.

"Lisa!"

"Popovitch, Kradic, Jones, and"—she took a breath—"and you."

Now I knew what had been bothering Susanne.

"It's okay about me. They're not interested anymore, but do the others know of the high honor you've accorded them?"

"No, just Sylvia."

"Why?"

"I guess she's the only one they questioned."

"Questioned! Here? While she was on duty?" I knew the interviews would be scheduled at the convenience of the police, but I'd naively assumed they'd start with off-duty doctors and conduct the sessions in private, not ambush a doctor trying to run the ER at the same time.

"No, not here. They took her to their interview room before her shift started. She told us what they asked about when she got back. That's the worst part—they asked about her mother's death."

I couldn't have heard right. "Her mother's death?"

She nodded, and the incredulity of the other nurses matched my own.

A year ago her mother had been admitted over Christmas with severe flu and aggravated heart disease. She'd come in with acute respiratory distress, cardiac failure, and chest pain. She was eighty-seven, and we prepared for the worst. To our surprise, she recovered and went home in a couple of weeks. Two days after that, she collapsed at home in acute pulmonary edema and arrested in the ambulance on the way back to the ER. When she got here, it was too late.

It wasn't that anyone had been negligent on discharge, but more could have been done. An echocardiogram to better assess the function of the heart and the use of an ACE inhibitor to reduce the load on the heart were options available but not taken.

The echo had a waiting list from budget cutbacks. The additional medication simply hadn't been thought about at the time.

While neither omission was cause for a lawsuit, Sylvia had been bitter. I'd held her hand while we sat together in the nursing station. She'd told me how her family had been prepared for her mother's death but gained hope again when she'd recovered, been discharged, and seemed to have beaten the odds.

At that moment Kingsly had gone stumbling by. Sylvia had looked at his lurching backside and started to sob. "That's the son of a bitch who cut the very echo time that might have made a difference. Maybe I could have had her a while longer. Just a little while."

I'd been unable to say anything then. Now I was furious that this moment would be used against her. And how did they know?

I spun out of the room and went down to the examining cubicle, where I found Sylvia dutifully preparing to repair a gaping facial cut on a young girl.

I waited until she finished replacing a dressing pad, then excused myself to the patient and led Sylvia out to the hall.

"Syl, I'm furious. Those cops were way out of line!"

"Damn right they were."

I put my arm around her shoulder and gave her a hug. "Listen, for what it's worth, I'll scream bloody murder to stop those jerks from harassing you and any of us around here."

She looked a little mollified. "Us?"

"Yep, they've been on my case since Monday. At least they were until someone tried to run me over yesterday."

"Oh my God! I thought it was an accident. Who was it?"

"I've no idea."

A slow, sardonic smile transformed the horrified expression on her face. "If that's what it takes to get clear, I'll settle for staying on the list."

"I need to ask you something. When your mom

died, who else did you mention Kingsly cutting the echo time to?"

Her mouth became a hard, thin line before she spoke. "Hurst!" she snarled.

I only half heard the PA as I walked out of the building. A code 44 was being called for nine west. Nothing unusual, a code 44 means a psychiatric disturbance and brings a gang of orderlies to restore peace, one way or another. I hear it announced a dozen times a day and never really pay attention.

It was 5:10, and the parking lot was already dark. In the distance, low rolls of thunder mixed with the drone of commuters heading home. The resultant grumbling noise made this daily evacuation seem more desolate than usual. The air was something to be chewed before breathing.

Lightning danced up the hospital walls, then left them invisible again in the black, but not before I glimpsed a lone bowed figure, like a cathedral gargoyle, on the roof of the west wing—the wing that had only eight floors.

Nine west was the roof.

The next flash caught a huddle of white figures creeping up behind the figure in the dark suit. In the dying illumination I saw the man step forward as calmly as if entering an elevator. The return to black enveloped his drop, but not even thunder could mask the wet, soft thud of his impact on the pavement ahead of me.

Fluttering down after him in the soft descent of a wounded cardinal was a wisp of scarlet. A flicker of lightning caught its brilliance until it landed and disappeared in the spreading ooze of mud and blood.

Chapter 13

The chief of psychiatry leaping off the roof of his own hospital was the lead story in all Buffalo's TV, radio, and newsprint media. Even the trashy tabloid *Police News* out of New York City, which usually focused exclusively on their own body count, led off page three with a wire photo of poor Gil's remains—only the feet poking from under a sheet, of course.

"Psychiatrist Jumps!"

"Suicide!"

"Killed!"

The stories underneath contained a spatter of quotes.

"He'd seemed distracted lately."

"He'd stopped caring about how he dressed."

"He hadn't looked well recently."

Now everyone was saying they'd known something, but no one had done anything. In medical circles we called it the retroscope, perfect hindsight.

I couldn't read the stories. I kept imagining that moment when his brain was still cognizant of onrushing cement and inevitable death was milliseconds away. Was there time for a final no?

Immediately the media recounted the details of Kingsly's murder they'd been reporting for nearly four days. Most of them hinted at the possibility of a connection between the two deaths and left the question tantalizingly up in the air. There was no mention of embezzlement so far, but it would be a while before our story even got off the front page or was relegated to the end of a newscast.

We buried Dr. Gil Fernandez that Sunday, and with him, Bufort buried his murder investigation.

The cemetery was a large green oasis around which the rest of the city sprawled. Covered with trees and slopes of mowed grass, it would have been the perfect place for families to have picnics—except there were a few centuries' worth of tombstones. Rich and poor, black, brown, and white, people whose ancestors had come from far continents; all lay at peace together. It was the inverse of the American ideal—men and women equal in death, not quite having managed it in life.

The questions I'd not had the chance to ask Fernandez thudded into my thoughts with each ritual toss of earth on the closed casket.

Was the money in the unexplained account that Bufort found actually the surplus that Fernandez had bragged about so often? Was that what Fernandez meant when he'd boasted that psychiatry paid its own way?

Was it dirty money, Gil? Otherwise, you would have stood up and proudly claimed responsibility for it and pulled Bufort back from a false lead. That's what I finally realized was missing from our last meeting together.

I also remembered Voyzchek requesting the emergency psych roster for last July. I'd thought it peculiar that she would ask us, because Fernandez drew up the psych on-call schedule. *But had she noticed something, Gil, and wanted to check it out behind your back? Obviously Bufort had, and when he announced he was looking closely at the salary pools, you knew you were going to get caught. For fraud.*

A man of God started some words. Some more dirt hit the coffin.

I thought I knew how it was done. It had to be with fee-for-service patients, and their care had to be government funded. Psychiatrists in a teaching center can bill both for patients they see themselves and patients the residents see in their name under their supposed supervision. So even legitimate billings to Medicare or Medicaid might not seem familiar to a psychiatrist looking at computer records six weeks later. They'd just put an unremembered session down to an uneventful supervision signed off to them by a resident. This happened a dozen times a week per psychiatrist. When billing records showed increased claims, no one would remember enough about the exact amount of their supervision activity to suspect an error. Supervision was sometimes done too much at a distance anyway, but residents liked the apparent autonomy. They got to play real doctor and erroneously rated staff who kept out of their way as "good teachers." And it suited the staff. If their billing statements showed they did a lot of this "teaching," in a university center it was the currency of tenure.

The secretaries for the salary pool would prepare and submit bills in the name of supervising psychiatrists, having power of signature in billing claims for the entire staff. *So, Gil, you could add hours of claims for sessions never done, hours per day per week per psychiatrist. With a staff of twelve, at a rate of one hundred an hour, and two to three bogus supervised hours a day per doctor per year, an extra million would be easy.*

A last handful of earth arched into the grave. A wisp of dust hung in the air, then vanished. The mourners had finished. The man of God hadn't. His words drifted in and out of my thoughts.

It could be done only in a salary pool, Gil, and only in a psych pool at that. Your docs would bring into the pool an annual income reflecting both their work with patients and money generated by supervised sessions. Out of this total, two-thirds would be paid back to the physicians as salary. The balance would be used to cover operating expenses. Even so, your docs would end up innocently taking home a little extra—and who questions a raise, or a year-end statement that shows increased productivity?

"Look what I'm worth," each would think, or *"I knew I was working harder."* The documented increase would be readily taken as a well-deserved pat on the back.

We were now in a moment of silence. A lone plane droned overhead.

Nor would Medicaid or Medicare officials handing out these funds call psych patients and ask for a detailed account of their treatments and the hourly breakdown. The bureaucrats got away with checking with Mr. Jones if indeed Dr. X had seen him on such-and-such a date for pneumonia, thus verifying the billing. But no way would the public tolerate bureaucrats delving into psychiatric matters, even at the excuse of avoiding fraud, such was still the stigma of mental illness. So they acted only on patient-generated complaints, and those would mostly be for some claim of abuse, usually sexual.

So, Gil, you could bill a little extra here, a little extra there, and as long as your staff didn't diddle the patients, you'd be safe.

But you got careless. I know now why Voyzchek wanted July's roster. Because she was on vacation then, had switched with someone at the last minute, had let us know, and found a substitute. But she probably hadn't changed your master list. As long as the roster's covered, none of us really keeps track of who's away. So you did your usual creative billing, including her name. She might not know how many hours she supervised, but she'd catch supervision billed to her while she was on the beach in Acapulco.

How did it start, Gil? The dashing champion of care daring to steal from the bureaucrats and deliver it to the healers? More funds for research? Special patient pro-

*grams and equipment? I'd like to think so; at least I'm
pretty sure it started that way.*

*If it had ended there, you wouldn't have chosen to die.
No, you would have been a hero—in trouble, but a hero.
You would have been a masked protector of the mentally
ill undoing the evil bureaucrat kings and rendering
better means of care to the sick. No, if it had ended there,
you would have stuck around, played Zorro against the
technocrats and basked in the glory of the docket, a
pulpit for your cause.*

But it obviously hadn't ended there.

The clouds begrudgingly shifted enough to let a needle
of sunlight through to our little graveside band and then
snapped it back.

Hunched in pain, an older version of Fernandez cried
silently. His hands were weathered. He had the leathery
look of a man who had worked outdoors most of his life,
probably to give his son the education that, till Gil Fernandez, I'd been told, no one in the family ever had.
Beside him, her face invisible under veils, erect and
silent, sat Fernandez's wife. She was surprisingly young
and slim-figured. I winced at the chilling mix of grief and
rage that came out of her stillness. I didn't know if Fernandez's mother was sedated somewhere, unable to bear
this, or long dead. I hadn't read the obit.

But the pity I felt for Fernandez's father and wife was
a fraction of what I felt seeing the horror and agony in the
hollow face of his young son. I estimated his age at ten or
eleven. He stood at the side of the grave, a brittle sen-
tinel, looking as if he were on the verge of speaking, of
calling his dad back. I felt no one in that sad huddle loved
or needed Fernandez more. Certainly no one had been
more betrayed than that poor boy. He would always
wonder why his dad had chosen to desert him so finally.
From the grave, Fernandez's suicide gave an answer the

boy would dodge all his life. "My love was enough for you. Your love was not enough for me."

I left that graveyard hating Fernandez.

It was Sunday morning and the traffic was sparse. The hospital was a twenty-minute walk, but anger would get me there in ten. I wanted the time alone.

During the service Hurst had quietly gone from chief to chief asking us to meet briefly in his office afterward and hear his strategy to get the hospital back to normal, starting tomorrow. It looked like he was giving condolences, but he was really counting on our respect for the family to prevent us from making a scene and telling him to get lost.

As I walked, I returned to my one-sided conversation with Fernandez.

It was probably Kingsly's strategy all along. He snagged you to play Zorro, and then he got you dirty.

Were the prints and etchings offered you as a tribute to your noble work and the service you were doing the hospital? He'd say, "You, more than anyone, both deserve and can appreciate a collection of fine art. Savor it. You've earned it."

But here, my dear psychiatrist, your ego bought a bill of goods, allowed your fantasy as superhero to excuse and explain going on the take.

And Kingsly had you; he owned your soul. Probably less and less of the pilfered money went to extra care, while more and more went to him. You must have hated him and feared that one night in a haze of booze he'd do something that would expose the scheme and your part in it. Is that why, at every meeting, every encounter, on record, you ran your boast that psychiatry gave back funds to the hospital? To warn him that he was also under your control and force him to at least make some show of funds back into research and patient care?

But your position was the more precarious. He had

what he wanted, a cash cow. You had lost what you thought justified larceny. The money going to research and treatment programs became a barely maintained trickle. Now most of what you stole went to a pathetic alcoholic who'd trapped you with your stupid ego and a moment of greed.

You probably didn't need a lot of time to figure your options when Bufort's investigation seemed poised to expose you. Hell, you'd been living with imminent exposure for years. I don't think it was being a thief or a fool that you couldn't live with. Even jail, if you got that far, I think you'd have taken.

No, I think what killed you was the automatic loss of your license to practice medicine ever again, the consequence of a criminal conviction. That, and the even more immediate loss of your reputation. The adoration of grateful patients would change to shock and outrage. Your articles would be relegated to trash cans the world over. They would never be refuted scientifically; no one would bother. It would just be that Gil Fernandez, world-famous psychopharmacologist, would now become "That fraud, convicted, in jail, on parole." And academic psychiatry would move on to its next hero.

I stopped at a streetlight and admitted I'd never know for sure how Fernandez had slipped and crossed the line that doomed him. But cross it he had.

The light changed. So'd my thoughts. I kept seeing the grief-stricken face of Fernandez's son and his hand reaching out and dangling empty at the grave's edge.

My own hands were fists in my raincoat pockets by the time I reached the hospital drive. I scowled my way through the stone arches and automatic doors. A security guard was too busy eating a doughnut to challenge my ID.

In the lobby, a gaunt old man was pushing his IV pole through the racks of get-well cards by the gift shop. The wheels made muted squeaks. My own steps cut through the echoing hush that settles over a hospital on weekends. It's a brief respite, a truce between the weekday hustle of white coats and shuffle of patients scurrying to endless probings and tests. Both sides need the pause before going back at each other Monday morning.

While I was waiting for the elevator, the old man's IV pole stopped its whimpering. He reached for a card and then studied it carefully. The racks were full of treacly verses; maybe he'd found one he hadn't seen before. The noisy arrival of the elevator rang through the lobby, and the old man looked up. His face and eyes were yellow. He watched me as I stepped in and in turn watched him through the closing doors. He looked terminal. He probably envied me for having a place to go.

My mood got no better walking the deserted corridors to Hurst's office. I couldn't help seeing Fernandez, stepping to oblivion, and that old man downstairs, clinging to his remaining moments when just a guy taking the elevator was an event.

As much as I was raging against Fernandez for betraying his son, and as readily as I could find him capable of fraud and a lethal mix of greed, shame, and pride, I couldn't go the rest of the way and label him a murderer. When a patient's condition was a mystery, when the residents were trying too hard to force an easy diagnosis onto symptoms and signs that didn't fit, I had an instinctive sense, developed over the years, that told me not to trust their conclusions. And now, with the same intangible intensity, I knew that Fernandez was not the killer.

This was Hurst's meeting, but when I entered, it was a victorious Bufort I saw strutting around the room.

"—obviously this case is closed," he trumpeted. "Since there won't be a trial, the hospital will be—"

"You're out of line!" I blurted out.

Everyone looked at me in surprise.

"We just buried Fernandez," I said hotly. "I watched his family at the graveside. I don't want to watch you dance a jig on his grave, Bufort."

"Dr. Garnet!" Hurst was horrified. The others glanced nervously at one another.

"And what are you doing here anyway?" I demanded. "We were told this was a meeting to agree on the best way to get St. Paul's back to normal." I was still standing, and Sean reached over to put his hand on my arm, trying to get me to sit down beside him.

"Detective Bufort is here at my request," answered Hurst. "The first step to help everyone move on from this tragedy is to explain what happened."

Bufort pompously held up his arm to me as if I were oncoming traffic. "Why, Dr. Garnet, you of all people should be grateful it's over. Fernandez tried to kill you and gravely injured your dog. Now, I understand how upset you are, but go home. It's over. You and your family are safe."

"Why did he try to kill me? It makes no sense!"

A Gallic shrug. "Perhaps Kingsly had secretly started to blackmail him while overtly being his partner in crime. He might have sent Fernandez anonymous letters, demanding money orders for cash, funneled through a series of post office boxes. Who knows? I've seen that method used many times before. In any case, Fernandez couldn't be sure it was Kingsly, but he'd certainly suspect him. He already had cause to feel it was too risky to let him go on, what with him drinking more and more. The chance of Kingsly babbling was just too great, so he killed him. Then you made some crack to Fernandez in the parking lot about finally checking the books." He stopped, stepped over to his briefcase, and lifted out a sheaf of papers. "I read that in your own report," he continued, holding the document up for the others in the room to see. "Suddenly Fernandez thinks he made a mistake. Thinks that you were the blackmailer all along, and that you'd probably heard Kingsly burble out the truth one drunken night. But now, in Fernandez's mind, you also could expose him for murder. You had to die, and fast."

I felt stunned. Bufort had taken the dictated report of my movements and conversations he'd insisted I write and was using it to dismiss my doubts. He'd even made sure he had it with him today. Given that I had little more than my instinct to go on, I was pretty easy to dismiss. He rushed on, waving my own statement at me, the better to demolish my protests.

"Already terrified, he feared his worst nightmare had come true. On impulse, he followed you out of town. He probably couldn't believe his luck, that you'd let yourself be so isolated, so vulnerable. If he were thinking right, he'd have realized that had you been the blackmailer and were willing to take on a murderer, you wouldn't have been so foolish. But he was probably in a panic. That chance comment about an audit confirmed you were dangerous and set him off."

He stopped, obviously enjoying the theatrical hush, and then delivered the denouement. "The first time at your cabin, the dog chased him off. The second attempt was better planned. You survived only by chance." He turned his back to me and added my report to a stack of files on Hurst's desk. He appeared done.

"Why a cardiac needle?" I asked quietly, slipping into a seat beside Sean.

Bufort whirled around. "Why not?" he snapped. "It nearly worked."

He glared at me. "It was pure luck you found the needle. It was his bad luck it broke off. Probably his original plan was to insert and withdraw, but Kingsly struggled, or convulsed as he died, and it snapped, just as you and Dr. Watts originally surmised."

"And what about the wino?"

His cheeks flushed. "Winos die, Doctor! You know this as well as I do, and no one makes a thing of it. And I suspect you never have before either."

"Because they don't die of cardiac needle stabs."

"Winos die with everything under the sun inside them. From drain cleaner to gasoline."

Mistake, Bufort, I thought. Now you're on my turf. "This guy's tox screen was clean."

He backed up. The expression on his face told me he wasn't about to get suckered into a slugfest with me on medicine.

"Quite right, Doctor, but didn't he have some medicines in him that we hear on TV not to take together because they stop the heart?"

Good move, Bufort. Reduce it to civilian medicine. If I clobber you here, I'll seem an arrogant prick.

I answered quietly. "The post showed that the needle killed him. The rest may have helped, but that needle went into a live man and stopped his heart."

"Fine, Doctor, then Fernandez killed that homeless man. Wherever he killed Kingsly, the derelict was hiding for the night. Too late, Fernandez realized he had a witness and got him as well. Later he moved the body out to an alley, and it was picked up as a DOA. Again it was you, Dr. Garnet, who told me homeless people sometimes sneak into the hospital to get out of the cold."

I sat there, speechless.

I glanced at the others. They were looking at their watches, shuffling their feet, shifting restlessly in their chairs. Someone murmured, "Come on, let's go. It's over." I heard similar mutterings behind me. Hurst nodded in agreement, almost encouraging the protests. If he'd organized this little show just to kill any arguments against Bufort's "solution" of the murders, he'd succeeded. The increasing unwillingness of everyone in the room to put up with any more of my questions proved that.

Bufort quietly gave me the coup de grâce. "Haven't bag ladies and derelicts been found on cold nights hiding in stairwells and in the basement to keep warm?"

I didn't answer, but he wasn't about to let me stay silent. "Haven't they, Dr. Garnet?"

"Yes," I conceded.

With operatic show, Bufort finished putting his papers away. "I want to thank you for your cooperation in this difficult time. Without your help, I—we wouldn't have been successful."

I nearly pointed out that in our profession, a man's brains all over the parking lot is not a success. I looked over to Watts, but he gave a me a dismissive wave. There'd be no mention here of checking other dead street people for signs of intracardiac stab wounds. The others in the room began pushing their chairs back from the table. They all wanted out of there. So did I.

As the meeting broke, I saw Riley standing in the doorway, his jaw muscles working overtime. When I got near, the side of his face relaxed and he seemed about to say something to me. Instead, he glanced at Bufort, stepped aside, and let me leave the room. I was halfway down the hall when Hurst's call from behind made me wince. "Dr. Garnet, could I see you a minute?"

He hurried along the corridor, pulling on his coat as he came up to me. I knew he often used the walk to the lobby after a meeting for a conversation he didn't want to be official or recorded in a set of minutes. "I've canceled elective activities tomorrow as part of the memorial to poor Kingsly," he began to say, falling into stride beside me. "That means you can have surgical beds for emergency until Tuesday, providing, of course, your staff withdraws their threat to withhold service."

I'd expected this. It meant Hurst's hospital lawyers hadn't found a way to prevent us from shutting down emergency—yet. This was to buy time until they could.

"Of course."

He stopped walking. My ready agreement must have caught him off guard. Until I turned to him and added, "For the duration of the day's memorial to poor Kingsly."

Had he been anatomically equipped with venom and fangs, I'd have been looking for shots. As it was, I left him standing there, narrowing his eyes and making do with his lizard imitation while I continued down the hall. When I reached the next corner, I looked back and saw him still watching me.

I'd bought a day of respite for emergency, but I wondered what I'd bought for myself.

I took the stairs down to the main entrance on the ground floor, but even on a Sunday, I couldn't leave the hospital without walking over and checking the ER. On my way, I wondered about Hurst and Bufort's curious need for quick closure on the murders. I guessed each had different reasons—Bufort because he had no one but Fernandez to blame the murders on; Hurst because he wanted the scandal over with . . . or because he was the killer.

When I stuck my head in the door, I saw Jones down the hall and overheard her quietly reassuring a very relieved-looking older woman that her son would be okay. The young man on the stretcher beside them was about thirty and didn't appear too bad, but he was hooked up to a portable monitor, IVs, and an oxygen tank for the transfer to the ICU. The nurses were putting away the crash cart.

"What's up?" I asked the charge nurse, who was standing at the nurses' station.

"Another one of Jones's miracles," she said appreciatively. "He's a dialysis patient who came in with florid pulmonary edema. I don't know how she did it, but she kept him alive until the renal guys got here and dialyzed him."

She was obviously impressed, and so was I. Not many in the department were both good and aggressive enough to pull it off. I watched Jones give a final reassuring pat to the man's mother, a few more supportive words to the patient himself, and then start back toward where the charge nurse and I were standing. The contented smile she was wearing faded a bit on seeing me, and I started feeling my usual ambivalence toward her.

"Beautiful work, Valerie," I said quickly. "Congratulations!"

Despite the praise, she seemed genuinely, but not pleasantly, surprised to see me here on my day off.

"I just dropped in after a meeting," I explained without waiting for the question. I wanted to make sure she didn't think I was checking on her.

She hesitated, then started to smile again. "Thanks" was her only reply. She moved over to the work counter and started writing up her chart.

"She's a wonderful doctor." It was the man's mother passing us as she followed her son's stretcher to the ICU.

"Yes, she is," I replied, finding it hard to reconcile the decisive clinician I'd just witnessed with the departmental brat she could sometimes be. Yet the only medical criticism I could make against her was that like most prima donnas, she was less enthusiastic about the smaller cases and left them more to the residents. I sometimes worried what subtle but serious problems might get overlooked this way, but in her case, so far, nothing of consequence had happened. Ironically, during the entire eight years she had worked at St. Paul's, not once had I ever gotten a complaint about her behavior from a patient or a patient's family. No one else, not even I, had that clean a record. I guess, with them, she was in control, and therefore secure.

"Everything else okay?" I asked the back of her head while she continued to write. I really didn't want an answer.

I didn't get one.

I reminded myself I hadn't called her in about Todd yet, but today—after Fernandez's funeral and while she was on duty—definitely wasn't the time. I promised myself once more I'd do it tomorrow.

I left the hospital and located my car in the parking lot.

Under the windshield wiper I found a card. Written on the back was "Please meet me at the Horseshoe Bar in thirty minutes."

It was not signed, but on the front was the logo of the Buffalo police, and printed on the bottom, "Detective G. Riley."

The Horseshoe was near the hospital, but it was a place I'd rarely visited. Ten years before we'd get a stabbing victim from that bar nearly every weekend, usually drug related. It was a student hangout for the university, but it wasn't a watering hole for philosophy and suds like I'd known in the sixties. Kids went there to score hard drugs. I'd learned my toxicology on pretty teenagers with a thousand-dollar-a-week habit from this place. I'd asked one of those girl-women how she managed it. I'd just resuscitated her from a deluge of pills, cocaine, and booze. She'd been brought in naked and unconscious. Her body was young, breasts and hips maturing at odds with her still-present baby fat. After I intubated her and lavaged out her stomach, she was a bedraggled, coughing mess of vomit and the charcoal used to neutralize whatever she'd downed. Yet her face held the pudgy features of the little girl she'd once been.

"How do you pay for it?"

The hard eyes that flashed back were older than I'd ever want to be.

"Guess!" she dared.

A year later I'd pronounced her dead on arrival. By then she'd become so wasted I didn't even recognize her until I saw my note from a year earlier in her chart. The stillness of her parents when I told them in our grieving room chills me still. There was not a move of either the father or mother toward each other, nor any show of feeling. The father, my age, had coldly signed for the body and left. The mother, dark like her daughter but with a face set hard long ago, walked out stiffly a few minutes later.

Now the drug wars had spread throughout the neighborhood. The stabbings and ODs came from everywhere.

The Horseshoe, its job done, had gentrified itself. The owner had put in a few plants, added some mirrors, and updated the green walls to a dark tone seen in a lot of home digests this year. It hid the blood and fitted the nineties, but it didn't do it for me.

As I entered, the stench of cigarette smoke mingled with the odor of stale beer. Four guys in raincoats at a booth looked me over as my eyes adjusted to the pink neon that lit the place. They looked like police, or soldiers for one of the gangs. Gloomy veterans from one side or the other toasting old battles and what-if's. Riley was alone at the bar.

"This place still active?" I asked as I joined him.

"Only for old cops and crooks. Kind of a club. Has-beens telling lies and drinking booze to dull the memory. What'll you have, Doc?"

Hell. It had not been a good day. I needed something strong. "A Black Russian would be most welcome."

Riley looked relieved and approving. I guessed he felt more relaxed with a guy who took a real drink.

He caught the bartender's eye, a bodybuilder in a black T-shirt wearing a ponytail. He ordered doubles and downed the remnants of the amber rocket fuel he'd nursed waiting for me.

The drinks arrived. We both stirred, sipped appreciatively, and settled back to face each other.

I started. "What's up?"

He took another sip. My first was still burning its way down my belly, reminding me I hadn't had lunch.

Finally he began. "To start, I'd like to keep this meeting confidential and unofficial."

"Why?" I already knew, but I wanted him to say it, still unofficially, of course.

He took a sip, raised his eyebrows, and went on. "Because my boss is a brilliant prima donna prick, and if he knew I was doing an end run round his legendary judgment, he'd put me back on the street directing traffic."

I smiled at his candor and toasted it with another sip. More burning. I remembered I hadn't even had breakfast.

"I can't ignore the questions you raised earlier," Riley said. "Your uneasiness with pinning the murders on Dr. Fernandez leaves *me* uneasy." He paused, sipped, and continued. "Have you got anything hard you can give me to back up your doubts?"

The glass was cold in my hand. The ghosts of all those pathetic kids who had poisoned themselves here were making me colder.

"No," I admitted.

"Why are you so sure he didn't kill Kingsly and the wino, just like Bufort claims? He had the motive. You know we found the artwork hidden in the attic of

Fernandez's cottage. His wife told us it had been hanging in their home until a few months before, when he suddenly cleared it out and claimed to have sold it."

"Because murder, for him, doesn't make sense. Fraud, arrogance, and greed, yes. Then shame and a loss of face, that I buy too."

I stopped and looked around the deserted bar, then back at Riley. "And there was the search of my office at home. Fernandez didn't need anything from me. Hell, what he had to fear was in Kingsly and Laverty's files. You guys found them."

That was it. The biggest incongruity of all. I leaned toward Riley. "If Fernandez killed Kingsly for fear of exposure, why didn't he search the files then and there and destroy what ultimately nailed him? The chaos of financial records in this place is legendary; nothing would have been missed. Why didn't he search when he was alone in Kingsly's office, middle of the night, after supposedly killing him and moving the body there?"

"Maybe he did and couldn't find them."

"How hard was it for you guys?"

"What do you mean?"

"For you to find the anonymous account and the art receipts. How long?"

"Well, not too long. Remember, we didn't know what we were after, and everything was such a mess anyway, but it took a few days."

I sat stirring my drink. Fernandez would have known what he was looking for. But he also would have known the confusion of records might make it hard for even him to dig out the incriminating material. No, he couldn't count on even a hurried hour alone at night producing what he had to destroy to be safe. And what about Thomas Laverty? Surely as director of finance he was in on the embezzling as well? Wouldn't he have to be silenced?

Riley prodded gently, "I'd like you to let me in on your thoughts."

I smiled. Exactly what I always said to residents struggling to find the "right answer." I wanted to hear their process as well as their conclusion.

"Okay," I agreed. "Fernandez didn't kill Kingsly, at least not hurriedly without a better chance of it kicking up what Fernandez really needed, Kingsly's evidence. Fernandez would have had to destroy those records and therefore needed time to find them. And to be consistent, if he was going to murder Kingsly to cover up their scheme, he probably would have needed Laverty dead as well, but there isn't a hint of that kind of logic here. From Fernandez's point of view, stabbing Kingsly with a cardiac needle and dumping him nude in his own office just doesn't make sense; it wouldn't achieve the result Fernandez would be after. Why not just make Kingsly disappear or, better still, search the office first, over several nights maybe, until he found the evidence, and then make him disappear?"

"Maybe he was doing that," answered Riley. "Kingsly staggers in, nude from a prowl, catches Fernandez in the midst of the search, and Fernandez grabs the nearest weapon at hand and stabs him."

"Come on, a psychiatrist doesn't carry cardiac needles around. Hell, nobody does. They're kept on a crash cart for arrests and in surgery." Then I smiled. "Besides, Detective, you're forgetting, there was no blood in his office. He was killed elsewhere."

Riley gave me a grin. "Just checking, Doc. You amateur sleuths have gotta be kept on your toes." He began waving his empty glass around to catch the bartender's eye. I was looking around the lounge again. They once sat here, all those ODs. "Empty chairs at empty tables." It was a phrase from the musical *Les Misérables*.

Except these dead students had poisoned themselves.

Then I had it. "Poison!"

My outburst startled Riley. "Poison?" He was perplexed. He gave a guilty glance at his still-unfilled tumbler and quickly replaced it on the bar.

"Yeah, Kingsly wasn't poisoned."

He frowned at me. "So? We know that."

"Precisely." I paused, then leaned forward, enjoying this. It's amazing what a few sips of a Black Russian with no breakfast can do. I lowered my voice. Cheap melodrama, but hey, I don't get out much. "If Fernandez had murdered Kingsly, he would've poisoned him."

Now the detective was looking interested.

"Elaborate for me."

"Fernandez was a psychopharmacologist."

"Huh?"

"Sorry. That means he has special expertise in psychiatric drugs. More, he was a renowned researcher and was studying a number of new, unreleased drugs. He investigated their effects, therapeutic and toxic, as well as their properties when mixed with other medications or, better yet, with each other."

"Better yet?"

"Better yet to murder with."

My Black Russian no longer burned. Or maybe my stomach was numb. Riley didn't even notice the bartender slip a refill in beside his elbow.

"Look, some of his studies found drugs too toxic to be released. I'm sure he found mixtures of drugs that were particularly lethal. Approved tricyclics used to treat depression can cause cardiac arrest when taken in excess. Who knows what other toxic effects he discovered in experimental drugs never released for public use? And while these formulas would be available to him for research, they would never be part of a pathology tox screen. A drinker like Kingsly would be a perfect target. But first Fernandez would find the evidence he wanted, then he'd coax Kingsly to take his favorite but final beverage. Heart attack, and who needs needles?"

Riley leaned back. He rolled his glass back and forth between his hands as if he were trying to make fire. I knew he was also rolling my scenario around in his head.

I downed my drink, waiting for his verdict.

Finally he stopped rotating the glass, and I figured the movement in his head had stopped too. "You must be very careful, Doc." He spoke quietly—too quietly. He then went on to say what even I, Black Russian and all, was just figuring out.

"If you are right, and I'm afraid what you say makes more sense than the conclusions of the genius *I* work for, out there is a killer who thinks Fernandez's suicide has closed the case. Right now this killer feels safe, which means for now, you're safe. However, the instant you voice these doubts, all that changes. This killer will feel threatened again, and you, sir, will be a target again."

Chapter 14

It was only 1:30 when I left the Horseshoe. The afternoon light had dimmed to premature dusk. I hadn't seen the sun in weeks and knew how the dinosaurs must've felt at the end. Maybe we were having an eclipse. Hell, was there even still a sun out there behind all those clouds?

Riley had done the bureaucratic shuffle as far as I was concerned. He'd made it clear he'd enjoy taking on his boss, but it was also clear that I'd have to provide him with more than hunches to get him to do it.

As I got back to the hospital grounds the rain began falling again. It was cold, and the drops were like sludge on my glasses.

I paused by my car and realized I had nothing to do for the rest of the day. I wanted to see Janet, but she was on call at her hospital. I unlocked the driver-side door, slipped the key in the ignition to activate my car phone, and dialed the case room. They informed me Dr. Graceton was busy in the OR. I called the vet and learned Muffy was sedated, afebrile, but still fragile. So, I couldn't even drive over and give comfort to my dog.

I sat staring out the windshield stained with rain. Without the women in my life, I was at loose ends. The parking lot was foggy, and I couldn't see past the few cars parked nearby.

But out there, somewhere, was a killer. Was I safe for

now? Maybe. Maybe not. Probably not. Not until I figured out why I'd ever become a target. Fact was, I still didn't even know how to "be careful," as everyone advised.

Again I thought of the ER stats. If I was a threat because of some information hidden in the those studies, then I wasn't safe at all.

It wasn't only because I loved an excuse to go to the cabin that I did my computer work there. I was so electronically stupid that Carole wouldn't let me use our office computer unless she was physically present. I'd once crashed a complete hard disk attempting to find something on my own. Since then she wouldn't even trust me with the pass code. She routinely duplicated all departmental information with a separate set of disks formatted specifically to work on my clunker at the cabin. I knew how to work the routine programs for the terminals at the nursing station. In fact, any innovations there were tried on me, on the principle that if I could do it, anyone could. But getting into the hospital network without Carole to guide me, code or no code, was beyond my trying. Yet I didn't want to call her in to help. This wasn't going to be the conventional analysis of QA data she'd helped me with two days ago. Now I was going to use those numbers to go after a killer. She'd have to work along with me and know what I was doing, and until I figured out what was going on, I wasn't about to endanger her or anyone else.

To be alone in the woods on this shrouded weekend was not a soothing thought, but I needed my own computer again. If I was going to unravel anything today in private, it would be in front of that forgiving relic in my beloved cabin. I pocketed my keys, got out of my car, and headed toward my office. The QA material was still in my trunk, but I needed some other disks for an idea I was getting.

I stopped by the coatroom to check my mailbox. Behind the coat racks was a wall of open mail slots, each with a doctor's name over it. For once I could see easily into mine. Usually the slot above, which was Jones's, was so stuffed, the overflow flopped in front of mine. Today hers was empty. Mine held a notice for a hospital bake sale.

Emergency was bustling, but the nurses were smiling. A steady stream of orderlies and nurses were pushing gurneys along the corridor to the elevators that would empty those patients into real beds upstairs. Hurst's beds, finally. The vacated hallways and stretcher stalls had the debris from a week of crowded living. It looked like the morning after a wild party. A small group of cleaning people waited to move in.

"Congratulations, Chief!" It was Sylvia, in for the evening shift, but three hours early.

The nurses echoed their relief at the reprieve. I didn't tell them it was only for a day.

"Where's Jones?" I asked. She should still be on.

"She got a phone call, some personal business. She asked if I could come in early. Baby was asleep. Daddy was sitting around; no sense both of us watching the angel. Besides, someone has to put her through college."

Graceful as usual. I knew she'd love to have spent a few extra hours just watching their new daughter. Like most older parents, she and her husband treasured the additional joy of affirming and reaffirming that "Yes, it's finally, really true." I wondered if Jones's lonely life left her incapable of realizing what she cost others.

The call came minutes after I'd entered my office. "Dr. Garnet, you're wanted two-three in the morgue."

I needed a second to get it. "This is a joke, right?"

"No, sir. Call came a few seconds ago. Said you were

in your office and wanted you called, to come down two-three."

"Who?"

"They didn't say."

"Why?"

"Just said it was urgent."

A 2-3 call would get me running, normally, no questions asked. But this was weird. A macabre joke in hospitals is about mistakenly sending a live one to the morgue. Had one of Watts's tenants suddenly sat up?

"Sir, are you going?"

"Yes, operator, but have security meet me there right away."

I grabbed my stethoscope and was out the door and halfway through emergency before I saw a nurse.

"Sandy, grab the resus cart and meet me in the morgue!"

She was taken aback. Obviously she also presumed this was a bad joke.

"I mean it!" I snapped, and headed for the door. I grabbed a ventilator mask and intubation gear hanging there for resuscitations off the premises.

The stairwell was empty for my run to the basement. The echoes of my own steps followed me down. I had a bad feeling about this. The only way someone could have known I was in my office at that minute on a Sunday afternoon was by watching.

The thin line of overhead bulbs led off into the distance toward Watts's lab. No one else should be here on a weekend, but I listened and peered down that string of light pools inviting me farther in. I had thoughts of a spider and a fly. I took a breath, remembered with relief that a security guard and a nurse were on their way, and picked up my pace.

The anteroom was just a pocket off the hallway right in front of the lab doors. Two stretchers were parked on either side of the narrow passage. There were no bulbs suspended above this area, but there was enough light from the hallway behind to show me that one of the stretchers was occupied. To me, the shrouded figure was more suggestive of death than an uncovered corpse would have been. Obviously Watts planned a weekend dissection. I edged my way around the body and approached the lab entrance. To my right was the heavy wooden door of the walk-in freezer, where bodies waiting to be picked up are kept. It was ajar. Instinctively, I clicked it shut. My mother had always taught me to close the refrigerator. Ahead were the double swinging doors to the dissection room. Light seeped under the sill. I knocked, feeling foolish, especially for still keeping an eye on the sheeted figure behind me.

"Hello? Anyone there? Robert?"

There was no reply, but coming from inside the lab I could hear a fast, steady beeping that was familiar, yet out of place.

I opened the door and stepped into the bright interior.

Watts was spread-eagled on his own autopsy table, naked from the waist up, white, not breathing, and wired to a portable monitor. He had a large bruise on the side of his head, but it was his sightless stare, the wet mark at his crotch, and the stench of fresh excrement that told me he was clinically dead. The jagged run of ragged peaks across the monitor screen meant ventricular fibrillation. I could still bring him back.

At the far end of the counter that surrounded the room a tap was open full, and water was sloshing over the edge of the sink, spilling onto the floor. Damn, but the place would be flooded soon. What the hell was going on? I didn't have time for that question—or anything else, if I was going to save Robert.

Quickly, but still moving carefully so as not to slip on the wet floor, I stepped to the monitor and grabbed the paddles. They were already greased, and the machine was charged to 360 joules, ready to fire. None of this made sense. But my training took over. Though hardly necessary, I checked his neck pulse and verified its absence. I placed the paddles at the appropriate landmarks on the chest and got ready to attempt to recapture a normal heart rhythm with a jolt of direct current. These moves in preparation for discharge were automatic. I leaned over Watts to assure a good electrical contact, but inside I was recoiling. What monster had set this up, made Watts a specimen, like a drill dummy, and then readied everything to lead me through his resuscitation like a training exercise?

Positioned, not even having to think about it, I moved my thumbs over the red discharge buttons. Even though I was alone, I automatically glanced around the table. We give our residents holy hell if they miss taking a look around and calling "stand back" to prevent a member of the team who may still be touching the patient from getting shocked. This omission can result in having two cardiac arrests to deal with. In spite of myself, to no one I muttered, "Stand back." The harsh dissecting light glinted off the steel surface of the autopsy table and the wet floor as I completed my look around. Maybe that glint was what broke my unthinking rush through the steps.

"Shit!" I shouted, slapping the paddles back in their holders as if they were snakes.

I had to insulate him—and myself—from the water and steel. An uninsulated shock would hit me and stop my own heart.

Far off down the hall I heard the distinctive crashing noise our elevator makes to announce its arrival. Then came the excited chatter of the security guard and Sandy running down the long tunnel pushing a squeaky resuscitation cart.

To buy time, I positioned Watts's head, sealed his lips with my own, and gave him two quick breaths. Then I moved my hands to his midchest and gave fifteen brisk compressions. At one moment I felt the dry snap of his ribs, but if he lived, I knew he'd forgive me. It took three cycles of this before Sandy and a puffing, fat security guard pulled the cart inside the room.

"Sandy, call a ninety-nine. You, sir, we've got to insulate him, and us." I was speaking between puffs. Watts's chest rose each time I blew into his lungs. "Grab that backboard!"

The guard moved to the cart. On it was a folded six-foot board for lifting people with back injuries. Sandy made the call, then came to Watts's side. She started pumping his chest. That left me free to assemble the bag and mask, slip in a curved airway to keep his tongue from blocking his throat, and start ventilating him. The guard wrestled the board to the table. Sandy pumped. I bagged. The rigors of giving compressions loosened a few buttons on Sandy's blouse. She wasn't wearing a brassiere. The guard slipped on the floor trying for a better angle.

"Okay, here's what we'll do." I got his attention away from Sandy. "On three, we'll stop, roll him toward us, and you'll slip the board under him."

We got the count right, but rolling Watts on the narrow table nearly dropped him over the edge. The guard dinged the overhead light and then nearly hit me trying to get the board into position while watching the developments of Sandy's blouse. With our feet sliding in the water and all three of us pushing Watts onto the board, we landed on his stomach, but at least the board was between Watts and the metal table.

"Right, Sandy, keep pumping." I kept bagging. The guard kept ogling.

"You!" I snapped. "Quit that crap." He went red.

Sandy rolled a stare of contempt his way but kept quiet and continued pumping.

"We have to insulate our feet!" I ordered. "We're still too wet to shock him. Turn off the water, then go out to the hallway and grab a mattress from a stretcher. Hurry!"

I was watching the monitor. The ragged activity persisted, but it was weaker. We were running out of time.

The guard went without protest. He didn't seem to mind that he'd be alone with a corpse out there.

Sandy was getting flushed and breathing hard.

"You want to switch?" I asked her.

"No! Just keep that bozo away from me."

"You're just too sexy when you save a life."

"Creep. Watch it or I'll tell Janet."

The banter. Whistling past the reaper.

While pumping, she took a look around the room. "What's the story here?"

I kept bagging. "I don't know. I found him like this."

"Like this!" The surprise interrupted her rhythm.

The guard stumbled in the door with the mattress and plopped it at our feet.

We stepped up on it. I took a final glance at the monitor; the tracing was a mere flicker. I reached for the paddles, placed them, and glanced around. "All clear!" Sandy stopped pumping and stood back, still on the mattress. I pressed the red buttons.

The charge arched Watts's back. He smacked back down on the board like a slab of sirloin hitting a butcher block. But I was watching the monitor. The zigzags flattened into a wandering straight line, nothing else. "Come on, Watts, come on!" Still a flat line. The steady whine of the machine mocked our effort.

"Shit! Keep pumping."

Sandy resumed chest compressions.

"Grab that high stool over there," I told the guard.

He dragged it over. "Up you go, Sandy. You'll have more downward force on your push."

I squeezed four full puffs of air into Watts, then dropped the bag and foraged in the cart for an ET tube and a working laryngoscope. I found the size I wanted, flicked the blade of the scope open to activate the light, and stepped to Watts's head.

"Hold it, please!" I ordered.

Sandy stopped pressing down on his chest. The guard held his breath. I scissored Watts's mouth open with the fingers of my right hand, inserted the blade with my left, and slid it back to the base of his tongue. There were the cords, clear, no vomit. I threaded them with the tube. The monitor was barely quivering now, almost flat. "Okay, pump."

Sandy moved to compress, and I'd just hooked up the bag to give more air, when we heard the first beep, and a healthy complex leaped to the screen. "Hold on," I said quietly. This would be it. A few salvos and then death was sometimes all we got. Another beep, another complex, then more line, then another beep. "Any pulse with that?"

Sandy touched his neck. A beep came and went; she shook her head and started pumping again.

"He needs help." I grabbed three ampules of Adrenalin, drew them into a syringe, and emptied it down the ET tube. Then I bagged that little cocktail home. There was another beep, then a line again. I heard loud clanking at the door. Our 99 summons was beginning to produce help. The respiratory technician struggled in with oxygen tanks, saw Watts, and silently hooked up his cylinders. In seconds he took over the ventilation, bagging pure oxygen into the lungs instead of air. "What happened?"

"I don't know."

Beep, then another, then a few staggered beats, then,

like a car in winter, they started and kept coming in a
steady, regular stream.

"Yes!"

"A pulse."

"Great."

"We got him!"

Sandy dived into the cart to start an IV. "Put some
Xylo through that, will you, Sandy? Seventy bolus and
two a minute drip?"

A resident touched my arm. "Earl, did you inflate the
cuff?"

I hadn't. "Sorry, is it leaking?"

He answered by injecting a syringe full of air through
a catheter running down the outside of the tube in
Watts's trachea. This would inflate a small balloon
around the tube and block any oxygen from escaping
instead of going on down to the lungs.

Two more residents charged in.

"Pull some bloods and a gas, you two," I said.

I moved to take Watts's pressure. Not bad. Hundred
over sixty, and getting stronger.

Ever-increasing numbers of residents, nurses, and students swarmed over the now-alive Watts, securing lines,
slipping in catheters, hooking up monitors, and cleaning
up spilled blood and other bodily fluids. He even began
to look a little pink, but he needed a respirator. Whether
or not he still had a brain was the real question.

Stewart Deloram from the ICU arrived. I gave him the
story of the resuscitation, added I'd just found him, and
left out the peculiar details. He slipped the strap of the
portable defibrillator over his shoulder, and I stood back
as the whole chattering, caring collection clanked and
bumped their way out the door. I followed them into the
hallway and watched the stretcher shrouded in a web of
IVs and winking monitors recede through the dark like a

departing train. They reached the end of the corridor and turned into the elevator.

Alone, I stood in the antechamber. Dripping noises were coming from the dissecting room behind me. I felt a coolness at my side and turned to find the freezer door open again, this time wide enough that I could see the interior. All the racks were empty. I was about to close it when I noticed a bunch of half-melted boot prints outlined in the frost on the floor just inside. I leaned against one of the stretchers. It held a stained, rumpled sheet. It took a few seconds before I remembered that twenty minutes earlier, on my way into the morgue, the stretcher had held a corpse.

A quick call to the nursing supervisor, Mrs. Quint, confirmed my growing fear. No one had died in the last twenty-four hours. No autopsies were scheduled for the weekend.

"So far," she added, probably thinking of Watts. "By the way, good work." She paused, then asked, "Is it true what Sandy told me, about you finding him, hooked up and all?"

I didn't know what to say. Tales of missing corpses and hidden killers were not going to assuage Hurst's attempts to keep me categorized as the resident nut.

I minimalized. "I don't know who called me, but whoever found him and hooked him up probably was goofing off and shouldn't have been down there. Maybe a smoker." I waited to read the silence on how this was going over. It was a pretty skeptical silence. I tried putting her on the defensive. "Maybe a nurse," I added softly.

I heard her breath hiss in. "Now, really, Dr. Garnet, you've no call to implicate my girls and boys." Some of her "girls" were forty-eight-year-old women, her "boys" about the same age, and too many of them still snuck off to smoke since cigarettes had been totally banned. At least we were arguing about who was goofing off and I wasn't having to explain killers and corpses.

I let her run on, then picked my spot and made my pitch. "Look, relax. What I'm saying is, it was probably one of your 'girls' who saved Dr. Watts's life, and she can't come forward about it."

The silence returned. It held a "maybe."

I pushed. "*Whatever* she or he was doing down here, that person's a hero."

More silence. She knew I'd just inferred her "girls" and "boys" sometimes did other secret deeds in hidden places besides illicit smoking. Sometimes the cigarette was included, after. Long ago, as a resident, I'd had my own induction to these liaisons, and, a half century ago, so probably had Mrs. Quint.

"Amazing" was her only comment, and then she hung up.

I'd made the call from the wall phone in Watts's lab. As I replaced the receiver, it dawned on me I might have smudged fingerprints left on it by the person who had called locating. But now I wanted out. With the dark corridor outside the door, the weight of the hospital over my head, and my second near-miss, I began to get the creeps.

An unknown killer was still hunting me, already setting up the next attack. Was it Hurst? But what did he care about ER stats? Had it been Kradic? He'd know how to set up Watts, but he had no connection with Kingsly. Yet he would have a connection with the ER data. For that matter, could it be someone else in the ER? I began to wonder if maybe, just maybe, Kingsly's death and the ER stats were completely unrelated. I had to get away—had to run. My breathing was openmouthed, and I kept trying to find some saliva for my dry tongue, but fear wouldn't have it. We learned as students in physiology how the adrenaline response mustered a fight-or-flight syndrome. I was all flight.

But I made myself do one last thing: I went to the edge of the locker and kneeled to see the boot marks better. At first they seemed indistinct and blurred together, but the warmer air through the open door increased the icy condensation over the prints and made them clearer. I could see two definite sizes.

Then I started out. The nearer I got to the stairwell leading up to light and air, the faster I moved. I heard nothing in the dark behind me, but I straight-armed the door leading to the steps and went up three at a time.

Adrenaline, we were also told, gives us a sense of impending doom. I was getting a good dose. That, and a full-blown panic attack.

I blew out of the stairs and halfway across the hospital front lobby before I pulled up to a trot. The same lone man, tethered to his IV, and the gift shop lady, equally elderly, gawked together at my noisy entrance. I could see her thinking "escaped psych patient," but before she could reach for a phone, I waved my stethoscope at her. "It's okay, I'm a doctor," I said, and made for the ER. "Emergency," I called after me, and felt like an idiot.

I managed to reach my office without the nurses getting a good look at what must have been a white and sweaty face. Had they, I would have found *myself* tied to a monitor and en route to the CMU. Instead, I pulled an old paper bag out of our recycling box and started breathing into it. I don't know how long it had been there, but it still held a faint odor of onions and something fishy. Nevertheless, rebreathing my own carbon dioxide began to slow my heartbeat and alleviate the numb tingling in my fingers. I've treated hundreds of patients with panic attacks, but now I know why they all think they're going to die.

My own chest finally lightened up by thirty pounds, and my breathing slowed. Okay, I thought, I'm okay.

Then the fish smell and my own stress got me, and I barfed into the bag.

"The horny-nurse story will make more sense to Bufort than a killer still running around." It was Riley over the phone. After cleaning up my mess, I had decided, for the record, to report what happened. In case I could ever prove any of this, I wouldn't be nailed for withholding evidence.

I'd figured the shrouded body back at the morgue was alive and well as I slipped by it heading in to find Watts. The open freezer might have held a couple more buddies, all ready to finish me off if I didn't zap myself first. I'd inadvertently shut them in on my way past. They were wearing boots, probably rubber, to protect themselves from the water if they had to "help me" fibrillate myself. Their shrouded buddy was likely letting them out to come in after me when the noisy elevator door announced Sandy's arrival and scared them off.

Riley interrupted these musings. "Or more to the point, he'll like it a lot better than admitting he was wrong."

"I know," I replied curtly. "Just memo this, will you? So if anything comes of it, I'm officially on record as having reported it."

Riley didn't answer right away. Perhaps he sensed how fed up I was with his reluctance to defy his boss, or maybe he was thinking over the politics of my request. "You got it, Doc," he said finally, but I suspected he'd probably forward the message to Bufort through channels, knowing full well it'd be lost there for weeks. "And, Doc—"

I waited.

He finally asked, "Why did they want Watts?"

"He was bait to get me" was my immediate reply, but I remembered something more. It was so speculative that I was hesitant to tell Riley.

He sensed my holding back. "Okay, Doc, let's have it."

I felt reluctant, but added, "Watts had started phoning around to the other ERs to see if any of them had noticed unexplained cardiac needle tracks on their DOAs."

After a few seconds of silence, he asked, "What did he find?"

"He didn't find out anything. The run has apparently dried up."

"Still, Doc, it's a hell of a thought."

"Are you willing to follow it up?" I demanded.

I could almost hear the lid snap shut on his own moment of speculation. "Like you said," he replied coldly, "Watts didn't find out anything."

I was about to hang up in disgust.

"Okay," he added after a few seconds, "obviously I was wrong. Someone is still coming at you."

No kidding, I thought bitterly. He was my best bet on the police force, but I wondered if someone else would have to die before he'd risk insubordination and stand up to Bufort.

"I'll alert a patrol car in your neighborhood," he continued, his voice no longer cold, "and ask them to make extra passes by your house. But be careful, and call me tomorrow. Maybe we can work out something else."

Swallowing my anger, I thanked him, and hung up without further comment.

I sat at my desk, doodling on a pad of paper, and thought some more about Watts's questions and our own dead vagrant. On impulse I made a quick calculation and wished I hadn't. If the other hospitals had been getting DOAs at the same rate as St. Paul's, one or two a month, there had been one helluva lot of them delivered to Buffalo-area ERs over the last year. Watts's hunch couldn't be right, not with the kind of numbers that could be involved. Yet I remembered his grave mood when he first raised the possibility in the coffee shop. He was earnest, almost grim, and clearly convinced it needed to be checked out. Over the years I'd found it unwise to dismiss any idea he put forward without looking at it pretty carefully first. His track record was too good. But if some of those corpses, now long buried, did have undetected cardiac needle marks in them—and those marks would be easy to miss in a routine autopsy—I hadn't any idea how that remotely related to Kingsly, or to me.

As Riley said, it was a hell of a thought, but pure speculation. Without evidence, even I had to admit I'd be a lunatic to suggest opening a few of their graves.

I shivered and called Janet's hospital again.

"Dr. Graceton is doing another C section. Can I give her a message?"

Janet had kept to her plan to work that weekend. She believed my suspicions that Fernandez wasn't the killer, and had agreed to continue to take precautions.

"Just tell her I called, and that everything's fine." Yeah, sure. "Tell her I'll call back later."

I gave the vet yet another call. This time I got one of Sophie's assistants.

"Good news, Doctor. The fever's gone. Muffy's lapping up a little liquid and starting to put out urine."

Thank God for "gorillacillin." "Great. Do you want me to see her?"

"No, she's alert enough now to get overexcited. Wouldn't do her a bit of good, so just leave her with us, Doc."

Chastised, I thanked her and hung up. I gathered the computer disks I'd originally come for, and left. My loved ones were safe for the moment, and I was starting to get a little more sense of fight than flight. By the time I reached my car, I even had a plan.

Over a beer, Doug listened to what I was going to do. He'd sat motionless in a quiet corner of our kitchen while

I told him everything. Elsewhere in the house the comforting banter of his men mixed with the racket of hammers and saws. They were working throughout the weekend to get us back in our home as quickly as possible.

The late afternoon light gave a sheen to the top of Doug's bald head. Explaining my plan had sounded strange and impossible, but his absolute stillness reassured me he was taking me seriously, very seriously indeed.

"I don't want any of your guys to endanger themselves, Doug. I have to have your promise on that." I couldn't see his eyes. They were in shadow, but I saw his slow nod.

"I want them there only to call in the cops, to get help when it's obviously time." I handed him Riley's card, the one I'd found under my wiper summoning me to our meeting.

Doug took it but played with it and looked off into the increasing dark of evening. He knew violence. He'd told me of the times when, as a private contractor, he'd had to protect his building sites with shotguns from union goons. The thugs still roamed the labor movement, but now they wore suits and used laptop computers.

"Time's the problem."

His sudden speaking took me by surprise. For a moment I was afraid he was going to tell me he didn't have time for this nonsense.

"You're too alone," he continued, "and too far from help, even with a good response. It'll be too long before the cops will get to you. We need something closer."

He was with me.

Stiffened by this reinforcement, I began to think a little more offensively. "Give me that card a second." I reached for the phone. This time, with the help of information, I talked to another police station, near where we were going to play. They understood, and would be available to help. Easy. Cooperation assured. Of course the county cops had no idea I wasn't really Detective G. Riley of the Buffalo police force.

Doug went upstairs to select the men he'd need for his part of our plan. I went downstairs and collected my waterproof hiking boots and changed into long underwear and heavy socks. I put my dress slacks and socks over the outdoor stuff so no watcher could guess my destination. I replaced my sport jacket with a heavy ski sweater and hid this with my regular topcoat and white scarf. The bush would ruin the coat, but it would be warm enough. I dumped out my doctor's bag, actually more a small suitcase, and hid my boots in there. I added my computer disks and made sure I had all the keys and money I'd need. Finally I squeezed into a pair of black oxfords. To all appearances I looked city bound. Doug and I met quickly back in the kitchen, checked our watches, and he started getting the men he was taking with him ready to leave.

I wasn't hungry, but I made myself heat up some soup. It was going to be a strenuous night. The cold itself would take its toll. The soup was tasteless but hot. I downed it like coffee and was out the door.

My first task was to lay a false trail. It was completely dark now, and the air was fresh with frost. I walked a block south to the corner of a main thoroughfare, where I grabbed the first cab I flagged. Buffalo still partied Sunday night to buffer facing the gloom of Monday, but it was early. I asked for the downtown train station, then watched as we entered the east end and passed by blocks of buildings long gone out of business and boarded up with plywood. A few stores remained lit up but were nearly empty of goods and not far from the inevitable slide to bankruptcy and more plywood.

The station, little more than a redbrick house, was a

cruel testament to the abandonment of the train travel that was once so prevalent in this city. But it was where a lot of taxis could be found. I paid the fare without comment, hopped out with my briefcase, and walked up to the lead cab in the line. It was strewn in back with old mud-stained papers. I'd just passed cleaner versions using more recent editions, but to avoid a fight with the driver, I ignored them and jumped into his more lived-in offering. Besides, the bus terminal was only four blocks away.

The driver must have figured he had a real tourist who didn't know the city, because I got another tour of plywood tombstones, in silence, before he finally deposited me back where I could have walked in three minutes flat. My tip evoked a slightly raised eyebrow. I didn't ask for a receipt.

I ducked into the bus station. It was an overlit, echoing cavern designed for hordes coming and going. No one was leaving or arriving that night. Expectant vendors eyed me hopefully as I clacked across the tile floor. I felt their disappointment when I headed straight over to the Ellicott Street exit. Back outside I turned right, walked two blocks north to Clinton, and turned west. This brought me to the side door of a large hotel that squatted beside Lafayette Square. It had once been grand but now seemed faded among the refashioned buildings that surrounded it. A perfect place to hide out, I wanted my pursuers to think.

I slipped into the lobby. The interior was dusty and the carpet worn. Bored bellhops didn't even look up. They'd come to take vacant rooms for granted.

I walked by the front desk without a glance and pushed my way out the revolving front door that jammed only a few times. The security guard eyed me suspiciously from where he was sprawled on a feeble-looking wooden chair reading the *Police News*.

Back on the street, it took me three minutes to reach Main, where the tram cars ran. Here I would make sure no one followed.

Since the events in the morgue, it seemed pretty evident I was being stalked by more than one person.

I really didn't care what they made of all my skulking about. I wanted them to see me running and perhaps assume I was trying to hide in the city. Or think I was trying to leave town but presume I'd head where a train or bus could take me. Their confusion would buy me time to get set up, yet I had to do more than confuse them. I had to really lose them, and here was my key move to accomplish that, if they were still out there, tracking.

I dropped ten quarters into the fare box, got a round-trip ticket, and then stood by the tracks for a northbound tram. As I waited, I looked up at the city hall building, a huge layered obelisk that hulked thirty stories over downtown Buffalo. The windows were narrow, pointed at the top, and set in deep vertical grooves running up the height of the walls. In the mist they resembled scales on loose folds of skin. The final hundred feet of the tower was eight-sided in shape, and the peak was a series of ever-smaller octagons stacked on top of one another to form a ridged hump. Decorative patterns of yellow and red had once been stained into the sand-colored stone, and the entire structure was touted as a monument to Art Deco. To me it always looked rather shabby and rusted, like the sides were about to slough off. Ironically, it was these upper floors that housed Zak, his staff, and the command center from where they dispatched ambulances in response to 911 calls. But instead of overlooking the city as a beacon of help, the place brooded in the fog. I shivered and glanced back down the darkened street behind me. I was still alone, yet I welcomed the distant bells of the approaching tram.

Once on board, I relaxed slightly. It was a three-car train less than half full, and for the next few stops we poked along the aboveground tracks through the theater district. I found the light and laughter as people got on and off briefly comforting. All too soon we went underground, where the tram picked up speed and I got ready. I let the first station go by and got off at Summer-Best. On this platform there were nearly as many people as I'd seen on the tram. At first I thought waiting for the subway had become a night out in itself. On closer look, the bags carried by these withered, dirty women told me I was in their home.

I stood at the platform's end near the stairs. Across from me was its mirror image for southbound travelers. More people were gathering on both sides of the station, but the place was full of the hush that marks a crowd of strangers. I watched every newcomer on my side of the tracks but saw no likely candidate. Not surprising, since I'd no idea who *they* were anyway.

Another northbound train arrived first. I let it go by. A few people got off and went upstairs. Most of the people on the platform entered the train, were shut in and whisked away. The taillights and sound of the last car faded up the tunnel, leaving me alone with the bag ladies and their suspicious stares. This uneasy silence lasted until in the distance I heard the approach of a southbound train. I bolted for the stairs, ran over the crosswalk above the track, and descended on the other side just as the doors slid open for business. A quick glance behind assured me none of the bag ladies had followed. There was no one else. I felt an odd little spurt of elation. I had lost them.

Still wary, I jumped off the train after only one stop,

ran up the stairs, found a cab, and gave him the mother lode of fares, at least in this city on this night.

Any initial sense of advantage began to fade as the city dropped behind us. The deserted highway led my cab south through the farmland toward the mountains. Some of the bungalows that had seemed so bleak midweek looked cozier. Through the lit windows of kitchens and sitting rooms, I caught glimpses of happy children bobbing around gray-haired elders. It reminded me of Sunday nights long ago on my father's farm—family and neighbors gathered to share and lessen the worries.

My cab made a sorry comparison. The floor was littered with more wet, shredded newspaper. The driver looked concerned about what he'd gotten into and kept glancing nervously back at me, chewing his lip.

The plan Doug and I hatched at my kitchen table had seemed simple, plausible. Now, in the dark, and with increasingly cold feet, I had the feeling that same scheme was rapidly becoming pathetic.

"Could you turn up the heat back here?" I asked.

Without answering, the cabdriver grudgingly turned some dials on the dash and sent a blast of hot air directly into my face. It just made it hard to breathe and my feet seem colder.

"Thanks."

He missed the sarcasm. He'd gotten over his first enthusiasm at the hundred I'd handed him in Buffalo. Out here on the highway, alone, it was little wonder he was visibly afraid. Someone in the city had recently taken to hunting cabbies. It had been a front-page headline recently that three had been killed in the last month.

I knew how he felt.

Waves of sludge from southbound traffic arched over the median and thudded onto the hood of the cab.

In the glow of theory, I'd thought coming north would be unexpected, that I'd be safe for a while, and Doug would have time to prepare for his part in what lay ahead. But I kept looking out the rear window and didn't feel safe at all.

A heavy ridge of slush caught the cab's front wheels, and we lunged back and forth until my reluctant driver regained control. I heard some muttering, but he didn't dare turn his eyes from the road to give me an accompanying glare. His grip on the wheel was so tight, his knuckles were nearly white enough to glow in the dark.

My thoughts were no less erratic than the movement of the cab. The attacks had to have come from someone near me. They seemed based on an intimate knowledge of my life and where I was at work. Tracking me to the cabin, the move on me in the alley, the search of my house, the call to the morgue within minutes of my arriving at my office, unscheduled, on a Sunday; it all suggested they knew my movements. Whoever they were, they obviously could keep track of me from close by and remain unobserved. They also appeared capable of taking instant action. The person—or, now, I assumed, people—who wanted me dead must have been right in the thick of the attempts to kill me. It would probably be a hands-on killing, not an anonymous hit ordered through a chain of command. At least I'd know my killer when the time came, I thought bitterly.

But the elaborate setup with Watts betrayed even more. One of these killers knew modern resuscitation routines and techniques, knew how I'd react, and counted on my shocking myself into oblivion. Electrocuting myself. My pulse raced.

Evidently my death had to appear accidental now. They had to know Bufort was about to blame Fernandez for the murder of Kingsly and the derelict. Otherwise, why all the trouble and risk of staging the show at the morgue to make it seem like a bizarre yet deadly mishap, not another murder? I could just hear Bufort and Hurst explaining it. "Tragic!" they'd say. "Obviously Dr. Watts had a cardiac arrest while working in his lab at the sink. He must have hit his head as he fell. Dr. Garnet, in his rush to defibrillate him, forgot to turn off the water and insulate himself. Terrible loss." There'd be a lot of unanswered questions, but for sure Bufort and Hurst wouldn't ask them.

Only someone at our meeting earlier that day could have known for certain that Bufort was holding Fernandez responsible for the murders. Was it Hurst? But if he had murdered Kingsly, would he now risk trying to kill me simply because I hadn't accepted Fernandez as the killer? And while he might know how to use a cardiac needle, was he up enough on cardiac resuscitation to have pulled off such a cunning plan?

All this begged the real question: Why did whoever it was think I still had to die? Why didn't they lie low and let Bufort's closed mind do the rest? Somehow I was still a threat to them and could possibly, even probably, stumble across what had really happened. I looked at my briefcase on the seat beside me.

My plan in heading to the cabin this way was twofold— lose them long enough to find the secret of the ER stats and, after, use myself as bait to lure them into a trap.

More slush splatted across the windshield, then slid down like dirty egg whites. The wipers smeared this mess into a greasy film. Apparently our budget for the trip didn't include windshield fluid. The driver just hunched farther down to peer through a bare spot. Like Quasimodo with a day job.

My questions raised even more gruesome possibilities. Was there a connection between the citywide increase in DOAs and the murders at St. Paul's? Did my ER data hold evidence of an even blacker secret rotting in God only knew how many paupers' graves? No! That was just too fantastic, too paranoid. But as my cab brought me nearer and nearer to where I'd intended him to drop me in the night, a little paranoia didn't seem inappropriate.

I brought myself back to the odds. Doug's precautions in case the attackers were able to watch the cabin presumed they'd have to do it from a distance. Otherwise the people who shared our road might spot them or their vehicle hidden in the woods. We'd also presumed they wouldn't break in and wait in the cabin, since again they might be spotted by a neighbor.

In this cold, they'd have to have a shelter, a vehicle they'd turn on now and then for heat. Or a tent with some kind of heater, or fire.

At least that's how it played back in my kitchen. Now, nearing my drop-off, the inside of my mouth blow-dried with the blast of the heater and my cold feet becoming unpleasantly metaphorical, the chances of our plan working out seemed to depend on a lot of assumptions being correct. If they weren't, I'd probably end up dead.

We rose out of the farmlands and onto the dark, twisting road that started the climb into the mountains. The course of the black pavement ran back and forth like a metronome timing my thoughts. Occasionally the entire road disappeared into sheets of blowing white snow.

My jovial chauffeur slowed and muttered, "Shit!" For a moment I feared he was going to dump me right there.

"It's only another twenty minutes!" I implored, hoping for a shred of empathy. He didn't bother with an answer but kept going.

I began preparations and tried to shut out any more gloomy thoughts. I pulled my winter hiking boots out of the briefcase and switched them with my oxfords and toe rubbers. My feet warmed, and I quickly felt better. I stuffed my shoes back into the briefcase. Snapping it shut pretty well wrapped up getting ready, and I again began to think maybe my plan was a little thin. I sank back into nineteen more minutes of such morbid thinking.

For a change I looked out the rear window—as if I hadn't a hundred times already. Whatever vehicles had accompanied us from Buffalo had long turned off to saner and safer destinations. No lights followed for any distance. Local traffic getting on the road and then getting off again was all there seemed to be. At one point a flashing red light caught my attention. The vehicle came up fast, its siren soon audible. We'd just passed the Holi Mont ski area, which was where the police I'd called earlier were located, and for a minute I wondered if Doug's boys had already sounded the alarm and called the cops prematurely. But in minutes the yellow truck body of an ambulance was clearly visible. It swirled the snow sweeping by on our left and went speeding on into the night. Only once did it slow, at the curve ahead, the brake lights illuminating the yellow rear box and doors. It skidded a bit, warning my own driver to slow. By the time we rounded the corner, only the flashing red could be seen disappearing over the next hill. Good luck, I thought grimly. Whoever needed help out here so far from ER miracles could use good luck.

We were about fifteen minutes from my chosen spot, and I was feeling downright stupid. Any cleverness in my idea to hole up in the cabin and crack the secret of the ER now seemed pathetically obvious. Still, once they— whoever *they* were—figured I was there, they'd assume just that: incredibly stupid. That was the bait. Hopefully, they'd then come on in, arrogant and careless, not suspecting it was really a trap for them.

I didn't feel a lot better, but maybe our plan had a chance of working. Yet springing the trap—having the cops catch them red-handed trying to kill me—was going to be tricky. The final village came into view.

Five minutes to drop-off.

A distant lit steeple, even some early Christmas lights, glowed in the fresh snow. A luminous Nativity scene was the centerpiece of a deserted parking lot, the glare of green, red, and blue bulbs muted by swirling flakes. The rest of the village sparkled up the hillside in a spray of tiny amber lights. It was like a vision from childhood, full of magic and promise.

If my night's work went awry, I thought, I might never share the world with my son.

The feeling hit me like a jolt. It was new. Till now, fear, worry, doubt, and anger had driven me through the last few days. But about to come face-to-face with who-ever was trying to destroy me, I felt a cold rage.

I sat motionless in the dark cab. I'd never felt a similar emotion. I'd wanted safety for Janet and me, for our home, and for our child-to-be. But even in our wrecked house while standing by the baby's crib and feeling ready to kill anyone who might hurt our child, I'd been ready to let the cops stop them. This was different. I was shaking, but not from any chill now. I felt a strength and focus I'd thought were unique to the insane or soldiers going into battle.

I'd blundered into a killing game. To get out, I was set-ting a trap. But it remained a killing game. On the brink of my own son's birth, I felt a savagery that had always revolted and disgusted me when it exploded out of others. I'd spent a lifetime putting back together the human pieces that resulted from those eruptions.

Maybe it was as simple as self-preservation, an in-stinctive preparation as old as the cave, the getting ready to do battle with the beast that slouched toward it. No-body was going to kill my chance to see my son and rob him of a father.

If they came under my hand tonight, I'd be capable of killing them myself.

We were passing the last of the village. Brash red bulbs lit the local coffee shop. They shone harsh against its year-round color of canary yellow. Neither snow-flakes nor a full blizzard could soften the effect. They usually left the bulbs up all summer, unlit. Janet and I had ended many a warm weekend here, ordering hot dogs and ice cream to hold off the evening and the melancholy of returning to the city.

Four minutes more. I leaned forward. "Only a few miles to go. I'll tell you where. And slow down, now!"

The cabbie gave me an uneasy look, as if this were where I was going to jump him. I chattered on, to make sure he got it right and hopefully to reassure him. "Drop down to twenty. Up ahead is a hollow in the road. When I say stop, exactly at the bottom, stop dead. The second I'm out, go on, but drive slow. Leave your light off and keep going south, about ten miles. Then you can turn around and get back to Buffalo." His silence eloquently said he still didn't like it. I began to fear my whole plan was going to fall apart here.

"Look, I need you to do this. There's nothing illegal involved, but if you don't let me off this way, some very bad and big men might spot me." This rattled him even more. We were only three minutes away, and I realized too late he might suddenly refuse to stop in the middle of nowhere, where he could be jumped by "bad big guys." I improvised some more, trying to undo the effect of my last effort.

"My wife's brothers are watching the entrance to my place up here. I ran around on her, but they come from a family that cuts your nuts off for that. I just gotta get in without them seeing me and talk to my wife—you know, get her to forgive me and call off her brothers. Then it'll be okay. Please, you gotta do this for me." I had his attention. His jaw stopped the grinding movement that had gone on since we left Buffalo.

We were only two minutes away. I went on with my wheedling.

"So I'm not a nice guy, but do you want to be party to me getting my balls cut off?"

I sensed him flinch somewhere down in the region of his crotch. He must have known the kind of relatives I meant.

"Okay," he grunted, "but it will cost you another fifty." Human kindness. I crossed his palm with two twenties and a ten.

We crested the final hill. Here the road dipped down about a mile before our turnoff. Anyone watching from near that entrance could still see the glow of the lights but would lose sight of the actual car as it went into the hollow. I'd be able to jump out of the taxi without anyone spotting me. All an observer would see was the cab as it came up out of the hollow and headed south. They'd assume it was driving slowly because of the storm.

I got ready. "Just along there, at the bottom of the hill. Remember, stop dead! The second I'm out, go on, but at the same slow speed."

He said nothing. I could only hope.

We rolled to the spot.

"Now!"

I opened the door, and lugging my briefcase after me, I hit the pavement with my boots even before he stopped.

"Now go," I said softly, closing the door. The cab crept forward and continued up the hill. In the glow of his dash, I could see him immediately hunch forward to go on the radio mike—probably to tell his buddies about the kook he'd just dumped in the wilderness. Then his taillights disappeared over the crest and he was gone. That he would keep his word and continue south to complete my cover I could only hope.

It was so still, I could hear the snow fall. It made a gentle, steady hiss. Big flakes descended slowly and stuck to my cheeks and eyebrows. The cool was welcome after the blast of the cab heater.

There wasn't any light, but it wasn't dark either. A luminous glow reflected from the white surface and made it possible to see quite well.

I took a few steps through the ditch and up the shallow bank that ran along the highway. The snow was fluffy stuff that barely reached my knees and fell away easily when I walked through it. For the moment, I wouldn't have any trouble.

I climbed over a broken fence, then stopped and looked back. My tracks were visible if you were looking, but the fresh snow would soon cover them. Once in the woods, my trail wouldn't be seen from the road.

Ahead lay a mile-and-a-half trek, all uphill, to reach the cliffs behind the cabin.

Going in this way should take care of any watchers. Make them sweat where I was and make my hiding out seem real. But was it clandestine enough to bring them in, unsuspecting?

Before heading into the woods, I looked across the highway. I could hardly make out the black shape of the clifftop opposite, bulky against the sky and trailing off in each direction until, like the road, it became lost in swirling snow. That's where Doug's boys were to wait, watch, and spring the trap.

He was moving a pickup and a vanload of his men over from their village, Colden, east of us, but they were coming on a back road. A mile from here, they would turn onto a logging cut, known only to locals, that would bring them up the back side of the cliffs facing me. There they would be overlooking the highway from Buffalo I'd just arrived on, and the entrance to our property. Any watchers already hidden by the roadside couldn't drive up to the cabin without being seen. All newcomers would be spotted.

"I sure hope you're there," I muttered, and turned to enter the woods.

Chapter 15

My first mistake was gloves. My socks and hidden longjohns had been clever, but I hadn't thought to bring warm gloves. My stylish black calfskin pair were a soggy wad in minutes. The underside of the large evergreens rising away from the highway was far darker than the roadside. I was stumbling along the uneven ground, one arm forward for balance, the other dragging my briefcase, and I was pitching frontward on a regular basis. This methodical plunging of my arms into the snow soon filled my short gloves and froze my wrists. With each fall I also clobbered the back of my legs with my briefcase. Unseen twigs attacked my glasses and repeatedly tossed them into the snow. Finding them didn't help. A frozen coating of ice impossible to see through had glued itself to the lenses. I pocketed them.

The next time I fell, I simply lay there. The highway was mockingly nearby. My flailing about had given me sweaty thermal underwear, frozen hands, enough facial scratches to mimic a cat fight, but little distance. So much for clever. Time for practical.

I needed to free my hands and warm them. The double socks were redundant and making my feet swim in their own sweat. I carefully unlaced my boots, got them off without too much snow falling inside, and peeled off the outer layer of wool. Chucking my useless gloves, I pulled these smelly, thumbless mitts over my hands and coat sleeves to halfway up my arm. I managed to get rebooted with only a few chunks of ice puddling under my toes. Then, fumbling with my improvised mitts, I opened my case and quickly transferred my computer disks to an inner pocket of my coat. I separated the sheaf of printouts into smaller rolls and stuffed them into various pockets, down my trouser legs like hockey pads, and inside my shirt and waistband flat against my stomach. Bending over to tuck my trouser tops into my boots made the papers at my waist dig into my chest, but it'd do. Then I chucked the briefcase. Optimistically, I tried to note where I was beside the highway so I could find it later. But it didn't seem so important now.

I turned again to the mountain, this time with both hands free.

I made slightly better progress, yet it was slow going. I could grab overhanging branches to steady myself with both hands now. But since these were the lower stubble of ancient fir trees, half of them broke off, resulting in an unwelcome slide backward. Even when I got enough traction to step forward, my boots would often slip out from under me, and I'd again drop to my knees.

The cabin lay four hundred vertical feet higher than the highway, but the mountainside itself rose and then descended into gullies, then rose again. Going down was even more treacherous than climbing up. The snow hid pockets of rocks and fallen tree branches ready to snag and snap an unsuspecting ankle. I had to inch down these slopes, testing with one foot forward. I couldn't avoid repeated wild descents on my backside that slammed me into the next lower tree trunk. Usually my legs cushioned the blow, but some smaller saplings managed to reach more sensitive parts.

As the night wore on and I was out of sight and sound of the highway, I began to wonder about keeping my bearings. I had hiked the area many times, but usually in summer and always in daylight. I was heading generally up, but even in the dim light I could see my trail of footsteps had meandered to avoid more forbidding sections of rock and cliffs.

By now the snow was falling heavily, and not even stars were available to give me some sense of direction. All my thoughts were focused on finding footholds. In some places where the snow was over my knees, the effort of walking nearly doubled. My breathing was hard and loud enough to be heard, but I didn't care. My pursuers would not be stupid enough to be out in this. Then with a giggle of fatigue, I thought, "Great, I've out-stupided them." More giggles, and a particularly slippery outcrop of rock launched me down the next gully and plopped my behind in an unfrozen spring-fed stream.

"Shit!" My yell was involuntary. Even after realizing the noise I'd made, again I didn't think it mattered. Besides, my immediate concern was the ice water percolating through my trousers, the printouts, and down my legs.

"Damn!" I was on my feet instantly, but my clothing was soaked enough for the water to continue on into my boots. I started to wade out of the pool, giving a pretty good imitation of someone who's peed in his pants.

It would have been funny except for the cold. From the waist down I was soaked, and cooling fast. The papers were probably ruined.

I squeezed what water I could from my pant legs but managed only to wet my hands in their improvised coverings. Before I fell, I'd been warm with all my exertions, hot even. Now I was shaking with cold. I had to start moving again and get to the cabin fast.

But any hope I had that I'd reached the downhill run to our lake finished with a sharp upturn in the slope ahead that was even steeper than before. The snow was falling thickly. My only choice was to continue uphill. The routine two steps up, slide back ten, was happening more often now. I was unable see if I was even making some forward progress. I had a panicky image of becoming a frozen Sisyphus condemned to struggle up, fall back, and get nowhere. My pant legs had become hardened into corrugated iron tubes. Burning seared any remaining skin that wasn't numb.

I was lying at the bottom of one of these many descents, listening to my own breathing, when I heard the plodding behind me.

I spun around and pressed my back into the hill. In the white and black below, there was a definite steady thudding, coming right up at me. Suddenly I wasn't cold anymore. I squinted, but I couldn't see anything. The heavy, uneven thudding moved nearer. How could they have found me? How were they coming so steadily, and what made their steps so heavy? I could feel the vibration as well as hear them. Nausea and fear rose hot to the back of my throat.

Then I saw a wall of black behind the white, a wall that moved. I made useless scurrying movements backward and tried to fight away an evident hallucination. Hell, I wasn't that cold or gone yet. But I was looking at a moving black wall plodding at me that suddenly stopped. Then it moved at me and stopped again. Next, from above the wall I saw a great head topped with antlers the size of a small tree. Nostrils and large, forlorn eyes glided down to my face, took a sniff, then receded as the great beast turned away and began steadily plodding up the hill, past me to my left.

The moose was soon gone from sight and sound, leaving me with only the thud of my own heart.

They'd been around for years, but never came close. They felt safe here, a small refuge from hunting, but mostly they wandered quietly and alone. On rare occasions we would see one in a sheltered spot on the lake, where they came to take water. Mostly they wandered by night.

This moose seemed to be on his routine prowl. His large hoofprints looked like they might be good footholds in the snow. I wondered if he was heading to the drinking cove. If so, crazy as it seemed, my only chance at surviving might be to follow him. The cold was going to do me in if I flailed around much longer.

It was a risk—I had no sure idea where he was headed—but I decided to take it. Getting to my feet provoked a sickening wave of numbness and fire from the waist down. This solitary creature had better be on the shortest route to our shared cove, I thought, or it wouldn't matter for long where he led me.

Though only a little off my path, his trail rose steadily and was free of the hidden boulders and pockets that had made my chosen route so hazardous. It also provided the foot- and handholds I'd hoped it would, and climbing was infinitely easier. Ahead only the occasional snap of a twig confirmed his presence. For all his two-ton size and antlers rising six feet above my head, he glided through the forest like a spirit. My huffing and coughing must have been an unseemly din to him.

In minutes we crested the ridge. A blast of wind in my face confirmed we were over. His prints kept their measured pace, but trusting his affinity to find known pathways even in snow, I started the descent with new confidence. Picking up speed, reaching from one tree to the next for support, I pirouetted down the mountain in a mad slalom of "allemande left, allemande right" from trunk to trunk. So invigorating was this senseless speed into thick snow, I began giggling again at the absurdity of my situation. Hunted by killers, saved by a moose.

I crashed right into the forming ice at the lake's edge. A few seconds of teetering on my toes like a drunk kept me from diving outright into the open black water.

Regaining my balance and my bearings, I knew the cabin was minutes away on my left. The creature I'd staked my life on was nowhere to be seen. His prints led to a few yards from the water's edge, then wandered off north, to nowhere. He hadn't come to drink.

In the light of day it would seem that plain blind chance had caused our paths to cross. But here, jubilant at my reprieve, readied for war, I felt I'd been blessed and delivered to safety through that solemn beast.

The snow blurred his empty path. I turned in the opposite direction and trudged toward the cabin.

In a few minutes I was going by the boathouse where the trees reached the edge of the lawn. I stopped in the shadows of a large pine and peered through the storm at the darkened, familiar refuge.

This lakeside path was farthest from the front entrance. Anybody already there wouldn't expect me to arrive from this direction. The downside was, I couldn't see the front entrance and if any snow had been disturbed.

No telltale tracks or depressions covered by new snow ran around this end of the cabin, but the structure was about a hundred and thirty feet long. I stared at the large black picture windows overlooking the lake. If anyone was inside, they would see me before I saw them.

I hung there, listening, watching. There was nothing but the snow.

I was getting ready to hurry to the end wall when the gravel-covered area in which we parked and the entranceway at the far end burst into light.

"No!" I breathed, and froze, still in the cover of the pine's shadow. Expecting catastrophe, I waited. A light breeze caught the boughs above me. They made a soft hushing sound as they swayed in response.

No shouts, no running boots, nothing. After thirty seconds, the light went off.

The wind. It had swayed the trees and fired the

movement sensors that automatically went on when we arrived at night. It always happened in a wind. I had learned to ignore it. But this night it made me jumpy.

Any jerks in the house wouldn't know it was just the wind. They'd be watching now, but they'd be looking down the road, where they'd think I'd be coming from.

Time to move.

My pause in the shadows had left me stiff. I groaned out loud as I lugged myself awkwardly over the snow-covered lawn to crouch under the gable end of the cabin. I peered around the corner but saw nothing in the murk ahead.

I began creeping along the front wall, staying low to keep under its many windows. I was a quarter of the way up when another gust of wind whirled down the cliffs behind me and once again tripped the lights. This time everything around me, myself included, was bathed in beams of light in which the falling snow danced madly. Pretty, but deadly, if it was still important I remain hidden.

But again, there were no shouts, no hands from anywhere to grab me. Nothing.

Ahead the snow in the parking area and the path to the front was level and undisturbed. While the light stayed on, I stood up and walked the remaining sixty feet to the door. The glass was intact. The lock was on. There were no signs of it being forced. No tracks led around to the windows on the opposite end of the cabin that I'd been unable to see a few minutes before. All I saw were soothing gusts of snow swirling against the log walls.

No one was here. For the moment, I'd gotten ahead of them.

Once inside, the warmth compared to the outdoors and the wood smell of pine logs provided its usual solace and comfort. I felt heady, defiant. I could win this thing.

Doug's boys had binoculars. At the first sign of a hidden exhaust plume, smoke, or an unidentified vehicle entering the property, they'd be using the cellular phone to warn me and then summon the police from nearby Holi Mont to "assist Detective Riley immediately." Then I would have to make a choice. If I preferred, I could play it safe and clear out into the woods. The killers, once on the property, were trapped. Doug's boys would move their truck down and block the road and then hide out until the cops came. If the killers got tired of looking for me or sensed the trick and tried to get out, they'd be stopped by the roadblock. Then they'd either waste their time trying to get their vehicle around it or take off on foot, in winter, in the mountains. Easy prey, either way, for the cops when they arrived. I'd finally know who my attackers were, except this way all I might be able to charge them with would be trespassing.

I hadn't told Doug my other choice. He never would have agreed to it. I'd head out to the woods as the killers came in, but only to have more room to maneuver. Instead of hiding, I would show myself and provoke an attack. Until I found the secret of the ER data that they so feared, I had no proof. I had to let the police catch them actually *trying* to kill me.

In the vestibule, I dropped my frozen clothes and grabbed the phone.

I dialed the number of Doug's cellular; he flipped on instantly.

"Earl?" he asked, obviously waiting and worried.

"Yeah. I'm okay. The snow made it slow. I'm in now, and all's quiet here."

I glanced at my watch. 10:30. Three and a half hours since I began my run. The trek in had taken over an hour.

But Doug had other news. "Earl, get ready to move. We've got company here."

I stopped undressing. "Already! Damn!" So much for outmaneuvering them. "How? What have you got?"

"Look, it just may be watchers, like we anticipated. Here on spec, without a clue that you're already in. But I want you ready."

"What are they doing?"

"Watching. But get this. These guys have a pretty distinctive choice of transportation."

"What do you mean?"

"One of them's in an ambulance."

"Shit." It had passed me on the road. Then I remembered the box van that had been behind me when I drove south five nights ago. I'd seen its brake lights in my rearview mirror after I'd taken the turnoff to the cabin. It could have been an ambulance too. It was making sense fast. So fast, I was holding my breath and going cold in my guts.

I exhaled into the receiver.

"Earl?"

My mind was racing ahead. What was implausible before was becoming a hideous possibility. If Watts's hunch was right and the rise in derelict DOAs was from some maniac knocking off drunks with cardiac needles, an ambulance with the help of equally ghoulish attendants was the perfect cover. The calls would lead them to possible prey. Once they had a victim inside, they could do whatever manipulations they wanted. Screams wouldn't be heard over the siren. And if they were, what the hell. It was an ambulance with yet another maimed and screeching patient en route to an emergency room. And then they'd spread the corpses around the city. I shuddered. It might be the how of the DOA epidemic, but not the why. And not the connection to Kingsly. Nor to me.

"Are you there?" Doug asked again quietly.

"Yeah. But if I'm right, Doug"—I faltered, still stunned at the probable scale of systematic killings—"Jesus!"

"Earl, tell me later. Now, just get ready to run!"

But I stayed on the phone. "Doug, this afternoon I estimated the number of DOAs in the city this year. It's maybe what's behind all this, and they may all have been killed like Kingsly and the derelict at St. Paul's. It took over a year for the medical examiner to notice. Hell, it took me that long to realize that one DOA every few months had crept up to over one or two a month. If the other hospitals in and around the city have the same, we're looking at a mind-boggling number of murders."

"Lord!" he exclaimed. "Are you sure?"

"No, I'm not sure, not at all. But like it or not, I just figured out a way so many people could have been murdered." And slipped in unnoticed under our overworked, preoccupied noses, I thought. Whoever was doing this had cynically relied on our fatigue and usual indifference—born of overwork—to a dead vagabond. Again it had to mean that at least one of the killers knew emergency and knew emergency physicians but this time had played us like a program to hide corpses.

My distracted silences were obviously making Doug edgy. "Earl, figure it out later. Get ready to move! They're here. Let's call the cops!"

"No! We have to wait till they come in," I insisted, "just like we planned, or I'm back to square one."

I heard him sigh heavily, but he didn't refuse to hold off our call for help. Thank God I hadn't told him I intended to be more of a decoy than we discussed. Then another thought fell into place, like a tumbler to a lock. "Wait a minute, what do you mean 'one of them'? There's more than the ambulance?"

"That's right. About ten minutes ago, another car arrived, slowly, from the north, just like you in the cab. It went on south. A few minutes later we see it coming back on the northbound, lights out, and it pulls in behind the ambulance."

"What are they doing?"

"Like I said, sitting there."

"How many?"

"Can't tell for sure. No one's gotten out."

"Did the ambulance try to arrive on the q.t.?"

"Nope. It drove up, lights flashing from the north, did a U-turn at the intersection near your entrance, and parked with the lights doused."

"Did my cabbie go out of sight way farther south like I asked?"

"Yep. As ordered."

"And their car went farther south before turning around, like the cab, and afterward snuck back?"

"Right."

The car had taken the same precautions I had; the ambulance hadn't.

"Do you figure they don't know you're up there yet, watching them watch?"

I didn't like the pause Doug took before answering. Finally, the best he seemed able to muster was a quiet "Probably."

"Probably! Hell, not exactly a battle cry of confidence."

No answer.

"Doug, what's bothering you?"

A wave of static came and went before he answered.

"You mean besides the fact I'm looking at a nest of vipers who kill on almost a daily basis? Well, it's that I think there's not enough of them."

"What!"

"Your escapade at the morgue involved at least three people. We know there's at least two down there, but I think that's all."

"How? I thought they didn't get out of their vehicles."

"They didn't. But one of my guys saw a cigarette tip

glowing in the driver's seat of the ambulance, and the same thing just now in the car. Nothing in the passenger seats, and the glow just staring at your entrance each time; no turning toward a passenger to talk."

"Maybe they don't talk."

"Maybe, but the way the tips are bouncing up and down, the two drivers are talking to each other, or someone, on the ambulance radio or car phone. Seems funny such chatty types wouldn't say a word to someone beside them."

He was reaching. I was beginning to feel guilty for involving him at all. It was turning out a lot worse than we had guessed back in my kitchen. "How can you see all this?"

"One of my guys has night binoculars."

"Where'd he get those?"

"Souvenir from 'Nam. Arnie and Norm are vets."

I wasn't surprised. Over the years I'd enjoyed the quiet closeness of these two large men. Even in a crew of characters like Doug's team, their easy humor and un-flappability were a pleasure to be around.

"I'm impressed."

"Yeah, except they don't work so good."

"Which, Arnie and Norm or the binoculars?"

Doug chuckled. "Both. The vets are fat forty-five-year-old warriors." I heard mock protests from somewhere in Doug's cab. The morale was still good at his end. "And as for the binoculars, well, let's say they worked better in 'Nam, where it didn't snow."

How many killers there were had always bothered me. "So we're missing a viper. Maybe it's still in Buffalo, looking. Maybe we've confused them as planned."

"We might get a better count on how many are here soon; the snow's letting up. Meantime, stay ready."

He hung up without waiting for my answer.

My pants and half-removed longjohns were twisted

into partially thawed ropes that lay in a cold puddle at my feet. I stepped out of them and then extracted what was left of the computer printouts I'd stuffed around my legs from the soggy mess on the floor. They were unusable, at least for now, but might be legible if they were dried. I placed them on a marble table over an electric heater. I gathered up the rest of the clothing and carried it to the washing machine, where I dumped it.

Next I salvaged the disks from my inner coat pocket. Thankfully, they were fine. Most of what I needed to start with was on them. I'd need the printouts only if my first ideas didn't work out.

I peeled off my sweater and T-shirt, more soaked with sweat than snow, and found that the printouts wrapped around my waist were just as wet as the others. I added them to the table and put the remaining clothes into the washer.

Naked and shivering, I quickly headed to the master bedroom at the far end of the main floor, where I'd find something dry to put on.

This room was the windowed end of the cabin overlooking the lake where, fifteen minutes ago, I'd been peering in from the outside, unable to see anything. As I found my clothes and dressed in the familiar darkness, I could see outside relatively easily. The snowfall was letting up, and the lake was becoming visible to the end. The dark trail of my tracks where I had run from the deep shadows at the edge of the woods to the outside of this bedroom wall was obvious. But I wasn't going to worry about that at the moment. It shouldn't matter anyway.

Warm and dry, I grabbed the disks and headed back to the other end of the house and the small room over the kitchen that held my computer. I turned the screen on, and the gray glow bathed the keyboard enough to work without turning on the room light. It didn't make sense, but I felt better keeping in the dark.

* * *

The sprawl of numbers and abbreviated diagnostic categories spilled down the screen and gave me a sense of security. I was back in my own realm of expertise. Here, amid the maze of a functioning emergency department, if one of the killers had left aberrant signs, I had a good chance of ferreting them out.

I entered the DOA category into the most frequent diagnosis menu so I'd be able to subject it to the same profile breakdown I'd already done for the major emergency case categories. DOAs would hardly ever command such attention, apart from a footnote as to their proportion of our overall mortalities. The killers probably counted on that too. The posts on those derelicts would be done cursorily by frazzled pathologists wondering what bureaucratic idiot was wasting their valuable time.

All pretty safe for our murderers, until Kingsly.

The screen flickered and retrieved the diagnostic categories I was waiting for. I punched in the keys to call up a coded cross-reference with individual physicians for the frequency of DOAs. The screen hummed and clicked again to follow this unusual command.

I was looking for a fiend with the knowledge of someone close to the ER. Hurst gave me the creeps, but he wasn't part of emergency or linked to the data in front of me. Besides, he simply didn't have the ER mentality that I'd sensed driving the work of the killer, especially the way Watts had been set up—an ER drill with a live victim.

I sure had my suspicions about Kradic, and I had to control my dislike of Jones long enough not to exaggerate what I thought she might be capable of doing, but I also thought again about other doctors and nurses I'd worked with for years. With a few exceptions, I realized I knew nothing of their private dreams, desires, hatreds, or burning causes. All I ever saw was their outward professional conduct. Did the repeated rudeness of a triage nurse mean stress and insecurity, I wondered, or a pathologic cruelty? Was the distance I'd seen some doctors take from pain and fear a blundering defensiveness or a carefully concealed sadism?

I winced, remembering an old school of so-called thought where respected emergency physicians would roughly perform a not-so-necessary gastric lavage on an overdose patient to "teach her a lesson." Thankfully those days were over, but was one of them a fiend, hungry for a reason to inflict pain?

Surely, though, killing, repeatedly and almost clinically, went beyond any of the scenes I had witnessed.

I stopped myself, a little aghast, not because I had failed to guess who might be the monster among us but because for too many I couldn't say for sure who or what they were outside our peculiar cell of work. The medical field had hidden murderers before. So-called doctors and nurses had performed atrocities in Dachau and gone home to play with their children. One such "healer" had dedicated his life to humanitarian clinics in the third world before being tracked down after the war. In the past year an esteemed physician in Oregon had slashed and strangled six prostitutes over a ten-month period, then moved over to Europe and was caught after a series of similar killings there. The DOA profile by individual physician popped onto the screen and pulled me back to my hunt for a current creep.

Nothing.

Fifteen physicians, identified by code numbers across the bottom of the page, me included, made up the ER roster. A black bar rising above each number indicated the number of DOA cases. No one stood out. Most had one or two, a few had three or four, and a single physician apparently had none. I shouldn't have been disappointed, but I'd thought maybe I was smarter and more clever than whomever I was after and that a bar graph would point to the killer. Obviously not.

I hadn't broken open the number code yet, so I had no idea who was who. I'd do it later. At least I could eliminate suspicious thoughts about the doctors with low numbers. Perhaps I'd have to look at the two or three with the higher bars. As Doug had reminded me, this was a nest of vipers, and we had at least three snakes to trap.

I pressed the copy button, and as my noisy printer started drawing up the apparently innocuous graph, I laid in the program to compare the incidence of DOAs by shift. The noise of the type head stopped, and while waiting for the new table to pop on the screen, I ripped out the first graph and dropped it unthinking on the floor.

The grid for a week of work appeared, broken into three eight-hour shifts—days, evenings, and nights—starting at seven A.M. By these hours doctors and nurses the world over live their lives.

A superimposed grid then made an hour-by-hour subgrid, and a spatter of dots finally appeared spread out over the screen. Each spot was a corpse. The groupings told us the times and days we were most busy with the already-dead over the space of a year.

Visually I couldn't read much into it; the picture looked like a space map with over thirty stars, a few more than I'd estimated. I then punched in the analysis program that would plot any significant time and day groupings.

This took a little longer. Carole had given me the program in a simplified version for my lowly skills and PC. The same exercise went much faster at her desk, with her machine, and, more important, with her hands tapping in the commands.

Waiting out the hums and clicks, I stared at the first graph as it had fallen upside down at my feet. I had been foolish thinking a simple flick of a computer switch would give me a singular accusing bar graph rising up over a killer's name.

Viewed from upside down, a black bar graph changed. The white background became the bar. The white bars measured the negative finds. And seen this way, one number had a massive white bar under it compared to all the others. The negative find, no DOAs, was made significant.

The code to identify this doctor was on another disk. I didn't want to stop the program already plotting DOA times midrun, so I waited, growing steadily excited that the absence of bodies might be the slip-up I was looking for.

The screen sprang out an ordered collation of times and days. There was no preference of days, but twenty-five of thirty-one DOAs had arrived in the morning hours. Most of those arrivals were between eight and ten.

This was a huge bias, but it could mean nothing more than that the derelicts who had died or been killed overnight got found in the morning and were sent in then.

Our doctors worked shorter blocks of time than the nurses and overlapped their shifts. This strategy lessened the stress and fatigue inherent in ER work. I requested that the schedule of individual doctors over the last year be correlated with the exact time slots in which there'd been DOAs, and that the result be represented by a bar graph again. As I expected, no single physician worked these slots more than any other, but this time I was ready for the negative find. Long white bars rose over several numbers, distinct from the black columns over all the rest.

The numbers with white bars hardly ever worked mornings. They included the same code number that had no DOAs.

Again, by itself, there was nothing sinister about this.

Some doctors simply preferred afternoons and evenings and didn't work mornings because of competing schedules and commitments outside the hospital. That had been my own preference before I became chief.

I played some more with the schedule data and asked for a list of the M.D.s preferring evenings and afternoons. As I expected, this consisted of about half the department. This group included the number I'd started to track.

Then I played a hunch. I shifted back to the DOA time and day graph and combined it with the year's schedule. I asked for a correlation between the DOAs and whoever worked the preceding shift.

This was a very unusual request, and the computer had to whir and click much longer than before. As I waited, a cold draft stirred at the back of my neck. I absently added this room to the list of ones that Doug was to caulk against leaks. It was an early winter routine that mercifully lessened each year as the logs in the newer parts of the cabin finished settling. The older sections, permanently cozy, gave me faith the process would end someday.

As I sat there in the dark, listening to the machine while the gray light on its screen flickered, I felt chilled despite the warm clothes I'd put on. I'd get a sweater as soon as the program finished.

Just then the screen snapped into yet another horizontal spread of vertical bars.

Except this time I had my markers, two in fact, one white and one black. The black bar rose like an obelisk above all the rest, but not over the number I now knew by heart. Above that number was a white column.

It was like looking at a positive and a negative. The physician I'd been tracking virtually never did a shift prior to the arrival of a DOA. The doctor represented by the black bar was on duty before most of them were brought in.

I spooled back over the graphs I'd constructed and tracked this new number through their grids. I began to see what it might mean.

Before changing disks and activating the program to the identity code, I wanted printed backup of what I already had. Years of being computer stupid included some bitter "save-it-while-you-got-it" lessons. I also no longer completely trusted my ten-year-old clunker; it sometimes jumbled text and then showed a little bomb sign that meant I was out of luck. Before risking yet another disaster with the drawn-out routine of switching disks to make duplicates, I started running off paper copies of all the graphs. The printer sounded like a sawmill, laboriously grinding out each line I'd just concocted. While waiting, my fingers tap-danced the passing seconds on the blue surface of the disk containing the names.

One minute; one sheet finished. Five more graphs, and five minutes to go. What a dinosaur, I thought, and decided to go back downstairs to get a sweater.

As I walked through the kitchen and started toward the other end of the house, I could hear the stutter and whine of the printer overhead. It got quieter while I made my way through the cozy sets of chairs, couches, and small tables in the darkened living room, our chatting areas and reading nooks in happier times.

Soon the noise became a dull whir in the distance behind me, stirring my thoughts. I figured I understood why one physician was never around and another was nearly always present prior to the arrival of a DOA at St. Paul's. And if I was right, that same telltale pattern would hold for most of the other DOAs recorded around Buffalo—if I lived through the night and ever got a chance to check that data.

I walked down the hallway that led to the master bedroom. It was even darker here, and I had to feel along the walls. I still didn't want to turn on a light.

So many DOAs; so many statistics—yet some numbers had a vague familiarity. More chairs and nooks. I felt my way by them in the dark.

What other riddle involving numbers had I looked at recently? Stats related to the emergency study? Probably, and possibly of no significance.

I entered our large bedroom. After the darkness in the rest of the house, I found the blue glow of moonlight coming through the big corner windows more than enough to see by. Outside, the snow-covered lawns and surrounding thick forest were now equally visible. Doug had been right; the storm had stopped.

I found the sweater I'd remembered stashing in a bureau drawer and put on the pullover. The lake, still open, stretched out darker than the night, black glass set in a shore of white. I could even see under the pines at the edge of the lawn, where an hour ago I'd huddled in the shadows and watched for signs of someone inside.

It was probably a good thing they weren't, I thought. From the dark in the room I would have been spotted easily as I ran to the cabin.

The cut of my tracks stood out like a laceration in the moonlit snow, deep with shadow. It looked darker than before, like a line of dried blood. Not much snow had fallen since I got in. But as I watched, I let my memory wander, struggling to recall what relationship these pieces of data had one to another.

Possibly. For some reason the word drifted into the back of my mind. The word *probably* floated in as well. Why did *possibly* and *probably* connect with the elusive numbers I was trying to recall? Three hundred? The number seemed to come out of nowhere. Three hundred what? My memory refused to divulge the source of that figure. I was ready to dismiss the silly little words as one of those trivial loops the mind can fixate on. But the loop continued to play, and the word *study* joined the others. They all swirled around like an annoying anagram that defied solution until, just as abruptly, the words settled and changed for me. *Probability. Possibility.* The chance of error of a *study.* The source of a p value.

I knew whose name I was going to find under the white bar on the code disk.

The phone rang like a scream in my ear.

I yelped without realizing it and spun around. Quickly I picked up the receiver of the phone beside the bed. I didn't even have a chance to say hello.

"Earl, get out!" Doug shouted. "Get out now! A second set of tracks followed you in. Get out now!"

"Second tracks?"

"Don't talk! Just get out. They've pulled an end run. The car that came up after the ambulance must have pulled the same maneuver the cab did with you and dropped at least one of them off at the same spot. We didn't see it at first because of the storm. They're coming for you through the woods."

"Doug, I think it's just a moose!"

There are qualities to a silence in which you know, with absolute certainty, that people have decided you're insane. This was one of those moments.

Finally, Doug asked, "Earl, is this a code? You're in trouble, right, and talking gibberish is meant to tip me off?"

"No, Doug, I met a moose. It followed my tracks. Hell, it led me out of the storm to the lake. It's just a moose."

"I don't believe it."

"Christ, did you call in the cavalry yet?"

His stony silence started a rising dread he'd blown our cover, but finally, reluctantly, he said, "No, I wanted you out first." More silence, then, "But I don't like this."

"How'd you just see the tracks?"

"The night binoculars are great once the snow stops."

I knew now the computer was going to give me a name, a suspicious pattern on a schedule, but no proof. I could accuse, and arouse suspicions, but not necessarily convict. I still had to get Doug to wait. "Well, relax. It's nothing," I said to him. "Let's watch a bit longer."

There was more doubting silence on his end. "Hold it a sec," he said.

I heard him carry on a hurried conversation with one of his guys in the truck. I could hear a snatch of Arnie's twanging. "No fuckin' way that's a moose track. Moose leave prints; that's a steady human track. And it's too fresh. Dr. Garnet's tracks are already half covered, barely visible. These couldn't be more than an hour old. Get the idiot out of there."

Arnie had hunted both men and animals. He was edgy. As I listened, I found my mouth going dry. I involuntarily pressed my back to the wall. I peered across the dim room and out the window to the dark trees where my path left the forest.

Upstairs the clatter of the printer abruptly stopped. A shutter thumped the wall in another part of the house. The logs creaked in the wind, and a puff of snow flew against the panes of glass across the room from me. The printer sputtered to life again in the distance. It must be almost finished.

Doug came back on and diplomatically translated. "Uh, we got a serious difference of opinion here. Look, I want you out of there till we sort it out. Have you got that dinky little portable phone that works near the house?"

I'd bought it for work in the garden. Doug had borrowed it during projects here in the old days before he got the cellular.

"Yeah, I got it. What are the two watchers up to?"

"Nothing. Just sitting there."

"If someone else is on the way in, how'd they know I was here?"

"I don't know! Look, just get out of there. Go up and hide in the cliffs behind the cabin. We'll watch these turkeys here. If they move or anyone shows up where you are, we call the cavalry. Phone me when you're outside, to check that your cheap walkie-talkie talks."

In a flash I saw what we'd forgotten. "My tracks! They'll see my new tracks heading out again and follow them right to where I'm hiding." Even though I'd decided to be a decoy, I thought I'd have control of when I'd allow them to see me. Then I could have timed it to happen just before the cops arrived. The Holi Mont police were about ten minutes away, and we'd told them to come in without sirens when they got our call. But now, instead of dodging the killers for a few minutes, hopefully long enough for them to incriminate themselves, I might be at their mercy a lot longer, no matter how quickly the police got there.

Doug's silence confirmed he hadn't thought of this either, even with his safer version of our plan. We were improvising now, and our scheme, either way, was coming apart.

"Earl," he said urgently, "it's gotta be that you head up the cliffs and watch for them from there or I call the cops now and scare them off." He let this sink in, then added, "It's your call."

I was getting scared, but leaving these killers free frightened me more. If the secret of the bar graph was what I thought it was, my "accidental death" was not only to keep me from trying to expose a mass murderer, it was to allow the killings to continue. "All right," I agreed, "I'll hide in the cliffs, but we wait and watch. I'll call you when I'm outside."

"Remember, take off through the woods back toward the highway as soon as we call the cops. They'll probably check out the cabin first before they start tracking you again. If the cops get here fast, we might even trap them while they're still in the house." But he sounded pretty tense about our prospects.

"Okay," I answered, "but did anyone ever call you cheeky and bossy?"

"Wait till you see my bill." He hung up.

The click that ended the call stuttered and became a dial tone. The drone was unpleasant, like a fly in my ear. I'd wanted to tell him what I'd found on the computer and whose name I expected to reveal with the identity code in case anything happened to me. I decided I'd call him back as soon as I was safely outside.

I glanced back at my outside track through the windows.

How did they get on my trail, get a car up here, and replicate my slow drop-off?

I visualized rolling out of the cab; the hollow was completely invisible to the rest of the road. Hell, I saw the dimming taillights of the departing cab go out of sight over the rise between the watching ambulance and me. They couldn't have seen me.

As I stood in the darkness looking out, I replayed the image of the departing cab. In my mind I saw the shadow of the driver hunched over the dashboard, then taillights.

Suddenly I had it: The dash. The radio. The ambulance must have been monitoring the cabbie when he'd radioed in. He probably mentioned dropping off some lunatic in the woods. The ambulance driver would have realized it was me. And now they were coming in the same way.

I moved away from the window and turned toward the hallway. The portable phone was at the other end of the house on a charger in the guest bedroom. I'd grab it and call Doug once I was outside. Time for the cavalry. I was halfway through the dark passage before I remembered what I'd find: a phone unplugged.

I always unplugged the damn charger when we were away. It got too hot while charging, and I was worried it would short and burn.

I'd use the phone at the entrance and then get out to the cliffs.

I had reached the long hallway that passed from the living room to the kitchen. The vestibule and entrance-way were about halfway down the corridor that stretched ahead of me. I heard another burst of noise from the printer upstairs.

Then a gust of cold air caught my face.

I went still. The door was open! Or was it another draft? I'd stopped breathing. More cold air blew against my skin. My thoughts raced ahead. The tracks outside hadn't been darker, they were deeper. They'd already gone by. My tracker was in the house!

I was too still. I had to buy seconds to get out, which meant I had to keep moving. I couldn't let on I knew the killer was already inside.

As I made each step, I thought I'd be jumped.

I crept up to the entrance of the vestibule and peeked around the door frame.

Empty. The outer door was closed, but a cool, steady breeze came at me from where the pane of glass beside the lock used to be. I slipped into the vestibule but kept watching the dark corridor by backing to the door. With my left hand I made a grab for my boots; my right fumbled blindly behind me for the handle. The floor was wet with melted snow. I stepped on the missing pane of glass and crunched it. The suction cup that had removed it was still in place. If I cut my foot, I didn't feel it.

Above me the whine of the printer stopped. The silence was as still as my breath.

I felt the thudding up the dark end of the hallway before I actually heard the running. I was more startled by a steady rising beep, familiar as a heartbeat, but grotesquely out of context here.

I got the door partly open behind me as a figure in a black ski suit, gloves, and mask neared the vestibule. The beeping increased its crescendo. The intruder was holding out two paddles, like lethal suction pods. They were connected by coils of wire to a small monitor slung on a shoulder strap. The beeping had reached a steady scream. The paddles were fully charged and ready to deliver. A single jolt and my heart would be a fibrillating sack, useless as a bag of squirming worms.

Before I could get out, the partly open door behind me was slammed hard into my back. It sent me flying face-down on the slate tiles at the boots of my attacker with the paddles.

The air flew out of my lungs with an involuntary roar. One of the boots came down on my head, and pain exploded over my skull and down my back while my throat burned with surges of vomit. A heavy knee dropped on the back of my legs. My sweater and shirt were ripped up my back to the bottom of my neck. The one with the boots—I could feel the heavy corrugated ridges on my scalp—plopped the paddles, cold with lubricant, on the back and side of my chest behind my heart.

I was going to die. I started to flail and squirm, but pretty weakly, given I couldn't get my breath. I clutched feebly at the boot on my head. I thought of Janet, of my unborn son, and finally gurgled in enough air to sob, "Please!"

All I got was a gruff "Stand clear!"

The knees went off my legs and the boot lifted off my head, but the full weight of the hooded creature bore down on the paddles, crushing my chest into the tiles. I still couldn't breathe in. I weakly raised my head and spat out vomit. I started kicking jerkily with my legs but touched nothing. Drooling and sputtering more vomit, I strained my head up a few inches higher. Above me, my attacker stretched in a grotesque push-up, arms straight and pinning my chest to the floor with full body weight on the paddles. Legs akimbo and out of reach.

Behind the oval mouth hole in the ski mask, I could see a red leer.

A little flick from within the black eye slits invited me to turn my head farther around, to watch the paddle handles and the gloved hands. The screaming tone kept shrieking in readiness. Knowing I could see, the black-gloved thumbs moved with sadistic slowness to finger, to caress the red buttons.

Then a familiar voice, a voice I knew, the voice I expected, hissed, "So long, Doc."

The thumbs hit the buttons before I could curse the name.

Chapter 16

The juice kicked through my chest. The whack of its force hit me like a train. White light shot up over my eyes and head. My ears recorded a loud *whump,* like kerosene rags igniting. Then they sealed off, filled with a hollow ringing.

An unsynchronized shock can restart a stalled heart, but it will stop a healthy heart cold. Mine was no longer beating. It had been reduced to a quivering, disorganized mass of muscle. But I wasn't out. Not yet. That would, could, take thirty seconds. That was the point. I had enough time to know I was dead.

Shocked still, my heart no longer pumped blood. Air hunger mounted in my chest, then drove me to make useless gasping movements—my turn to endure, like a stranded fish, the longest seconds at the end of a life.

I didn't like it. I felt no peaceful ascending and looking down at my remains. This hurt. I remembered the eyes of men and women I'd seen die over the years, awake and knowing as they shut down. I'd pampered my horror with the platitudes "It was quick; they didn't suffer." This wasn't quick; the suffocation was slow, sure, and the tips of dying nerve ends hurt like hell. I strained for a gulp of air but got only futile twitchings from muscles that no longer worked.

I wanted the end, I wanted out of the agony. Please, I begged, let the blackness come. End it!

But that fight for air is the most powerful drive in the human body. Life begins and ends with it, and it's as ancient as the first primitive gasp that hauled life out of the swamp. It wouldn't let me go. There were no childhood memories, no rerun of my life; only that squeezing urge to breathe.

Vaguely, in spite of the pain, I realized that thirty seconds must have passed. Why wasn't I dead?

I must have been rolled onto my back, because I started to sense someone pushing, not unpleasantly, on the front of my chest. Next, bursting into my lungs, I felt a rush of air explode the vise of asphyxia. Again, again, and again. It was like sex, like coming, release.

More pushing, more volleys of relief.

The whiteout in my eyes began to clear. Shadows speckled with light moved above me. The ringing dimmed a notch; voices vibrated through the din.

More pushing, more relief. I could feel a mask applied to my face.

These creeps were resuscitating me. They were bagging air into my lungs, compressing my heart.

The voices organized to speech. I still saw only shadows dancing above me.

One of the shadows barked, "All clear!"

The other form withdrew. The precious puffs of air stopped, the vise in my chest clamped back down. They were stopping. I wanted seconds more. Don't stop. Not yet!

I sank back into the airless pit. I still could see the remaining shadow lean over me. I felt more pressure on my chest.

Another ignition of white light exploded up my eyeballs, arched through me, and flopped me back on the floor.

My world stayed white, but the vise on my chest was lifting. This time I could even feel the press of the reapplied mask on my face and a delicious flow of air bagged into me. My ears were back to ringing. I couldn't move, couldn't twitch a muscle, but I knew my heart had been restarted. Hey, when you've been down to the last ticks of the second hand, you take what you can get, although even in my recently fried state, I figured I wasn't exactly in the care of a concerned team of health professionals.

I tried taking inventory. Breathing on my own was slowly coming back, the mask assisting my still-feeble efforts. Talking was impossible. My tongue felt the size of a salami. I could only gurgle pathetically. My sense of smell was all too functional; I was lying in a pool of my own urine and feces. Everything hurt, nothing moved. *Anoxia, acidosis,* and *postresuscitation myalgia* were the medical terms. In reality, it was the wall of screaming muscle pain marathoners hit when their bodies run out of oxygen. I was powerless, effectively paralyzed. Their specimen. They had turned resuscitation into an instrument of torture. Any move by them could plummet me back to a slow and lingering horror, death.

The flashing lights subsided. The hooded shadows became silent ski masks. Behind the odd "O" eyes and mouth shapes, I looked for some shred of pity, doubt, or change of heart. Instead, the eyes above me revealed a cold indifference. In the one bagging me, the lips were thin, grimaced, neutral. The other, hunched over in front, leered at my increasing fear. The mouth was hideously familiar. I knew she would speak, would no longer take the trouble to hide. She would leisurely savor a running commentary on my death, or deaths even, repeated over and over, as long as the cruelty pleasured her.

"Go check his computer. See how far he's got!" Jones's voice was cool, matter-of-fact, the voice of a practiced clinician, familiar with the process. The other figure left without a word.

"So, who'd you tell, Doc? Or did you figure it out yet?

Before you go, we have to know." Her leer returned at her own accidental rhyme. My attempt to reply was still a gurgle.

"Fuckin' Kingsly. Came up on me in the path lab that night. I think the slob went there to hump the corpses when he couldn't find a stray woman to paw. He caught me with one of my subjects. Even stewed, he knew I was being a bad girl. He started loping off down the hall, hollering. I had to run after the dumb fuck. I grabbed my cardiac needle and caught up with him easy enough, but he was thrashing around like a cornered pig."

I heard more gurgling. It was my breathing. I tried to turn my head to get rid of the drool and vomit, but I couldn't move.

"Oh, airway trouble, Doc. You were always the stickler about teaching the importance of managing an airway." With a vicious twist, she wrenched my head to the side. A sour goo ran out the corner of my mouth, and I stopped choking. But every part of me felt encased; I couldn't seem to move at all. Even my eyes had trouble turning back toward my tormentor's voice. I gave up trying to see her. If she was talking, she wanted me able to hear. That's all I was reduced to—listening and gulping air, grasping a few more seconds.

Her voice dropped the clipped neutrality. "Did I do that good, Doc!" she exclaimed. I could feel her breath on my ear. "You hear me, Doc!" she shrieked, and snapped my head back around, grabbed my chin, and pinched hard, putting her face right up to mine. Her eyes, dead before, now seethed with fury, a ferocity I'd diagnosed and felled with Haldol many times. This was one sick cookie.

She switched back and donned her cool indifference like a gown. She studied me, her specimen, and continued her dissertation.

"So I had to settle him down, Doc, get him positioned,

you know what I mean. So you know what I did? Hey, you're going to love this one. I ripped open my shirt and showed him my titties!"

At this revelation, she snapped her head upright and waited, real delight on what I could see of her face, as though she expected a laugh from me. When none came, she shrugged and went on with her tale.

"Dumb fuck went for them, like a bull to a red flag, sucking and slobbering all over the place. I had to get my back up against the wall to support his weight. As he entertained himself, I got his shirt unbuttoned, slid in the needle tip, and did an underhand into the heart." The recollected moment brought another smile. "Funny, he was so into my little titties, he didn't realize at first he was dead. Kept sucking away." The smile faded, the voice hardened. "Then he dropped; broke the needle. Sprayed blood everywhere and peed all over me as he went down."

She seemed transfixed as she continued. "Stripped off his shirt and pants, cleaned up the blood, got him into a wheelchair, and bagged his clothes. I covered him with a sheet and had to switch into OR greens myself, in case a stray guard saw us, but they didn't usually go to administration at night. I got him up the freight elevator to his office without being seen."

She'd started out by taunting me but now was staring off into space as I'd seen her do so often at staff meetings. It was as though she'd repeated what happened many times before, compelled to reiterate her downfall, like a liturgy for her own undoing. "I dumped him on the carpet," she continued, not even looking at me, "wiped off his chest again with alcohol swabs, and cranked up the heat to dry him off. By that time the blood had clotted and the puncture site was just a tiny scab. With what everybody knew about him, they'd still think he'd tried to have sex somewhere, stumbled back to his office in his underwear, got cold and turned up the heat, and then died from a heart attack. I slipped back to the morgue, cleaned off the wheelchair, called in my ambulance, and whipped the derelict I was working on, the bloody clothes, even the sheet, out the back door." She stopped, seemed to see me again, and added, "Did you know you can move a body in a body bag in and out the back door of a hospital morgue at almost any time during the night and nobody questions it? Everybody assumes it's a pickup for a funeral home."

She looked proud, but seconds later the smug expression faded and her face took on a hardness again. "Who would've thought a stupid civilian would pump a corpse? Hell, no doctor would have. Even with the heat, Kingsly would have been stiffening up after five hours." Her eyes were filling with rage. "And you," she snarled, grabbing my hair and leaning toward me, "you homed in on the call, noticed the blood, and found the needle. Then you just kept pushing, Watts's little pointer. When you called to ask Kradic about needle stabs and the DOA, I knew you were getting close to what was really happening and you had to die too. Even without Watts, it'd be only a matter of time before your damn ER data gave you my name. The rest, as they say, is history, and so are you, you pompous, self-righteous prick." She slammed my head back on the tile floor.

I had at least started swallowing again, but the stench of her breath and the pain in my skull promised new vomit to choke on. I tried to pull my face away, but instead she gripped my chin again with her fingers. "How about you, Professor?" she whispered. "Do you want to suck my titties while you go?" She suddenly brought her head so close to mine, I could see only her eyes. "Don't worry, I won't tell your precious Janet."

My fury snapped through me like a jolt of current. If I

could have moved, I would have torn into her like an animal, with teeth, hands, fingernails—anything.

Just as abruptly, she moved back, and I was being eyed as a specimen once more. She returned to the defibrillator monitor on the floor beside us. Quickly she set the machine at ready and picked up the electrical paddles. She began slathering lubricating gel onto their surfaces. Over her shoulder she bellowed to her partner, still upstairs, supposedly with my computer records. "Did you find anything yet?"

The reply was muffled but satisfied her, something about "in a minute," which was probably how long I had. I tested if I could move anything. I got a finger to twitch.

She kept circling one paddle on the other, languidly spreading the lubricant as if absently stirring a bowl of batter. I noticed she'd taken off her gloves.

"You know," she said softly, "if mag sulfate had been the magic bullet to resuscitate arrests the early studies had hinted at, my trials would have discovered the standards for the most effective dose and administrative protocol long before the rest of the world. Other researchers in the study were tied to the tedium of double-blind randomization and limited by having to wait for natural arrests to occur." She kept circling one paddle on the other and staring off into space. I tried to move my hands.

"And the delays, they always had the delay before they got to the subject. I had them fresh; time didn't obscure my results. Sometimes I could run up to ten treatment protocols on a single specimen before they were gone for good."

More silence, more circling. A faraway look glazed over her eyes. I knew her fever. It was like Fernandez's, but on a much greater scale. Jones was after the adulation of *sensational* health research. The same forum of recognition and respect that so enthralled Fernandez, but multiplied tenfold. At this level there was the possibility of big bucks. The drug-company cash available for backing a winning record was phenomenal. Discovering a drug protocol that dramatically increased survival after heart attacks and cardiac arrests would be heralded everywhere and set its founder up with research funds for life. Jones had been after a breakthrough in resuscitation, a kind of Lazarus protocol, a new and better way to raise the dead that would catapult her to the head of the field.

I could hear her bitterness. "It wasn't there. Mag sulfate, the cheap heart saver, didn't work much better than the usual treatments." Then she stopped circling the paddles and looked down at me. "But Doc, I couldn't let all that risk, all that work go to waste. No, I grabbed one corner of resus protocol and made it mine forever." She leaned forward. "Did you figure it out yet, Professor?"

It was a command, an order to see and acknowledge her genius. And I *had* figured it out. Torsade de pointes. An obscure, rare dysrhythmia, never frequent enough to give the opportunity for much definitive study, had started turning up unexpectedly as one of the dysrhythmias in patients on allergy medication, like terfenadine, in combination with antibiotics, like erythromycin. Those were the drugs found in our DOA. When the health warnings first came out, Jones had seized on the knowledge to salvage something from her failing murderous quest for recognition. Alcoholics had been injected, probably intracardiac, to produce torsade de pointes and give Jones enough cases to get the best protocol with magnesium sulfate. Then she buried her data in the Buffalo cardiac arrest study.

But the p value for her results, the probability of certainty over chance in scientific studies, was far too good for the small number of cases the Buffalo area should have had. That's what twigged when she ran her study by me—her possibility of a result due to chance was below a probability of one in ten thousand times. She must have had nearly three hundred cases to have such certainty.

Of course, she'd never spelled out her study size. She never had to. She was sentenced to having her name confined to a minor find, just a footnote added to a larger investigation. A mention, a p value, nothing more. There were no detailed numbers or data. She couldn't afford closer scrutiny. But the rarity of naturally occurring torsade de pointes wouldn't invite much interest. Her study would be a little oddity in the literature of cardiac arrests. To end with so little; to have hungered after so much. To have caused so much evil.

I had to stop her.

She placed one of the paddles on my chest and languidly spread the gel, absently, almost tenderly, like greasing up a lover. Her eyes were far away again, as if locked on her failure.

I could still feel the cold slush from melted snow under my palms. I could move my hands enough now to press them against the wet tiles.

She stopped stroking my chest. The paddle had smeared itself dry. Sticking to my skin, it tugged her focus back on me. She troweled on some more gel, but roughly this time. "What the hell's keeping you!" she screeched over her shoulder.

There was another distant murmur. I heard the floorboards above creak, followed by the heavy thud of returning steps.

The other figure loomed behind her.

"Anything?" She was curt, clinical now.

The figure stepped around in front, shook a masked head. My sight was clearer. I could see white stubble lining the silent mouth. Older; male.

"Good for you, Doc. No entry to the identity code logged. Got here just in time." She turned to the dials.

"You hadn't gotten my name yet." The click of the sync switch going off sounded like a cocked pistol.

"So now a little heart attack. All that paranoia, running around, and sneaking in through the snow. Too much stress. Popped your mind; blew your heart."

She spun the charge to full. "Nobody likes their easy answers messed up. Not the cops, and definitely not Hurst. They're gonna love this."

She plopped the paddles on my chest. I tried to strain away. My fingers flexed, my arms budged a little, but I was still unable to move the rest of my body. The beeping steadily rose toward ready.

"Grieving widow, unborn infant already fatherless."

Any reserve I had went into a gurgled roar.

It surprised her, then tweaked her interest. I felt her lean on the paddles. She put her thumbs over the buttons and wiggled them.

"So, a little response. I thought this was going to be boring. That you'd be classy to the end with this stiff-upper-lip bit." She brought her mouth down and exhaled. "Want to beg?"

I started moving my head, tried to spit in her face, but managed only to drool.

"Oh, so fierce," she mocked. "Good. Hate me! I'm taking away your miserable high-class fucking life."

My legs shuffled uselessly, but my hands were opening and closing, squeezing the slush between my fingers.

"Ah, that's good," she crooned. "I like them writhing." She was breathing hard enough now that I believed her.

She pressed just one thumb down on the red button. I braced. She kept the left thumb up, twitched it. I tried not to close my eyes but kept staring at it. I was going to get only a fraction of a second to do this, and it would have to be the right fraction.

"Yes, yes," she teased, caressing the button now.

"Fuck this shit!" hissed the figure behind me.

The voice. I knew that voice.

Jones reacted as if she'd been slapped. She glared up at him, forgetting me for the moment but still leaving the paddles in place. "Don't you ever speak to me like that," she said. "Do you hear me! Don't ever interfere with what I do!"

I saw the large shape turn and heard the latch behind me snap open. Cold air ran over my head while his footsteps crunched as he walked away over the snow. He didn't bother to close the door.

Jones squatted, hunched over her machine, her shoulders drooping. After a few seconds the piercing tone of the monitor seemed to revive her. She gave it a final look, then turned abruptly back to me. I got ready. I was going to die, but I had a chance to take her with me.

She pressed the paddles hard down onto my chest. I gasped one final breath and grabbed for her hands.

Her thumbs dropped. I exhaled a scream. The white explosion roared back through my brain. I felt the current lock my wet hands to hers and curl our fingers into spasms, clamping us to the paddles. Through the pain, I heard her shriek—an explosion of sound blown out of her lungs as the direct current convulsed her diaphragm. I'd gotten her! Then my hearing sealed off, and the searing grip of electricity snapped through my back, arms, and legs. It shot my muscles into a fixed seizure. My back jerked into an arch, my arms jammed into my chest, my grip on her increased. For that fraction of a second we were arched away from each other, yet fused in the extended agony of a violent convulsion. When the discharge ended, we both flopped back down—released, and dying.

I could feel her twitching on top of me, fighting for air, the same as I had done. She must be aware, gasping in pain and terror, as I'd been, and as so many others had done under her cruel watch. I felt no forgiveness, no pity as we hurtled toward death together. I wanted her to fight it, to feel the horror of knowing she was already dead, to strain for air that would never come. To endure the long seconds at the end of her life knowing I'd sent her to hell.

I went easier this time. Already weak, and with no one pounding my chest or shoving air into my lungs, I fell back to black.

The rush into silence was unseemly. I tried not to struggle, to just let go. A vision of Janet came, then vanished. Even the rage and anger faded. My last thought was that I'd stopped Jones. I felt an acceleration, but it was more a dispersal in all directions than any real movement— spreading out—like a drop of water going back into the ocean. Death as a diluent.

Suddenly there was a flash, followed by another. They were more whiteouts of the black than anything I could actually see. This wasn't part of the ride. The hurtle slowed, reversed. The sound of surf began rushing in and out of my skull. I was going back. That bitch wasn't dead! I thought, suddenly terrified again. She was bringing me back! The surf got louder. A tunnel burrowed into my throat. I was rising fast, welling back to life with the surge of vomit that flew out past the tube now snug in my airway. Seconds later I became very worldly and simply fainted.

The sounds of surf were back; steady, running in, running out. It was the sound of my own breathing, noisily pushing up and down the tube in my windpipe that felt like a garden hose. I seemed buried alive, so heavy was each limb, every finger immobile. What flicker of brain activity I had left was enough to fear more games. It became essential to open my eyes. What was she going to do? Why was I still alive? Why was she? The rushing sound of my own breathing blended with a tinny rumble. A voice? Was someone speaking to me?

I felt hands on me. I got ready. I still couldn't lift my lids. Had the bitch stitched them closed? I could barely manage a good flinch.

But the hands were gentle. The breathing got less loud, and the rumble organized itself into a man's voice.

He kept saying two words, but they were garbled. He repeated them, and finally I could hear what he was saying.

"I'm sorry."

All at once the hands, and the voice, were gone.

Everything hurt, even my eyelids. I finally opened them, but it didn't matter. The hallway was dark, and I wasn't past seeing just blurred shadows anyway.

My breathing kept me company. Any gagging I felt didn't amount to much. I was too feeble to vomit.

I heard a sound, rising and falling like my breathing. Except it was higher, annoying, getting louder. A siren. It seemed to be right in my ear before someone mercifully shut it off. I heard doors slamming, boots crunching on snow. Then I felt a shot of cold air over my head as the door flew open and my new visitors arrived.

I sensed more than saw one of them kneel by my side. "Are you all right?" he demanded.

Sure, I'm lying there in my own pee and crap, had been dead twice, and now I didn't have the strength of a polio victim, but sure, I'd reassure my rescuer. My brain said "nod." What my head did, I don't know, but it must have budged.

The man, who was still blurry and unrecognizable to me, leaned back as if relaxing. "Wait till you get my bill."

I couldn't see yet. My vision remained a blur of speckled lights. Any effort to speak left me gagging on the tube in my throat. I could hear their voices, but they sounded pretty far off and faded in and out like a poorly tuned radio. In the background I recognized the steady hum of a vehicle moving fast.

I was still barely able to move, but I had to get that cursed tube out of my throat. It was making me cough and retch continually now. I tried to move my arm and feebly brought my hand up to the part of the tube sticking out of my mouth. I got my fingers around it and pulled. Whoever had intubated me hadn't inflated the cuff to keep the tube secure. It slid out easily, and while the extraction had left me coughing and spitting, I immediately felt better.

Someone supported me when I tried to turn on my side and clear my mouth. I heard Doug's voice say, "Easy, Earl."

"What happened to Jones?" I managed to croak after I caught my breath.

Doug didn't answer at first. "Was that the woman we found beside you?" he asked after a few seconds.

"Yeah," I answered. I'd forgotten he didn't know her name.

He waited, then told me, "She's dead, Earl."

At first I didn't feel anything in particular. Not relief, not triumph, not even a sense it was over. It worked, I thought almost neutrally. My grab at her hands had worked. I seemed to accept this outcome the same way, as a physician, I'd have accepted the successful outcome of an attempted therapeutic act. Then a horrible feeling of emptiness came through me—a hollow, sick feeling—absolute, final, irrevocable. I felt dead inside.

Chapter 17

I could finally see. Arnie was driving the commandeered ambulance with full lights and siren. I was trying to stay in the bouncing stretcher. I found my voice enough to ask Doug a few more questions on the ride into Buffalo.

"What brought you in?"

"You didn't call."

"You sound like a mother," I quipped, trying to hide how shaky I was, inside and out.

Arnie whooped with glee as yet another column of traffic pulled over to let him pass.

When I hadn't phoned in, Doug told me, he radioed the cops. Then he and his boys drove down to the highway and with their trucks cut off Jones's two thugs waiting in the ambulance and car before they even could start their engines. The sight of him and his men jumping from their vehicles, armed with crowbars, ball-peen hammers, and a few hunting rifles did the trick. The two came out, hands up. Doug trussed them in bandages, threw them in the back of the ambulance, and roared in to find me.

"When we arrived, no one else was there except you and that woman. Scared me shitless, seeing the two of you stretched out like that," Doug continued. He paused, having trouble finding the words to recall the scene. "With that monitor thing wired to you and a tube down your throat, I thought we were too late."

I was still confused, but I started to get it. "You mean you didn't shock me back?"

"Me? No way. You were already beeping away with a pattern on the screen—the pointy pattern, like you see on the TV shows when it'll be okay. Still, we didn't want to take any chances with you by waiting for the cops to arrive. That's why Arnie and I have you in this ambulance. We left Norm and my other men back there guarding the bad guys."

The man with the familiar voice must have somehow slipped back and resuscitated me. I was still wondering why when I went unconscious again.

The next time I woke up Janet was holding me.

"You turkey!" she yelled as she burst into tears. She was still giving me a hug when I slipped away again.

The next few days were a series of comas. In between I slept a lot. They hooked me up to every piece of equipment they had in the ICU. Then they went out and rented some they didn't have just to make sure. When they finished, I looked like a pinball arcade paying off in free games. But they needn't have bothered. My best monitor was Janet. She was there each time I woke up, watching every blip, every digital printout.

"Hold my hand?"

"Sure."

"Rub my head?"

"Don't press your luck, turkey!"

There were no windows in the ICU. The mornings were marked by how many times the powdered egg stuff came by. I could tell it was night when all the needling and testing stopped.

I could tell I was doing better when I awoke and the chair where Janet kept her vigil was empty.

By crossing my eyes I could see the tube running out

my nose. The needled catheters inserted under my right collarbone and into both arms were easier to spot. Another permanent arterial line was stuck in my wrist with a spigot on the end for immediate access to my blood. I felt like a keg of draft on tap.

But the ultimate humiliation was the tube running off the end of a condom I now peed through. For some strange reason, they called this contraption a Texas catheter.

Stewart Deloram, the chief of intensive care, seemed to enjoy having me under his total control. He strutted to the end of my bed and boomed, "How are you today, Chief?"

It wasn't a question. It was a gloat. A look-at-you-there-and-me-here kind of gloat.

"Deloram, you're a sick, sadistic son of a bitch in a control frenzy!"

"Ooh, nurse, has Dr. Garnet shown signs of delusional paranoia, an ICU psychosis?"

"You're the only psychotic on these premises. Hell, I don't need half this crap."

"Is that a professional opinion, Chief, or does all this crankiness mean you're really getting better?"

"Apart from being pretty sleepy, I can't tell there's anything wrong with me."

"Frankly, neither can we."

"Why not back off all this mother-hen stuff?" I waved my arms and the attendant tubes at him. The attached bottles of varied green and yellow secretions rattled noisily. The bells and whistles on all the machines lit up. Five nurses ran over to our cubicle.

Deloram waved them off. "He's just being expressive again. It's all right. Everyone back to work." He turned to me. "You keep crying wolf like that, Doc, no one will believe it if you really need us."

"How do you know I need you at all?"

He pouted, then did something really scary. He got serious. "We don't know. Nobody's done studies on stopping and jump-starting a normal heart before."

"You find any damage?"

"None we can measure."

"Do you think it'll affect my life expectancy?"

"Like I said, no studies. There've been a couple of series on dogs who had tickers tocked and restarted with a shot of juice. They did okay, but by that I mean you can expect to be burying bones in the backyard to a ripe old age of twelve in doggie years."

This time his humor felt a little thin. The look on my face must have betrayed a wee touch of the cold, crawly feeling I was getting inside. He put a hand on my shoulder and became very gentle.

"Look, Earl, what you were put through is as weird as I've ever seen, and probably ever will. Those creeps seem to have kept you pretty well aerated while they had their sick jollies. In that regard, they were at least technically competent, but monsters with expertise are somehow even scarier."

For a moment I didn't see Deloram. I saw a pair of older eyes, eyes of a man who kept saying he was sorry.

"Any word on the fourth guy yet?"

"Apparently the cops got him. They picked him up coming out of the woods about two miles south of you. So you don't have to worry about any of them. It's over."

I still had a dead feeling inside. In some ways I knew it would never be over.

"By the way," Deloram continued, "some big detective's taken a special interest in you. He's been here regularly for the last two days to see if you were ready to talk to him yet, but I told him you weren't going anywhere and needed the rest. I suggested he run your name for unpaid parking tickets while waiting."

Riley. "Let me speak to him next time."

"Sure."

"Where's Janet?"

"Asleep."

I must have looked lonesome because he said, "Hey, give your guardian angel and us a break. She's been like a one-woman accreditation visit since you got here. It took her twenty-four hours just to trust us enough with your precious skin before she agreed to a little nap herself. She's in the residents' room, wondered if we'd changed the sheets since she rotated through here ten years ago. Let her rest."

"So this is day two?"

"More or less."

"How much longer?"

"Now, that, my son, is a closely guarded medical secret."

"Dammit, Stewart, quit kidding around. When do I get out of here?"

He slid off the side of the bed where he'd been sitting, strode to the cubicle curtains, struck an operatic pose, and answered, "Soon, my son, soon, or never." Then, with a maniacal grin, he left.

Outside from the nurses' station I heard his deliberately overloud instructions. "Oh, Nurse Mandy, I think it's time to change Dr. Garnet's Texas catheter, please."

There were giggles, and Nurse Mandy, who regularly modeled swimsuits in the ad section of the *Buffalo Gazette*, jiggled into the curtained area to do her duty. Then he must have hit the alarm-set switch at his desk because every bell and buzzer at my bedside went off again.

"You're a sick person, Deloram! Sick!" I yelled against a rising wall of laughter from beyond my curtains. Nurse Mandy never missed a beat, so to speak.

I figured the stay at Deloram's little kingdom would end when he got bored with me or I could stay awake for more than an hour. The first occurred pretty quickly. I didn't see him much after our chat. The second feat proved more difficult.

A few awakenings later I found Janet back in her chair. She looked tired, but she smiled my way and softly said, "Hello."

"Hi, yourself."

I enjoyed just watching her for a few quiet minutes. She looked pleased that I was awake and reached for my hand. It felt wonderful.

"I was afraid you'd still want to brain me," I whispered.

"That would presume some brains in the first place." Her voice was a little less soft.

"You *do* still want to brain me."

"I'm letting them fatten you up here first."

"How's Muffy?"

"Better than you. She's out of intensive care."

I was left to stew in an uneasy silence for a while. Then Janet added, "She's going to be all right. Probably will be home next week."

"And how is home coming along?" It wasn't exactly a roaring conversation, but I figured sputtering talk was better than icy silence.

What I got back, however, was ice *and* talk. "Let's just say," she began rather coolly, "that Doug's wife was as thrilled as I was with the great bozo escapade. Now that she's let him back out of her sight, the work is going quite nicely." A pause. Then a hint of melting, "Especially the baby's room." More thought. "It's really quite lovely."

"You look like you could use some of the sleep I'm getting."

"It's the two men I run around with. One keeps me up all night with worry, the other kicks me awake when I sleep."

"I'm sorry, Janet. It was a pretty boneheaded idea."

She rolled her eyes and said, "Oh, great! You decide on your own to play Hardy Boys with our contractor, without so much as a word to me, and then bring the Wicked Witch of the Night down on us, and you think a big doleful 'I'm sorry' is going to cut it!"

As Janet's voice rose, the rest of the ICU suddenly got very, very quiet.

"C'mon, Janet, this is embarrassing me."

"Ahh, scare me half to death, then poor you gets embarrassed."

She was up off her chair now, obviously enjoying my discomfort. "You can just lie there in silence and contemplate your sins," she proclaimed rather loudly, then walked over to my array of monitors. She gave me a big wink and started shutting off the alarm switches one by one. "No! Not another word." She started undoing her ponytail. "Just let me read in peace" was her final, very public instruction.

Then she leaned over me and let her hair shower down around our faces. For the next half hour, not a bong could be heard. At least not in my cubicle.

My next awakening was not so pleasant. Bufort sat huddled in the chair like a hulking toad. Riley prowled restlessly back and forth in front of the curtains.

I wasn't sure what time it was except that another serving of the dried egg stuff lay congealing on my bed tray. Must be day three.

Bufort didn't even wait until I was fully awake. "Dr. Garnet, do you know the penalty for impersonating a police officer?"

"Why, Bufort? Is someone threatening to charge you with it?"

"What!"

"I wouldn't worry. It'll never stick. At least not for impersonating a competent one!"

A few of my bongs had started going off. Janet must have reattached them. Bufort's eyes bulged, he was so enraged. Riley had gone perfectly still.

"That's right, you pompous prick, your silly, conceited posturing left me at the mercy of a serial killer, a maniac. If I hadn't done what I did, I'd be dead by now, and you'd be clucking your tongue and pronouncing it an unfortunate end by stress."

"That's absolutely—"

"It's absolutely true, and you know it! You bother me one more time and I'll give enough depositions to bust you to traffic tickets!"

A few nurses swished by the curtains and busied themselves with the alarms my rocketing pulse and blood pressure had triggered. A very stern Nurse Mandy said, "Gentlemen, you are out of here." Forcefully, she levered Bufort out of the chair by the elbow and showed him the door. Riley winked at me as he trailed after his boss.

The rest of the afternoon crept by. Popovitch and Sylvia Green dropped in to wish me a speedy return to work. Sometime later a rather morose Hurst hung around the end of my cubicle for a few seconds, mumbled about reopening the hundred beds, then left. I guess he figured it was politically unwise to continue our battle while I was so helpless.

I had a couple more sleeps and then was gently shaken awake. It was Riley. "Hi, Doc," he said quietly. "Dr. Deloram said you wanted to speak to me?"

He'd pulled a chair up near my bed and kept looking nervously over at the curtain. I guessed he'd snuck back in and was afraid of being found again by Nurse Mandy.

"Yeah," I answered sleepily.

But before I could say anything else, Riley interjected, "I wasn't part of what that idiot boss of mine pulled today, but I couldn't prevent it." Then he gave me a big grin. "You really got him!"

I smiled back at the compliment. Then I got down to what I wanted to ask him. "I've got a lot of questions about how it all happened. And with Jones dead, are you going to be able to make a case against her thugs? The thought of them getting out scares me. And who was the guy that came back to resuscitate me? After all the killings that Jones had involved him in, why'd he bother?" Slept out, I was eager now to talk.

Riley leaned back in the chair. "First of all," he began, "the guy who saved you is going to testify against the other two goons who worked with Jones in exchange for a lighter sentence. You won't have to worry about them. Apparently they used to beat up on strikebreakers for the truckers' union before they got to be ambulance drivers. That's where Jones found them. Since they know we have a witness, their lawyer advised them to cooperate, and they're talking now as well, though we haven't made them any promises. They claim they never actually killed anyone, but are admitting to working with Jones for more than three years, snagging derelicts off the street for her 'research,' and then scattering their bodies around town after she was done with them."

Three years. That was longer than I'd figured.

"They also did her other dirty work," Riley added, "like trying to run you down, helping her trash your house, and setting up Watts. We found the Dobermans in a cage behind the house where one of them lived. They said it was for the money she paid them, but I got a creepy feeling they liked watching people suffer and would've done it for free. One of them also told me she really liked getting it on with them, together." He related her sordid story with the neutral cynicism I'd expect from a cop. But I couldn't suppress a shudder on hearing what she'd kept hidden all these years.

"A few of the vagrant DOAs' bodies are being exhumed," he continued, "to get evidence of needle marks in the heart. By the way, why was she so afraid of your ER data?"

I sat up. "The data covered only twelve months of her activity, but it contained enough information to expose her, if you knew enough to ask the right questions. It showed that DOAs came in only on the mornings when she was off duty the night before, or, to put it crudely, only when she wasn't stuck in the ER and was free to go out and kill. I'm pretty sure the same pattern will show up for the times the other DOAs turned up all over the city. At first I made the mistake of looking for the shift with a lot of DOAs, but then I realized that didn't make sense because they weren't being killed in the ER. What pointed to her was the lack of DOAs when she was on duty. Show that same pattern for all those derelicts murdered with a cardiac needle and Jones would stand out from every other ER doc in Buffalo. I don't know if she always used Watts's lab to kill them, or if she sometimes ran her codes right in the back of the ambulance. If so, it might also have been possible to link the deaths to the nights she was on the road with the cardiac study."

Riley reached for his notebook. "Can I get copies of the data that shows this?"

"Sure. See my secretary."

Then I remembered Jones's words back at the cabin. "All that risk, all that work. I couldn't let it go to waste."

"Oh my God!" I exclaimed, suddenly realizing the obvious. "The torsade de pointes killings were only part of it. There must have been earlier murders as she tried to get a breakthrough treating V. tach. and V. fib."

Riley looked puzzled, and I took a moment explaining the terminology. When I finished, he stayed silent, then reached into his briefcase and handed me a folder. "Does this mean what I think it does?" he asked. "We found it in her apartment."

I opened the file and recognized Jones's familiar handwriting. It was an outline of the research she'd intended to pursue in phase two of the cardiac study, but it was never intended for presentation to any ethics committee.

"My God!" I said again as I handed it back to him.

"She intended to go on killing, didn't she," he replied.

"I think she'd already started," I answered.

"What!"

"Her idea in there," I said, nodding to the file, "was to see if magnesium sulphate would be a breakthrough in the prevention of deadly heart rhythms as opposed to their treatment. She proposed loading up her derelicts with magnesium sulphate and *then* challenging them with her erythromycin/terfenadine cocktail or unsynchronized electric shock, like she'd tried on me, to see if they'd be more resistant to developing abnormal rhythms."

"I thought those medicines usually produced torsade de whatever, and it was too rare to make her famous."

"Torsade de pointes is still a variant of V. tach., and preventing it might have given her a useful lead on how to prevent ordinary V. tach. and V. fib. I'd already figured she was onto something new, using her old techniques, because the DOAs had kept coming. And even though she'd finished her paper on torsade de pointes, Watts had found terfenadine and erythromycin on the last John Doe." I paused, thinking of all the poor souls who had died in such fear, then tapped the grisly document still in Riley's hand. "She'd obviously begun her own phase two."

"Christ!" whistled Riley as he returned the file to his briefcase. I thought he was going to close it, but he hesitated before snapping the clasps shut and took out a small cassette instead. I noticed his jaw was bulging as he looked at it. "Doc, you also asked about the fourth man, the one who saved you. I wasn't going to put you through this yet, but if you're well enough, I'd like you to listen to part of his interrogation."

"Sure, but why wouldn't I be well enough to hear it?"

"Because it's going to take you back through all that happened to you, but from their point of view. And there are some nasty insinuations about you, at first."

"What do you mean?"

"Let me start by telling you about the guy who saved you. His name's Vito Manley, though that wouldn't mean anything to you. What's important is he's different from the other two. He worked for the same company as them, but he'd been transferred to dispatch at 911 about four years ago as part of some program to improve standards when MAS took over. A few months later, Jones appeared on the scene and started riding the ambulances for the research project. He noticed she preferred his old company and later realized it was because the types there suited her purposes."

"How'd he get involved?"

"Listen for yourself. The full session was formally videotaped, but I recorded the parts I wanted you to hear on a cassette." He pressed the Play button. Even with the hollow sound of a recording taken in a room, I recognized the familiar voice of the man who had saved my life and who had kept saying, "I'm sorry."

"She'd slipped me a few thousand to direct any calls to pick up street derelicts to her and not make a record of it. Hell, I thought it was a Medicare scam—that she was copping their cards and running up a bunch of bogus claims payable to her. It seemed safe enough, at least for me. It wasn't until last year, when someone started blackmailing her, that she told me what was really going on. Then she threatened to pull me down with her unless I helped her find out who it was."

His words kept coming in a rush, as if he felt compelled to talk.

Riley leaned over and stopped the machine. "Did you know anything about a blackmailer?" he asked.

"No!" I exclaimed, astonished.

"The next part is going to be hard for you to hear," he warned, restarting the tape.

After a few seconds of room noise, the man spoke. "At least, at first it was to find out who was blackmailing her. After the Kingsly fiasco, *whoever* it was hit her for a last big payment, probably figuring she'd soon get caught and the cash flow would end. The way Garnet had kept the pressure on, discovering the needle in Kingsly and exposing the derelict's murder, she actually figured for a while that it might be him. That made her nuts. She thought he was lording it over her that he was a medical bigshot while he was bleeding her dry. But she didn't want to kill him outright until she was sure. That first night she had her goons use the dogs on him, it was a warning, like, to back off."

The man coughed, then said, "The next night she had the two of them follow Garnet to his country place—at that time she only wanted them to steal the analysis of the ER statistics. You see, she was also afraid Garnet was preparing a record of dates based on the data that would show her connection to the DOAs. She figured it would have been good strategy on his part, had he been the blackmailer, to have it as a kind of insurance policy against being killed if he was ever found out—to be opened if he died. Something like that. If she found a document like that she'd know for sure he was the blackmailer and could kill him. But his dog chased the guys off before they could get what they came for. She tried again herself and broke into his hospital office early one morning. She didn't find anything. But when he had that resident ask about using cardiac needles on derelicts in front of her, she was sure it was him, and that he was still playing with her to get more cash out of her. So she phoned her goons and arranged his hit-and-run accident on the spur of the moment. I think it was as much revenge as a need to get rid of him. When it didn't work, she got away from the hospital long enough to join the men in searching his house while we were on the way to the vet's with his dog. Boy, did she go berserk when she couldn't find his analysis."

Riley stopped the tape again. "Does any of that make sense, Doc? Or was this guy blowing smoke to try to get a better deal?"

My mouth was so dry, I could barely swallow. "She thought I was blackmailing her?" I finally managed to croak.

"Apparently, at first."

"What do you mean, 'at first.' "

"There's more. But what about his account of what happened? Does it jibe with how you remember things?"

The swirl of events he described ran through my mind like fragments of a movie—familiar, yet seen from the other side. "I guess so," I said haltingly. And then a detail popped into place. "He said he drove me to the animal hospital. That's where I remember him from. He was the older attendant! Good God, does that mean he was the one who tried to run me down?"

As an answer, Riley continued the tape.

This time I heard the detective's voice echo my own question.

"Was it you who hit Garnet and the dog?"

"Oh, no! That was those two goons of hers. I was only told to be in the area. Like I said, it was a last-minute call just twenty minutes before. She said that she was gonna take care of the blackmailer. I had to be careful because my partner had nothing to do with it."

"Were you supposed to finish him off?"

"No!"

"Level with me! What were you supposed to do with him?"

"If he was okay, just shaken up like, I was to make sure we took him to the hospital for a checkup. To get him away from the house so she could search it."

"And if he wasn't okay?"

I heard some shuffling noises and another scrape from a chair leg.

"If he wasn't already dead, but near killed, I was to tip him over, an accident like. Drop his neck, leave his airway blocked, stuff like that. You know, our usual screwups."

There were a few more seconds of shuffling sounds.

"Hey, I didn't do it, did I?"

"Because he wasn't near dead, and it would have been too obvious."

"No! I couldn't do that." There was another pause, then he added very quietly, "At least I found that out."

Riley pushed Stop and waited.

I felt angry. "He probably saved my life only to get a better deal with you guys, once he saw Jones was dead."

"Maybe. Either way, he's going to do time. But I don't think he had the taste for killing the way the others had."

"You said there was more . . . about the blackmailer?"

"That's the next bit," he answered. The tape came on in the middle of his next question.

"—Garnet the blackmailer?"

"No! That Sunday evening she calls me and says she's taken care of the *real* blackmailer and that it hadn't been him after all. But she told me Garnet was still a threat because he wasn't buying that Kingsly and the derelict had been killed by that crazy psychiatrist who dove off the roof. She knew he hadn't figured out it was her *yet* or he would have already gone to the cops and had them arrest her. If we moved fast, she said, we could stop him before it was too late and make it look like a heart attack. That we'd all be safe forever."

Riley snapped off the machine and moved to put it back in his briefcase. "Do you know who might have been blackmailing Jones?"

"No. Did he, Vito, what's his name?"

"Manley. No, he said she never told him. The other two men had no idea either."

"Did you really think it was me?"

Riley looked embarrassed. "He brought it up. I had to ask the question. No offense. I only wanted you to hear in case you'd felt there was a blackmailer involved somewhere and hadn't been sure enough about the idea to mention it. But if you've no idea, you know what I think? *Here* this guy's talking ten pounds of fog, trying to get us hooked on chasing some crazy story about a blackmailer so he can get a better deal. No, I think it's a crock. There were four creeps. One's dead, and we got the rest. For once I agree with my boss. This case is closed."

That evening I got to sit in a chair for half an hour. Carole came up and would have put me to work had Nurse Mandy not shooed her off. But before she left, Carole sat on the edge of my bed, hunched forward, and started rubbing her palms together. I waited. Still looking at her hands, she said, "The police returned the articles they found in Jones's locker that they didn't think were important." She reached into her sweater pocket and handed me a small envelope. "I thought you should have this."

I opened the flap and shook out the contents while Carole continued to look down at her hands. It was an old newspaper clipping, a photo taken a few years ago of Janet and me in formal dress at the annual hospital ball. We wore polite smiles. We usually had the best fun of these evenings while getting ready, with Janet doubled over laughing as I struggled into my tuxedo. This kind of social circuit definitely wasn't our style.

Clipped to the picture was an unused ticket. My first response was so what, but by the way Carole's palms were rubbing together, I figured there was more. "What does it mean?" I asked, truly puzzled.

Carole stopped rubbing her hands, then looked up at me with a kind of smile you bestow on a child who's too naive to get it. She started talking very softly, careful of her words. "With a woman like that, I wouldn't use the word *love*, not at all. But she was interested in you. I could tell by a lot of little things, the sort of things only a woman might notice: the way she would watch you when you weren't aware; all those green outfits she wore—in the early years I think they were mainly for your benefit. But you never caught on."

"Why didn't you warn me?" I asked, incredulous at what I'd just heard.

She laughed, leaned back, and said, "Hey, I'm your secretary, not your mother. Besides, you didn't need warning. You weren't going to do anything about it. Everyone knew that."

"What do you mean 'everyone'?"

"Well, not everyone. Just some of the more observant women in the department who could see what was going on."

Jesus Christ! I thought. My old nemesis. Denial. Maybe that was why I'd become so aware of her sexuality recently, since it was safely directed at others. I'd spent years denying her overtures to me.

I needed no reminder of the demonic rage Jones had exhibited while straddling me back at the cabin. *Good. Hate me! I'm taking away your miserable high-class fucking life.* I'd hear that shriek in my dreams the rest of my days.

I looked back down at the unused ticket and the old picture of Janet and me in our evening clothes.

"You see," said Carole, leaning forward, "I think what Jones really coveted was this." And she tapped the photo of Janet and me, decked out in the full regalia of a *high-class fucking life*.

A few hours later I had the strangest visitor of all.
Kradic.

He stood at the curtain, fingering it, before giving a little cough. "Hi, Dr. Garnet," he said hesitantly.

"Dr. Kradic," I acknowledged, genuinely surprised.

"Can I talk with you for a moment?"

He was so uncertain, almost shy, that I was actually curious what was up. I was also relieved he'd no idea how much I had suspected him.

"Sure, have a seat."

I was back in bed; he took Janet's chair.

"How are you doing?" he asked, uneasy and obviously bad at small talk. He wanted to get on to what he came for.

I answered, "Okay," and waited.

He coughed again, took a breath, and then started. "With Jones gone, I wondered if you'd give me her nights."

I gave a laugh in spite of myself.

Kradic didn't even look offended but pressed on with his case. "Look, I know it's indelicate and that you don't particularly like me, but I can do the job. You know patients are safe on my shift. Who else are you going to get to replace her?"

He had me there. Carole and the others had all assured me they were muddling through, but without Jones, the schedule would be a holy mess, and with Christmas coming up, it'd be worse yet. Nobody would admit it, but even increased doses of Kradic would be acceptable if he did more nights, worked holidays, and kept the rest of us, me included, from having to double up on these difficult shifts.

But I wasn't prepared to pay any price for his help. I stared back at him, still not answering, and calculated my terms. "Since we are being frank, Dr. Kradic, let me say that the entire department, including myself, is fed up with your rudeness and your complete lack of professional behavior with your peers. I'll give you the shifts on trial, for the holidays. Then the rest of the staff, nurses and clerks included, will decide if they want you around anymore."

He looked taken aback but said nothing.

I continued. "I am offering you this last chance only because you are an excellent physician. I would trust you with the care of myself or any member of my family, but your skill doesn't give you a license to disrupt the department. If anything, it gives you an obligation to help, not clobber, other physicians less gifted than yourself."

The compliment surprised him. His face flushed. He swallowed hard and started blinking a lot.

I watched him as he regained his composure.

"Thank you," he said simply, but he was looking down at his hands so I wouldn't see his face.

"Al, I want to know why you've started to come late. Punctuality is part of the deal."

My question broke his reserve. I watched his whole body tense, his hands tighten into fists. "Because my wife divorced me and is suing for custody of my two little boys." He was spitting out his words. "I took some extra shifts at other hospitals to help pay my lawyers." He looked straight at me, and his voice softened. "The additional nights will give me the income I'll need, and I'll be free in the days to take care of them." He took a deep breath, swallowed, and very quietly added, "I can't lose my boys, Dr. Garnet, I can't. They're all I have."

Then, embarrassed, he got up and left. When I fell asleep again, I was worrying about the schedule. Things were returning to normal.

The morning I was discharged, I walked out of the ICU and went directly down to the ER to work a shift. My doctors had been livid, but Janet had understood. "Go to it," she'd whispered in my ear, giving me a hug on my last night as a patient.

Susanne unceremoniously stuck a chart in my hand. "Welcome back. There's a guy with multiple trauma in Resus A. The residents are losing him, and I mean losing!" We started for the room, and she told me the rest while we walked. "He's a jumper. The medics said he must have fallen forty feet. He was still conscious when they found him, but he screamed when they tried to move his legs."

I glanced at the ambulance sheet and learned he'd jumped from Oratory Steps, a shrine that some faith healers had erected on top of a fifty-foot staircase in an escarpment overlooking the Niagara River. A lot of cripples crawl up there to try to walk again. Apparently this guy had reversed the procedure.

When I stepped to the side of his stretcher, he was already half dead. The surgical residents had been fiddling with him an hour and fifteen minutes without calling their staff.

"What's his pressure!" I asked, snapping on gloves.

"Sixty over zip," hissed one of the nurses up by the guy's head. "Like I been telling these two!" She glared at a pair of baby-faced kids in greens. New rotators. Lord help us.

"Shit, he's in shock!" I roared at them. "What the hell's he still doing here? He should have been in surgery an hour ago." I spoke quickly to Lisa, who was nearest the door. "Call a code blue." Then I turned to my new residents. "Gentlemen. This is unstable multiple trauma. It needs a trauma team. No one, not even you two, can save this man's life diddling over him alone. Now get me two more lines, big ones!"

Thirty minutes later I stepped out to the parking lot. It was a clear morning. The small amount of snow covering the ground crunched under my shoes. My ears tingled. I could see my breath when I exhaled. All over the city, vertical white plumes were rising into the blue sky as Buffalo started its day.

Half an hour on the job and already I had staff problems, inexperienced residents to worry about. And I'd barely arrived in time to save a patient's life.

Slowly I blew out another cloud of frost, and smiled. I was back.

Epilogue

Four Months Later

It was a Tuesday afternoon at the end of March. The remnants of winter were at last reduced to a few crusty ridges of silt and ice and a gritty covering of sand left on the roads. Even the sun, for a few minutes at two in the afternoon, seemed to remember what it was there for. I couldn't take my coat off, but I could open it, and the back of my neck felt warm if I stood out of the wind.

I was driving north out of Buffalo. On my left the Niagara River surged toward its rendezvous with the falls. It had broken free of winter's bondage weeks ago, though the currents here never really surrendered in the first place. The waterfront back in the city was still snarled with ice.

I'd put off this trip, but his secretary had told me he was setting sail that weekend. His house was sold. His phone was disconnected. When the ice went out he'd moved onto his boat. Now it was stocked and seaworthy, and I was out of time.

Power lines ran overhead; telephone poles ticked by on my right. An old freight train rumbled the other way. Everybody was going somewhere.

The light danced across the water, giving it a sparkle and the illusion of being clean. A sign said it was twenty more miles to the village of Youngstown, where he kept his boat.

This morning Janet had actually put bedding on the new crib. Three weeks to go, but staring down at that little flannel sheet and quilt had made the arrival imminent for me.

The ER was in better shape too. There were no more bed closures without my approval, and I'd been made chairman of the new financial ways and means committee. We didn't have much means, but we'd shut down Arnold's "pet farms," and at least I was able to protect emergency from more idiocy.

Kradic was still a pain in the ass, but he'd started teaching seminars for the staff. So far everyone was willing to let him stay.

The parking for Watts's yacht club was on a small bluff above a series of rickety steps leading down to the boat basins. To my right I could see the open waters of Lake Ontario. The smell of seaweed and dead fish got fresher as I descended. A bunch of boats leaned crookedly on dry land cradles.

Most of the slots on the water were still empty. His was the only sailboat. No one else was there. They were all probably working at the jobs they needed to try to pay for this stuff.

The wharf was a series of floating docks. My steps on the wooden slats and the creaking of the adjoining hinges announced my arrival. He'd been coiling and stowing ropes on the front deck, and he spun around at the noise. I hadn't called ahead. He was clearly surprised. And puzzled.

"Earl, what a pleasure," he said with a big smile.

I forced one in return. "I came to say good-bye, Robert."

"Well, come on board and let's do it right," he said with some real enthusiasm and a trace of relief.

He helped me across the gap between his bobbing boat and the dock and onto the thirty feet of rich, glistening deck he planned to make his world. I couldn't help my own twinge of excitement at the allure of it all.

"Very nice," I said, and meant it.

"Sit down, sit down," he replied, relaxing, and waving me toward an expensive-looking set of black canvas and teak deck chairs.

Sitting in them warranted another even more enthusiastic "Very nice!"

"How about a drink?"

"Sure."

"What do you like?" He strode to an on-deck bar.

"A Black Russian would be great."

"What's a Black Russian?"

I told him. He made it.

I settled back and looked at him over the rim of my glass.

He looked casual enough, what with his mackinaw over a white turtleneck sweater. And he looked a hell of a lot better than when I'd last seen him in his lab. He'd been discharged before me, and hadn't come to visit. But now his eyes had the hardness they'd always assumed when he was standing over a particularly problematic case, scalpel raised and ready to start.

I lifted my glass, took a sip of the liquid, and savored the icy warmth. I'd come to like Black Russians. It was time to begin.

"I'm here to say I know."

He remained still, just staring at me.

"Jones was your investment."

He was dead still.

"The police dismissed a statement from one of Jones's accomplices who claimed someone was blackmailing her, but I couldn't. His story made too much sense and explained too well the events of that week. It even began to answer the questions I had about you."

I set my glass on the table, keeping my eyes on him.

"You probably noticed the increase in DOAs before anyone else. You got curious. You got thorough. Anyway, long before Kingsly's murder, you had discovered what Jones was up to."

Nothing moved. Not in his face. Not even in his eyes.

"I can only guess why you then did what you did. I mean, besides for the money."

I hesitated. About this I wasn't sure. "I figured it was your wife's death. It must have left you devastated. Not only with grief but with anger. Anger at the very profession you had dedicated your life to."

Here he blinked. He looked a little startled.

"For all your attention to detail, a lifetime of teaching us to be better doctors, no one had caught your wife in time. When she died, you had to have felt betrayed that your profession had let her down."

His upper body tensed.

I went on. "But even this wasn't enough to make you turn against what you'd served your whole life. There had to be another reason you hadn't put a stop to Jones and why you chose to let her continue the killing and to blackmail her. It had to be a specific hatred to drive you to that." I paused, then told him, "Before I came out here, I went down to the medical records archives and pulled your wife's chart."

He started breathing through his mouth. His lips thinned, and he bared his clenched teeth. That familiar face suddenly looked ugly and sullen as he glared at me.

I waited, felt the calm would hold, and went on. "I found the notes from her last admission before she died, when the cancer was diagnosed. They were straightforward, tragically so, but appropriate and in order. Then I leafed back through her dossier and came to the records of her visits to emergency. There, I found she'd presented to our department a full six months prior to the discovery of her cancer with a complaint of abdominal pain. The clinical notes were written by a resident. Quite complete, they described your wife having a monthlong history of cramps and reduced bowel movements. The exam was unremarkable, and she was told it was constipation. The staff signature validating that 'diagnosis' was Dr. Valerie Jones."

He still didn't move.

"If the proper follow-up had been done then, the cancer in your wife's colon might have been caught in time to save her. Or if she hadn't had those false reassurances from Jones, maybe she would have mentioned her problem to you. For whatever reason, she obviously remained silent until it was too late. You chose to let Jones go on killing vagrants for more than a year so you could torment her with blackmail and punish her for your wife's death . . . punish her over and over."

No denials.

"After Kingsly's murder was discovered, you really tightened your hold on her. Feeding me the pathology evidence on the cardiac needles, first for Kingsly, and later for the DOA, you cocked and pointed me like a pistol. That's why you delayed 'finding' the needle track in the derelict and reporting it to the police. The better to keep her terrified of being discovered and force her to give you a big final payment by first threatening to expose, then making good on your threat. Trouble was, she thought I was the blackmailer. You must have made your last demand the day after Kingsly's murder. Maybe you anonymously slipped her a copy of my note to you. Remember? 'Pigmented lesion vs. small scab at left xiphoid-sternal junction. Check it out'? I knew something had driven Jones to think she had to try to warn me off with the dogs later that same night. She didn't see the ER statistics in my office until Tuesday morning."

The stare continued. I took another sip of the Black Russian. He hadn't touched his drink.

"When she was trying to kill me, she said something about me being your little pointer. I wasn't paying much attention, considering the circumstances, but I thought it was just a general slur, part of her fury. You probably hadn't counted on pushing her to actually try to knock me off. That day at the meeting, when Bufort announced the attempted hit-and-run, you were truly shocked, more than the rest of them. I'm sure it gave you pause. Hell, later in the cafeteria, I think you actually considered putting a stop to it, but in the end you let your play ride. Let me be the decoy while you turned up the heat."

I took another swallow. More warmth. He turned his glass by its stem.

"Oh, and I figured out how you did it. Prior to Kingsly, you probably just mailed your threats and demands to her apartment. But after Kingsly, to save time, I bet you used that mailbox of hers, the one she hardly ever emptied. You could have delivered your anonymous notes through the hospital in-house mail or even slipped them in there yourself. By the time she got it, she wouldn't know what day it had arrived, let alone who'd been around to do it. That's why she started to keep her slot clean. I ought to know. Her uncollected mail always used to fall over into mine."

His gaze had slid off me now and was somewhere out over the water. The sunlight was starting to thin. Now I needed the warmth of my drink.

"Did you use the technique Bufort described as common to blackmailers? Have her send money orders to different post office boxes, pickups she couldn't trace? At first I thought it was simple convenience that she used you as bait for me. But I think you'd screwed up. That Sunday you probably didn't wait for the in-house mail to put another of your threats in her box. My tirade at the meeting that Fernandez wasn't the killer must have convinced you I was on the verge of nailing her, so you wanted that last payoff fast, before I found her name and exposed her to the police. I'll bet your note even told her that I'd challenged Bufort and wanted the case kept open, then made it look like the tactic of a blackmailer increasing the pressure on her. But she'd begun keeping an eye on her box and must have seen you slip the note in."

He didn't answer. It didn't matter.

"I don't suppose you ever got that final payment." I paused and waited until he finally looked back and faced me. The hardness was gone. His eyes were dead.

The sight of him hunched over in his chair suddenly disgusted me. I slammed my empty glass on the table between us. "You'd kept her too busy trying to kill me!"

He flinched at my fury.

I leaned across the table at him. His mouth opened. He made swallowing movements.

"Don't worry," I said through clenched teeth, inches from his face. "I'm not going to the cops. I'm going to do something a lot worse. I'm going to leave you to yourself, with what you've become, and let you go crazy with it. You will, you know. All that instinct for nasty truths turned in on yourself, in this floating jail of yours."

He suddenly looked a little puzzled. Maybe I was wrong, perhaps he would let himself off the hook. I really didn't care. "Even if you don't drive yourself mad, I'm not going to tell the cops because there's no good in it to drag your dirt into the open. Not for me, not for the hospital, not for anyone. And personally it doesn't really matter to me what happens to you. I'm a physician, not some avenging angel or Lady Justice herself. I've got my life back. That's all I ever wanted."

At this point I was standing over him. I nodded toward my glass. "Am I going to need an antidote for that?"

He was still gaping at the chair where I'd been, but he managed to shake his head. I believed him, and left.

I didn't look back until I was up in the parking lot and getting into my car. He hadn't moved. His drink, still untouched, sat on the table beside his motionless arm. He seemed to be fixated on my empty chair.

I felt cold. I once thought he was a friend. Maybe once he was.

The sun, low now, cast him in the glow it saved until the end of the day. It highlighted the ropes and rigging that coiled about his yacht, like snakes ensnaring it. In widening circles around the white hull bobbed the wreckage and silt of the end of winter. The debris at the end of a life.

Arched across the stern was the name of his boat. It was once intended to celebrate his cleverness, his success. Now, like a verdict, it hung there.

THE PATH O LOGIC

THE BUFFALO GAZETTE,
APRIL 25, 1997

DEATHS.

Dr. Robert Watts, lost at sea during a squall in the waters of Chesapeake Bay. Physician, teacher, and former chief of pathology at St. Paul's Hospital. Age sixty-three. Survived by his daughter and two sons.

THE BUFFALO GAZETTE,
APRIL 29, 1997

BIRTHS.

Brendan Garnet, seven pounds, six ounces, was born this morning to Dr. Janet Graceton and Dr. Earl Garnet. All are doing well.

*Watch for Peter Clement's next novel
of medical suspense,*

DEATH
ROUNDS

Coming in early 1999.

Published by Ballantine Books.

What booksellers are saying
about LETHAL PRACTICE . . .

"What a thrilling first novel for author Peter Clement. Not since Robin Cook's first couple of novels have I enjoyed a medical thriller so much! It was really hard to put down and do other things like go to work!"
—BRENDA ELLIOTT, Oxford, Alabama

"The most exciting book I've read in a long time. I couldn't put it down. I hope Peter Clement is working on his next medical thriller because I can't wait for more!"
—VICKY JACOBSEN, Missoula, Montana

"Really great! Moved so fast I didn't try to figure it out! I just went along for the ride and enjoyed every minute of it."
—SANDI LOCKE, Saugus, California

". . . highly engrossing and entertaining . . . It's a medical thriller that doesn't get bogged down by medical jargon! It's fast paced and read-able, and I will definitely recommend this book to anyone who reads Robin Cook or Michael Palmer."
—SUE MCHUGH, Northville, Michigan

"Great debut novel—the story moves and carries the reader quickly from start to finish. Dr. Clement's background keeps the story authen-tic and urges the reader to continue on this heart-stopping suspense tale. Keep writing, Dr. Clement!"
—PATTY WACHTER, Harrisburg, Pennsylvania

"Mr. Clement writes like a seasoned pro! If his medical skills are as polished as his ability to relate them, I'd trust him anytime. Just enough medical detail to make it real, just enough suspense to keep me reading instead of doing other responsibilities. Great book and unexpected twist to the ending. I hope he writes more in the future."
—TISH MURZYN, Hartly, Delaware

"I loved it. I couldn't put it down. Very suspenseful!"
—MARY VECELLIO, Flint, Michigan

"An extraordinary medical thriller . . . contains plenty of believable scenarios with plenty of twists, suspense, and surprises. It kept me riveted all night long. I'm ready for more by Peter Clement."
—GINNY HIARING, Clarinda, Iowa